EVERYTHING HAS CHANGED

KENDRA SMITH

HEAD
of ZEUS

An Aria Book

BY KENDRA SMITH

First published in the UK in 2021 by Head of Zeus Ltd
This paperback edition first published in 2021 by Head of Zeus Ltd
An Aria book

9 7 5 3 1 2 4 6 8

A CIP catalogue record for this book is available from the British Library.

ISBN (PB): 9781800246256
ISBN (E): 9781789541892

Head of Zeus
5–8 Hardwick Street
London EC1R 4RG
www.headofzeus.com

Print editions of this book are printed and bound by CPI Group (UK) Ltd,
Croydon, CR0 4YY, on FSC paper

All we are given is possibilities — to make ourselves one thing or another.

JOSÉ ORTEGA Y GASSET

1 VICTORIA

At the precise moment Victoria's finger found the sticky liquid at the back of her head she wondered if she was dreaming. The one where her husband James was in the car with her, and they were both usually naked – stress someone said once – and he'd be shouting at her. Asking her *why*. Always 'why'. It was the look on his face that normally woke her up. She touched the back of her head and winced. No, this wasn't a dream.

There was a voice talking to her. 'Victoria? Victoria? Can you move?'

A memory: lights dazzling her, the terror. She glanced quickly in the passenger seat. Empty. Her heart lurched. A voice was telling her it was alright.

'Where's Lulu?'

'She's with us. She's in the ambulance and they are checking her over. It's OK.'

It was *not OK*. 'Is my little sister alright?' Victoria sounded croaky. She couldn't stop shivering.

'She's going to be fine, her injuries are minor, but we're

doing some tests.' The voice belonged to a paramedic who was reaching over her to unclip the seatbelt. Both airbags had deployed. Victoria sat, frozen with fear, looking at the scene unfolding. She glanced at the bonnet; smoke. She felt a lurch of terror. Was the car going to burst into flames?

The paramedic reached for her hand and squeezed it. 'Don't worry, love, I'll get you out of here,' he said warmly, releasing her seatbelt gently and, painstakingly slowly, eased her out of the car. The blue flashing lights of the police cars lit up the sky and were reflected in the sheen on the road. Victoria could just about make out an ambulance; the firm grip of the paramedic holding her was real and solid as she leant on him. She tried to take a deep breath, but felt a stab of agony in her chest. 'Steady now.' He helped her limp to the ambulance where she collapsed onto the bench and passed out.

———

When she woke up she was in a bright room with a doctor leaning over her and a nurse fussing by the trolley. Her head was pounding, and, she thought, the doctor could do with a shave.

'Victoria, Mrs Allen, you've been in a collision, we're taking you for a scan. There's a morphine drip attached to you, just squeeze this button here,' the nurse pressed a cold plastic tube into her hand. 'Like this,' she guided Victoria's fingers around it then heard a click. 'For the pain. Good girl.'

She felt herself moving on the bed and being wheeled out of the room, down a long bright corridor with yellow-painted walls. Busy people rushed past her and then suddenly she was in a much dimmer room with the scanner. People with kind smiles were telling her to stay calm, clips were put on her clothing and she was told to lie still as she was placed on the scanner bed – the scanner looked like a giant plastic donut on its side.

'My sister?'

'Victoria, don't worry.' A doctor leant across her, adjusting her positioning.

'People keep telling me not to worry,' her head was throbbing with the effort of explaining everything to these people, 'but I know she was in the car with me, I just can't remember, well, much at all.'

'That's perfectly normal. Your sister is being checked over in A&E too. She escaped with very little damage, a broken finger, some scratches. Now lie still.'

Victoria didn't argue as the machine made a noise and she slid into the mouth of the donut.

———

A nurse was wrapping a Velcro bandage around her arm.

'Where am I?'

'You're at the Royal Brighton Hospital, I'm just taking your blood pressure.'

'Royal Brighton? The new one? That was quick! But they're still building it, surely?'

The nurse patted her arm. 'It's been here for six years now, not really new, love.'

Victoria's head throbbed. Visions were coming and going from her brain, a flash of a headlight, the terrible sound of scraping metal: what happened just before the accident? Why did that car come into their lane? She wondered again how Lulu was. She was just a baby – only twenty-four, her little sister. These things can scar you for life.

'Can I have my phone?'

The nurse pulled a chair up next to her and placed a strange bag on it. It was one of those bags that organised women had. Neat. Tidy. Navy. With a large gold clip. It didn't have tissues spilling out of it, and biro marks on the outside and there were probably no half-eaten Hob Nobs in the side pocket. 'Here's your bag, I think your phone's in there.' Victoria looked in the bag and saw a phone she did not recognise; and it was out of charge. Someone must have given her the wrong bag. She felt dizzy again.

'Has anyone told my husband?' She gripped the sheet on the bed.

The nurse turned to her. 'Yes, but he's abroad, with your children; they're coming back soon.' She patted Victoria's arm again. *Pat, pat, pat.* 'Don't worry. It's half term, remember?' she offered by way of explanation, brows furrowed.

Half term? Where was James? He'd never go away without her! And the kids! How on earth would he manage with ten-year-old twins for goodness sake? He'd been going for a three-day interview the other day, she remembered, in the Lake District, something about Helvellyn and management skills. He had been pacing the floor because he was up for promotion. And if he *had* got the promotion, why on earth had he just upped and gone skiing? 'You'll be fine darling,' she remembered saying that morning and had reached up and given him a kiss, then, as she'd backed away he'd grabbed her wrist gently, glanced at his watch, said he still had half an hour to kill and knew what would be good for his nerves. She blushed. It was as if they were still newly-wed sometimes. She tried to recall a memory of her wedding in her head… wedding, wedding? Any memory would do. Where had it gone? She must be able to remember her wedding! The most important day of her whole life. She tried to replay it. It was all a bit foggy. She could see James's face –

4

but was that memory from their wedding or some other time? Why hadn't he called? What had her dress been like? Oh heavens, what was wrong with her? How in God Almighty could she not remember her wedding dress? It seemed to really matter somehow. She leant back on the crunchy hospital pillow with a thump. Bridesmaids? Had she had bridesmaids? And flowers? Was Lulu there? She certainly hoped Lulu had been there. What's the point in having a fantastic wedding with the love of your life if you couldn't remember it?

Twins, she knew she had twins. Focus on what you know. Ten years old and adorable. Izzy and Jake. She loved them more than the centre of a Creme Egg. They hadn't got to the awful stage that some of her friends' older children had. The grungy teenagers, the nose rings, the greasy hair, faces constantly in their phones. No, her kids were still angels. Annoying sometimes, especially if they left the lid off the milk in the mornings – this was a very strong memory – but she could still suggest what they wore, organise playdates and make sure they only watched PG films. Only the other day they'd snuggled up with her on the sofa to watch Mary Poppins. Popcorn. Messy house, yes it was all coming back to her. Thank God! Piles of ironing. Yes, nothing wrong with her memory – some bits anyway.

'The weather's meant to be lovely there,' the nurse offered, tucking in the sheet at the end of her bed.

'Where?'

'Where your husband is! And your kids. He called late last night and the Duty Nurse updated him on your status.'

My status. What *is* my status? But why hadn't he called again? Spoken to her? Perhaps he had and they'd told him she was resting. She'd seen that in TV shows. She could see his face: the fair freckles that splattered across his nose, the

5

relaxed smile, the one he'd give her after they'd have sex, when he'd lie with his head leaning on his hand; warm grey eyes as he smiled fondly at her. She could just about touch that memory. She could almost smell him: Soap. He would be *very* worried.

'Did he say where they were?'

The nurse was straightening her blanket. 'Verbier. Something about black runs.'

Victoria leant back into her pillow and stared at the nurse. Her children had never been skiing in their lives.

———

A man in his late forties with greying hair at the temples pulled back the curtain as Victoria had just managed to doze off. But it was a miracle that she had. Machines were bleeping, people coughing, and that poor lady next to her; she'd heard the word 'terminal' and had clutched the bedsheet. Good grief, Victoria was just grateful to be alive! She vowed she would turn over a new leaf, she'd really sort out that to-do list, join that new gym place that had opened in the village and get in shape, she'd stop snapping at the twins about their rooms, they were tiny after all. Stop watching all that daytime TV. She would go to more of those parent tutorials on algebra, yes she would, and she'd also lose that pesky stone she'd put on after having the twins. Get fit for her kids! Life was for living! She loved her family!

The car crash had made her lie awake last night thinking about her life. She'd listened to the orchestra of hospital noises, buzzing machines, the clip of shoes, the swish of next door's curtain and realised she was grateful, *so* grateful for all of it, for the daffodils that came up every year in the garden, for the squirrels that pranced in the grass, for her darling twins, for her gorgeous, successful husband. She tried to imagine their next holiday. Camping in France – she hated camping, but never mind; a coastal walking holiday in Wales – they'd cross off how many miles they'd covered each day, find places to buy ice-cream; or perhaps they'd go to Cornwall and visit award-winning beaches. Perhaps a farm experience? The ones where the kids milk the cows, collect eggs from the chickens, that kind of thing. Life was for making memories – well, in her case, she needed to hurry up and make some more memories. She wanted to grasp the holy grail of her beautiful family with both hands and enjoy it – not many people were as lucky as her. She felt, despite the agony of her broken ribs, evangelical. She wanted to shout from the rooftops. People died in car crashes. She hadn't.

'Mrs Allen?' He took his glasses off and wiped them with his tie.

'I just need to take a look at your chest, where you've broken your ribs. The scan is showing a slightly complex fracture. You're lucky you didn't puncture your lungs. But first if you'd let me take a look.'

Victoria let the doctor lift up her hospital gown. She was beyond being modest, especially after the ordeal with the twins, my goodness. First one twin was born, and then she had to go through the whole rigmarole all over again. She loved her twins with a passion, but honestly, the whole of the hospital had practically seen all her private places; she really wasn't bothered. He lifted up her gown and was gently pressing the tissue under her breasts.

'Ah, looks like some scarring here. When did you have the breast implants?'

Victoria sat bolt upright, then put her hand across her chest and winced in pain. Breast implants! Was he joking?

'I don't have breast implants!' She almost wanted to

laugh. Was this some kind of sick YouTube hospital joke doing the rounds? She hated breast implants, used to snigger at one of the school mums who everybody knew had been to somewhere in Europe last summer to get 'work' done. What was her name? Began with a Z? Why interfere with what nature had given you?

He looked up at her and frowned. 'You most certainly do, Mrs Allen, there is still some mild scarring and um, from the look of your breasts, they have certainly had some enhancement.'

Victoria whipped up the gown and stared at her protruding breasts which sat, quite pertly of their own volition, requiring no support whatsoever.

'Good God. I don't think they're mine.'

'Right.' The doctor scratched his head then changed tack. 'Well, from your CT scan that you had we can see you have fractured two ribs. I'd like you to focus on breathing deeply please and rest.'

What was happening to her? Why did she not feel like her normal self? Where was James? All the air had left Victoria's lungs anyway, she realised, as for some unknown reason she was walking around with someone else's breasts.

2 LULU

Do you love him?

I'm not going there. It's the last thing I remember before the awful screaming, the lights, the noise, the black. A nurse is sashaying up to me. Her rubber shoes squeak.

'How you feeling?'

I have been in a car crash with my sister and I feel like shit.

'Fine.'

'Right, well, we'll just give these grazes a wipe and then you can go see your sister,' she puts a strong hand on my forearm, produces a wipe with her other hand and says 'this-wont-hurt-a-bit' but of course it does.

Simon's in a state. I don't blame him. Imagine your first wife dying in an accident. When he told me, my heart went out to him. They had been living in a rented flat, and she was poisoned by carbon monoxide; he broke down when he told me and I didn't want to ask any more questions. I suppose if your new fiancée has a crash, you *would* go to pieces. To paraphrase Oscar Wilde, to lose one partner would be unfortunate, but to lose two looks like carelessness. It's not funny, I know. He was beside himself when I called. Said he'd get the next plane down from Manchester, leave the company's annual accounts conference which he was heading, but I persuaded him to stay and to catch a flight tomorrow morning. I pointed out that I would be groggy, and just wanted to rest in my own flat. 'Wish you weren't going back to that poky little flat,' he'd said. '*I'll* be fine. It's Victoria I'm worried about; the doctors have mentioned amnesia,' I said to him on the phone.

'Right, that's you.' The nurse smiles at me and I look down at my patched-up arm.

'I'll get a porter to wheel you up to your sister.'

'I don't need a wheelchair.'

'I think it's wise. You are not to walk after what's happened.' Her head tilts to the side. 'OK?'

I nod and let the porter help me into the wheelchair. The porter presses the lift button and we silently ascend to the fourth floor in the little box smelling of antiseptic and cabbage.

Victoria looks like a tiny doll perched upright on pillows on the bed. Her eyes are closed and somehow, miraculously, her hair is immaculate. For the first time in a long while, our roles have changed. My big sis looks very little. I take her hand. It feels small and warm.

'Victoria?' I whisper.

Do you love him? It's going round and round my head in a repeated loop. I want it to stop.

'Lulu!' Victoria yelps and releases my hand. 'What have you done?'

'What?' I manage, my fingers fly to my face and I feel my cheeks. Perhaps it's some kind of impact of the accident?

Dried blood, a black eye? Or some glitter left on from my
Fairy Glitter Party.

'You look—'

'What?'

'Older.'

I smile at a passing nurse and ask if by any chance she
has a small mirror. When she pulls one out of her pocket I
hold it up and look. Tired and shaken, yes. Hair covered in
glitter from the Fairy Party, but no blood. Basically, I look like
you would look on the day of a car crash: a bit crap. I decide
to veer off-topic and concentrate on her. 'The doctor tells me
you had a bad head injury; might take a few weeks for, um,
things to heal, like your ribs.' *And your mind.* I smile at my
older, capable sister. The one who carries notepads and has a
schedule.

Victoria nods. 'Have you told Dad?'

'Yes.'

'How's he doing, you know? Because he often says he can
cope, and I wonder if he still thinks of mum passing and I
wonder how he's *really* getting on up there.' She looks
urgently at me.

Mum died nine years ago. And Dad and Mum had moved to
Yorkshire ten years ago. It took them both by surprise how much
they fitted in to 'her' world there; it was where she was from. But
then suddenly, Dad was left on his own, fending for himself. He's
got used to the fells now, found some 'new old friends' as he calls
his walking group, and especially in the shape of a four-legged
friend, a beautiful border collie called Billie. The fact that Mum
had been the fittest person I knew, meant that it came as such a
shock when she died of a stroke. I lean forward onto the hospital
bed and flick off some invisible dust from the bedsheet. 'Victoria, Mum died nine years ago, remember?'

'Nine?'

'Mmm-hmm.' I'm staying calm here, I don't want to frighten her.

'Right.' She presses her hands down on the sheets, smoothing them and doesn't look at me.

'I spoke to Dad earlier, he wanted to come down but I told him not to worry at the moment, it's mid-February and the roads are icy. I said you were OK. I promised I'd phone and update him later, alright?' Victoria bites her lip. 'And Simon sends his love. I told him to stay put in Manchester but he'll be back tomorrow.'

'Who's Simon?' She stares at me blankly.

Dear, dear Lord. I need a consultant – I need to find out what they've done with my sister's memory. Instead, I smile as brightly as I can. 'Simon's my fiancé, remember?'

'Fi-an-cé,' she repeats in three syllables after me, as a foreign language student might do. 'But you're a, um, yes, a rock chick! You can't be getting married, like *married*-married?' She rakes her fingers through her hair. 'I don't understand?'

I'm glad I'm in a wheelchair. Victoria won't be able to see how much my legs are shaking and that I'm shivering. This is a disaster, but I have to remind myself that *she's* come out of this worse, *much* worse. In fact, she looks like she might cry at any minute.

'Lulu.' Her voice is croaky. 'Where *on earth* is James? Why hasn't he called? I thought he'd rush here.'

Dangerous territory. My sister is now not only the victim of a car crash and a couple of broken ribs, she is also teary. This means emotions are involved. I don't like emotions. They don't get you anywhere. Best to keep them well hidden. Victoria is meant to be in control, the older sister, I was the one who was allowed to be a bit bonkers. And why on earth is she asking about James? As if *he*'d run to her side. We're entering a pin-out-of-a-hand-grenade situation here and I don't know how to break it to her. I weigh up my options.

'Victoria?' I say softly, using my Talking To Children Voice.

'Why do you keep calling me Victoria!' she sniffs. 'Like I've done something terribly wrong, like Mum used to when she scolded us? What's happened to "Vicky"?'

That's exactly what I want to know. 'Sweetheart.' I'm back to hand-squeezing, it seems safer with what's about to come. 'Look, first, you have insisted on being called Victoria for the last five years; second, James is skiing with the kids in Verbier, remember?' I clear my throat for the final blow. 'And third, he's filing for divorce.'

3 LULU

'Darling!' Simon bounds up the stairs in the shared hallway of my Victorian flat as I open the door to him. He's carrying a shopping bag, his overnight holdall and a bunch of lilies. He squeezes past me in the narrow door frame as I open the door wider for him, then pecks my cheek. I smell wet rain on him, newspaper and a sort of chemical dry-cleaning aroma. I close the door and sigh. It's good to see him but I'm just so tired. 'Thank God you're alright!' He hands me the flowers. 'I've come straight from the airport. These are for you. You like lilies, don't you?'

The truth is that I don't like lilies. Their scent gives me a headache. 'They're lovely.' I move swiftly, closing the door and then head into the kitchen, grab a vase from a top cupboard and then place them out in the hall, away from me.

'You should sit down!' He comes up behind me and snakes his arm around my waist. I smile. He's always been tactile. 'How's Victoria?' He squeezes my waist and looks at me in the hall mirror. He's in a pair of chinos, red-checked shirt and navy jacket. I stifle a yawn.

'Well, she's a bit odd, actually,' I say, turning around and looking at his short-cropped blonde hair, his pale, watery blue eyes.

'Bound to be after what you both went through. Come on, you need to sit down, you look shattered.' He leads me by the hand back into the kitchen and instructs me to take a seat at the kitchen table.

'No, I mean *odd*-odd, Simon.'

'I'm sure she will be just fine. She's in the hands of the consultant, he knows best. Hospital is the best place for her.' He turns to the kitchen counter and starts to rummage in the shopping bag.

'Yes, I'm sure you're right.'

'I thought we'd make *moules mariniere*.' Simon is very engrossed rustling through the plastic bag, laying out ingredients on the counter with a flourish.

'Sounds great.' I manage a smile. All I can think about is Victoria.

'Going to cook it with parsley and thyme, double cream, what do you think?' His eyes light up. 'For my invalid.'

I think I'd rather have fish and chips from the chippie. 'Yes, lovely.'

'Have you got any *bouquet garni*?'

'Bouquet of *what* flowers?' I smile. He stares at me. Humour, I've found, doesn't always work with Simon. I stroll to the fridge tripping up slightly on the ripped linoleum next to it. Simon looks round. 'Have you spoken to your landlord about that yet?'

'No,' I say as I open the fridge and pull out some white wine, frown at the amount left. 'Drink?'

His head is burrowed deep inside my store cupboard, the one where I keep stock cubes and supermarket instant gravy powder that he disapproves of. He peeks out at me. 'Yes please.' He nods, then turns back to me. 'Should you be having one? I mean, what did the doctor say?'

The doctor *might* have mentioned something about not drinking today, but I choose to take my own advice, I need it for my nerves. 'It's fine.'

I sit at my small wooden table and pour out two glasses and knock one back quickly then refill my glass. Simon washes his hands vigorously and then starts to haul things out of my cupboard, pots and pans banging on the floor; a lid falls out. I hear him swear under his breath. Cooking is always such a pantomime.

I pick up my glass and study my engagement ring, sparkling on my finger. He'd been so persuasive. I study the tiny gold claws holding the ruby in place, thinking about the security it offers. And, let's face it, right now my life isn't exactly a raging success, is it? Twenty-nine and my list of achievements read like a series of cartoon shows: Little Bo Peep, Bubble Disco, Hungry Caterpillar… Simon might be on the wrong side of forty, but as a widower, it's the whole package. Home and husband – I think about that word and say it to myself. It's time to stop being a children's entertainer and grow up. What was it Simon had joked, 'time to give up that silly little business'? It had hurt at the time, but maybe he's right. My glittering West End career hasn't happened. Four years at drama school just landed me voiceovers for a cartoon monkey for a cereal brand, and then it was a slippery slope to children's entertainer to pay the rent. I take another slug of wine. The audiences are still live, I sniff, it's just that they're normally toddlers.

'I thought we'd look through some venues online tonight, what do you think?'

I hadn't even thought about where I want to get married, I've been getting used to actually being a fiancée, the fact that there's an end point is quite scary – but we're getting married in two months, Simon's right, we need to get on with it. I just feel exhausted.

'What's up?' He comes over and kisses me on the head. 'It'll take your mind off that nasty little prang you had with your sister.' He hesitates then adds, 'If you like?'

'I'd love to,' I lie, sipping my wine. But perhaps we should. And the little girl in me, the one who used to hide behind Victoria's legs at Christmastime when the house was full of grown-ups, *does* want the fairy tale, and after a glass of vodka or red wine it's much easier to forget about ambitions and dreams and what you *think* you want. In fact, it makes you much more *chilled* about everything, and the demons that lurk in my head are silenced for a while, too.

'Can't wait,' I say, running my finger around the rim of the wine glass and watching him as he throws open cupboards and mutters about sea salt. He's wearing one of my aprons and looks faintly ridiculous as I study his frilly outline. But he's a kind man. I pour myself another glass of wine and cast my mind back to meeting him. He'd been hanging around the back door to the garden at one of the children's parties. He'd been there with his goddaughter, who I assumed was his daughter, but when I asked where his wife was, his eyes had clouded over. 'Died. Three weeks ago.' I'd been lost for words. I'd reached out and touched his arm and he'd seemed surprised. He'd fiddled with his cufflinks, mentioned a dreadful accident at their rented flat, and said something ridiculously British like, 'These things happen.' I'd wanted to hug him there and then, he'd looked like a wounded teddy bear, so I'd pressed my business card into his hand – it's all I'd had on me, *Lulu your Chameleon Children's Entertainer* – and told him to call if he needed to chat.

And he had. The very next day. I was gobsmacked. He'd

flattered me ridiculously, but I'd enjoyed the attention. He wasn't my usual type, but all my other 'bohemian bad boys', as Vicky used to call them, where had they got me? It seemed that you couldn't have the bad boy without them being – well, bad. They were either unfaithful, or they'd lie to me, or worse, they'd be lying to themselves, telling me that they would change.

'Lulu, don't you have *any* other saucepans?' Simon turns from the stove.

I shake my head. I've had to make do with what I've got. It's not easy coping on a children's entertainer's salary. No sooner do I pay off one 'final demand', another one thumps onto my doormat, or in my inbox.

'Sooner we get you out of this dreadful flat, the better, eh?'

I like this flat. It's my haven. It might have a wonky table in the kitchen, the shower may be leaky but I feel safe here, tucked up on the first floor of a Victorian semi on the outskirts of Little Norland overlooking the fields. But Simon's just looking after me, that's all. He's kind and caring and wants the best, wants to look after me and that feels good. I close my eyes, enjoying the feeling of the wine relaxing me. I like feeling looked after – it doesn't mess with your head like love does, that's way too emotional for me. And emotions can let you down.

'There you go, darling.' I open my eyes as Simon places a steaming plate of little shells in front of me and breaks my train of thought. They glisten, the little creatures inside shrivelled up, suffocated with a creamy sauce. I look up at his sweaty forehead as he puts his hands on his hips and smiles triumphantly. He's so kind. Love can start from many places, I remind myself.

4 VICTORIA

A nurse was helping Victoria to the bathroom in the corridor. The one on her ward was being cleaned. They shuffled along in amicable silence, Victoria leaning on the nurse's strong, freckled arm. She glanced at her nurse's name badge. Sarah. She had kind eyes and reddish hair swept into a neat pony-tail. Victoria managed a smile. She imagined her smile as 'being brave' as her mother used to say. This was all a silly mix-up and she needed everyone to understand that. But first, she needed to wee.

The nurse pulled open the door of the bathroom. 'Will you be alright? I'll wait out here.'

She nodded. She may have lost some memory, but she could still remember how to go to the toilet. She yanked the door shut and took a breath, inhaling the musty mixture of damp and bleach. It was a roomier cubicle than the one on her ward. There was a shower for a start, with faded blue shower curtains and a white plastic seat, presumably for those who could not shower standing up.

She glanced to the right – then screamed. Across from

her was a woman she didn't recognise. An older woman, a woman with chestnut highlights. The woman was staring blankly at her in a hospital gown. Her hands flew to her face. It was her. *She* was that woman. The nurse banged on the door.

'Are you OK Victoria?'

She coughed. 'Yes, fine, I just – slipped. Won't be a moment.'

'I'm still here.' Sarah's muffled voice came through the door.

Victoria leant on the basin under the mirror. The bathroom on her ward had no mirror, she suddenly realised. Is *this* how she looked? She smiled into the mirror. It looked odd. She smoothed her hand over her jaw. It was so angular. And when she frowned, nothing happened. And her eyebrows! It was as if someone had drawn them in using a Sharpie pen. How dreadful. She closed her eyes and opened them. No, same woman. The woman did look sort of *good*, she thought as she scratched at her eyebrows to see if they could be removed or something, but not like *her*. Her hands skimmed over her bust. She pressed them. They felt hard and unreal. She pressed again. They didn't budge. She clung on to the edge of the sink, watching as her knuckles turned white.

A light knock on the door. 'Won't be a minute.' Victoria sat down on the toilet with a thump. She was shattered.

———

The consultant was standing looking at Victoria's notes at the end of her bed. Which was a good thing. She'd just had another X-ray for her ribs and he was here to discuss her MRI brain scan, she hoped. She really needed to understand where this whole divorce business had come from. Perhaps the MRI scan would show up the 'divorce' section in her brain. I'm happily married, for goodness sake, she mused, pulling her sheet up sharply between two fingers. She loved her husband. She had pictures of him on her screensaver at home – she knew she did – and on her phone, she and James were the annoyingly cute couple at dinner parties who still held hands under the table when nobody was looking. They were in *love, goddamit*.

'So where exactly is my memory, doctor? Has it taken a vacation? And if so, when will it be back?' She found the absurdity of her situation simultaneously amused her (Oh, you lost your memory? Maybe it's hiding in the cutlery drawer?), then terrified her. It was easier to joke with herself than face stark reality: she had lost years of her life.

'These things take time to come back, Mrs Allen.'

'How long?' Perhaps Lulu was the one with the brain injury and had got it all wrong.

He shifted from one foot to another. 'We don't really know. You've had a mild brain injury, a concussion. It has disrupted your brain's ability to receive and send signals. It's called retrograde amnesia.' He smiled at her.

'And how do I recover from this, um, retrograde amnesia.' She tugged at the neck of her hospital gown.

'Rest, for a start. But if you were to go back to your house, look at pictures on your phone for example, to time-travel as it were, back in photos, old emails, that kind of thing, we've found that can be useful. The brain is a complicated thing, Mrs Allen. Patients often have short-term memory loss after such an accident, that's very normal. What we don't know is how "short term"' – he screwed up his nose when he said this bit, 'it will be, and what it affects. It's all about the different areas of the brain and where long- and short-term memory are stored. Longer-term repeated memory, if you will, like how to ride a bicycle, that's harder to erase.' He beamed at her, as if she'd be very pleased that she could still ride a bicycle. Probably.

'Meantime,' he glanced at his notes, 'the good news is, your breathing has returned to normal and your ribs are slowly healing. You must take it easy. No vigorous sport. Make sure you rest. These ribs will take about six weeks to heal properly.'

Retrograde amnesia. What she had, had a name. She felt oddly pleased. Suddenly there was a flash of a memory. Vigorous sport? Tennis! Did she *play* tennis? She really didn't know. Somewhere, lodged into her brain, was a kind of memory, a squishy sort of memory, some sensation she was trying to locate. A distant joke. Where had the joke gone, the memory? It was just – yes, just out of reach.

'Mrs Allen?'

'Sorry, miles away.'

'Good memories I hope?' he smiled at her.

'Not sure.' She leant her head to the side and looked at him. He pulled at his collar, the way people do when they're a bit agitated and need to go.

'Your sister, I believe, is coming tomorrow to take you home in a taxi, is that right? I'll get your release papers ready. There are some quite extensive notes that, er, somebody needs to read. Your sister perhaps? About your head injury – but we're satisfied that you are out of the danger zone. Your Glasgow coma scale is normal. But you must take it easy for a few days – no stress, and if you have any headaches, or vomiting, you must let us know. We've prescribed paracetamol, the nurse will explain more, and some codeine if your ribs get too painful.'

'But my *memory*, doctor?'

He put his clipboard under his arm. 'We just can't tell if you'll get all your memory back or just some. However, normal functions seem to have resumed and your working memory will not be affected – like I said, you'll remember how to say, type, for example, that kind of thing. The good news is, memories like your schooldays will be crystal clear, childhood memories, if you will. That's because the neural pathways are much older, stronger than newer ones, ones that were formed nearer to the accident, so the older memories survive, you see? You'll be able to remember *skills*, like how to drive or swim, for example, but you won't remember facts so well, like what kind of car you drive, *where* you used to swim, that kind of thing. Recent memories will be the most affected.' He coughed.

Victoria glanced out at the incinerator through the window, then back at the consultant.

'Some patients find that "jogging" their memory, looking at significant items helps. Does that make sense?'

Nothing made sense at the moment.

'You'll have another MRI scan in about six-to-eight weeks with the neurologist, just to make sure all is well.'

All most definitely did not feel well in Victoria's world as she pulled the bedsheet up and stared back out of the hospital window at the grey tower of the incinerator, plumes of smoke rising above, feeding the skies with black, putrid waste.

5 LULU

Caterpillars can dance! Treat your toddlers to a funny and fabulous wriggling creature who will gobble up lots of things but also hand out sweets from a secret caterpillar pouch! *
*(NB A Strict Health and Safety form has to be signed & measures in place at your property before we can allow the Crafty Hungry Caterpillar to enter the premises).

A thwack. *Ouch!* Another kid lands on me as I lie on the floor.

I yank the green Velcro neck of the caterpillar suit and wince as my broken finger throbs. I hate the Caterpillar gigs – the suit makes me itch for days. Vicky used to read the Caterpillar book to me when I was little. Sometimes she'd skip a page, but I always knew. I would poke her in the ribs and tickle her until she owned up. I loved her soothing voice. It was fun to pretend she hadn't read some of the books, then she'd have to re-read my favourites. I scratch my neck and think about her – always been the capable one. But not since the crash. *Who am I, Lulu?* she keeps saying. *I just don't know anymore.* It unnerves me. Changes our places in the universe.

I lift my mask up to see a wobbly toddler clinging onto his mother's legs. The mother is speaking in a pseudo-child's voice, as if speaking in baby-talk will win me over. I smile. Is this where all my training at the London College of Performing Arts has got me? I sigh and reach for my handy water bottle. Half water, half vodka, it's perfect to get me through these gigs. I take a sip.

'Mr Caterpillar, we *have* paid you for an hour and a half,' says the Mummy in her sugar-coated voice. My gaze falls on shiny red patent shoes. I look up. But then suddenly I grin, because Markie has just struck up on his guitar. Markie is my boss and the brains behind these children's parties. I could listen to his lilting voice all day. I look at him effortlessly strumming the guitar, he's got a great sense of rhythm and such an easy manner with the kids. It's that Irish charm or whatever you want to call it.

'*I'm a caterpillar, I'm a caterpillar…*
'*And I want to eat a massive dinner…*
'Lulu?'

Oops, it's my cue to wriggle and say I'm hungry… I pull myself up onto my knees. 'I'm so hungry!' I say, rubbing my caterpillar tummy, but then I wobble slightly and steady myself. 'What else can I eat?'

'My mummy!' says Leg Cling Boy.

I stifle a snort. 'How about I find some yummy things that *you* can all eat! Are you hungry?'

'Yes!' they yell as I reach into my hidden pouch and produce several packets of mini Haribos.

'Yippee!' I lean back on my haunches. A swarm of children floods over my lap like hungry bees, ripping open packets. As I help a child open a packet, my engagement ring glistens in the sun, sending shards of deep red light sparkling across the wooden floor like a glitter ball. It wasn't Simon's fault that he didn't know I don't like rubies. My mind wanders off. Thinking about the whole wedding shenanigans gives me the jitters: the dress – Simon's mum is piling on the pressure, the WhatsApp wedding group she's created has made me feel suffocated, not supported. Marjory wants to meet tonight to look at shoes. *No Marjory*, I texted, *the shoes can wait, Vicky's in hospital.*

'You alright?' Suddenly Markie's hand is on my shoulder, reassuringly, and I'm back in the room.

'Yes,' I smile. But I'm not really. Ever since I've come out of hospital I've been at odds with myself. The crash, Victoria still in hospital; something's shifted. My focus has changed. Before the accident I had my eye on the future, and I knew where I was going. It's different now. I feel different. Maybe my brain got a jolt too, like Vicky's.

'Look, let's call it a day, get cleared up, you look shattered, you've probably done too much,' Markie winks at me, then he tilts his head to one side and stares at me. 'You're still worried about your sister, so you are.' Markie's soothing Irish accent washes over me, bringing me back to earth.

I *am* worried about Victoria. I'm fetching her from hospital today, seeing as James has made no attempt to come back. How's she going to cope?

'Hey, it's not your fault your sister lost her memory,' Markie adds, as if reading my mind. I look up at him packing away his guitar and shrug. 'No, I guess not.' A wave of guilt hits me like a force field, square in the chest. I hope he can't smell the vodka on my breath.

Once we clear up, we clamber into Markie's van, or 'portable office' as he likes to call it.

'Want to talk about it?' he offers, pulling away from the kerb.

There's something about him which makes me want to

confess, to talk, to lose myself in the calm of the space between us. No, that sounds ridiculous – but it's true. His van, the way I can just be myself and not have to think too much – until we pull up at the next party.

'Trouble is, I don't know where to start, Markie.'

'Have you talked to Simon?'

With the mention of his name I feel a weird sensation in the pit of my stomach. I should talk to Simon. Trouble is, I already did last night. And it's all practical, do you want a sandwich, are you cold, shouldn't you go to bed, should you go to work? He's never asked me how I'm actually *feeling*. I'm being unkind, I should try again. Simon's been great since the accident, he even let me watch Love Island Extra last night, and other stuff he normally rolls his eyes at.

Pull yourself together, Lulu, a little voice pipes up. Simon will know what to say next time – won't he? Tell me it isn't my fault… be my comfort blanket, the one I've ended up turning to, he'll heal me. He'll tell me – what? There's that knot of guilt again.

'Look, why not start at the beginning?'

I glance at Markie and offload. Tell him about the Wedding Fayre, the free prosecco, the car, the drive, those lights. But I don't tell him about those endless refills, the deep nagging or the demons I keep hidden. Abruptly I stop, tears threatening, and I feel conflicted, I want to go on, but I can't. 'Actually, you're right,' I say shakily, 'I should talk to Simon.' I hesitate. 'But Vicky's not right, Markie, I mean really not right.'

'How do you mean?' Markie glances in his rear-view mirror.

'She thinks she's who she was ages ago, like, before she and James, her memory—?'

'She doesn't remember stuff?'

'No.'

'That's not good. So she still thinks her and James are pally?'

'Yeah. It's a nightmare.'

I've told Markie loads about my family, about what happened to my mum and dad when they went to Yorkshire, about Vicky, or Victoria as she has wanted to be called in the last few years. ('It will give me gravitas,' she said. I just burst out laughing. I asked her if 'gravitas' was a kind of Spanish tapas. She didn't find that funny. Even when I poked her in the ribs.) I've told him about my dreams and he's shared his family story with me. I know that Markie's 'mam', as he calls her, and dad still live in Dublin, he's an only child, he went to a local grammar and then on to the Royal Irish Academy of Music on a scholarship – he was in a band in the Nineties, playing gigs around Brighton, but they split up after two years. And then he started the children's party business.

'Why don't you drop a few hints, see if her memory comes back a bit?'

Markie drives us through the dark streets of Little Norland towards my flat; houses flash past on either side, windows glow in the dark. He pulls up behind a queue of cars.

'Penny for them.'

I turn to him. 'It's like the accident has made me question everything. I know Vicky got a bump to the head, but I feel really rattled.'

'What are you questioning?' He is staring straight ahead.

'Well, who I am, too.' It sounds pathetic, saying it out loud, but well, I kind of mean it. 'Sorry, no that sounds ridiculous—'

'No, no it doesn't,' he moves gears and pulls away. 'It's bound to shake you up – I mean these major events – death, birth, near-misses, or, you know, weddings, have a habit of doing that.'

Major events… I close my eyes and shake my head. I want to rid my brain of those black thoughts. When I open my eyes Markie's smiling. 'Look, it's your big day soon. That could be stressful, no?' he says, with an edge I don't recognise – is that sarcasm? – as he slides the car into the next lane.

My 'big day'. I feel overwhelmed and sweaty. It's probably just this ridiculous outfit, green and crumpled and hot. It's bound to give me a headache. I yank at the collar just as my stomach rumbles really loudly; I blush. Markie turns to me and grins. 'Well, pet, it's no wonder, because,' he makes a comedy face: 'you are a *really* hungry caterpillar.'

I snort out loud.

He can always make me laugh.

6 VICTORIA

'Do you recognise this?'

Lulu was sitting next to her in the back seat of the taxi; she put a hand out and touched her forearm gently. 'Victoria?'

'Will you stop calling me Victoria! I'm Vicky!'

'Have a look around,' Lulu soothed.

Victoria sat back and took a deep breath. The ride home had been like some sort of nightmare. While she couldn't process what was going on in her head, her body had another idea. Lulu had laid her hand on her arm as she'd taken short, shallow breaths as the taxi swung out of the hospital car park, recognising that her body was having some kind of reaction yet her mind was blank. She'd pulled at her seatbelt. *It's OK, Victoria*, Lulu had said. She hadn't felt OK. Now, she looked at her unfamiliar surroundings. They were sitting on a perfect resin-coated driveway with tidy borders, punctuated by little pockets of wild primroses and snowdrops. The little white flowers were bobbing up and down in the wind, as if greeting her.

Friendly flowery faces in an unfamiliar driveway. Her driveway.

The house was a 1950s two-storey double-fronted detached building. The outside walls were painted white, and there were grey weatherboard beams running across the top floor, rather like a New England house. It was a nice house. Two very neat bay trees sat elegantly in brushed metal containers on either side of the door. Victoria found that she rather liked it. But it didn't feel hers.

'I don't know where I am.' She had recognised some of the streets on the way back from the hospital, especially as they drew nearer to Little Norland; there was a café that looked oddly familiar, but when they had stopped at the junction just before her driveway, they could have been anywhere.

'It will come back to you, I'm sure.' Everyone kept telling her this. Bits will come back to you. But what if they didn't? What had happened? What had she and James done to their marriage for goodness sake? She looked around again and then caught sight of something and gasped. 'Good lord, Lulu, we have a tennis court.'

She heard Lulu sigh. 'Yes, Victor— Vicky, you have a tennis court. You really don't remember, do you? Come on, let's get you inside.'

Victoria followed Lulu to the front door and watched her turn the key in the lock, then they both nearly jumped out of their skin as an ear-piercing siren started. 'Jesus, I forgot you had an alarm,' shrieked Lulu.

Calmly, Victoria walked inside and stared at it on the hall wall. Then, without realising what she was doing, tapped in a few numbers and pressed the key icon on the keypad. The alarm stopped.

'We have an alarm?' she turned to Lulu.

'Yes, you do. You remembered the code?'

Victoria's handbag slid off her arm and it fell to the floor with a thump. She turned around and leant against the wall. Her head was spinning. 'It's weird. The doctor said this might happen. Some things will be lodged in my brain and stuck there – like the code for the alarm – but other things,' she shook her head, 'have vanished, and nobody knows for how long, or if they'll come back.' She felt her throat catch.

'Come on,' Lulu said, yanking her away from the wall, 'let's get into your kitchen and I'll make you a cup of tea.'

She let Lulu lead her into the kitchen. 'Oh my! It's incredible. And so tidy! When did I get this tidy?'

'Probably around the time you lost— well, you said it kept you busy. Gave you something to do,' Lulu said, filling up the kettle.

Victoria gripped the kitchen surface as Lulu came over to her. 'Sweetie, let's sit down, you're probably still in shock.' She led her over to the table and pulled out a chair. Victoria sat down and took in the kitchen with its tiled floor, grey marble surfaces and glass-fronted cupboards and stared at Lulu as she busied herself with making tea, putting biscuits on a plate. When she sat down opposite her at the kitchen table, Victoria shivered. There was so much she didn't know. Most importantly, why was her husband divorcing her? Surely when he got back they could all sit and talk about it? Hold hands, and she'd make his favourite Moroccan chicken, the one they'd had on honeymoon and she'd hunted out the recipe for. She'd add the flaked almonds, plus the Greek yogurt and it would be melt-in-the-mouth gorgeous and he wouldn't dream of leaving her. *No, said a little voice, it will take more than a chicken dish.*

'Lulu, I can't remember any of this. It's starting to scare me.' She took a sip of tea. Nice mug.

'What, er, what do I usually *do*?'

Lulu looked at her. Victoria took in the curly blonde hair framing her face, the slightly more tired-looking face – she'd got used to it now – and watched as Lulu tilted her head, as if summing something up, then she flicked her hair off one shoulder decisively. 'Well, you like a tidy house, and you're pretty busy with that new Pilates place in the village you joined, and your friend Zoe – and um, manicures, Botox, and of course ferrying the twins here and there, school committees. You're – you know – busy.' She shrugged then took a sip of coffee.

'Manicures? Pilates? But I hate sport.'

'Um, well you don't really "do" sport, Victoria, you sort of like to wear the gear and – have coffee.'

What was the point of *that*? 'And this Zoe, is she a good friend, is she nice?'

Lulu picked up a biscuit and bit it in half. 'Remind me what the doctor suggested. You know, about your memory?'

'He told me to look at some photos, that kind of thing, to see if it jogged my thoughts. Triggered any events.'

'Right, I'll get a few photo albums – wait here.'

Victoria gripped her arm on the way past. 'Lulu, why hasn't James called? I mean, whatever's happened, surely we're still talking?'

Lulu gave her a weird look. 'Let me get those photos.'

When she came back, Lulu had a collection of photo albums and pictures in frames. They sat and pored over some old photo albums – the old-fashioned kind with little stickers under each one saying when it was taken. Victoria pulled one from the pile, it had a green velvet cover which had faded; it was oddly familiar.

'That's the one from Mum and Dad's house.'

'Dad – he's?' She scratched her head. Oh, blast these memories.

'He's OK. In Yorkshire, remember?' Lulu was nodding with eyes wide. The way you do when you're talking to small children. 'He wanted to come down but I told him to wait till you were settled back home.'

'Look, here.' Lulu stabbed at the picture with her fingers, silver bangles clanked around her wrist. 'When the twins were born.'

'I do remember that!' Victoria's heart thumped in her chest. She remembered! She flicked through the pages of the worn album and took in the tiny bundles, one in the crook of each of James's arms. 'My darling babies.' But there was a dark memory too. She frowned. A haunting feeling, of being sucked under – was it water? Then a pillow wet with tears. When was that? But then she looked at James beaming from a hospital chair in the photo, in a blue wrinkled shirt with a twin on either side of him, bundled in blankets. She traced the outline of his face with her finger. She *did* recall that day, pieces of it. The shock of the twins arriving early, going into labour, being utterly terrified, James being calm by her side, his thick thatch of strawberry blonde hair sticking up because he kept running his hands through it, saying it would be alright. She smiled at the memory. Eventually they'd had to whisk her off for an emergency caesarean, but James had stayed right by her side, holding her hand. The tiny wail of Izzy coming out first was a sound she *could* remember, thank goodness.

'Hey, how about this picture?' Lulu held up a silver-framed photo of her with James on what was clearly her wedding day. Right, memory, *come on*. She screwed up her eyes, tried to focus. Images were there somewhere, she just had to find them. It was like ploughing through a vast picture file but they were all foggy, the pictures out of focus. She looked up at Lulu. 'No,' she said shaking her head.

She looked back at the photo. She was in a cream satin figure-hugging dress, spaghetti straps over her shoulders and, from what she could see, a delicate, shoulder-length veil and daisies in a ring resting on her hair, which had been tied up in a messy bun. But it was her face that she noticed most – staring up at James, radiant. And James, in a grey morning suit and purple tie, had both his hands clasped around hers and was bending to kiss her fingers, eyes fixed on the camera. It was such a sweet moment, James looked not conventionally handsome, but there was that cheeky smile, the dimples, the way his neck curved round. She remembered *him*, she just couldn't remember the wedding. None of it. She quickly wiped away a tear from the glass frame and looked up at Lulu, then out to the garden.

'Have a look at this.' Lulu held out a wooden frame with two surly teenagers glaring at the camera. 'Last summer. You went to Florida.'

You could see the girl's bright orange bikini top tied round her neck, her hair pulled back in a high ponytail, arms folded and – oh— Victoria peered closer. 'What's that in her ear – and, er, eyebrow?'

'Oh, yes, Izzy's piercings. You weren't very keen on them. Especially the eyebrow.' Lulu raised her own eyebrow at Victoria as she processed this information. As images of a ten-year-old in a pink gingham hairband flashed through Victoria's mind. Something told her Izzy would no longer be wearing gingham. Anywhere.

The boy frowned at the camera from underneath a long, dark fringe. He was in a black T-shirt and his skin was pale. 'Is— is that Jake? My ten-year-old? The one who's just collected all the football stickers from M&S?'

Lulu nodded. 'Well, yes, no. He's nearly sixteen, Victoria.' She put a hand on her knee. 'Look, I'm going to get you upstairs for your nap, James and the kids will be back soon. And you don't have to come tomorrow, really, I'll be fine.'

'Of course I'll come to your wedding dress fitting!' Even Victoria could hear the faux joy in her voice. 'I just can't believe it, that's all.' Victoria tried to smile as she pushed back her chair. Something was niggling her. She could remember some things. 'Lulu, what about the West End? Wasn't there an audition?' The last proper memory Victoria had was of a Lulu who was too excited to tell her down the phone that she'd secured an audition for *Mamma Mia* at the West End. Lulu had been screaming at her, yelling '*I did it, I bloody got the audition!*' The unstoppable Lulu, the force of nature, the girl who came alive behind a microphone.

A look flashed over Lulu's face. 'Didn't work out,' Lulu said with a tight smile as she placed a hand on Victoria's elbow to help her up. 'I'll explain it all later.'

She heard the car before she could see it. She clutched the windowsill and stared at the huge grey Land Rover as it headed confidently into the driveway and stopped just outside the garage door. Land Rover? They hated four-wheel-drives, didn't they? Used to make jokes about people who owned them, *didn't* they? Her hands were trembling. It was two o'clock. She'd been asleep for an hour and had come down to the kitchen to make a cup of tea.

She felt like an extra in her own movie. James got out of the car, and rolled his broad shoulders, the ones she used to rest her head on. He was wearing a navy ski jacket and beige chinos. Two, tall, lanky kids got out the back. Her kids. Her *teenagers*.

It was still a sunny day, a glimmer of spring in mid-

February, but the air was bitter. She shivered at the window. As James slung the strap of his bag over his shoulder he glanced at the house and she could see him sigh, the mist of his breath swirling round his face. Was he taller than she remembered? Had her memory played tricks on that too?

He opened the boot, and they all grabbed various duffel bags and headed to the door. Her legs suddenly felt weak. She sat down at the kitchen table with a thump and looked around her wonderful, tidy, foreign kitchen.

The key turned in the lock with a click at the same time as her heart rate sped up. She shoved the letter from the lawyers about mediation that she'd found on the pile in the hall under a stack of free magazines on the kitchen table – she'd tackle that later.

And then there he was. Standing right in front of her, the man she had ached for in hospital, the only person she had wanted to see, whose skin she'd wanted to feel next to hers, the only shoulders she had dreamed of leaning her head on: her husband, his eyes boring into her, standing in the kitchen doorway. His face was tanned; he leant it to one side, summing her up. His sandy-blonde hair was still short, but there was that funny bit poking out at the front. It made her want to laugh. Sort of. He was looking at her. 'Victoria.' One hand in his pocket. No wide grin. He looked older, slightly stockier, but still *her* James. Still *him*.

'James. Good to see you.' She smiled her best smile and started to get up, then sat down again as her legs felt strange and her breathing was tight.

He nodded at her then walked stiffly over to where she was sitting. 'Don't get up, I expect you still feel very shaky.' He pecked her on the cheek. Soap and a smell of the outdoors, stubble. No arms finding her waist, telling her it would be alright, no fingers laced through her hair. He

37

towered above her. He'd clearly brought some frostiness from the slopes with him: he could barely look at her. He took his glasses off the top of his head and placed them on the counter. 'How are you feeling?'

Awful, nearly came out of her mouth. *Lonely. I want you to embrace me, call me Squishy Vicky. Anything but this.*

'Better,' she lied.

'Good.' He walked back to the door and then turned around. 'I'm going to take a shower.'

'Hey, Mum.' Izzy was standing next to her. She looked up at her now-teen and blinked. She was willowy and, well, grown up... What had happened to those gorgeous chubby ten-year-old cheeks, the ones she'd pinch sometimes to squeals of 'leave me alone!' – where was her girl who'd worn plaits to school, who'd still sucked her thumb, had stolen Victoria's nail polish one night, waking up in the morning with it smeared all over her duvet because she 'wanted to look like Mummy'? Her chestnut-brown hair was long, in one single plait resting on her shoulder, her eyebrows were dark brown semi-circles framing her eyes – and there was that tiny diamond eyebrow stud. Victoria shivered involuntarily. Izzy had applied thick, black eyeliner across each lid and finished it off with heavy mascara, a dramatic contrast to her alabaster pale skin. Victoria smiled up at her, this woman-girl of hers.

'Hey, sweetheart, how are you?' Victoria stood up and put a hand on the back of the chair to steady her and started to give Izzy a hug. Izzy froze.

'Mum, weird!' She pushed her away, then cocked her head to one side and their eyes met. 'You don't normally, like, hug me,' she mumbled.

'Rubbish! Come and give Mummy a hug!' Victoria pulled

her closer, but Izzy was motionless. Reluctantly, Victoria released her.

'*Mummy?*' whispered Izzy. 'What's with "Mummy". What, like, has happened to you?' Izzy stared at her as if she had green hair and two antennae. Victoria's heart was pounding. She felt alone – very, very alone. This was her *daughter*, for chrissake.

Just then, Jake popped his head round the door. 'Yo. Mum! Alright?' he looked at her from under his fringe.

'Yes, well, Izzy and I—'

'Yeah, girls' stuff.' He held up his hand like the traffic police. 'I won't interrupt. Don't worry.'

'Who says don't interrupt?'

'You!' they both chorused, as she tightened her grip on the back of the chair.

'No, Jakey, it's OK.'

'Jakey? Mum, hey, that's just weird.' And he flicked his fringe off his face. 'I mean, nobody's called me that since I was about ten.' He screwed up his nose and looked at her. 'You OK?'

She fought the urge to shout 'No!' at about the same time she reminded herself that 'Jakey Wakey' standing in front of her really *was* nearly sixteen. She used to call him that in the mornings, his hair sticking up, legs akimbo, strewn across the duvet and pillows as if he'd been wrestling all night. She'd never known a messier sleeper – that was a strong memory. She could recall his face, breaking into a beam as she chided him it was time to get up. There was no beaming right now. 'I'm fine,' she managed.

'Good. I'm just going round to Blake's house. Leave you two to catch up – OK?' But without waiting for an answer, he just shouted, 'See ya.' She stared at his ripped jeans as he walked out the kitchen, heard the front door bang shut, then, seconds later, a screech of tyres as he whizzed by on his bike, a flash of black against the grass.

'Does he, erm, always ride that fast?'

Izzy glanced over her shoulder. 'Dunno. Yeah, suppose so,' she said, and clicked the kettle on. She turned round and folded her arms. 'So. Mum,' she shrugged, 'like, what happened? One minute we were all skiing down this red run, then at the bottom Dad was waiting for us with this weird look on his face. He said you'd been in an accident with Aunty Lulu, that you were in hospital. He seemed really odd about it. Me and Jake said should we go home,' she flicked her plait over her shoulder, 'but he said he'd spoken to the doctor and you'd be fine. That hospital was the best place for you.' She poured some water in two mugs, then turned back round. 'I was kinda worried. You weren't replying to my WhatsApp messages. Dad said he wasn't going to cut short his ski trip coz he'd badly needed the break.'

What's-what messages? Izzy placed two mugs of tea on the table as she sat down and Victoria looked at her daughter's pale blue eyes, at the smattering of freckles across her nose, just like her father's, and frowned. *Needed the break.* How bad had things become that he'd rather stay skiing than come to her side at hospital? *Bad*, said a voice in her head.

'Mum?' Izzy leant in towards her and she caught the scent of her daughter's perfume and suddenly she was overwhelmed with a memory – it was, where was it? James shouting at her, Izzy in the kitchen, her shutting the door to the garden outside. James turning to her, his face, it was – it was haunted, Izzy's voice asking her 'Mum?' and tears, hot tears, streaming down a face – her face or Izzy's? And the perfume, the embrace, the wet tears sliding down a cheek. A hand, a wedding ring. She glanced down at her left hand and noticed with a shock she wasn't wearing her wedding ring. Where was it?

'Mum?'

She needed to be cool in front of Izzy. She could see that. She didn't want to scupper any fragile relationship they might have had. Only, *what* relationship did they have? 'Sorry darling, I don't know, that's the problem, Izzy. Me and Aunty Lulu were driving back from a Wedding Fayre, it was dark, Aunty Lulu was laughing a lot, I just remember headlights, Aunty Lulu screaming. Then suddenly it was the paramedic, trying to get me out. I don't remember the actual accident or much before it – that's probably a good thing.' She could hear her voice break, so coughed instead.

Izzy took a sip of tea. Victoria did a double take. Long, red talons were wrapped around the mug. Her daughter stared at her and she felt herself prickle under the scrutiny. 'You don't have to talk about it if you don't want to.'

Izzy was right, it was probably too much for her. Victoria wracked her brain for something to say. She studied her daughter as she tilted her head, looked at the fluffy pink jumper and didn't know what to say. 'Show me some photos, of your trip, I'd like to see.'

Izzy smiled briefly then pulled her phone out of her back pocket and started swiping; on the screen were shots of a perfect slope, sun shining on the runs with the snow glistening as if someone had laced diamonds through it; the three of them, grinning madly, slightly out of focus. Izzy must have given someone her phone to take the shot. Jake in an all-black ski suit with a snowboard under his arm, sort of smiling. Izzy in a sky-blue ski suit, cream woolly hat, holding up a glass of – *what?* – wine? She decided to tackle that later. James waving his ski poles in the air, and grinning. *Waving his poles in the air and grinning as she lay in hospital with amnesia. Why was there this distance between them?*

'Izzy, I know this is going to sound weird, but what happened – to me and Dad, I mean, my memory – I just can't—'

Izzy rolled her eyes. 'Seriously? Ask Dad. I'm done with the moods between you two. I need to unpack.' She pushed back her chair, grabbed her bag and walked out the kitchen.

Victoria sat there in her marble-topped kitchen with its Neff appliances and stared around the unfamiliar room. Where had the wooden floors gone? Who had chosen a tiled floor? Where had the old Ikea kitchen table gone, where were her wonky cupboards that didn't quite shut properly? Where were her ten-year-olds? Where was her *life*?

———

James was standing by the French doors looking out to the garden when she went into the sitting room. It was one of the memories she could just about recall about the house. Her and James looking through brochures and poring over which way to have the patio built. They had a half-acre west-facing garden, which caught all the afternoon sun, and a view over the Sussex Downs in the distance. She studied the white shirt collar beneath the navy jumper. It had a small fleck in it. Had she bought that jumper? She had an overwhelming urge to go over and straighten it, then wrap her arms around his waist, smell his smell. But instead she curled her fingers into fists and looked at the view. It was not the time. He had made it perfectly clear that his whole body – his mind – was out of sync with her. She shivered. How had they ended up at opposite sides of their marriage?

She stared at the petite moss-green ceramic pot plants

lining the edge of the patio, housing pansies, Christmas roses and daffodil stems poking through. The paving stones were wet from an earlier shower and the weak sun was casting a shimmer across them. James rolled his shoulders then suddenly turned around and leant against the door frame. He caught her eye. He had his reading glasses perched on top of his head, a tuft of hair caught in them, poking out comically, like Tintin.

'James, can we—'

'Victoria, I really don't want to have a row now.' He turned back round to look out at the garden. Why such acrimony?

'Neither do I,' she said quietly. 'I'm just trying to piece things together; I need your help.'

James walked towards her, but then turned and sat heavily on the blue velvet armchair. When did they buy blue velvet? It would be a nightmare to get yogurt stains out of that. 'Since when?' His voice was quiet. Before he worked for Town and Country Architects he'd had a job with the local council, she did remember that. And he used to tell her about his boss there, 'The Incompetent One'. He was using the same voice with her.

'James?'

'I don't know where to start,' he said quietly. She cast her eyes over the shelves behind him; they housed a gallery of photos chronicling their life as a perfect family: baby shots, some black and white, toothless toddlers grinning at the camera; holiday snaps of the twins with buckets and spades in their hands, squinting in the sun, curls escaping from sun hats; James skiing, the twins at a festival with ear defenders on, grinning on top of James's shoulder – where was that? Then the wedding photo Lulu had shown her; him looking at her tenderly under a stone archway. The man looking at her now did not seem to be the same man who had looked adoringly at her – ever. He rubbed the heel of his hands into his eyes and looked up at her.

'James I've been wracking my brain – so much is gone, and yet other parts are crystal clear, like the twins' seventh birthday, here in the house, the big party we threw, the bouncy castle, that kid throwing up in the garden, what was his name, Ben? And you wearing a silly hat. I—' she hesitated. 'I just can't remember some bits before or after that; I mean, some things are there, like the birth of the twins, some fragments of the accident, the lights coming towards us. Then suddenly it's now, today – I seem to have lost nearly six years of my life, and it's awful. When I charged my phone I was sure my screensaver would be the twins grinning at me, ten years old, like I remember. Only—' She chewed her cheek, 'it's not. It's some dumb picture of me in sunglasses. Someone must have taken it for me, it's weird.'

'It's a selfie.'

'What's that?'

'When you take a picture of yourself,' James sighed loudly.

She had wanted to remain calm but it was proving too hard. Who took pictures of themselves? And how would you do that, anyway?

She glanced at the photo of the twins in the pearl frame and her mind went back to that special party. Izzy and Jake had been wearing matching fancy-dress bumble bee outfits. For some reason that was a craze. Izzy with little black antennae bobbling from a glittery hairband, Jake in his black and yellow socks which kept falling down. *They're adorable*, James had told her, his phone poised capturing them on the side of the bouncy castle.

'Yes, and we made them. Not one, but two! Imagine! Remember when we couldn't even get pregnant?'

'Yes, and you surpassed yourself, Mrs Allen. Not only did you get pregnant, you gave us two for the price of one.' And he'd leant down and kissed her, right there, right in front of Lulu and she'd gone quite pink.

That had been their little phrase, *two for the price of one*. Well, really it hadn't quite been 'two for the price of *one*', because as anyone who's had twins knows, it's really double trouble and double sleep deprivation and double vomiting, and doubly-sore tits. But she and James hadn't minded; they hadn't minded one jot. They had stared down the abyss of maybe never becoming pregnant, three years of dreaded period pain heralding no pregnancy, so that when the sonographer had said 'there's two in there' she and James had cried, actually cried at the hospital in front of the purple-haired woman with the frown and the ring on her thumb which looked really odd – but then suddenly she was handing them both tissues and smiling. Their twins, their children.

For the party, they'd had ice cream cake as the birthday cake – it was from that new café in Little Norland next to the village hall, she couldn't remember the name right now. But she knew it had been strawberry with glittery candles on it. And later that evening she and James had sat with a glass of wine in the garden when the twins were finally in bed – she hadn't bothered to bath them that night, they had been high on sugar and the bouncy castle they'd hired, she had just put them to bed in fresh pyjamas and she probably hadn't worried about their teeth.

'I'm so lucky.' James had turned to her and squeezed her hand. And she remembered that feeling – like sinking your teeth into warm toast that had had honey drizzled onto it, mellow and comforting – and recalled how she had never wanted that day to end.

She stood up and went over to the wedding photo and picked it up, then sat down on the arm of his chair, traced the outline of his face on the photo with her finger. 'Look at us here, it's magical – we look besotted. What happened?'

James jerked his head abruptly and looked at her. 'I don't know, you became someone else, Victoria. Our lives changed, *you* changed. I mean after the—' he hesitated, 'well, anyway, what we had, you made fun of it – you were someone... someone I didn't know.'

'After the what?'

Just then, Izzy breezed into the room wearing very high-heeled boots and abruptly stopped. 'Oh! Sorry, I didn't know *you two* were in here.' She said 'you two' like a vegetarian might say 'hamburger'.

'Should she be wearing such high shoes?' James shot Victoria a look, as if seeking the right response.

'Um, well, maybe not?' Victoria was at a loss. She glanced round the room for another adult to consult. Wait, this was *her* teenage daughter. What shoes did a sixteen-year-old wear? She didn't have a clue. Last she remembered, Izzy was beside herself in a new pair of red trainers with neon laces. She did look great, though. 'You look marvellous, darling! But maybe they *are* a tiny bit too high.' She glanced at James. Was that the right response?

Izzy narrowed her eyes and looked at them both. 'Marvellous? You think I look *marvellous*?' When she said it, her mouth twisted into a weird shape. 'Since when did you ever say I looked marvellous, Mum? And what's with the cosy chat, you two? On the ski holiday I overheard Dad talking to Uncle John – he called you "controlling" and before Mum's accident, you were both shouting at each other, I remember.'

If Victoria hadn't been so gobsmacked about the 'controlling' insult, she would have said something.

'I'm going out.' Izzy flounced towards the door, but not before James shouted, 'Where?' To which she stopped, smiled sweetly and said, 'Shopping. In town. With Bella. We're getting the bus. Then we'll buy some more "marvellous" clothes.' And with that she swung the door open and pranced out of the room.

James rolled his eyes. 'Bella. She hasn't been the same since she started hanging out with her. You need to look into that.'

How did you 'look into' that? She turned to James for some kind of solidarity, but when she looked into his eyes she saw hurt. She studied his long eyelashes, the dark circles underneath, reached out to touch his face, but he flinched and she pulled her hand away.

'You said I was controlling?'

'Victoria, you don't remember, do you? You changed. I mean, all this didn't seem enough for you anymore,' he said, sighing, and leant back heavily in the chair. '*I* didn't seem enough for you anymore – you wanted a bigger, better kitchen, a smarter car, I don't know, like you were competing with someone, and then, you know, you started to make "improvements",' his eyes flitted to her breasts, '*your* words by the way. I'd go away on client trips and come back and there would be more changes, Botox, I just don't know what else. And the problem is,' he stood up abruptly – 'I was never sure if they were for me.' He caught her eye for a moment and there was such sadness there that it took Victoria's breath away.

Victoria touched her hair. 'I don't—'

'Look, we shouldn't do this right now – I read your notes. No stress.' His expression altered and there was a tiny glimmer of the old James as he stood there in front of her.

'James, the accident wasn't my fault.'

His face softened a fraction and her James was still there. 'I know.' He pulled his hand out of his pocket and for a tiny minute Victoria thought he was going to reach out to her. He hastily put it back in.

'James, what happened to us? I mean, I'm hearing a lot about how I changed; well, I can see that.' She waved her hand vaguely up and down over her body. 'But what about "us"?'

'It's— it's complicated. Listen, I have to make some calls now, I said I'd be back in the office tomorrow – will you be alright?' He looked her up and down as if assessing something, then started to walk towards the door. And with a sideways glance at her, her once-more-distant husband left her alone in the room.

7 LULU

Simon opens the door to me. It's midday on Friday and for once Markie and I don't have any party bookings. 'Lulu!' he booms. 'Come in! You'll catch your death out there.' He grabs both my shoulders and pulls me in for a hug on the doorstep. Then he stands back. 'Don't you have anything else to wear but that tatty leather thing? You're freezing!' He kisses me on the cheek. His nose is slightly wet, like a dog. 'We must get you some new clothes!' he says walking back in.

I look at my blue leather jacket. I like this jacket, I've had it since drama school. I follow him in, shrug off my jacket and hang it on the banister. 'Not there, darling.' Simon slides it off, holds it at arm's length and gives it a shake. He then hangs it up on the pegs in the porch. 'Come in, come into the kitchen and sit down. I've made lunch.'

Simon loves to show off his Cordon Bleu skills. He cares about ingredients, looks at something called provenance and reads all the reviews for new restaurants in Brighton. I'm at my happiest with a takeaway – Chinese, anything – and bottle of wine in front of the telly. He's told me his late wife was 'a whizz in the kitchen'. From what I can make out, she was 'amazing' at almost everything. I feel daunted if I even pick up a spatula in front of him. I pour myself a glass of wine from the open bottle at the table. Simon reaches for the bottle. 'Let me do that!' *Does it matter?* I take a sip and tell myself to stop overreacting. 'Mum will be round soon. You two girls have lots to chat about! It's flowers today isn't it? And I think she said she had some sample menus too.' He places a hand on my shoulder as I twist the wine glass stem around in my hand.

I let out a long breath and take another sip of wine. Marjory seems to be involved in every aspect of this wedding, and of Simon's *life*. I'm not ungrateful for her help, but I feel I'm sitting on top of an avalanche of wedding plans, as it zips down a mountain, taking me with it. It's been all wedding, wedding, wedding. I take another slug of wine. I need to just *be* sometimes. Alone with my thoughts. Figuring out—

'Darling?'

'Sorry, miles away.' I put my glass down on the table.

'Will you set the table please? With the serving spoons.' He turns back to his cooking with a flourish. His precision shouldn't bother me, it really shouldn't. I guess when your wife dies in a tragic accident it's no wonder you want to try and control what you can, poor man.

'Well done!' Simon puts his arms around me. 'Just think, in a few weeks, you'll be out of that cold flat and here all the time!' He spins me round to face him, 'In fact, why don't you just move in now?' He fixes me with a pretend pleading look. I kiss him on the cheek and move away.

'Helloo!' Marjory is shouting through the letterbox.

'Mum's here, I'll go let her in.' Simon lunges towards the

hallway and somehow an image of an eager Labrador flashes across my brain.

―――――

'Turn to page forty – what do you think Louise?' Nobody calls me Louise. Simon knows that I'm called Lulu, but I did tell him that I was christened Louise and he seems to have told his mother and she's got it into her head. When I was born, Victoria used to read to me – she was twelve then – and we both loved this heroine called Lulu. She started calling me that. It stuck. And I love it.

I dutifully turn to page forty. 'Um, it's Lulu.' I look up at Marjory, who's peering over her glasses at me.

'Sorry. Lulu. Anyway, I can't decide between E and B – see, have a look, B has more of a vintage feel.' Marjory jabs at the laminated page of flower bouquets with a pink polished fingernail.

Does it? 'They're *all* lovely, I just can't decide.'

Lunch is lovely: some kind of asparagus soup, swirls of single cream, and lashings of that delicious Viognier. I can't really pronounce it, but so what? 'Just wait till you see my sample menus!' Marjory clasps her hands together as Simon beams at her. Just then my phone bleeps and I turn it over on the table and glance at the screen. Markie.

So sorry. Are you free? It's pretty urgent. Like, now-urgent. Had call from a friend of clients who's been let down. Kids party. We'll ad hoc. Can I pick you up?

I register a tiny tingle of anticipation to get away from sample menus, but stamp it down.

I text him back with Simon's address then put my phone down. 'Simon, Marjory,' I look at both their eager faces. 'I'm *really* sorry but I need to go. My boss is stuck – this woman's entertainment has fallen through and she's called him as a last resort. Another client recommended him. He does need the business.' I look pleadingly at them both as they stare at me. 'Sorry,' I mutter and take a swig of wine.

Simon's face falls. 'That's a shame, darling. I thought we'd watch the Grand Prix together later? I mean you're giving up all that children's entertainment business anyway, so what's the point? Can't he cope?'

A little nugget of indignation bubbles up inside me. 'Not really, Simon. He can't sort the lights, the bubble machine and entertain twenty kids – that's why he's got me. And I really don't want to let him down. I do work for him.'

'No. Of course. We'll do this another time. Sorry, Mum.' He glances over at Marjory, who's closed the folder and is leaning back in her seat. 'I know you're worried about the timescales, Mum, and it *is* rather annoying, but,' he snatches a look at me, 'Lulu here needs to go, don't you sweetheart?'

'I can see that,' mutters Marjory.

'Marjory, I love the vintage one, actually, let's go for that – E, right?'

Marjory folds her arms. 'No, B.'

'B it is then, splendid!' I finish my wine and jump up from my seat, steadying myself and peck Simon on the cheek. Just then there's the sound of tyres on the gravel. 'See you both later.' As I grab my leather jacket I'm reminded of a time I sneaked out the house to a school disco aged fourteen. Mum and Dad hadn't known and the flutter of excitement as I scuttle down the drive is almost the same. I stifle a giggle, looking at my reflection in the windows: a woman with mad blonde curls and a flash of lip-gloss grins back at me.

———

'Hi there,' Markie smiles at me as I slip into the passenger seat. 'Thanks for doing this. Sorry to take you away from your lunch.' He puts the car into reverse, then drives a few feet and stops and turns to me as I fumble with the seatbelt. 'Lulu, have you been drinking?'

I stare straight ahead, the buckle in my hand. 'You called *me*, remember? We were going through wedding menus, flowers and, um, things and celebrating.'

'Of course. Sorry. Sounds fun.'

I snatch a look at him. Is he smiling? I feel bad for snapping. The rest of the trip is in silence as we are left alone with our thoughts. I close my eyes for a while as the wine has made me sleepy and images of lilies and menus dance in front of my eyes. Half an hour later, we pull up to a set of black wrought-iron gates. Markie leans out the car to push the buzzer on the keypad. 'Thank *God* you're here,' gushes a woman's voice.

'What kind of party are we doing?' I ask as he puts the car into gear and slowly moves forward.

'Anything we can,' he laughs. 'At this late notice, we will just throw it all at them: I've brought the disco decks and the bubbles, and the UV light. If you change into Disco Diva with the sparkly dress, is that OK? We'll do a conga, I'll do some magic tricks – we'll smash it.'

He's always upbeat, so sure of himself. 'You don't see problems, do you?' I lean back in my seat and smile. I probably *have* had too much to drink.

Markie stares straight ahead as the gates move apart and grins. 'Try not to. Why?'

'Just an observation.'

Half an hour later and we've set up the music in the 'playroom' – a huge room with a wooden floor, perfect for five-year-olds to dance. Markie's started the bubble machine and I've changed into Disco Diva in the downstairs bathroom – I tripped over the shower tray and ripped my dress; it doesn't really show. Now I'm snapping the glow sticks to hand out to all the kids. Music is pumping through the speakers, the sound of the bass throbbing with my own heartbeat and the messy playroom has morphed into a mini nightclub with strobe lights and bubbles. It's a fabulous transformation.

The mother bustles into the room. 'Brilliant! Holly is thrilled this is going ahead! Here's some wine, it's open.' She places a tray with a wine bottle and two glasses on the table. 'And I'll pay you guys double!'

'Nah, no need to do that.' Markie grins at her, then turns up the music as I fill two wine glasses to the brim and take a gulp.

'Let the party begin!' I say, holding up my glass to Markie. He takes a sip of his then puts it down as a gaggle of youngsters rush into the room and grab the glow sticks from me. Half an hour later as they're jigging up and down, Markie motions to me to start a conga. I grab a girl by the hands and show her how to put her hands on my waist and we start. Reluctantly, a few girls join her, then, half a song in, the whole party joins in, whooping and cheering as Markie turns up the bubble machine. Then, suddenly, he's in front of me and I grab his waist and loop my fingers through the belt hole on his jeans, and we're all doing the conga together. At one point, I nearly lose my grip, so I grab his waist firmly and have a sudden urge to wrap my arms right around him.

Which is the thought that's looping round my head as he turns and stares at me. 'Lulu?' He's put the music to Macarena on and is gesturing to me that I should start. I've made up my own moves as well as the standard ones and the wine is really helping me make this fun for the kids now! They're screaming with laughter and Markie has joined in, hamming it up, pretending to get the moves wrong. We stand in front of a sea of kids, smiling and clapping and jumping forward, both singing the words to the Spanish hit song. As we belt out *Hey Macarena*, throwing our arms in the air, I realise my jaw is aching from all the grinning and I feel *alive*!

'Right boys and girls,' shouts Markie as I get my breath back, 'last dance of the night! Baby Shark! The kids start to scream even louder, then begin to copy Markie with the hand movements; he's larking about and being such a clown, but the kids are lapping it up. I start to jig up and down and polish off another glass of wine. Eventually, Markie has to turn the music off. 'Awww,' the kids all moan together, but Markie's still laughing.

'This really is closing time, lights on!' and with that he flicks on the main switch and we are blinded by the awful bright lights. As we pack away our guitars, the speakers and load up the van with all the paraphernalia of the evening, my heart sinks just a little that the party's over too.

Back in the car, Markie holds up his hand for a high-five. 'Good work partner.' I stare at his large hand with a ring on his middle finger, lit by the streetlight in the driveway and I want to reach out and hold it. I smile at him and instead I reach over to slap his palm to give him a high-five, but he moves it away and grins. 'Too slow!'

'Very funny,' I say sinking into the familiar musty smell of his van, hidden away in my cocoon where we talk, swap ideas for ever-more crazy parties we can host and have a laugh.

'What's on the cards for you now then?' Markie says as he puts the van into reverse.

'Oh, an evening of Grand Prix highlights and scrolling

through wedding menus.' I sigh. As Markie steers the van carefully through the black gates, I wonder how the girl who was good enough to audition for *Mamma Mia* could have changed like this. Tomorrow's my 'bridal hair try-out', whatever that is. I reach into my bag and make sure my 'water' bottle is there. I'm going to need it tonight.

8 VICTORIA

Victoria gripped the steering wheel of her car. She'd peered outside earlier at a BMW convertible and screwed up her eyes. *Is that my car? Will I remember how to drive?* She'd been driving her 'other' car, apparently, when they'd had the accident. What other car? she'd been dying to ask, but felt she shouldn't. Although the damage wasn't extensive, the car had still been written off by the insurance company. Her life was one long game of putting together puzzles. Except some pieces of the puzzle eluded her. The kids were back at school – that had been weird. The hugs from some school mums, the kind stares, the nods to her from those she, presumably, knew less well. She'd found herself being centre stage in the play Victoria Loses Her Life. James had driven them off from the first school drop-off as she sat in tears in the passenger seat, unable to cope with driving that time. It had been like a sluice gate of emotions had been opened up – only she didn't know quite what was behind all the sensations she was feeling.

Suddenly, everything came together: seatbelt on, ignition,

lights, a flick of the windscreen wipers. Yes, she could do this. This kind of memory was working. She *wanted* to do this. To prove things were getting better, that *she* was getting 'back to normal'. Even if it was a new normal. She twisted in her seat as her ribs were still tender. But it wasn't that. Her heart was somehow beating rapidly and some part of her was registering deep distress. She took a steadying breath. She was determined to gain control of at least a fragment of her life again, so she navigated out of her drive and found the shop in the middle of the High Street. Lulu had told her where to find it. Thank God it wasn't far.

She pulled into a parking spot and turned the ignition off and leant back in her seat, quite exhausted. She flicked the visor down and looked at her reflection. Who was this woman, in the BMW, with the long bob – she looked down at her chest for the umpteenth time that day – would she *ever* get used to them? Sleeping was a nightmare, she just couldn't get comfortable. James was in the spare room. 'It happened months ago,' he'd explained on the first night, almost amused, when she'd asked.

'Hey!' Someone was tapping on the window. It was Lulu, grinning. Seeing her was like a warm blanket was being thrown around her, especially as last night everyone had been so chilly. It had been excruciating at dinner. Everyone was trying to act normal, whatever that was. Although Victoria couldn't actually remember how she *would* ask for the mashed potatoes to be passed, she was bloody sure it wasn't with a sugary sweet voice and met with a dull stare by her teenage daughter. Everyone was avoiding the massive elephant in the room, and that elephant had been getting larger and larger as the minutes ticked by. *Where is my memory, dammit? And where is my marriage?*

And she hadn't been able to find anything in the blasted

kitchen either. Who keeps Tupperware boxes *inside* each other? Russian doll Tupperware. 'You used to insist it was like that, Mummy.' Izzy had stood, smirking, arms folded, watching her struggle. 'Said it was neater. Complete 'mare.' Was it Victoria's imagination, or was there a real frustration burning underneath Izzy's fake smile? She *knew* she was a teenager now, she *knew* things had changed between them, but she sensed Izzy wasn't quite herself. Or perhaps it *was* her blasted memory playing tricks. Izzy and Jake had rushed away from the table the minute they had finished, as if their pants were on fire, claiming jetlag. Much later, she'd seen the eerie glow of white light under their bedroom doors. Time with a screen was obviously preferable to being with her.

She'd been too tired to argue, too overwhelmed. The politeness was killing her. James had sat through the whole dinner with pursed lips, like she'd served them mashed hedgehog or something, then he dutifully made sure she had taken her painkillers, helped her up the stairs as he said she looked pale, then taken himself off to the spare room saying a curt 'good night'. She'd crawled under her duvet without washing her face and started to sob.

'Hey, sis! You alright?' Lulu yanked open her door. Victoria couldn't help but notice how dull her eyes looked.

'Think so. Well, no, actually. It's all a bit weird.' She took another look at her little sister. 'Big night?'

'Oh, um. Not really. Last minute booking. A kid's party at a woman's house.' Lulu stood back to let Victoria get out the car.

'You were out late,' said Victoria as she shut the door and seemed to know which button on the fob to press to lock the car. 'When I couldn't get hold of you I called Simon – well, I found the number on my phone – and he seemed very nice but he said you'd been out late, then just crashed into bed.'

'Yeah, it was exhausting and it took a bit longer to tidy up – hey,' she said, glancing at the salon behind them, 'let's get us some "me-time"!' As they walked into the salon, Victoria was embraced by a fug of warm air. It smelt of hairspray and singed hair.

'Victoria, hell-*o*. How are you?' An older woman with grey hair in a choppy cut, dressed in all black, was almost bowing. 'Here for your usual? Let me take your coat. Oh, I *love* your earrings!' Victoria touched her earrings and looked around for clues. Who did they think she was? Meghan Markle? Lulu had vanished round the corner for a 'bridal hair try-out'. Victoria tried to find some images she recognised. As she sat down in the chair, the woman staring back at her was certainly not one of them. What *was* her usual? She nodded – much easier to agree, rather than risk her hairdresser bundling her out of the salon as a nutter. Maybe having her hair done might spark some synapses to remember more about herself – including her hairstyle.

Debbie, as the woman turned out to be called, was the salon manager. Apparently Victoria would only have her do her hair. She gave her a glorious head massage. (*Pressure alright? Good, because normally you're very fussy.*) Then she set about snipping a tiny amount off her fringe, her layers. Products were applied, her hair was rough dried and then the straighteners had come out. Straighteners? What a performance. Normally she just washed her hair at home and let it dry. Didn't she?

When she looked up from the magazine she was reading, there was a woman in the mirror with poker-straight hair looking at her. It looked good, yes – but it didn't look like *her*. Certainly not like the Vicky she remembered, not like her *at all*.

'How's that for you?' Debbie was holding a mirror up to

the back of her head. She looked at the immaculate way the layers fell and found herself nodding.

'Are you sure?' Debbie rested her hands on her shoulders and looked at her in the mirror. 'Because we don't want you having one of your fits, like when I let one of the juniors dry your hair! Do you remember?' She smiled at Victoria in the mirror but it didn't quite reach her eyes. Then she fussed around, flicking hair off her gown and chattering about everyone in the salon. Victoria didn't have a clue what she was talking about.

As she presented her credit card to pay, Debbie said, 'Oh, just touch it, dear,' as Victoria tried to put it into the little slot of the card machine. She did as she was told and, magically, the screen flashed up 'paid'. She smiled tightly at Debbie wondering what had just happened.

Walking back to her car, Victoria thought about what Debbie had said. I'd have a fit if a doctor gave my children the wrong medicine, thought Victoria, I'd have a fit if James had an affair, she reasoned. But to have a fit over how her hair was dried? She shook her head. She had to find a way to convince James that the Old Vicky was back – and was giving the New Victoria a run for her money.

9 LULU

'What do you think?'

Markie swallows a smile. 'Grand. I mean you look like you've been to the hairdresser.'

'What does *that* mean: "like I've been to the hairdresser"?'

'Well, you've got a new hair "do", right?' He scrunches his brows together quizzically at me, as if guessing the right wording. 'Hey, it is grand, so it is.' He leans back on the leather chair in The Little Norland Coffee Shop, the one by the village hall, and it makes a kind of whoosh noise.

'So you said.'

'Why are you looking at me like you just bit into a lemon?'

I burst out laughing. 'I am not.'

'You're kind of snippy, so you are.' A smile twitches at his lips.

'Snippy? I'm not snippy!' But as I say it I can feel my face twist into, well, a snippy kind of look.

His eyebrows fly up before he looks back down at his laptop. I sit down heavily in the chair next to him and yank my hair. I knew it was all wrong. My normal bouncy blonde curls have been tamed with what looked like a cooking utensil and I resemble a TV presenter on one of those American shopping channels. When I looked in the mirror at the hair-dressers I nearly screamed. *We'll give you a full bridal*, the girl had said, see if you like it. Markie certainly doesn't, in fact he's glancing sideways at me now, looking like he's trying really hard not to piss himself.

'You hate my hair.'

'Lulu, my darlin'.' He says this in a lilting way, dropping the 'g'. 'I am not the one wearing it.'

'You don't *wear* your hair.' I fold my arms across my body but my mouth is involuntarily smiling.

I catch Markie glancing at me as he angles his laptop closer. 'You'll make a lovely bride, so you will. Anyway, have a look at this.'

Get Paid to Have Fun!

We are looking for an enthusiastic part-time children's entertainer in Sussex to work for us!
The ideal candidate will have:
Bundles of personality; a desire to succeed; love working with kids! Driving licence. You will be working with 4–12-year-olds in a fast-paced environment, using cool disco decks, letting off bubbles, snow or using a smoke machine, one day you'll be Bubble Bo Peep next, A Hungry Caterpillar! Experience not essential. Full training given. You will be accompanied by Markie Music, who will provide the musical accompaniment to all the events.

He's wasted no time trying recruiting for my job. Why am I not delighted? I'm giving up this 'kids' party malarkey' as

Simon calls it. But a thought lands on my brain like a butterfly gently flapping its wings to get steady and the idea circles around and around. *What will I do after I'm married?* You'll be safe, Lulu, a voice tells me. Safe. Married.

And *bored*.

The truth is I haven't been able to think about it – it's been all 'wedding dress this' and 'wedding flowers that'. The snarky voice is quietly whispering to me – you *have* been able to think. 'Art classes' Simon said a few days ago as if a light-bulb had gone off in his head, as he stirred some béchamel sauce. As if, just because I am 'creative', I'd suddenly be able to wield a paintbrush and be any good at that. 'It's completely different Simon,' I'd said patiently, 'painting, to singing, to being on an actual *stage*, you know, in front of people instead of being in front of a canvas. There's a live reaction when you perform. The canvas doesn't give you that.' I tried not to sound sarcastic. How could he think those things were similar? His world is figures and spreadsheets, I know, but still. And then I tried to explain to him about my dream, about the West End, I couldn't tell him *why* it had all gone wrong – that will have to wait till I'm ready – but I needed him to understand it was where I felt alive. 'You don't want to bother with all that, you'll be married soon' was his response. I'm still processing it. But it was the most annoyed I've been with him since we met.

'Well?' Markie seems oddly pleased with himself. 'I've got fifty CVs to look through! Result!'

'You'll need the right person, not *everybody* can do this job you know.' I close my mouth, because I do sound prickly. I'm glad he's getting on with it. He needs to, as he's running out of time.

Markie looks towards the café door. 'Course they can't. Nobody can replace you!' Is he serious or messing with me?

'No, well, I'm trained, you know, and I'm only doing this—'

'Because you haven't got anything else.'

'Thanks a bunch.' I cross my legs and sit back.

'Whoa, Lulu, I mean it,' he places his hand on my forearm gently. I'm acting like a four-year-old, but I don't seem to be able to stop myself. 'It's a shame you haven't got anything else,' he takes a sip of coffee. 'I happen to believe that this is actually quite a difficult job, and, for what it's worth, you're great at it *because* you're trained. But you're wasted here, Lulu. And I shouldn't be saying that about my own business, but it's true.' He leans in closer. 'And you know you are. But I've been lucky to have you.' He smiles at me and releases his grip. There's an odd whirling at the pit of my stomach.

'Just don't you forget it.' I use my best schoolteacher voice.

'Hey, will you help me interview? Got a girl lined up who I think is perfect. I'm meeting her here.' He glances at his watch. 'In ten minutes.'

A surge of unease lands in my stomach as I nod.

———

'Hiya! I'm Katia – you must be Markie, good to meet you!' A girl with an elfin face is grinning and holding out a hand expectantly to him. She's about five-foot-seven, with long blonde hair pushed jauntily in place by a polka dot hairband; pink raincoat, tight black jumper and short pink netted skirt; opaque black tights and thigh-high boots. Is she in fancy dress?

Markie stands up instantly and takes her hand. 'Great to

meet you Katia.' He's grinning from ear to ear. 'Have a seat. This is Lulu.'

'Hi,' I say, folding my arms across my chest. Markie snatches a look at me.

'Oh wow, this is exciting! Thanks for seeing me!' Katia sits down on the chair next to Markie and, with a flurry of hair flicking, takes off her raincoat.

'Shall I hang that up?' Markie bounds out of his seat and hooks the coat on a nearby peg.

Markie chats animatedly as I try not to notice her perfectly polished fingernails, her tiny waist, and try to focus on what she's saying: she's doing teacher training at college, is a trainee drama teacher, looking for extra work, she just *loves* kids, been on the stage herself since she was ten years old, parents couldn't drag her off it – bet they couldn't. I look away at the door to distract myself from this nauseating Mary Poppins of a girl. When I zone in again I hear her tell Markie she's come up with a new song for the Bo Peep character. *Couldn't help myself and thought I'd just sketch something up.*

I think I might be sick. I cough and excuse myself to the Ladies'. When I get back, Markie is tapping away at his laptop. He looks up at me when I sit down. 'She was perfect! Don't you think?' He turns to me.

'Yeah, she was great.' I bite my fingernails. But as much of an actress as I am, I can't hide my feeling of unease. Perhaps it's just a hangover, perhaps it's the stress of the wedding. I haven't been sleeping well. I'm waking up at 2 a.m. most nights, staring at the ceiling, wondering about life, about my past, about *it*. I shake my head. Markie is frowning at me. The concern in those green eyes is almost too much and I feel tears threaten. I don't want to burden him. I focus on the crinkly bit at the side of his eyes as he says he'll get us another coffee and gives me a friendly wink.

I watch him walk back to me, carrying a tray. His concentration is immense, eyebrows knitted, and I smile watching him. A bit of coffee spills from his cup and he swears under his breath. 'I got you a hot chocolate instead, with whipped cream, I know you like them.' He places the tray on the table and mops up the spilt coffee with a napkin, making a mess of it. Then he looks up at me. 'Are you alright for the gig later? Only I can't really fit into Bo Peep's frock?' He looks at me deadpan.

'Of course, Bo Peep at your service.' I channel all my acting skills and muster a fake smile and salute. As long as I have a few drinks back at the flat, I'll be the best Bo Peep *ever*.

———

Markie holds out his hand and I take it. It's soft and warm and for a fleeting second I imagine pulling him into the hay bale with me. I start to giggle. 'Did you see Stuck-Up Mum's face when I forgot the lyrics?'

I can tell Markie's fighting with his professional side and trying not to laugh; he's biting his cheek, one of his little habits. 'C'mon mo-stoirin,' he grins. That's his little name for me, his Irish pet name. 'I used to call my dog that,' he told me when I first met him. *His dog?* But still, it made me smile. 'I think that's enough for today.' He pulls me up to a standing position and then gently nudges me to sit on the hay bale. 'And I'll just have this.' He reaches out for my glass and puts it on a nearby table.

'But we're off duty!'

'Yes, but I have to get you back to your fiancé in a fit state.'

I yank down my bonnet and scratch under my wig. I hate the word 'fiancé', it's so priggish. And I hate Little Bo Peep parties, especially as we had to control two very horny sheep earlier on. I suggested to Markie that perhaps it should be the last time we use a ewe and a ram, but he'd just smiled his relaxed, lop-sided smile at me and told me to chill. The sheep had been tethered outside; earlier the ram had *baa*-ed at a nervous four-year-old who was now sedated with Calpol. I reach for my 'water' bottle in my bag. *One more won't hurt.* I'm seeing Victoria next and I feel a rush of guilt as I take a swig, but this always helps; helps to calm the clashing voices in my head.

'You'll not get us any repeat business, so you won't.' Markie winks at me. 'It's not every day you change the words in The Wheels on the Bus to "the wipers on the bus go piss, piss, piss" instead of "swish, swish, swish". I saw that lassie screw up her nose at you as she was singing along. And the mam was raising her eyebrows.'

'Serve her right. That *mam*, she's a madam. Capital "m".' I seem to be shouting. I steady myself on the hay bale.

'Lulu! keep your voice down.' Markie frowns at me.

'And the kid's a spoilt brat too!' I stage-whisper.

'Lulu!' Markie glances to his right.

I'd better stop having a go at the parents. It *is* Markie's business after all. It's just that sitting in a marquee in Sussex on a bale of hay isn't how I'd planned my life. What I'd planned – well, it's too late. I pull a strand of straw from out of my fringe just as my phone pings. I pull it out of my skirt pocket. It's Victoria, telling me she's early and is parked outside the wedding dress shop.

I sigh and reflect how I've got to this place. When Simon whisked me off my feet for a surprise trip on the Eurostar to Paris, where he produced his grandmother's ring, I was swept up in a tsunami of emotion, confusion – and I was *grateful*. Plus, I hadn't wanted to hurt him. Instead, I'd poured myself another glass of champagne, and we'd had *such* a fun week-end, not that I can remember much of it. But he *is* a good man. He's restored my faith in men. I take another slug from the water bottle. And anyway, all that glitters isn't gold, is it? I'm not sure another man would take me on, not after—

'Lulu?' Markie's packing away his guitar. He looks up at me with those sparkly green eyes. 'When do you need to be there?' He checks his watch.

I glance at the time on my phone. Oh shit. Like *now*. 'Now? Sorry!' I frown as we both speed up and pack away all the equipment. Markie shoves the small beanbag props into the huge duffel bag while I collect up sparkly wands. They've kept the bridal shop open after closing time for 'our special clients'. Marjory practically had an orgasm when she told me they were opening it up 'specially for us'. *And there will be prosecco there*, she'd whispered, as if she was telling a four-year-old there were Smarties in her pockets.

'All done.' He zips up the duffel bag and looks at me. 'Who's going with you?'

'Victoria and the battle-axe,' I say, yanking up my pink tights which seem to be constantly falling down.

'She'll be your mother-in-law soon, I'd save the "battle-axe" craic till later.' He tilts his head at me. I shrug.

'Right, c'mon, Bo Peep, or we'll be late. There's no time to change. If anyone can rock Little Bo Peep wedding chic, it's you!' Markie grins at me as we jump into his van.

'There you go again,' I say, opening the door. He looks at me over the van roof. 'Like I said, never sees the problems,' I smile as I hop into the passenger seat and slam the door shut on the outside world.

10 VICTORIA

Victoria forced a smile as Lulu walked towards her. She hadn't seen her leave the hairdresser – something about her boss interviewing her replacement. Her normal curls had been replaced by poker-straight hair, now sticking out of an absurd bonnet, tied under the chin with a bow; and not only that, she was sporting a pink-and-orange-checked full skirt, with netting over the front, her waist nipped in with a massive white bow and bubble gum pink tights. The effect was Little Bo Peep-meets-catwalk – sort of. She'd just leaped out of a van driven by some gorgeous bloke.

'Who was *that*?' she asked as Lulu approached her and immediately wrapped her in a hug as she always did.

'Oh, that was Markie.'

'Eugh, you smell.' Victoria pulled away.

'Oh crap, that's probably l'eau de sheep.' Lulu grinned at her.

'What?'

She opened out her arms theatrically. 'You can't have

Little Bo Peep without the sheep, can you?' And then she was tittering and wobbling towards the wedding dress shop. Victoria watched her little sister. When had this happened? When had the fiercely ambitious Lulu swapped her musical theatre dreams for children's parties? She was sure the parties were all very well, but Lulu had trained for four years. Why was Lulu always either making jokes, wearing fancy dress, or – she didn't like to admit it – mildly pissed? Victoria realised she couldn't have a heart-to-heart with her on the day of her wedding dress fitting, but she needed to find the right time. Yanking her handbag up her shoulder, she walked towards the shop door. Lulu was standing by the window, rummaging in her bag. She produced some perfume and started to spray herself.

'Did it go OK?'

'What?' Lulu steadied herself on the window pane.

'The children's party?'

'Oh yeah,' Lulu swung her fringed bag over her shoulder. 'You know, twenty pre-schoolers ran riot, I sang Little Bo Peep, then Wheels on the Bus – but changed the lyrics and saw Markie piss himself – then,' she leant in and Victoria got a whiff of alcohol on her breath, 'he was a *total* legend and covered for me when I forgot the words!'

'Lulu, sweetheart, have you been drinking?' Victoria touched her elbow.

'No,' she snapped. 'OK, maybe a little.' She held her fingers up in a pincer action. Victoria sighed and put her arm around her sister, and they both turned to look at the shop window. There were five dresses, held up by invisible nylon string, suspended in the air, like magic. One was tight and fitted with elaborate gold lace along the bust, another was the full fairy tale with a billowing, netted skirt, glistening with tiny diamonds sewn into the tulle net. Weddings. It made Victoria think of hers, or try to – nope, that bit was empty again. Her heart ached for James. For the memories she did have. And for the ones she'd forgotten.

For as long as Victoria could remember – well, this was the hard bit… what she *could* remember was that Lulu had always loved entertaining people. She could summon up sketchy memories of her with a hairbrush, singing into it, and making them all laugh. Christmas parties, then the four of them: Victoria, Lulu, Mum and Dad, round the table on Friday nights listening to the top 100 on the radio. Something changed when Lulu stood up to sing, she remembered. The awkward teenager, who as a child had hidden behind her mother's knee or Victoria's skirt, blossomed with a microphone – or hairbrush – in her hand. And she was good. She'd been an understudy for *Evita*. But now it was all 'wedding lists' and 'floral arrangements'. It seemed a U-turn from her sister's dreams. But perhaps Lulu had changed, perhaps she wanted all that now. Who was she to judge? She just wanted her to be happy. She placed a hand on her sister's shoulder and squeezed. 'Hey, let's see what they've got for you. Bet you'll look a million dollars. Shall we go in?'

'Sure,' muttered Lulu, pulling some straw out of her hair. Victoria glanced at her and caught a look cross her face.

———

'Darlings! How are you both?' The woman leant over and gave Victoria a kiss. Victoria was overwhelmed with strong perfume. Who was this woman in her too-tight navy-blue suit and pearls? She took Victoria's hand. 'My dear – what a dreadful time you've had.' Victoria noticed the pale blue eyeshadow, the fat fingers curled around her hand. This must be Marjory, Simon's mum. Lulu's future mother-in-law. Had she met her before? She suddenly felt a bit faint and sank into one of the purple velvet chairs. 'Just need to sit down.'

Marjory turned to Lulu: 'How are you? I hope you're as excited as I am!' Then she took a step back. 'What *are* you wearing, Louise?' She was holding her at arm's length. 'Anyway, I've been looking at the date in my diary and basically trembling with excitement as the day got nearer! I'm *so* relieved you're both alright after that horrific accident! Simon has been worried sick!' She patted Lulu on the arm as she headed to the dressing room. 'We'll get the nice lady here to get you a cup of tea, Victoria, you look very pale indeed.'

Once Victoria had her tea, Marjory sat down in the red velvet seat with gilt arms next to her. 'I'm a bag of nerves,' Marjory gushed. 'I can't wait to see how our Lulu will look in a wedding gown, I feel a bit teary actually. They've given her five to look at.' Suddenly Lulu appeared in front of them, fiddling with the pearls on the bodice of a fairy-tale dress.

Marjory put her hands up to her face in wonder. 'Lulu, that's simply dazzling. I think this might just be pushing me over the edge.' She stood up and fussed around Lulu. Victoria glanced at her sister whose cheeks were flushed red and thought for one awful moment that Lulu was going to burst into tears.

'Lulu, it really is stunning,' Victoria said gently. She watched as Lulu twirled round in the dress; when she caught sight of herself in the mirror, her sister's face did soften. The dress made her look spectacular. It had a tight bodice beaded with pearls, and the skirt flared out from her tiny waist in a mist of tulle. It was a bit over the top maybe, but it transformed Lulu. She was radiant.

Lifting her veil up, Lulu peeked out from behind it and grinned. 'Peek a boo!'

Then she was laughing, bending double. Slowly, she stood up wiping tears from her eyes. 'That was funny! Sorry, only kidding. It *is* lovely.'

Thank goodness, sighed Victoria. My sister seems to be getting in the spirit of things.

'Oh darling, you look splendid in it!' Marjory was standing next to her now and fiddling with the netting. 'My goodness, it's not every day that you get a second chance at a daughter-in-law. I just can't wait! Can't wait for Simon and you to be properly married – it was all such a dreadful thing when – anyway, perhaps you two will be quick off the mark to start a family, maybe?' She peered at Lulu, then gently pushed Lulu's veil over her shoulder as Victoria watched the colour drain from Lulu's face.

When she came out of the cubicle, Lulu handed the dress to the shop owner then turned to Marjory. 'Thank you.' The two women gave each other a hug and then Lulu raised her eyebrows at Victoria. 'Fantastic, now we both need to go, Marjory. Victoria needs to rest.'

'Of course you do, this has been splendid. See you soon dear. Send Simon a big kiss from me, won't you!' And as they left the shop, Victoria just made out Marjory asking to see the Mother of the Groom outfits please, with a little laugh.

———

It was getting dusky. It was only a five-minute drive back to Lulu's flat on the outskirts of Little Norland, and then she was going straight home to lie down. 'What was going on in there? You seemed very stressed?'

'I just feel a bit overwhelmed with it all, the shop, the

dress, the whole shebang. It's making it very, very real.' The laughing Lulu from the wedding shop had vanished and in her place was a sombre sister in fancy dress, slumped in the seat. Shouldn't she be buzzing?

'It *is* real, Lulu, he's asked you to marry him – or so you told me,' she paused and her voice softened, 'and you've said yes.' She pulled up behind a car at a set of temporary traffic lights.

A silence fell between them as they watched the oncoming lights of the stream of cars illuminate the bonnet then veer off. A mist had started to form across the road.

'So. Tell me, what's he like? Simon? Only, I just can't remember much.'

Lulu cleared her throat. 'Well, he's an only child, he's an accountant, he went to Southampton university to study Finance, he loves to ski, he's a good cook and he's – well, he's nice.' Lulu put her hands in her lap. Victoria released the hand-brake and pulled away.

'Lulu, sweetheart, I didn't want his CV, I wanted to know about him. What's he like, as a person? What do you *feel* about him?'

'He's great.'

They carried on a bit further to the sound of the wind-screen wipers swishing this way and that. Victoria concentrated on the road ahead. She was driving slowly. She wasn't going to let the accident stop her, but she acknowledged that she was finding it tough. She gripped the steering wheel.

'Lulu, can I ask you something?'

'Yeah.' Lulu sat up. 'What?'

'*Do you love him?*'

Suddenly those words took Victoria back somewhere ugly. Being in the car, with Lulu, a screech. *Do you love him?* It triggered something. It was bringing back powerful feelings and her palms felt sweaty on the steering wheel. She let out a sob.

'Victoria? Sweetheart, don't worry. Calm down. We're nearly home.' Lulu was rubbing her back, telling her to pull into their drive, soothing her. Had she asked Lulu that question just before the crash – or, worse, had Lulu asked *her*?

11 VICTORIA

'Coo-ee! How *is* everybody?'

A woman in tight navy jeans with a fitted blue-and-white-striped blouse and skyscraper heels clipped confidently into the kitchen. She was carrying a Tupperware box. Inside, Victoria could see, was a row of perfectly-iced cupcakes, magazine cover cupcakes with swirly lilac icing and silver balls. Lulu followed the woman in. James was at work in Brighton and the kids were back at school. It was three weeks since the accident. She was alone in the house with Lulu, who had popped round 'just in case you need me', as Zoe – her 'friend' – was coming around.

'Zoe, remember the doctors have said Vicky can't handle too much stress?' frowned Lulu. Lulu really emphasised 'stress'. Victoria wanted to giggle. Lulu was being *very* protective.

'Vicky? Who's that?' she screwed up her nose. 'Course sweet pea, only kidding.' Zoe grinned, there was an accent there. Was it South African? She placed the box on the table – 'these little beauties are totally fat-free!' – then immediately rushed over to Victoria and embraced her in a big hug. Victoria was enveloped in a cloying smell of jasmine. 'Sweetie! I was beside myself! I called your mobile, I messaged you, I sent you FaceTime requests, I checked your Insta account, but zilch!' She sat down with a thump on the chair next to her and placed a large pink leather handbag on the table. The clasp was just like the one on Victoria's bag. It was ghastly.

'Well, I was in hospital, couldn't use my phone,' Victoria began, 'in fact I didn't even recognise my phone, I don't recognise—' She stopped short of saying 'you', as this woman was clearly someone *very* familiar with her.

'I was so worried, but your dear sister here messaged me about you and told me not to worry, but I *so* did!' She squeezed Victoria's knee.

'Cup of tea, coffee, Zoe? Or maybe just a glass of water?' Lulu was standing by the kettle, hand on hip; the mannerism reminded Victoria of their late mother.

'Darling, I'll have one of those Italian coffees, from that darling machine.'

'We don't have a machine.'

'Yes, you do, sweetie,' she got up and pulled her blouse down. 'Right here, ya? You've got every gadget!' She clipped over to a cupboard at the back of the kitchen and opened a door, pulled out the coffee maker, then plonked it next to the kettle. 'Voila!'

'Right,' Lulu muttered, and turned it on. It started to roar into action, making a noise like a Boeing 747 was about to take off. Eventually the dreadful noise stopped.

'Tell me *all* about the terrible accident.' Zoe had somehow found three plates and she clipped back to her seat, put the plates down and looked sorrowfully at her. Victoria didn't know whether to laugh or cry.

'Zoe, listen, I well, I know this might sound a bit strange, but I can't really remember—'

'The accident? No well, that's not unusual. I've read about these things.'

'She doesn't know who you are,' Lulu cut in as she placed two mugs of coffee on the table.

'Sorry?' Zoe had a cupcake in her hand. She hesitated, batting her unusually long eyelashes at them. The silver balls on the top of the cake gleamed in the kitchen light.

'It's called retrograde amnesia,' explained Lulu, 'and a lot of Victoria's memory has been lost from before the accident. The last thing Victoria remembers is that her twins were about ten.'

'Sweet Jesus!' Zoe's hand flew to her mouth. 'Really?' She swept some hair off her face.

'It's been awful.' Victoria took a sip of coffee and stared at Zoe's dark blue fingernails clutching the little paper wrapper on the cupcake. She felt a wave of tiredness again. She just wanted to lie down, wake up and remember her life.

'Are you alright, Victoria?' Lulu asked and put a hand on her shoulder behind her. 'I'm just going to get something from the car.'

'God that must be awful,' Zoe placed her cake down and frowned. 'You really can't remember stuff from before the accident?'

'Not for about five, maybe six years before, no. And bits before that are sketchy too. Like I can remember the day the twins were born, but I can't remember my actual wedding day.' Had this Zoe been there? She took a deep breath. 'Life has moved on. But I haven't.'

'You poor thing.' Then Zoe leant in closer and quickly glanced behind her shoulder: 'And do you remember

"Andy"?' She did that funny inverted comma thing with her fingers.

Who? What? Victoria could feel a flash of something, but it was very loose, a memory trying to come to the surface. Wine. Laughing. It was very vague.

'Why?'

'Well, look, sweetheart,' Zoe leant in closer. Victoria could see huge clumps of mascara on her lashes and a thick layer of foundation. 'Because—'

'Everything alright?' Lulu placed a bag of shopping on the table in front of them. 'You look washed out, Victoria, remember what the doctor said?'

'I know, I know.'

'Zoe, I think Victoria needs to rest now, OK? If you don't mind—'

'Yes, of course,' Zoe scraped her chair back and got up, adjusted her bra straps under her blouse. 'Well, look, you call me if you need anything, OK? And enjoy the cupcakes. How about the gym soon? I'll pick you up.'

'The gym? Oh, I don't think so.'

Zoe yanked her handbag over her shoulder and turned to look at Victoria and smiled. 'Look, we'll just go for coffee, sweetie – check out the eye candy, eh?' She winked at her. 'Like we used to. Maybe it will trigger some memories.' She leant in for a hug on the way out, and whispered in her ear – 'I need to speak to you.' Her necklace clanked against Victoria's cheek as Zoe leant over awkwardly. It was like embracing a stranger at a wedding. It felt all wrong. She heard Lulu let Zoe out. Victoria suddenly felt like a tonne of bricks had been placed across her chest. She put her head in her hands at the kitchen table and sighed as Lulu came back in. 'Oh God, Lulu, what happened? I've missed so much. I've changed so much, or at least that's what people seem to think.'

Lulu sat down next to her and put a hand on her knee. 'We've all changed.' There was something so sad about how she said it that Victoria looked up.

'Tell me.'

Lulu glanced at her then carried on. 'Well, I wanted to change the world, remember? Go on stage – and now? It's sheep at children's parties.' She smiled but her lips were wonky; it didn't reach her eyes.

Victoria sat back in her chair and considered what Lulu had said. 'But what *about* your ambitions, Lu? You used to come alive when you got a microphone in your hand. Most people would be terrified, but not you. That school play you were in – what was it?'

'That was *years* ago!' They smiled at each other.

'But still, *High School Musical* or something, you were the lead, *the lead* for God's sake. It was your dream to be in the spotlight, you wanted nothing more than that, to get to the West End, I do remember that. But the rest—' She waved her hand around the kitchen. 'Not so much.'

Victoria looked out the window and then back again. She fixed her eyes on appliances she didn't recognise, willing them to shed some light on her life. She thought about Zoe – her 'friend'. She thought about the sadness in James's eyes. She thought about her body.

'Especially these.' She nodded to her bust and then both of them started to laugh, and after a while tears were streaming down Victoria's face with shoulder-shaking giggles… but before she could help herself, the next breath turned into body-wracking sobs. Eventually, Lulu handed her a tissue, put her arms around her, and they sat there, Victoria glad of the human warmth next to her. Eventually she pulled away. 'What happened to me, Lu?'

'Honey.' She touched Victoria's cheek. 'You sort of became obsessed with all the trappings of your life, if you want the truth, we – well,' Lulu ran her hands through her hair and looked straight at Victoria, 'we were all wondering what was happening to you. And you and me, we were kind of growing apart. It was complicated. I was making decisions you weren't sure about.' Lulu sat back. 'It's a really long story.' She closed her eyes and opened them again, as if summoning up strength. 'Anyway. I've got Simon now, things are different.'

If Victoria didn't know better – and actually, she didn't – she'd have thought her sister wasn't quite herself. The *va-va-voom* had vanished. She stared at her clever, sparkly blonde sister who could hold a crowd in the palm of her hand with a sweet ballad. 'Lulu, getting married mustn't stop you being who you want to be.'

'And who do *you* want to be, sis?'

That was the point, wasn't it? She couldn't remember who she wanted to be. But if it was anything like the woman she was discovering, this 'New Victoria' as she was calling herself in her head, she didn't want to be *that* Victoria *at all*.

'Hey,' Lulu said, sniffing, 'I think it might be a good idea for you to lie down, OK? Remember the doctor warned against any big stress, any emotional drain on you while your brain – and your body – is healing, right? And as for these cupcakes? Fat-free?' She picked one up, and then lobbed it in the bin. 'That's stress in itself.' They smiled at each other, and then Lulu carefully tucked a piece of hair behind Victoria's ear. Which almost made her cry again.

Upstairs, Victoria sat on the edge of the bath, and started to fill it. She wafted her hand through the mixer tap, waiting until it was the right temperature then let it fill midway, grabbed some purple bubble bath from the side, and then stepped in. Did she like purple bubble baths? After about five minutes she was bored counting the tiles around the wall. Enough. She stared at herself in the bathroom mirror and wondered where her soft, round belly had gone? In its place were perky boobs and a flat stomach. The boobs seemed to defy gravity and looked utterly out of place on her body. What had she been *thinking*? She had always been someone who made the best of what they'd got. She vaguely remembered talking to Izzy when she found her pinching her lipstick as a little girl. It was cute, but Victoria had a hazy memory of reminding Izzy that she was beautiful without make-up. And how much had they cost? Had she used her savings? What had she told the kids when she went into hospital? She dried between them gently and stared at her alien figure. Many women would be pleased, she realised. But it didn't feel like *her*. She had become someone else. A *different* Victoria. Not 'Squishy Vicky' as James used to call her; she smiled ruefully to herself in the mirror. Then she leant in closer and looked at her taut forehead again. Sighing, she pulled her dressing gown around her, walked out the bathroom and lay on top of the bed. Come on, memories. Where were they? A tiny spider scuttled across the wall and eventually stopped by the windowsill.

What if she could find more things that would jog her memory like the doctor suggested? Old clothes? From before her apparent 'transformation'. Didn't she used to keep boxes under the bed? There was a vague memory of things under the bed, important things.

She reached underneath and pulled out a shallow cardboard box. Opening the top, she found some very old summer dresses. Definitely pre-breast enhancement. Next, she uncovered a couple of small photo albums. One was of the twins when they were about two, they were both in high-chairs, creamy white skins with little pink cheeks, plastic spoons in their hands, and what looked like a bowl of pasta in front of them. There were two egg yolk yellow baby blankets in the box as well. She held them in front of her face and inhaled. It was musty and sweet and something in it ignited a memory in her brain of a twin pram, of covering the twins in these blankets, walking around the streets of Little Norland. She could feel tears leaking from her eyes and she pressed the soft blankets close to her face. Where were all her memories? The car crash had stolen parts of her life from her and she wanted it back.

Victoria rummaged in the box. Her wedding ring. She took it out and tried it on; the gold glistened and she was mesmerised, staring at it on her finger. Why had she taken it off? Half-formed memories were floating in her brain, like balloons she couldn't catch. Next, she found a little pink ribbon nestled at the bottom of the box tied in a bow. Was it Izzy's? Then, out of nowhere Victoria felt a dragging sensation in her stomach, a feeling of dread. She looked up and stared at the blinds framing her window. Bright red poppies on a beige background. There was something about those cheery poppies that unsettled her. She'd stared at them, hadn't she? For a long time and something had been wrong. Very wrong. She shook herself. Next to the blankets was a delicate piece of netting. Her veil! She pulled it out triumphantly. Lying underneath it was the silk daisy garland she recognised from her wedding photo. She traced the fragile little flower buds with her fingers. A surge of emotion ran through her and she felt light-headed. She would look at that later.

As she was placing the veil back in the box, something at the bottom caught her eye. She fished about and pulled out an old iPad. The blue cover triggered a memory.

She flicked open the cover, it was blue with tiny yellow glittery butterfly stickers on it; they were peeling off. She had a strong memory of Izzy sticking them on the cover, pulling off the backing paper and gently placing them on the front. She had flashes of carrying this iPad in her handbag. She opened up the lid and a few Post-it notes fluttered onto the bed. She picked one up. It was a list.

Izzy: ballet shoes!
Birthday cake! 14 candles!!
Bouncy castle?
Magic show?
Remember milk

Then 6/10 had been circled in red pen with '*Jake, maths.*'

The writing didn't look like hers. When had she written this? Fourteen candles? She had always made sure each twin had their own cake, so had they been seven? 2011? She got off the bed and plugged the charger in. She sat cross-legged on the floor waiting for the screen to light up. Then she pressed the home key and sat staring at the screen. She somehow managed to navigate her way to the email icon and pressed it. It took a while, but then stopped. They'd had a Hotmail account back then – she remembered that – and she stared at the email icon as memories came and went. Then suddenly, her fingers flew over the on-screen keypad with surprising agility and she was typing in a username and password.

The messages took ages to load, but one after the other, old emails started to appear. There were apparently 649 emails in her inbox – many of them junk, she could see that, but she started to scroll through, getting a weird sense of déjà vu. But there, amid all the mail for holiday cottages and mortgages, was an email from James, the subject 'Hi darling'. *There* he was, *her James*. It was like finding buried treasure under a mountain of spam.

She clicked on it:

Hey Squishy,

Still stuck in this crumby hotel in Newcastle. One more presentation to go. How are you doing? I thought about you yesterday. There was a woman at the indoor pool – no, she wasn't as good looking as you before you ask ;) – and she had twins too! They were adorable, they were about four. It made me think of our little six-year-old tykes! Made me really miss you all. Back on Saturday, for the birthday party! Did you get the bouncy castle? Can't wait to give you and the kids a massive hug. Right, I'm off to the gym here now, been trying to keep training up for the Suffolk Sevens! It's pouring outside so giving the treadmill a go.

See you on Saturday! Can't wait! Look after yourself. J. Xx

James had actually written to her like that? Her hands were trembling. This was not the man living with her at the moment. The man living with her could barely give her the time of day. She wanted *that* James back, *email James*. She climbed back onto the bed and hugged her knees to her chest. That was what she wanted to reclaim. But how? She picked up her phone from the bedside table and started to look through old photos. Something made her flick to the texts to see if she could find any feel-good ones from James too. She started to scroll through her messages and then suddenly her heart started to beat. Something was telling her this was *all wrong*. She scrolled down to one set of messages – they were from the same number but no name. All signed by 'A'. Who was that? Dear, God. They were *flirty*. Another caught her eye.

Where are you? I've been missing our chats… Andy x

Her hands were shaking and she nearly dropped the phone. *Ohmygodohmygodohmygod* who was *this*? And had she had an *affair*? Jesus sweet fucking Christ. She wasn't that kind of woman! She loved James. She'd married James, she'd had daisies in her hair for goodness sake – she'd seen it in the photo in the lounge – she was his *Squishy Vicky*.

She sat back and hit her head on the headboard with a clunk, her fingers wrapped around the phone. She shut her eyes and held on to the memory of James's email from the iPad, the twins' seventh birthday party, the garden, the wine, holding hands, even the vomiting child, they were such happy memories. *That's* who she wanted to be.

12 VICTORIA

'That's, like, *so* much butter! What are you doing?'

It was Saturday morning. Victoria looked up at her daughter, who was standing with her hands on her hips in the kitchen next to her. She had her hair tied in a high ponytail and her face was plastered in make-up. Her foundation was thick and her eyebrows looked as if she'd found two brown caterpillars in the garden and stuck them on – and that diamond piercing on her left eyebrow glinted at her in the kitchen lights.

'Well you need a lot to make brownies.' She piled more butter onto the scales.

'Butter? In those disgusting fat-free ones?'

'Fat-free?' laughed Victoria. 'What's the point of that?'

Her daughter's eyes widened. 'You tell me! Your mate Zoe was always bringing fat-free stuff round, and you started to bake it. Tasted like baby sick.'

She came round to where Izzy was standing and squeezed her woollen-jumper clad arm. 'Did I?'

Izzy moved away. 'Yes. You used to make revolting

Weight Watchers recipes. But if we said anything you'd snap at us, reminding us about childhood obesity and dental fillings.' Izzy flicked her ponytail off her shoulder. 'Remember, Mum, C-A-L-O-R-I-E-S?'

Had she actually behaved like that? What happened to the chaotic popcorn-eating, mother of ten-year-old twins who used to hide Maltesers in her knicker drawer so the twins wouldn't find them? Where had *she* gone?

'Well, um, I don't think it's wise to cook brownies unless they're totally moreish and that's what we're doing now,' she said, her hands shaking a little as she opened up the hot chocolate lid. 'The more the merrier,' she announced, almost to herself, and to prove that she could jolly well bake fattening brownies, she poured the whole tin of hot chocolate powder onto the mounds of butter. It slid down the sides of the butter making little brown sugary ski slopes. 'That should do it,' she said, mixing it up into a chocolatey pile. Then she lifted the spoon up and took a big lick.

Izzy was staring at her. She felt rather sick, but she had to go on. She licked off the whole tablespoon. 'Who's eating fat-free now?' She smiled and wiped some goo off her chin.

Izzy leant in beside her and, eyeing the mountain of chocolate and fat in the bowl, narrowed her eyes. 'Have you been drinking?'

Victoria studied Izzy. Her daughter's eyes sparkled under her heavily made-up smoky purple eyelids. They made her look twenty-six, not sixteen. What had she missed? Had Izzy had her first kiss? Sex? Dear God. She dropped the tablespoon with a clatter then picked it up and opened her mouth. 'Of course not. Listen, Izzy, erm, have you, you know, kissed a boy, do you need me to talk to you about—'

'This is *so* not happening, Mum!' Izzy flashed her a look

of panic and then smiled slyly at her: 'Maybe I've kissed a *girl*.'

'Right. OK.' What was the protocol here? Victoria plunged the spoon back into the mixture for something to do. 'That's fine.'

'Only kidding, Mum.'

'Oh, I see. OK,' she faltered, 'but Izzy, there's so much I've missed, or at least might have missed.'

'Don't worry, Mum, you were here, only you weren't,' Izzy shrugged and looked down, her fake eyelashes quivering, then she looked straight up at her.

Why had she missed so much? It couldn't have just been all her fault, could it? Perhaps they all just needed some time. Bonding time. Like now, making cakes. Surely that's what mums and daughters did. Even at sixteen? She arranged her face into a smile. 'Right, can you get me the mixer and we'll get to work on these.'

'Get it yourself,' Izzy said and then flounced off to a chair in the corner of the kitchen and pulled out her phone from the back of her jeans' pocket. Victoria's gaze fell on her daughter's face, lit up by the screen, as she frowned, then swiped left, then right. She was sure Izzy had said 'bitch' under her breath.

'What?'

Her mouth was turned down at the edges. 'Nothing. School stuff, a bitch of a project we've been set.'

Victoria scraped the mixture from the beaters and glanced at Izzy again. 'Anyway,' Izzy suddenly looked up at her. 'What do *you* care?' She sat frowning for another ten minutes as Victoria bit her lip.

'Izzy? I *do* care. Maybe pop your phone down?'

Izzy flicked her head up abruptly. '*Pop* my phone down? Are you for real, Mum? Just chill, will you? I'm surprised yours isn't glued to your hand, usually it's Insta, TikTok, Twitter, God knows what. You're never off yours! Looking at all your influencers.' Izzy said 'influencers' with the same disdain as if she was wiping dog-doo off her shoe.

Never off yours. Was that true? What the hell was TikTok? Or an 'influencer' for that matter?

'Izzy, put your phone down and come here.'

Izzy looked up from the phone, sighed heavily, pressed a few more buttons and swore under her breath and then came towards Victoria. 'What?'

'Are you OK?'

'Oh, here we go. Is it a mum-daughter counselling session? Have you got *time* for this?' She stared at her her mutinously. *How had her daughter become this bitter?* 'Course I'm not OK,' Izzy's shoulders slumped. 'My mum's had a crash and come back, like, as some weird person, one who *bakes*.' Izzy folded her arms. 'You're acting like me and Jake are like five years old. And all that stuff with Dad—'

'Look, I'm going to fix it, all right?'

Izzy flinched. 'Fix it? What, fix getting a *divorce*? I don't think so.'

'Look, your dad and I, we – er, nothing's been finalised yet, as far as I can see. I just need to talk to him. And I don't really understand what sort of mum I had become, either, Izzy, but I just need to get to the bottom of it—' She touched her daughter's cheek and registered that Izzy didn't move away as if she'd had an electric shock. 'I promise to do better, OK? All I know is that I love you, Dad and Jake. That's all I can manage at the moment.'

Izzy shrugged. 'Whatever.' And with that Izzy grabbed the spoon from the bowl and began licking it in front of Victoria, then tilted her head to one side. 'You're not going to tell me off?'

Victoria shrugged. 'Why would I do that? You love brownie mixture.'

'Yeah, I do,' she said, giving it a final lick, then tossing it in the sink before wandering out the kitchen.

One victory. Just one. I'll take that, thought Victoria as she picked up a spatula and started to fold the creamy mixture into the familiar brown comforting goodness she could remember. Folding it in and around the bowl, scraping it off the sides and then pausing. Why had Izzy become this uptight? She reached for a baking tray, lined it with greaseproof paper and scraped the mixture into the tin. Once it was in the oven she leant back on the side of the cooker and folded her arms. *Never off yours.* Was that true? She glanced over at the table where Izzy's phone lay.

Just then, Victoria's phone started to bleep and flash. Her dad's profile picture flashed up. *Oh, that's rather cool*, she found herself thinking. She pressed the button. 'Hi Dad.'

'Hello sweetheart, how are you?'

'OK,' she lied, trying to sound chirpy. She knew she'd been off-kilter when he'd last phoned.

'Good girl. Lulu's been keeping me posted but I was worried I hadn't heard from you in a couple of days. How's your head? The headaches? Memory?'

'Comes and goes.'

Her dad let out a laugh. 'I wouldn't worry about that, pet, that's probably ageing.'

'No, but Dad, important stuff like my wedding day – stuff with the twins, a lot has gone.' She let out a long breath.

'Oh.' A silence filled the air and she wondered if she was meant to say something.

'But I'm sure it will come back. And I've got my next scan, um, soon. I know it's soon.' She didn't want to worry him too much. 'Dad?' And although he wasn't in front of her, she sensed something was out of place with him. She may have lost bits of her memory but this was a *feeling*.

'Yes darling?'

'Is everything OK with *you*?' She wandered to the window and looked outside, noticing clumps of wild primroses in the border, their pale yellow flowers a cheery reminder that spring had just arrived.

'Well, yes and no. I'm fine, it's just that Billie's gone.'

'Billie?' Come on, memory, come on. Victoria stood staring out the window looking for inspiration. Was Billie his girlfriend? His car? Dear God. What?

'Gone?' she ventured, playing for time. 'Where?'

'Vet said there wasn't anything she could do. She passed away at 3 a.m. at the vet's surgery.'

'Oh God. Oh, Dad, my God, what happened? Why didn't you say she was ill?' Yes, yes, thank you, memory; Victoria raised her eyes to the ceiling. Billie was the dog who had stolen his heart. After Mum had died, Dad had taken in a Border Collie rescue dog and it had been the most loving bond she'd ever known. Dad wouldn't let Billie out of his sight – and vice versa.

'No. Old age. Vet said it would be cruel to let her carry on.'

Victoria bit her nail and listened to her dad's croaky voice.

'I'll be fine, pet. It's just, well, quiet around here now. And I miss our walks, up by the moors.' It was odd hearing her dad's frailty on the phone. As far as she could remember he'd been the capable one, her dad, the one who made things alright. But then, she reminded herself, he was six years older than when she remembered. She wished he wasn't in Yorkshire.

'Come and stay! For a bit, you know. I would love to see you.'

There was a pause and then he said: 'Are you sure? You don't normally say that. Normally you're, you know, too busy.'

Good grief, that New Victoria was some stranger to her. She needed to sort her out. 'Dad. Really. I think it would be good for you. Come next week, and tell me what train you'll be on.'

She could hear the relief in his voice straight away. 'Well, if you're sure sweetheart, I'd love that. I was pretty worried when Lulu told me about the accident, but I didn't want to be any trouble…'

'Dad, it's fine, I'll—' But she didn't finish as Jake appeared in the doorway.

'Yo! Mum, something's burning.'

'Oh crap. I forgot to turn the oven back down to low. The *brownies*! Dad, I have to go. Speak later.'

Jake burst out laughing as she grabbed the oven mitts and quickly hauled the smoking brownies out of the oven. 'Bugger,' she cried, burning her fingers, and then slammed the brownies down on the hob surface and turned round to see Jake smirking at her and James standing with his hands on his hips, trying to hide a smile.

'Alright? I could hear shouting.'

She folded her arms in mock protest and smiled. 'Never seen someone burn their baking, you two?'

'Well, not you! You're normally like some control freak,' Jake said, wandering round the kitchen table. Was she?

'And you *never* swear,' he whispered.

'Well, I do today.' She ran her finger under a cold tap and looked over at James.

'Are you alright?' he said. 'I was just passing, I can get you—'

'No it's fine,' she said, then after a beat, 'thank you.' He smiled at her briefly, opened his mouth as if to say something, then closed it again.

'Some work I need to finish off,' he said, heading for the door.

'Is it sore?' Jake asked, coming over.

'I'll live,' she said as they both watched the water cascade over her thumb and splash the back of the sink. 'Hey,' she turned to Jake, 'Grandpa's coming to stay.'

Jake's eyes lit up. 'Cool.'

Victoria cast her eye over Jake, with his ripped denim shorts and floppy hair, and had such a surge of love. Then she spotted some toothpaste on his T-shirt and her hand started to twitch, to reach out and grab the J-cloth to wipe it, but she stopped herself just in time. He was not ten anymore she reminded herself. 'Hey, do you know if everything's alright with Izzy?'

He pulled his T-shirt down and looked up at her. 'Yeah, guess so. Why?'

'She just seemed very agitated when she was on her phone.'

He shrugged. 'Been a bit of heavy stuff a year ago on social, but I think she's cool now.'

'Social?'

'Social *med-ya*, mum, like Facebook to you, you know?'

'Oh right. What sort of heavy?' She let out a long breath.

'Dunno.' Then he walked over to a cupboard and pulled out a glass, and turned to her. 'She won't talk to me. But girls can be bitchy. Just saying.'

'Bitchy? I hadn't realised.'

'No, well you wouldn't. I mean, didn't.'

'What does that mean?'

'You're—' he stopped and corrected himself. '*I've got my life*, you used to say sometimes when we needed stuff.' Jake's jaw was jutting out and his mouth was set in a line.

How had it come to this? 'Jake, I just don't know where you got that idea from—'

'From all the times you *were* busy, or distracted, or doing Pilates, or, I don't know,' he gestured with one arm, 'not around. Having appointments with, um, your doctor – women's things you used to say to me, or your beauty therapist, I dunno.' He was now back with her at the sink and was filling up his glass. He took a large gulp and then put the glass down and wouldn't look at her.

Doctor? Victoria turned off the tap and stared at her red raw thumb then used her hand to steady herself on the kitchen sink.

'Jake?'

He looked up at her from under his curly fringe. 'Sorry.'

'No, *I'm* sorry,' she carried on. 'I *am* around. I-I just need to remember who I was and what happened.'

'Maybe you shouldn't bother. The mum that's come back from hospital is way nicer,' he murmured. He glanced at her from under his fringe, as if summing up what to do, quickly touched her hand, and sauntered out the door.

She picked up Izzy's phone from the counter as tears threatened; the bitter smell of burnt chocolate filled the air. The screenshot was the three of them on their holiday. Their smiles wide, with the backdrop of the ski resort behind them, their faces tanned, the white slopes glistening in the background, a little bubble of three. And then a fleeting memory of something she couldn't quite place: *A family of five.* And then it was gone. Another feeling started to gnaw at Victoria's gut: would she be able to get back into that bubble again?

———

James was in the study when she went barging in – stopped and couldn't remember what she was in there for, frowned and said 'sorry' to his broad back. He was back at his desk working. Or hiding from her in there. She was never sure. She stared at his shoulders, at that navy jumper with the red flecks in it and wondered how many times she'd washed it, how many times she'd used fabric conditioner and lovingly folded the sleeves in, put it back in the cupboard. There was a strong memory of doing this.

He looked up from his desk. That little bit of hair at his crown was sticking out again. They had used to joke about it. Give it a name even. Henry the tuft of hair. Why Henry? But she remembered that. She smiled. For a man with such straight short hair, there was always a little bit that was unruly. She longed to touch it. She started to lift her hand, then saw him frown and pulled it away quickly. She stared at the screen instead. Sunlight was streaming in through the small window in the study, making it hard to see. There were tiny smudge marks on the screen, invisible in dim light but now, with the shaft of sunlight, it was like a little caterpillar with muddy feet had been scampering over the display.

'What, er, are you doing?' she ventured.

'Looking for our lawyer's postal address.' She glanced behind him at the screen again and it had changed to swirls of blue and green light as the screensaver started.

'Oh. Why?'

He sighed loudly. 'I think you know why.' His eyes flicked up to her. 'But I got distracted.' There was just the glimmer of a smile, a softening.

'Oh.'

'With this.'

He nodded at the screen then reached for the mouse and clicked it. An image appeared. Frozen in time, it was him with the twins as toddlers.

'Oh my babies! Look how little they are!' Her hands flew up to her flushed cheeks. 'When was it?'

James pressed the mouse again over the 'play' icon. Unfolding before her was a scene she didn't recognise at first – then slowly, like the fibres of a spider's web being spun back together, little fragments started to connect until the whole scene was a proper memory.

'James, I remember that!'

His eyes slid quickly to her and he nodded. 'That's good.'

Her young husband waved at the camera from the screen. Still the same James, but he was thinner, more wiry, with thicker hair. The same broad cheeky grin. He was in running shorts and a red T-shirt emblazoned with '26' on it.

'The Sussex Sevens.' He tilted his head at the screen.

It was coming back to her; a seven-mile fun run around the hills of Sussex. He'd done it every year before they'd got married and had kids. James was crouching down next to Izzy and Jake who must have been around four. He was waving at the camera, then it swooped to the ground, the sound of laughter – her laughter – 'oops!' said the voice. James and the twins again. 'Wave to Mummy!' James was grinning, doing that silly wave that people do when a camera is facing them. Then a look to the camera, a smile that was so deep it reached his eyes as they crinkled at the sides and his face lit up. Then blurry, branches of trees until the focus returned. He had turned the camera on her and him. Smiling, laughing; him giving her a kiss on the cheek. The twins shrieking in the background. Then James again, jogging, running off and waving back to her. 'Love you!'

She saw James tense up. It almost seemed like yesterday. Almost.

Another memory started to form. 'Did we, have a picnic that day?' She could feel her throat tighten as she watched her kids – her little butterflies then, free and spirited and so young. Where had that time gone? Izzy's spun gold for hair, bronzed skin, the smell of suntan lotion, lemons. It had been late August. Sweet-smelling watermelon juice dribbling down a chin. A finger, wiping it away. That had been James, across her chin. She touched her chin and looked at him.

'It was a long time ago,' James said quietly. 'I was just getting back into running and doing events as the twins were nearly four, they were sleeping at night better. Yes, we had a picnic. You and the twins had it all ready at the finish line. I loved you for that.' She looked at the little icon on the top of the screen which told her it was 2008 – nearly twelve years ago.

'And you came third that day, didn't you?' she said, remembering the sunshine, him panting across the finish line. A memory was forming: her running to him, being twirled in the air. She remembered the *feeling*. Like the beginning of everything; a town mayor handing out medals. Her heart bursting with pride. Back then, that was *her James*. He hadn't given up. Third place. A photo in the Sussex Gazette. She'd cut it out and sent it to her dad, hadn't she? The pride. They'd had a picnic, a rug on summer-burnt grass. Fragments were returning. Sitting cocooned between his outstretched legs, her back to him on the picnic rug. Warmth, a caress. Him resting his head on her shoulder and whispering: 'This is one of the best days of my life.'

'There are a few videos on here.' His voice was gentle, interrupting her reverie. 'You must have synced your phone to the main computer.'

What did *that* mean?

'Did I?'

He nodded.

And then his phone bleeped, interrupting their momentary truce. He snatched it up. She glanced at him as he pointed at his phone with the other hand, indicating that he had to take the call. They were back in today's world. The man she'd fallen in love with, the runner, the architect who built buildings 'to make people's lives better', was back at his desk. Emotions locked away, like the fragments of her memories – to come out another time. The shafts of sunlight had disappeared and the study suddenly felt chilly.

13 VICTORIA

'You used to love the Barre classes. Remember?' Zoe beamed at her from behind the wheel of her car as Victoria sat, too confused to argue. She'd set her alarm, crept out of the house and into Zoe's car. The night before, Zoe had phoned. 'Be ready at 9.30, I'll pick you up then. Remember we agreed?'

Rather than say, 'No, I absolutely don't remember and what idiot would get up early on a Saturday and go to the gym', Victoria figured she needed to live her 'new' life a bit to see if it brought back memories. 'I'll be ready,' she'd said.

Then she had gone upstairs, opened one of her drawers in the chest in her room and pulled out an array of workout items that looked utterly foreign to her. She wasn't going to *do* anything at the gym, her ribs were still healing, she just wanted to see what it was she *used* to do, who she *was*. She sat now, pulling at the fabric of some leggings as Zoe reversed the car into a space in the car park. According to Zoe, Victoria used to do Barre, Balance and something called Ballet Tone. Maybe being there would jolt her memory. And there was another reason she was going. But she couldn't remember it now.

'C'mon sweetie, let's go.'

Inside the coffee shop, Zoe placed a drink in front of her. People were waving at her and she smiled at these toned strangers. Zoe was babbling on about all of them, who they were, what classes they did. Then, from out of nowhere an instructor was standing right in front of them. He was in his mid-forties, hair the colour of dirty sand, cropped quite close, rough shaven, with piercing green eyes. He was about six foot, wearing a tight black T-shirt, long limbs encased in tracksuit. Fit. Sexy. He put his hand on the back of Victoria's neck very protectively. She tensed up. 'Hey girls!'

Suddenly Victoria couldn't breathe anymore. The phone. *Andy?* Dear God, could it be *him*? She felt her chest tighten, took a slug of her coffee and almost spat it out.

'What *is* that?'

'Soy latte.'

It was revolting. 'Haven't seen you around for a while? You OK?' A gentle squeeze. Before she could reply, he'd sauntered off. Victoria suddenly had a flash of memory, of James in the study, his face softening. Hold onto that memory, she told her brain, hold on tight.

'Zoe. Um, that guy, the instructor—'

'Is off limits, you cheeky thing! His *boyfriend* wouldn't be too pleased with you!' She nudged her in the arm playfully.

Oh, thank God for that. 'No, no, not that it's just—'

'Hi girls!' Lulu breezed in, walked over and plonked her fringed bag on the chair next to them and sat down with a thump.

Victoria tilted her head to one side. 'What are *you* doing here?'

'Meeting you, you lemon! You told me you and Zoe were retracing your steps.'

Had she?

Zoe glanced at her watch. 'Sorry to break up the party, guys, I need to get off!'

Victoria waved at Zoe then looked at her sister's drawn face. 'You feeling alright?'

Lulu took off her denim jacket. 'Yes, sure. Anyway, has this place, like, made you remember anything?' Just then a member of staff came up to their table with a chamomile tea for Lulu. 'Thanks,' Lulu said as they both watched her walk off in emerald green Lycra.

'No. I just seem to be surrounded by very fit strangers.'

They both laughed. Lulu leant back in her chair and took a sip of tea.

'You seem pale?' Victoria touched her knee.

Lulu rolled her eyes. 'Look, I had a bit too much last night. Simon and me kind of had our first proper argument. I guess that's normal, right?' She looked at Victoria for confirmation. All Victoria could think was, *Don't ask me, my marriage is hanging on by a thread*. Instead, she smiled brightly. 'Very normal.'

'After our row he stomped into the study and watched the Grand Prix highlights, left me alone in the kitchen. Thinking – and drinking,' she added with a weak smile.

'About?'

'The wedding!' she said with faux jollity. 'I just need to get on. Book stuff. I think that's the problem, I need to get a move on.'

This wasn't a tooth extraction; Victoria frowned and when she looked up she caught a look flash over Lulu's face. 'Look, Simon was getting stressed – said he couldn't understand why I hadn't done more organising. And I said that I'd had an accident and I was doing my best.'

'Sounds fair enough to me. Why don't I help?' suggested Victoria as a little voice piped up in her head. *Isn't it normally the bride who gets stressed?* 'Listen, Lulu, he's probably uptight because this is his second time around. Remember, you told me he lost his first wife,' she said softly, 'it will be making him anxious that he gets it right.'

Lulu nodded. 'You're right.' Her blonde curls tumbled across her shoulder. When they were young, Lulu used to make Victoria play 'hairdressers' with her. Lulu would sit in the front of the dressing table with the three-way mirror and Victoria would be the hairdresser. Lulu would tell Victoria to pile up her hair in a messy bun; she'd put in clips, spray a whole tin of their mum's Elnett hairspray over it and they'd both giggle at the result. *One day I'm going to be famous and have my own dressing room*, Lulu would say. Victoria took a deep breath. 'Right. Tell me, what do you still need to do?'

'Well the venue's sorted, it's at Treetops Hotel, near Heath Farm. Marjory's done all the food and flowers; I need music, I suppose, I need—' she screwed up her nose – 'bridesmaids?' She leant back in her chair, crossed her ripped-denim-clad legs and a look spread across her face.

'No, no you don't.'

'Please?' She tilted her head to one side. 'I'll buy you donuts. Jam ones. I already asked Izzy who said she wouldn't be seen dead in a dress so I'm a bit stuck.'

'I can't be a *bridesmaid*, Lulu, for goodness sake, I'm forty-one.'

'Maître d' then.'

'Matron of honour, you muppet.' Victoria grinned, smacking Lulu's knee playfully. It was good to laugh. Did the New Victoria laugh? Something told her she didn't. She pushed thoughts of phones and affairs out of her brain for the moment, it was time to help Lulu.

'Pleeese!' Lulu grabbed Victoria's hand. 'I'd feel less stressed. You'd be by my side.'

What about Simon? Victoria nodded. 'OK.'

'It will give you a reason to dress up!' Lulu pulled her phone out of her bag and started to scroll, shrieking with laughter. 'Look at this!' She pointed to a model wearing a red silk dress with a killer cleavage. 'You'd look fabulous in that! James wouldn't know where to look!'

'Neither would the vicar!' Victoria rolled her eyes, glad that Lulu was at last having fun. 'OK, but on one condition? Let me help you; it will be good to focus on something. I'll make a list. And anyway you've only got four weeks.' And as she whipped out a spiral notepad from her bag – did she now carry spiral notepads? – she had an idea. But it would have to wait till another day as right now she was done in.

———

When she got home, the house was quiet. She opened the front door and clicked it shut behind her, letting the silence of the house soothe her. The encounter with that gym instructor had unsettled her; the messages on her phone had unsettled her. She had the beginnings of a tension headache. But she was glad Lulu seemed brighter by the end of their chat. She kicked off her shoes and slowly climbed the stairs to her bedroom. She slid on to her bed, closing her eyes as a weight of half-memories and guilt and longing seemed to percolate through her brain. Then, suddenly, her eyes flew open. There was another photo album in that box, wasn't there?

She rummaged through her box again, letting the smells

from the baby blankets transport her back. She picked up the pink ribbon and placed it to one side. *I'll think about that another time*, she told herself. She wanted to look, to touch, to reach back into a happier past. She stroked the cover. It was made of purple and pink beads in the shape of a heart. She opened the page. Had she made this?

On the first page was a photo of her and James. Freeze-framed. She blinked a few times. Her memory went in and out of focus. She touched the image and willed herself to find the memory. They were standing side by side, the London Eye twinkling in the background, on a summer's evening. She was leaning her head on his shoulder, staring at the camera and smiling. She was in a white, embroidered summer dress, its ruffle hem turned up in the breeze. He had his arm flung around her. But it was the look on his face that made her catch her breath. He was gazing at her, an expression of tender disbelief, as if he couldn't quite believe that he was gazing at his wife. When had this been taken? She turned it over. In blue biro, James had written:

July 2004. London Eye. The day we found out you were carrying our little donuts! Love you. xx

She looked up to the ceiling. Harley Street? Why were they there? Oh yes, for a specialist scan the local health centre didn't offer. The sonographer with the purple hair. James squeezing her hand; she remembered the *feeling* of it. The walk along the Embankment afterwards, sitting, ankles entwined under a table, the Thames glistening in late summer sun. She could almost touch that happiness.

She turned the page and there were a few loose photos tucked into the back, and a collection of bits of paper. Her and James on the top of a snow-topped mountain somewhere, skis on their shoulders, sunglasses perched on their heads, wide grins. A group of them in a pub, all holding out their pints, some waving – there was Lulu – a TV screen in the background – football? James on a sun lounger. His long lean leg bent as he balanced a book on it, squinting under a baseball cap – a past life frozen in this little booklet. Victoria laughing, properly laughing, looking at James, who had his head thrown back, eyes shut. What had been so funny? We were somewhere hot, she thought, her with a silk sarong tied round her waist, James in neon green board shorts, a pair of flippers dangling from one hand. Tiny white dots on the hillside, an emerald, sparkly sea. Greece?

The next photo was James in a suit and tie. He looked about twenty, leaning against a cooker in a cramped kitchen. Suddenly a memory flashed up. Brighton! She turned the photo over. 'First day on the job!' That was *ages* ago, Town and Country Architects, his dream job. Before they'd had children, before this house. A one-bedroom flat, red front door. Sea views from the bathroom – just. He'd carried her over the threshold. She outlined his face on the photo. They hadn't made it to the bedroom upstairs. His wide grin when she said yes to him as they pulled a Christmas cracker and out fell a ring. He'd tampered with the cracker and put the ring in there, sealed it up; they'd shared more champagne and danced around their tiny table. 'A wedding in Winchester!' Hazy memories of planning it, lists, but not the wedding itself. She glanced at her left hand, with its small diamond cluster in the shape of a daisy, set on a platinum band. As she put the photo book back in the box, a tiny scrap of paper fluttered out. James's handwriting. She looked at it and smiled, then, silently, as the tears slid down her cheek, she put it in her back pocket. She'd had enough of an emotional roller-coaster today.

14 VICTORIA

It was Saturday, the first of April. Two weeks had slipped by and the mild tensions remained at home like a smattering of unwanted guests – popping up when she least expected them: sometimes civil, sometimes in the wrong place at the wrong time, sometimes friendly. How much longer could she go on like this? James had spent the morning in the office talking either on the phone to his architect colleagues or on Zoom calls to clients, and he'd finally emerged, and found her in the kitchen. He was looking drawn. What did she do in this situation normally? Ask if he needed a vitamin pill? Take a nap? Make him a coffee? Yes, that was it, she was sure. She pressed various buttons on the coffee machine. She was getting a bit fed up with New Victoria's gadgets.

He was sitting at the kitchen table now, going over some papers. He looked up at her. 'Does it always do this?' she asked, pressing another button.

He nodded. She could see him biting his cheek, as if trying not to smile. 'Every time.'

She fiddled a bit more, then some steam escaped and she swore under her breath.

'Need a hand?'

'Well, yes. This blasted machine, it's ridiculous!'

James came over and showed her how to heat up the milk, then pressed a few buttons. Water started to bubble up, make a huge din, then very slowly a drip of coffee emerged in the cup below. He put the milk to one side.

'Well there's a relief – but that'll take *ages*,' she said, peering into the drips gathering into a tiny amount of coffee in the cup.

'You wanted it.' He folded his arms and leant back on the counter. There was slight mischief in his eyes. Her husband in the photo album was there briefly, and then he was gone.

Victoria searched for something to say to unite them, but couldn't think of anything. April sunlight was streaming through the window; she glanced into the garden – what a *nice* garden. She smiled as she saw the daffodils bob their heads at her. The pink azaleas were flowering too, splodges of vivid colour in the borders; but the grass was pretty long now. What did they normally do? She wasn't sure. Did *she* do it? Or someone else? So many questions.

James went to the fridge, pulled out some soy milk and started warming it up in the metal jug and poured it into the second cup. When he finished he handed it to her. Their fingers touched briefly. Was he wearing his wedding ring? She didn't think so. Is that what she normally had, a milky coffee? She took a sip and nearly spat it out. It was dreadful. She puffed out her cheeks then let out the breath.

'What's up?' James glanced at her.

'Interesting coffee.'

'What you always have.' Was it? Well, the New Victoria

could keep her wallpaper-paste coffee. All this Victoria wanted was a normal filter coffee with one sugar.

'How's work?' she found herself saying, feeling like she was in a bizarre TV show, Wife Loses Her Memory. Perhaps this is what she should be doing, *showing an interest*.

He frowned at her from the coffee machine. 'It's OK. Major client in Newcastle wants me to come up and see him next week – new shopping centre. Then there's Hove County Council, they've asked me to bid for the new cinema complex they're working on. That's big. Lots of stress. Especially if I win the bid.' He smiled briefly, then wandered over to the kitchen table and sat down. 'Anyway, what's it to you?'

'It's your *job*. I'm so proud of you, you're a—'

'Architect,' he said patiently.

'Of course I'm interested, James.' Her jaw was aching from smiling. He took a sip of coffee and shrugged. Was he joking? Is this what their relationship had come to? Little put-downs. Surely not.

He seemed genuine, but why had it all gone wrong? Should she and James have tried harder? Seeing those photos had jogged her memory. The first day of his job. A packed lunch. They hadn't had much money. Post-it notes on a cheese sandwich, wrapped in tinfoil, she remembered doing that. And now? They'd gone from love notes on Post-its to snarky comments. He actually seemed surprised she was asking about his job.

'James, you know I have always been interested in your career, in what you do.' She almost said, 'This is your Squishy Vicky speaking' but she sensed that wouldn't work right now.

He was silent, then scraped his chair back, stood up and wandered over to the sink and started to rinse out his cup.

'I just,' she carried on, talking to his back, 'I'm struggling to understand what's gone wrong.'

He turned to face her. 'Quite a lot, Victoria, it's like dry rot – you know, in surveying terms, once it sets in, hard to manage – and it normally destroys the building.' He started to walk towards the door.

'James, talk to me.' She put a hand on his. It was warm and he didn't move away. 'Where has this dry rot come from? From me or from you? I'm not sure I can keep second-guessing all the parts to our marriage.' She rubbed her finger gently over his knuckles.

He stared at her hand until she removed it, but he walked back over to the table and sat down with a thump on one of the kitchen chairs. He pulled a pile of paperwork towards him. 'Neither can I. I'm so confused. You were always busy,' he said, looking back at her, '"up to your ears". I *was* away a lot, but I was building my career, Victoria, it was for *our* future – you didn't seem to understand that. You seemed – I don't know – fixated on the kids, the house – like that was all that mattered to you – I know you'd given up your job, we decided that was the best, but somehow in all of it, you were competing with me with everything you did.' He pushed his glasses up onto his head. She looked over at his stubbly face, the tired eyes and wanted to hold his face in her hands. She remembered the email. *Really miss you all.* 'I felt—'

She looked over at him and lifted her eyebrows, willing him on.

'Invisible sometimes.'

'Well, you're not invisible now,' she said brightly. 'You're right here.' She smiled her Best Wife Smile and walked over to him, but his eyes were dull.

'Yes, yes I am,' he said wearily, as she sat down in front of him. He rifled through the papers, and pulled two out. 'First, you need to look at this report the police sent about the accident and sign it. It's just a formality, we know who's to blame; our insurance company are dealing with it all, but there will be more paperwork.' Then he put his glasses back over his eyes and peered at the other form. He slid it right in front of him. 'And second, these are from the divorce lawyers. Can you read them and sign here please?'

She looked down at his long fingers and studied his hand resting on the papers. She thought of her family, she thought of the moments before the accident, then she thought about those messages on her phone, *who was it?* Perhaps this was some elaborate joke. James hadn't mentioned the papers for the last two weeks, she was hoping it would melt away, that by being back at home they would mend things.

'It's an April Fool isn't it?' She beamed at him. Went to poke him in the ribs, but drew her hand back when she saw his face, and started to bite her nail. He was shaking his head.

He tapped the paper with his index finger. 'You were going to sign them that day – of the accident. Only—'

'Someone drove into me – and everything changed.'

'Not this, Victoria,' he said, getting up from the table.

———

She closed her eyes momentarily and when she opened them she was looking at his dark silhouette, striding out of the kitchen. Her eyes flitted to the black cross next to where her signature should be and her shoulders fell. She took a sip of her coffee before she remembered it tasted like frog spawn and nearly spat it out. They were *both* to blame, surely? How had they let things drift so much? It was one thing for them to be on a flimsy bamboo raft, floating down the same river and facing bumps on the way in their marriage – it was quite another for them to be in different vessels, clinging on for dear life, not noticing if the other one needed rescuing.

Just what had happened to her? Had she missed her job so much that she turned her children into her career? Lost sight of what mattered? Her marketing assistant role for that charity had been good, but she was hardly the CEO – *was* she? And working part-time when the kids were little had eventually stopped, she did remember that, it was such a juggle – but there was a sense of loss – and relief. James had been earning a bit more money, she remembered, and they could just about cope. She had strong memories of parts of her life six years ago: on the side-lines of either a netball court or football pitch, helping decorate Jake's room – a trip to the planetarium, then later, sticking glowing stars on his ceiling – *'your own stars'*. Had she unwittingly been given her P45 from that role? Images of the pink ribbon and the iPad with the lovely emails in the box flashed through her mind along with an ache in her heart. *A family of five.* All she'd ever wanted was a perfect family. She glanced at the papers in front of her, mocking her fairy-tale memory as tears pricked her eyes.

She reached for a tissue in her back pocket and felt the scrap of paper from earlier. She pulled it out, looked at it and sniffed. She pushed her chair back determinedly; she needed to get her glasses. She wore glasses, right? James was in the study when she went barging in – stopped and couldn't remember what she was in there for.

'I found this,' she said clutching the paper.

'What's that?'

'A note you wrote to me.' She squinted at it. 'It proves—' She stopped abruptly, unsure what to say. He raised an eyebrow at her. 'That you love me.' She held his gaze for a moment, then looked at the silver rim of his glasses perched on his head.

'Loved,' he said, so quietly she almost missed it.

She decided to ignore that. 'It looks like a list you wrote for our holiday. It's your writing. I found it in a box under my bed.' She handed it to James. He took it from her and stood up and walked to the small leather sofa by the window. He slid his glasses down from the top of his head. She came and sat down next to him and leant over, their faces were inches apart.

Holiday list – it was underlined with a flourish.

Suncream
Upgrade to Premium Economy (yes, really)!
Two kisses on the neck 🖤 🖤
Beach towel
Shoulder rub
Sunset walk on the beach 🖤
Toothpaste
Swordfish in a taverna by the sea (I remembered!)
Charger
iPad
Board shorts
Bikini (the red one!!)
The best memories yet
(Love you xx)

Had he always been this romantic? She looked at the note in his hands. His fingernails were clipped short. His ring finger on his left hand was still bare. There was a tiny indent where a ring had been. She screwed her eyes shut. Maybe when she opened them again it would be there? She sighed and opened her eyes. No. Instead, she glanced at his long legs sticking out in front of him, crossed at the ankle. Those socks. Navy with ridiculous yellow ducks. A memory flashed past: Izzy, a birthday present.

'Victoria?' James handed her the piece of paper. She took it and rubbed the soft paper between her fingers.

'That was a long time ago. Greece,' he said quietly. She followed his gaze out the window. The dove-grey clouds above had no beginning and no end and the whole sky seemed to be pressing down on them.

'We can take a trip back,' she said, 'to that time, can't we?' She lifted a shoulder to her ear. Maybe humour would work.

James got up slowly and rubbed his temples. 'I don't think so.'

She stroked the piece of paper in her lap. How had they managed to let their love disappear through the cracks in their relationship? Had it *all* run out?

15 LULU

'Hungry?'

I nod. We're in the van. It's Saturday afternoon and we've just done a Bubble Disco for twenty-six kids over in Shoreham-by-Sea and the mother insisted we stay on a bit longer. It's been a four-hour shift and we're both exhausted. I lean into the soft leather seat and let out a sigh. I love this van, and I love our little chats on the way to various parts of Sussex looking for the party venues, people's homes, getting lost. Especially getting lost. That look on Markie's face when he's really concentrating, the furrowed brow, the slight twitch in his left eye as he peers at the satnav while I hold in the giggles. Him muttering about postcodes. Us laughing. 'Do you know what I really fancy?' I say.

Markie turns on the heating, raises his eyebrows at me. I feel a whoosh in my stomach but ignore it, and slap him play-fully on the knee as he takes the handbrake off. 'Fish and chips?' He glances at me.

'How did you know?' I blink at him. 'From a proper chippie, the only thing better than that is fish 'n' chips and a sea view!'

'That can be arranged.' Markie glances at his watch and smiles. 'It will only take us twenty minutes to drive to Brighton. It's only seven o'clock. Want to go?'

'Why not?' I find myself saying and grinning. Why not indeed. Because I should be spending the evening scrolling through wedding websites with Simon, but they can wait, surely?

'Let's go!' I throw my head back and laugh. I can't remember the last time I felt like this. After a few miles, I pull my phone out of my bag and text Simon to say the party ran late, I'm exhausted and I probably won't be round later. The nagging voice is back, asking me what I'm doing, but I quell those thoughts by taking a sideways glance at Markie and thinking that we're just getting food. What's the harm in that?

———

We're walking along the back streets of Brighton. The Saturday shoppers have left and there are still some lingering rays of sun in the sky. It's a chilly April evening but you can almost taste that summer is on its way. A seagull squawks above us and I breathe in the tang of vinegar. I hold up a chip between two fingers and inspect its crispy outer layer and anticipate the soft, fluffy centre. 'This is a perfect specimen.'

'Isn't it just?' Markie looks at me, then, at lightning speed, he pulls the chip out of my hand and rams it into his mouth, grinning.

After a while, we're nearly finished eating, walking side by side and I'm humming a song.

'That's a classic.'

'Well?' I raise my eyebrows at him.

'Walking on Sunshine. Katrina and the Waves.'

'Top marks, boss.' I throw my wrapping in a nearby bin. 'Not quite sunshine, I know,' I say glancing at the grey-blue sky, 'more like dusky evening light, but the waves are pretty cool.'

'Let's take a seat, over there, so we can see them better.' Markie points to a bench on the footpath by the sea. We sit side by side in silence for a while, staring out at the inky darkness, the noise of the waves rhythmically shushing us. I shuffle the soles of my boots on the pavement and can feel the gritty sand underneath, but I'm shivering.

'Here.' He takes off his coat, and places it across both our knees.

'Now I feel about 100 years old,' I laugh, but then fall silent again. There are a thousand thoughts tumbling across my brain as I inhale the briny air from the sea. My brain feels like one of those kaleidoscopes you had as a kid; you'd look through it and there were multi-coloured beads at the bottom, and when you twisted it, they were split into different prisms. That's my brain at the moment. I'm twisting and turning my thoughts and feelings, and they are coming out in different shapes that I can't decipher. Happy thoughts, haunting thoughts, they're all mixed up and I'm finding it hard to make sense of it all.

'Pure magic.' Markie breaks the silence. It is. Lights dance on the ocean's surface like fireflies as the mauve horizon melts into the sea.

I cast my gaze back to town. There are fairy lights twinkling and something that looks like a turret in the sky. 'What's that over there?'

'That's the Royal Pavilion, so it is. It's beautiful, they've got the ice rink there,' he says rolling up his wrapper.

'Is it open at the moment?' I ask.

He nods. Then we both turn to each other at the same time. I'm grinning. 'Are you thinking what I'm thinking?' I say.

Markie tilts his head at me and I study the way some curls are escaping from his woolly beanie, and furling over the top of his left ear. 'How good's your ice skating? If it's as good as your singing, I'm in!' He punches me playfully in the arm.

I open my mouth then close it again, uncertain. I grin. Then, for some reason, we both start to run towards the building. I'm trying to keep up with him as we belt down tiny side streets, following the glowing lights like children followed the pied piper. Suddenly, we're here. I stop abruptly. The palace is lit up with blueish lights from the inside, spilling over the ice rink – a purple mirror reflecting the tiny skaters above. A young girl, she must be about six, in a pink bobble hat, is clinging on to her dad's hand, slipping and laughing as he catches her falling time and time again, the sound of ice scraping under her blades.

'God, it's beautiful.' The twinkling palace reminds me of the stage show for Frozen I took Izzy to a few years ago – that was magical, Izzy still believed in Santa, she believed in Elsa, too. Before the eyebrow piercing, before the attitude. And before Victoria changed, says that voice, before she started to feel the kids didn't need her, and started to look for other things to fill up her life.

'Ready?' Markie nudges my elbow and we head inside to get skates.

It's another world on the rink: the aqua green and violet light from the palace are reflected on the ice making it glow like a planet in space. The only sounds are the quiet scraping of ice under my skates. Markie's gliding ahead, glancing back a few times to check I'm OK. He's a much better skater than me; I'm trying very hard to keep my balance and have wobbled my way to the centre of the rink. The air is freezing on my cheeks, but I don't care, my breath becomes white plumes in front of my eyes.

Markie's beside me, holding out his hand. I stare at it. 'C'mon, we can go round together, you look like you need help.' His lips are twitching.

'I do not!' But as I say it, one of my legs starts to slide outwards and before I know it, I'm heading for a face-plant in the ice. Markie quickly slides his hand under my arm and yanks me up.

We're standing face to face, inches apart. I'm aware of his strong arms supporting me still. He stands back, then holds out his hand for support. 'You were saying?'

'Well, maybe I do need some help,' I laugh. Then, slowly, we're gliding across the ice as one, speeding up from time to time as Markie leads me across the sheet of ice, skimming its surface in unison. It's still cold, and strands of my hair have escaped my clasp and are whipping across my cheek, but I hardly notice. All I can feel is Markie's hand squeezing mine tight.

16 VICTORIA

Later that Saturday she was sitting reading a newspaper in the comfy chairs at the end of the kitchen – she *still* had to look twice at the date on the top of the newspaper: 2020, not 2014. It had now been five weeks since she'd been out of hospital and life had taken on some kind of new normal – even with the spectre of those divorce papers playing on her mind. She hadn't signed the blasted things; she'd shoved them in the drawer in the hall table and slammed it shut. She just wanted some family time – space to figure things out. Was it too much to ask?

Every morning James got up from the spare room, showered in their bathroom, dressed and drove to Brighton to his office. The last two Fridays he'd worked from home. It was as if she was sleepwalking in her own life, trying to find those jigsaw pieces. Her phone bleeped. It was Lulu telling her she was in Brighton and wouldn't be home till late. She had said she might pop round. Victoria scratched her head. She was sure Lulu had said the children's party was in Shoreham-by-Sea. Just then, Jake sauntered in. He was wearing ripped denim shorts, slung so low on his hips that they revealed the colour of his underpants. She forced herself not to say anything about underpants and belts.

'Hi, Mum.' He wandered over to the cupboard, yanked out a bowl and proceeded to fill it to the rim with chocolate cereal, then he added maple syrup, and then he reached into the cupboard and pulled out multi-coloured sprinkles. He stared at her. She smiled. Was this a test? She bit her lip. She also found herself fighting really hard not to comment on the fact that he seemed to be wearing the same sweatshirt for five days in a row. Yet she also found a huge rush of love come tumbling out of nowhere and hit her with force. She smiled and tucked her hair behind her ear. 'Morning Jake. How are you?'

'Yeah, sweet – you?'

James walked in, turned the coffee machine on and she braced herself for the dreadful noise.

'I'm fine, thank you. Um, Jake, don't you have football training, or something? On a Saturday?' she said, getting up and coming over to the table. She swept some sprinkles from the surface into her hand. 'Did we forget last week?'

Jake's spoon stopped mid-way to his mouth. His eyes widened. 'So, Mum, I haven't played football for *two* years now. Me and Stanzy are meeting at the skatepark later.'

'Stanzy?' She screwed up her eyes as a memory flashed through. 'Oh, yes. Isn't Stanzy the boy who used to wet himself? He stayed for a sleepover here and we had to wash the sheets – the poor lad was so traumatised his mum had to pick him up?'

'Mu-*um*! That was *ages* ago. Stanzy's six foot now. Give the guy a break!'

Six foot? 'Right, sorry, yes.'

'Anyway, can I have a lift?'

'To where?'

'The skatepark?'

She looked wildly round the room for clues. What was her son talking about?

'S-k-a-t-eboarding park.' Jake said it very slowly and very loudly to her as if she was hard of hearing. Or in fact deaf. Or in fact, just stupid.

'Right, OK.' She nodded, looking for her car keys. *Where was the skatepark?*

'Jake.' The voice was low but loud. It was James. He looked at Jake and then swiftly up at Victoria as if making his mind up about something. 'Remember our chat? Your mother's *memory* has been affected – OK? It might take her a while to remember a few things, like your personal skateboarding schedule – OK?' He fixed his son with a special stare. Victoria bit the side of her cheek as her heart swelled. That sounded like a 'stern dad voice for teenagers'. She had never heard that before. She was grateful he'd stepped in, but she knew Jake didn't mean any harm. The Jake she *could* remember had been a boy holding hands with his father on the way to football practice, or playing in the garden, not issuing snide comments.

'Yeah, sure.' He shrugged. 'It's cool. Sorry, Mum.'

'It's quite OK, sweetheart.' Victoria went over to Jake and started to put her arms around him. 'Whoa! Mum, like, what's this?' He veered away, laughing nervously, then plunged his spoon into the chocolatey mess. She sat down next to him. After a few minutes of loud crunching, she turned to him, something was niggling her.

'Jake, you know you told me last time that Izzy had some "issues" with some girls? What did you mean?'

He screwed up his nose and looked between her and James. 'Ask Izzy. Like I said, girls can be bitchy. I saw something on her phone though, yesterday.' Then he dipped his spoon back into the chocolate-cereal-concoction.

'What?' said James. 'Jake?'

He glanced at both James and Victoria, as if summing up whether to snitch on his sister.

'OK, I looked at her screen and saw that there was a group chat and someone called her "Spot-face". Not very nice. I know she's my sister and I kind of am obliged to hate her,' he rolled his eyes, then carried on, 'but that's not funny. Pretty cruel.' He looked up at them both from under his fringe.

'No, it's not very nice at all,' said James, pouring milk into his coffee. 'Thanks, mate.'

'S'OK.'

James put the milk back in the fridge then said that he had some calls to make and Victoria was alone with the crunching of cereal. Jake was scrolling through his phone, which lay by his side on the table.

Victoria coughed. 'So, um, what are you looking at?'

'Nothin'. Just some Snapchat, bit of Insta.' He glanced up at her.

'Right.' What *on earth* was he talking about? 'So, how's things at school, you know, I can't really remember, um, what about exams?'

'Yeah mum, like G-C-S-Es,' he said this very slowly, then his face softened. 'Sorry. They're next year – remember?'

'Yes, of course. What, are – tell me your favourite subjects.'

'Seriously?'

'Yes, Jake, seriously. Like Dad said, I'm catching up, you know, trying to make sense of all this.' She touched his arm and he didn't move it away. 'I mean of course it will come back, I'm sure it will,' she said rapidly, 'but in the meantime, maybe you can help me out?'

'Sure,' he nodded. 'School's fine.' He seemed to be studying her face. 'Me and Izzy are doing our exams next year, remember?' He raised his eyebrows.

Victoria nodded even though she didn't really. She didn't want to freak Jake out too much.

'My choices are History, Geography, Spanish, and I'm doing the double Science plus Advanced Maths. You told me that Advanced Maths would be a good choice.'

'I did? Right. Advanced Maths.' She tucked some hair behind her ear. Last thing she remembered about Jake and maths was him getting his nine and eight times tables muddled up. Time really *had* flown.

'Mum?' He pushed his bowl to one side.

'Sorry, yes?'

'Skatepark?'

She smiled at him and reached out to ruffle his hair. He ducked and grinned at her. 'Too slow!'

As she gathered her things she tried to focus on her children. Jake doing Advanced Maths? And Izzy? What was going on there? They'd been called into school for a meeting tomorrow about Izzy's 'performance', so they'd bring it up there. Was her daughter being *bullied*? What else had happened that she'd been too busy to notice?

17 LULU

'How's Victoria doing?'

We're sitting in a café next to the ice rink with a hot chocolate and whipped cream on top. It's one of those American diners, with Fifties retro bench seats in red leather, the tables have ketchup and mustard in little baskets and a few people are perched on high stools up at the bar with milkshakes. There's a neon sign for Coca-Cola flashing across the top of the bar and the air is warm and fuggy, it smells of fried food and coffee. The Saturday evening crowds are gathering and its filling up but we've managed to get a booth at the back.

'Nice of you to ask.'

'Of course I'm going to ask, she's your sister – only one you've got, right?' A look crosses his face, then it's gone. 'And, anyway, you never know what's around the corner; you need to love the family you've got.' Markie twists his mug around, picks up his teaspoon and starts to play with the cream, taking little wisps of it on the spoon and licking them off. The atmosphere from the rink has vanished and his face is sombre.

Where do I start? 'She's all over the place with the memory thing – I don't know if she and James can resolve it.'

'They'll resolve it if they want to.'

'You think?'

He nods. 'Maybe it's a second chance for them, you know?'

'Possibly, but they just seemed to have lost their way.' I shrug. I'm not sure why it went so wrong. 'Sometimes, you know, it's better to say something, than nothing at all.' I look over at him and swipe at my cream with my teaspoon. 'She just can't remember.' I yank my skirt down over my knee and look up at the flashing sign. 'He started the divorce proceedings – I think he felt, I don't know, at a loss.'

'But what actually happened?'

'No one thing, it was just, sort of their marriage had kind of broken down, they'd drifted apart, she felt lost as the twins grew up, James was working away – then, I don't know whether it was deliberate or not, she probably thought another baby would fix things, but after they lost her – quite late on, they even had names… she went into a depression. But she can't remember any of it. She just thinks she and James were how they were six years ago. Happy as.'

'That's hard. She doesn't remember key things? Does she remember she lost the baby?'

I shake my head. 'I'm not sure when to tell her. I mean she's got enough to deal with.'

'Maybe that's a good thing?' He shrugged. 'If she can't remember then it can't hurt her, can it? And with her and James, well, it's almost like they've wiped the slate clean. Like a reset.'

'I hadn't thought of it that way.'

'I'm guessing they need to talk, like – don't get me wrong, but if the only thing messing with their marriage was, you know,' he pulls at his chin, 'life, right? Then maybe they can fix it.'

'Maybe you're right. There was, I suppose, a hole in their marriage. They need to mend that hole, they need to put in some – I don't know – underpinning.' I'm scraping the last bit of hot chocolate from the bottom of my glass and I look up at Markie.

'Very romantic,' he says, his eyes dancing, 'underpinning.'

'You know what I mean.' I grin and lick my spoon.

Markie nods.

'We looked at photos when she first came out of hospital: she remembers the day the twins were born – she remembers weird things like how to turn that scary alarm off – but not her actual wedding day.' Wedding day. I play with the word in my mind. It sounds funny when I say it. Markie reaches for a napkin and wipes his mouth.

'Do *you* remember, Lulu?'

'What?'

'The accident – what actually happened?'

And there it is – I'm being asked to lay bare my secret. To expose myself for what I am.

'Lulu?'

Something breaks in me. Maybe it's the first time I've felt able to talk about it, maybe it's the closeness between me and Markie, maybe it's because I need to explain, I don't know, but the resolve in me bends. 'It was my fault. The accident.' I pick up a paper napkin and start to fold it.

'I'm sure it wasn't.' There's warmth in his voice and he touches my fingers briefly and frowns. 'Was it?'

'No. Yes,' I let out a shaky breath. 'Well, not all of it but—'

And I tell him. I keep folding and unfolding the napkin and it all comes out. About being drunk; about pulling the steering wheel. About laughing, thinking it was so funny, thinking I was helping, Victoria's face, so serious all the time, all her *lists* for everything. That it drove me crazy, that something just snapped, and how I wanted to be taken seriously, wanted not to be the younger sister, the chaotic one, the ditzy one, the one with no proper career or life. The 'failed singer' as I'd overheard my uncle say to Dad one Christmas. Dad – to be fair – had defended me, but still, it *hurt*. It was the prosecco, the emotions, the terror of being at that prissy Wedding Fayre, feeling that I had to change. *Shoes? What's your dress like? Honeymoon?* And, if I'm honest, it was the thought of me and Simon alone for two weeks on some island that he'd booked. A hot island. I know most brides would be grateful, but all I wanted to do was say 'Why didn't you ask *me*?' I hate hot holidays. I'd rather go to Norfolk. How the pressure built up and something in that car that night had snapped.

When I finish, I realise my cheeks are soaking. Markie hands me a fresh napkin and I start to pat under my eyes. I must look a state. 'Sorry, Markie, I, um, I didn't realise I felt half those things until I started saying them.'

'That's often the case.'

'I'm worried she might think it was her fault; she can't remember, but it was mine. I mean it *was* the other driver's fault, but I think I made it worse.'

Markie leans back in his seat and puts his hands behind his head and is silent for a while. A waitress walks past and asks if we want anything else and we both shake our heads. After a few minutes Markie clears his throat. 'You know, I think that would really mess with her head, Lulu, if she can't remember. You should tell her, explain what happened, even if she's mad at you, she needs to know,' he frowns at me, those crinkly bits at the side of his eyes getting deeper. 'Tell her you just felt a bit dizzy, under pressure all of a sudden?' There was an edge to his voice. 'But it's important that you do. Really important.'

'You're right.' The air between us lies silent, charged with emotion.

I hesitate before I speak, not too sure what I really mean. 'But, well, I don't know if I—'

'I had a sister once.' He looks up at me and then back down to the table and moves the teaspoon to the right.

Had. I open my mouth to ask, when he clears his throat. 'My little sister was killed by a drunk driver.' He looks straight at me and somehow the glare of the neon lights above is intense, brighter.

'I was back home from university,' Markie carries on, 'in Dublin, staying for the weekend. Esme had been out with her mates – they were about eighteen, lethal mixture of new drivers and discovering booze. That was ten years ago. She was sixteen. They were driving back from a party, my sister was in the passenger seat in the front. Her boyfriend at the time, the gobshite, rolled the car into a ditch. He walked away. She didn't. It was a small car. Not a day goes by that I don't think about her. Like I said, you don't get a second chance with a sister.'

'I'm so, so sorry Markie,' I put my hands in my lap and look across at him.

'Well, it's no good being sorry,' he said breaking the silence eventually. 'What you need to do is tell your sister. I know you weren't driving, but you're in some way responsible for some of the mess.'

'I know, but she's got lots on her plate, perhaps I should leave it as it—' I begin.

'It's so *feckin'* dangerous. Lulu!' A waitress behind him turns to stare at us, then slowly turns back again. In all the two years we've worked together, I've never seen him this cross. Not when a toddler peed on his guitar, not when the Little Bo Peep 'friendly sheep' had yanked itself loose from its tether, not even when parents had cancelled at the last minute. A range of emotions bubble up from deep regret to shock. I sit rigid, staring at his face, his mouth set in a straight line and feel ashamed.

'Look, sorry,' he takes off his beanie and runs his hands through his hair. 'I shouldn't have shouted at you. It just hit a raw nerve. You've been through a lot. You said so yourself, it's like you don't know who you are anymore.'

'Or what I want.'

He looks at me then and I can't read his expression. We both sit for a while letting those words fill the air between us as I fiddle with the paper napkin, suddenly awkward with him. I hear him scraping his chair back and look up.

'We should go.'

———

We walk back to the car in silence. When we get in, we sit for a while staring at the strip of twinkling lights protruding out on the pier, like a bejewelled finger poking into the murky water.

'What if she hates me?'

'Lulu,' he says, reaching into his pocket to fetch the car keys, 'she won't hate you – nobody hates you, Lulu, but you need to love yourself. God knows you've got people around you who do!' He lets out a funny little sigh, 'You've got a man who loves you, who you're marrying. You're lucky.'

The trip is mostly in silence except for the change of gear, the flick of the indicator, the odd comment under Markie's breath about another driver at a junction. Something's shifted and I don't know what it is. It's as if there's a new wariness about him. Is it something I've said – or have I crossed some invisible line without knowing it? Putting my hands under my legs, I lean forward and stare at the road ahead. I really must give the future some proper thought. My wedding is only two weeks away.

The windscreen has fogged up and the orange glow of the streetlights is diffused by the semi-opaque window. It takes me a moment to focus on Markie's face as he's driving, the cinnamon lights from outside skimming his cheeks as he drives past each light. He bends forwards and turns up the windscreen fan. I should be thinking about Simon *a man who loves you*, but for the moment, my eyes won't leave Markie's mouth.

18 VICTORIA

'Mr and Mrs Allen?' A woman in a tight black two-piece suit and a crisp white shirt stood in front of her and James with her slim hand out to shake. They were in the foyer of Izzy's school, and Victoria marvelled at how bright it all was, how clean and tidy. She remembered looking at the school as they used to pass it on the way to the primary school. It always looked so big and intimidating. She summoned up a memory of watching the children there, and thinking how big they all were, how *grown-up*, as the long-legged girls leant on the gate, or the boys idled by the side of the road at the pedestrian crossing as she stopped in the car. She was aware of James coughing. Time to focus. Were they often summoned to meet Izzy's tutor? She couldn't remember what Izzy was studying, let alone the name of her tutor. She needed to get a handle on all this. Thank goodness Jake had filled her in a bit yesterday about him. But Izzy remained a much more closed book.

'My wife, she – the accident.' James fumbled his words and turned his glasses around in his hands.

'Oh yes, of course, your memory, Izzy's mentioned it.' She flashed them both a smile. 'I hope you're feeling better?' She didn't wait for an answer. 'That's why we're here, actually. I'm Jennifer, Mrs Allen – do you remember? Mrs Brown? Come with me.'

The name Mrs Brown rang a faint bell. Victoria followed her as she led them into a small, airless room with a spider plant on the table. Victoria wondered why people bothered with houseplants really. What was the *point* of them? Then, she wondered why she was thinking about that.

'So we just wanted to chat to you about Izzy, about her grades.'

'Which are?' James leant forward and put his elbows on his thighs and looked at Jennifer-Mrs-Brown.

'Perfectly alright, but she is capable of more. It's GCSEs next year.'

'And why isn't she getting better grades if she's capable?'

'Well, that's why I wanted to ask you both here – to ask if there was anything wrong at home.'

'No!' both Victoria and James said in unison.

Then James added: 'Actually, I think everybody knows that Mrs Allen and I are, in fact, separating, we are just in the process of the proceedings. But there isn't anything wrong with how we parent our children, Mrs Brown.' Victoria listened to him and felt like she was in some awful documentary about her own life. *Separating.* In her head she said it in an American accent. It sounded vile, it sounded like something other people did. She looked at James, willing something from him. She studied that little tuft of hair. Her stomach curdled. It was all so formal, so final.

'Call me Jennifer, please. No, I wasn't saying that there was. From all the years here, I know Mrs Allen has been a very committed member of the school community, very *organised*,' she smiled at them both and touched her hair. 'A very hands-on mum to Izzy, which is why I just felt that maybe there was more to it. You both need to know that of course if there's tension in the house from the break-up, this will affect your children, no matter how hard you try.'

Victoria felt chastised. She didn't want Izzy to be stressed about the break-up. She didn't *want* the break-up for God's sake. Was she *organised*? Since when?

'But I think there's more to it. Izzy seems distracted lately; and she's been late to a few lessons, which is very unlike her,' added Mrs call-me-Jennifer.

'Late? She's always caught the same bus. Surely being late a few times isn't a problem.' Victoria recognised the irritated-with-people voice James was using and tried to give him one of their secret stares. He looked blankly at her.

'Victoria?'

'Sorry, yes?'

'We were wondering if you'd noticed anything?'

'Well,' she glanced at Jennifer and then at the spider plant. Honestly, she hadn't even noticed that her son was good at maths. 'The problem is, I can't really remember Izzy the teenager, before my accident, you see. In fact, I can't really remember her after the age of ten, if you must know.'

Jennifer-Mrs-Brown inhaled sharply. 'Right. You mean when she was in *primary* school, not here?'

Victoria nodded. Images of Izzy in her long grey socks pulled up to her knees flashed through her mind, Izzy with her *Frozen* lunchbox, not the Izzy who wore trousers and the school's electric blue blazer, with the eyebrow piercing. What was the school's policy on *that*? 'But it will come back, I'm sure of it, I just need the right trigger.' She stared at the spider plant and wondered how often it was watered. Blast her bloody brain! *Focus.* 'She's quite moody with me too, but

I'm not sure if that's teen hormones, or if it's anything else. I just think we need to ride the waves and be there for her.'

'Yes, "being there" – it's something I wanted to bring up. When we did our psychoeducational testing for Izzy recently a few red flags came up.' Jennifer-Mrs-Brown crossed her legs and Victoria couldn't help wondering what denier her tights were. 'Peer group pressure came up as a "hot spot" when we looked at it – it can be perfectly normal, but I just wanted to check if she feels she can talk to you?'

Victoria sat with her mouth open, nodding. 'Yes. I think so—' she lied, thinking Izzy would rather talk to the binmen than her at the moment.

'I think it might be an idea to make sure you know who she's seeing, "hanging out with" as they say now.' Mrs Jennifer did that inverted comma thing with her fingers.

'For what it's worth,' Victoria added, 'I do feel that Izzy is a bit uptight. I mean, I know there has been an awful upheaval with me in hospital, the accident, the – possible break-up,' she glanced over at James to see if he'd noticed her edit. Part of her brain imagined him leaping up, a la Tom Cruise on *Oprah*, saying he loved her. But he sat quietly and fiddled with his jumper sleeve; 'but I don't know,' she carried on, 'there *was* something her brother saw on her phone which was a bit unsettling.'

'Ah yes,' said James.

Mrs Jennifer looked expectantly at her and James. She uncrossed her legs and leant forwards as Victoria expanded. 'She was called "Spot-face" in a group chat. Not very nice. It was the Year 10 chat.'

'That's interesting – who was the admin on that?'

'I don't know.'

'Right. I'll find out. We have a very robust anti-bullying policy here.' And she scribbled something in her notepad.

'Let's hope so.' James's tone was curt.

Suddenly a loud bell rang and Mrs Jennifer looked at her watch. 'Thanks for your time. If you notice anything else, or Izzy talks to you, you will let me know, won't you? Just keep your eye on her.'

'Of course,' James said. 'We'll keep an eye on her. She's our daughter. But I'd like you to do some digging too, please, especially about that WhatsApp group.' Mrs Jennifer nodded, then James stood up and the three of them awkwardly shuffled out the door as Victoria's phone bleeped. She glanced at it and put it back in her pocket.

She and James silently left the school; James said goodbye formally to her at the gates – he was getting the train to Brighton to get to work. She watched him walk away and took the phone back out of her pocket, then headed for the park. There was someone she was keen to meet.

———

Victoria walked to the park in Little Norland, glad to get out of the stuffy school. She could hear birdsong and the drone of a lawnmower. She ordered a coffee from the pop-up coffee shack, took it to a bench, and started making a list on her notepad. It was unusually warm for early April – the sun was flickering on her face and a robin, perched on a holly bush nearby, tilted its head at her. She looked back at her notes.

Timeline.
Cake cutting?
Speeches?
Izzy?
Taxis?
Champagne? Corkage?

Maid of Honour dress?

She had put an unsmiley face next to the last one. *Maid of honour.* It made her feel about sixty.

She looked up. There was a six-foot-two bloke with dark, shaggy brown hair walking towards her with a grin. He was wearing a purple beanie pulled to one side and a flash of sunlight reflected from an earring in his ear. His brown leather jacket was worn, and as he strode towards her, hands in pockets, his smile reached from ear to ear. He had a touch of the Michael Hutchence about him; in fact, if someone could be described as 'sex on legs – long legs' it was him.

Markie.

She'd looked up his number and called him after she'd been with Lulu at the gym. He'd been surprised to hear from her, but agreed to meet. *Anything to help Lulu's big sister.*

She stood up to shake his hand, but instead he brushed her hand off with 'away with you' with a strong Irish accent, and brought her into a friendly hug. He smelled of leather and lemons and for a second Victoria almost wanted to rest her head on his shoulder and let it stay there. It felt like forever since she'd been in the arms of a man who cared. But then she remembered where she was and pulled away. 'Nice to meet you,' she said as he pecked her on the cheek. They sat down on the bench and he stretched out his long legs, crossing them at the ankles.

'I can see the resemblance,' he said, looking sideways at her.

'Can you? Most people say we're very different.'

'Nope. Dead obvious you're sisters – it's in your smile. She's blonde, you're brunette, sure, but if you look closely, it's in the face, the way you both twist your mouth in a funny way to the side in a crooked smile. It's cute.' He sat up straighter. 'Anyway, how you doing? After the accident?'

'I'm OK!' She laughed nervously. *Crooked smile?*

'Really? Because Lulu's more than a wee bit worried about you – your head injury.' He leant forward and turned to face her properly, fixing her with his green eyes. She could study the earring now, it was a tiny silver guitar.

'I'm just a bit confused about a few things.'

'Lulu tells me you lost six years? Must be weird.'

'Well, yes I did, I have, but I'm sure I'll get back to normal. Anyway, Lulu's told me so much about *you*.' She didn't really want to talk about herself anymore, she was fed up analysing herself, second guessing James, her marriage, figuring out how to parent her *teenagers*. (*Mum, for Chrissake, where have you put my*... Since when did Izzy say 'Chrissake?') What she'd done. What she'd *not* done. No, she wanted to help Lulu, it would give her something else to focus on. It was important that she looked after her little sister. Her little sister was getting *married*, for heaven's sake.

'Has she now?' The lilting Irish accent was strong. 'All good I hope?' He grinned.

'I'm trying to help her get a few things sorted for the wedding, the timeline, the hymns, that kind of thing.'

'Hymns?' Markie looked surprised. 'I'd say The Killers might be more Lulu's thing.'

Victoria burst out laughing. 'Spot on. But we need to have a few hymns too, you know, tradition, for my dad. Anyway, Lulu loves singing – obviously.' Victoria rolled her eyes, then wondered why she was acting like a sixteen-year-old who rolled her eyes. 'So,' she carried on, 'I thought at her wedding it would be nice to have live music, not just hymns. Music, but proper singing. *You* singing.' She put her coffee cup down on the bench and pulled at the edge of her sleeve.

There was the tiniest hesitation, and then he beamed. 'Of course, if it's what she'd want. Grand. I hadn't thought I'd be there, to be honest.'

'No? I think it would be a nice touch.' She was sure Lulu and Markie got on. Lulu's face came alive when she talked about him, she seemed to really enjoy helping him build his company. But perhaps Markie was a bit of a cool customer?

'Oh,' she placed a hand on his arm. 'Just one thing?'

Markie nodded.

'Don't tell her, will you? It's going to be a fabulous surprise.'

'OK, I'm in.' He gave her the tiniest of winks. 'Only—' He sat back on the bench.

'What?'

'Ach, don't mind me. It's none of my business.'

'Go on.'

'I don't know.' He shrugged. 'She seems miles away sometimes. Like she's not quite "in the room" – do you know what I mean? Or she's worrying, maybe?' Victoria looked at his beautiful teeth as he spoke. He seemed to really care. And Simon? Of course, the voice scolded, of course he cares, he's *marrying* her.

'Sorry you were saying?'

He looked at her. 'I'm saying, with Lulu – there's something, a bit quare, you know, odd, out of reach, like,' his voice softened. 'She's got such potential,' he went on. 'A long, long time ago I worked for a record company, as a talent scout. Things didn't work out and I left, but it did give me, you know, clues about what to look for – for, well, talent.' He looked ahead. A woman walked past them pushing a pram. The baby was just visible, tucked up under a yellow blanket, blissfully asleep. 'Do you know why she walked away that day? When I ask her she just smiles, turns it into a joke, says,

Do you know how stressful it is to go to West End auditions? But really, she's just shutting me down. It's just—'

'Go on.' Victoria shivered as she stared at the pram. A tiny head covered in a white bonnet, eyes closed shut. Victoria was lost in snatches of muddled memories, the pink ribbon, glittering mobiles… Suddenly Markie was speaking.

'Look, it's none of my business.' Markie sat back.

'Tell me Markie.' Victoria took a sip of coffee. It was cold.

'I don't know – I just can't see her in a house, with a mortgage and two-point-four kids, so I can't.'

And that was the problem. Neither could Victoria.

19 VICTORIA

Victoria clasped the brooch tightly in her fist. The pin at the edge pierced her skin and she flinched. She was setting the table in the kitchen; everyone was coming for lunch. James had given her the brooch when they were on holiday in Greece. Since she'd found those photos and that list, more had come back to her. *It's beautiful, like you.* It was a white pebble, polished till it gleamed and there were tiny pearls surrounding it. She remembered the beach, Izzy and Jake had run into the waves and then come out and rolled in the sand. 'Chicken nuggets' they'd called them, pinching their toes. They must have been about five. And then James, holding a squealing twin under each arm, armbands bulging out the sides as he plunged into the water. She'd watched, her sarong gently flapping across her legs. There were flashes of vivid memory.

Life had been uncomplicated, hadn't it? They loved each other, they had two adorable children, James was trying for promotion and they were trying for another baby – or were they? It was a bit fuzzy. And then what? It seemed life had come along; the twins had grown up and they'd mismanaged their marriage. Had all the wet towels on the floor, the unanswered text messages, the late hours at the office, the headache of bringing up twins with two sets of everything from homework to nits – had that all seeped into the fibre of their marriage like rain soaking through a faulty roof, until the rot had set in?

It made her think of Rachel, an old school-friend, when she'd come round, sobbing. She could remember this clearly. Actual heaving breaths when she had opened the door to her. Told them that she and Rob were separating. They had been the golden couple, the ones who'd married young, Rachel and Rob. R&R everyone called them. Had they headed the same way? Relationships that hadn't worked out. Plenty of them. *We're not going to be like that*, they'd said to each other, tucked up that night in bed, holding onto each other, as if by pressing their bodies tightly together they could ward away any evil marriage spirits. Or other times, when she'd heard about yet another casualty at the school gates, she'd find herself holding his hand that evening, squeezing it tightly and saying 'I love you' to remind herself that she did and what she had. How did people do it? Walk away from years of love, of building a fortress against the outside world, a barrier made of stories, of love, of family holidays, of squabbles, of sex, of knowing it's sugar in coffee not tea, of leaving the light on at night, of sending flowers to say sorry, of sleeping on the side of the bed next to the door in strange hotels because your wife got scared, of quietly creeping out on Christmas Eve to check you'd hung the kids' stockings in their bedroom while your husband lay sleeping, of cleaning out a messy car and not getting angry. The cement in the bricks of marriage. How does that erode away? Not us, she'd thought. The twins will never tell a counsellor, 'Mummy and Daddy have fallen out of love.' Or will they?

How had it begun to rot? She realised with a jolt that maybe some of the fissures of their marriage had started with *her*. Had things become so desperate that her only way to flag up a failing marriage was to head for the Botox and beauty treatments? As if by wrapping up the present as sparkly as she could, she would entice her husband back. Why hadn't either of them realised that the decay had started, and that they should fix it, shore it up with love, or at least feed it with a proper conversation instead of silence? But that takes guts, doesn't it? It's hard to say 'is this enough?', to face the fact that midlife and older children mean the beginning of – what? The end? Certainly the beginning of a new era, of taking responsibility for your own happiness, accepting that shuttling kids to the school bus can only count so much as a shared hobby. Surely it could be the beginning of something new, too?

But I don't think it was all for me. James's barbed comment flashed through her mind.

What had she done?

Victoria moved round the table and mechanically placed knives and forks opposite each other. The napkins, the salt and pepper, it was all new to her. Household items were a surprise every time she opened another cupboard. Yesterday, she'd phoned the hospital and demanded to know when her next scan was – the secretary said she would send her an email. She'd been quite sniffy. It was alright for *her*, wasn't it? She wasn't the one who was a stranger in her own life. Who had messages on her phone. She'd peeked at them again last night. She felt sick. Yet she didn't really *know*. Everyone was being *so bloody polite*.

'You're wearing the brooch?'

She abruptly turned round as James walked towards her carrying a dish of salad. 'Yes.'

He glanced at it and she stared at his jaw, at his shirt collar and tried to remember how many times she might have lain against the crook of his neck, crying sometimes, laughing perhaps, sharing a secret? Where had his passion for her gone? The spark? *She* could feel it, she couldn't miss it, fizzing up inside her. What about him? She studied his mouth. It was moving. 'Where do you want these?' He stared at her.

'In the middle, please.'

'What time are Lulu and Simon arriving?' James stood next to her. So near she could see the pattern of freckles across his nose.

She glanced at her watch – nice watch, leather straps and little diamonds on every hour. Classy. Was she classy? 'About two-ish.'

It had been Lulu's idea to get everyone together. 'Might jig your memory a bit more, sis. Be good for us all to try to be a bit normal.' Whatever that was. 'Get to know each other, um, again, before the wedding,' she'd said. And she'd had a kind of weird look on her face, Victoria recalled, like she was summing something up.

She had made mushroom risotto. Izzy had announced she was now 'part-time vegetarian', and somehow, as she measured out the cream and the butter and the mushrooms, it came to her, the chopping, the right ingredients. 'It will be like that,' the consultant's secretary had advised when she'd asked about the next scan, 'remember? Procedural memory, but some other chunks of memory—' the secretary had sniffed down the phone and hesitated – 'will take longer to recover.'

'What about my wedding day?' Victoria had demanded of the poor woman.

'I'm sure it will come back. Look for triggers. Your wedding dress?' Her voice had been softer and Victoria had felt overwhelmed with it all, thanked her and put the phone down. Victoria had thought about her veil and knew it was in that box, the secret box that held memories of *her James*, her life, her past. And what else did her past hold? whispered a tiny voice in her head. Well, whatever it was, a new voice commanded, it wasn't *her*. They belonged to Another Victoria.

20 LULU

Simon is carrying a large bouquet of lilies, it's gigantic, bless his monogrammed socks. We're crunching across Victoria's gravel driveway, trying not to be late for Sunday lunch, Simon hates being late. Everybody likes lilies, he'd said. But I know Victoria adores roses. 'But she can't remember,' he'd said, 'I'm sure she'll like these.' His confidence is out of this world, it's one of the things which attracted me to him, feeling safe with him, valued; he can fight any battle. Fixes things. But he couldn't fix his wife dying and it's left a hole. *And should he fix you?* I hear my conscience asking.

Simon's nervous about seeing Victoria for the 'first' time. Only it isn't the first time. They'd met several times before the accident, it's just that she can't remember.

'Hello!' Victoria opens the door with gusto – and a frilly frock. Has she been drinking? Her face is super red. I glance at my watch – it's only twelve.

'Hey, sis, how are you?' I lean in and let the waft of Rive Gauche envelop me, it always gives me a sense of 'home', ever since Mum died and Victoria started to wear it. She used to get exasperated with my second-hand vintage 'finds', but, well, today it looks like she dressed head to foot in the stuff. I stand back. 'You look charming.'

'Charming?' she laughs. 'I'll take charming! Found this at the back of my wardrobe, isn't it fab?' She does a twirl then looks at us. '*Why* didn't I used to wear this more?' She glances at us. 'Simon, right? How are you?' She swoops towards him for a hug. My sister, the cool customer *hugging in a floral dress*. Next, she'll be barefoot.

'Good, very good, Victoria, really good.' He looks down at his shoes, then up again, suddenly remembering the flowers. 'These are for you.'

She clasps the flowers and smells them as I do a double take. The perfect hall is now trashed with shoes, muddy trainers and bags. Victoria sweeps them aside with one foot. 'Come and have a drink.' She presses her nose to the flowers again and starts to cough. 'Lovely.'

She ushers us into the lounge as James appears with a tray of prosecco. 'Hi Lulu, Simon.' He nods to us and holds out the tray formally. His face is drawn and there are dark circles under his eyes. I have no idea how these two are going to fix this. I can see why Victoria fell for him, on the outside anyway. He's not my type, but it's hard to ignore the perfect chiselled cheekbones and model looks you don't always see. Tall, blonde, assured, green eyes with a killer smile, a touch of the Daniel Craig about him. But the charismatic dude from the wedding photos has been replaced by an avatar of his former self, with worry lines etched into his forehead, and he's lost that confidence in his own skin.

After a while, I glance at my watch. Only half an hour has gone by. I down another prosecco to ease my inner demons. Memories of Victoria in hospital, the twisty snake of shame I feel about what happened starts to gnaw at me and I refill my glass again.

James turns to Simon: 'So, Simon, mate, good to see you, how's things?'

I down my whole glass and zone out as my fiancé explains to James about end-of-year accounts, losses, tax issues, and all I can focus on are the mini sausage rolls on the coffee table and how I want to stuff about ten in my mouth and shout 'boring'. But I don't. That's what ten-year-old Lulu would have done at Christmas parties, and then Dad would have sort of made a thing of telling me off, but be laughing really, and then they'd get out the karaoke machine – only I'd be the one up the most, the child they thought they wouldn't have. (*You weren't unwanted, sweetie, just unplanned! Imagine! Vicky was twelve when I was pregnant with you, pumpkin!* Mum's nickname for me as she washed my hair, scrunching it all up on top of my head and planting a kiss on me.) Twelve years between me and Victoria was quite a gap. Sometimes, Mum was mistaken for my nan at pick up. She'd come home, light a cigarette and not speak till she'd finished every last drag, her cheeks hollowed out as she drew on the cigarette, staring out the window.

———

'Lulu?'

We're at the table now and Simon is handing me something in a large earthenware dish. It's possibly mushroom risotto, but it looks like puke. Where's the roast beef?

'This looks nice.'

I glance at Simon's plate. He's taken a tiny portion, clearly expecting there to be some meat on the menu too.

'We're going vegetarian this week. Izzy has turned vegetarian, so we are too,' quips Victoria.

Jake glances at Simon. 'Yeah, I was looking forward to roast beef, too.'

Izzy looks up from her phone and shrugs. 'Whatever. I don't mind if you eat meat.'

'No!' Victoria announces. 'We are going to support you every step of the way.' I look over at Izzy who is scowling at Victoria. That kid sure is a moody teenager. A helter-skelter of emotions. One minute she's up, up, the next slamming her phone down like a drama queen and leaving the room.

It's like I've landed in some kind of reality TV show: '*Meet the fuck-ups.*' Simon is pretending to enjoy the risotto when I know for a fact he hates mushrooms. James's cheeks are so pinched with the effort of being polite; and Victoria, what has got *in* to her? She's acting like a 1950s housewife. Those synapses must be firing all the wrong way today. Where are the navy stilettos, the linen shift dresses?

'Terribly good risotto, Victoria.' Simon is helping himself to more, as I catch his eye and smile. He is a good man.

'Oh good! It did take ages, but I thought it would be a nice change. By the way, please call me Vicky, I don't know where Victoria has come from.'

'That,' James says in a booming voice suddenly, 'is what we *all* want to know.' He pushes his seat back and folds his arms. 'No, let me tell you, because I think I do know. It's come from about five years ago when you wouldn't answer to Vicky and decided to become Victoria.' I have a forkful of risotto mid-way to my mouth. James is staring at my sister with a look I can't place. I look across at my sister and her cheeks are flushed.

'Well,' Simon clears his throat, 'I love the chive on the top

– and I like the name Vicky.' Simon beams at Victoria. That pleasing Labrador image flashes through my brain again.

Izzy mouths 'Awkward' to Jake who lifts his shoulders in a tiny shrug.

Time to change the subject. 'How's school guys?'

Both Jake and Izzy say in unison: 'S'OK.'

Right, nowhere to go there.

'How are the wedding plans, Lulu?' James stares straight at me, trying to fix the awkwardness. I feel compelled to gabble a long list of explanations from flowers, to venue – that little hotel which has a chapel, remember, that small road off the A892, you know the one? – pretty remote, and yes, food's all sorted, Simon's a whizz with menus, and my dress, I start to explain as my sister sits in stunned silence.

Suddenly she pipes up. 'It looks fabulous,' she manages, picking up her glass and draining it. I don't blame her. It's like the worst kind of dinner party. Small talk, only *small talk with your family*. 'I wish I could remember mine,' Victoria fixes her gaze on me. 'Lulu, sweetie, I can't believe you're getting *married*, I mean, six years ago—'

'I was in a very different place!' My voice is shrill.

Victoria picks up the bottle of wine, fills up her glass and spills it on the table. 'The problem *is*, last thing I *remember*, Lu,' she leans on her elbows, 'is that you were going for that audition, for *Mamma Mia*? At that hotel. Meeting some hoity-toity producer person. You basically were about to give birth with the excitement of it. *Imagine, Mamma-bloody-Mia*, you said to me. A dream come true, you said…'

Her voice trails off as I hold my breath. 'And I suppose I thought you'd be – I don't know,' she shrugs then carries on, '—maybe in another role at the West End by now! That I'd see my little sister on those bus shelter adverts or something!'

She puts her hands into a prayer pose, as if she's about to say 'Namaste' or something.

Thank God the doorbell sounds. Vicky means well, but she has no idea. I glance at her glass. Or maybe it's the jolt she had during the crash. Or the strain of her and James. Anyway, the truth is, the day of the audition is not a day I want to remember.

21 VICTORIA

Victoria stood up and tugged at the dress around her bust. It *was* a bit tight. She was trying to channel 'domestic goddess', only it wasn't working. What with the risotto which frankly looked like cat sick and that outburst from James. Opening the door, she was nearly knocked over by a small bundle of fluff who charged straight at her, jumping up at her knees. The ball of fluff turned out to be an energetic puppy, bouncing around the hall, grabbing a trainer between his teeth and growling playfully. 'What on—?'

'Hello, pet!'

She looked up from the puppy to see her Dad surrounded by sunlight at the door. His hair was caught in a halo of light, it was as if her guardian angel – with bad hair – had just arrived.

'Dad! What are you doing here?' She felt overjoyed and confused all at once.

'You invited me, poppet, remember?' he said grinning.

Oh God, yes, yes, yes. Damn her memory. She did remember now, thinking about it, but sometimes all these pesky memories both current and past collided and her mind was a tangled mess. Rather like those phone boxes you see men kneeling at, by the side of the road, pulling at different coloured wires, and you wonder how on earth they can fix your BT Openreach by yanking at them. Her mind was just like that. Her synapses needed a tug. Of course he was visiting, she remembered now, staying even – Jesus, the spare room was a tip.

'I've been worried sick about you, pet,' said her Dad, offering his hand in support, then pulling her in for a hug.

'Ooh, watch my ribs. Little tender still.'

Her dad grimaced. 'Sorry love.' And as she pulled away she inhaled a smell of slightly damp clothes. She must ask if he ever did get the tumble drier fixed. A scratching at her knees told her the puppy was not going to be ignored.

'And who's this little one?'

'Ah,' her dad said, kneeling down and picking up the fluff ball in his arms, 'this is Pickle. He's a seven-month rescue Jackapoo and I just couldn't say no, not after Billie died. There was an advert in the local paper from the rescue centre.' Her dad stroked the little pup's forehead and cradled him in his arms. 'But I couldn't leave him behind, and so we've been on an adventure on the trains, haven't we Pickle?'

As if by answer, Pickle started to lick his face. He put Pickle down on the floor and she helped him take off his coat.

'Come on, Dad, let's get you in.'

She stroked the coat in her hands, felt the thin fibres between her fingers and noticed that the hem was down in places. Had her dad always looked this old? She glanced at her dad and she felt a rush of love. She also felt that she must get him to the hairdressers to sort out his fluffy hairdo. Since their mum had died he'd been coping on his own, he'd had to – those memories were quite strong, memories of the phone calls, the questions he used to ask, *What temperature should I put the wash on, love?* She did remember all of that. His new friends in the Dales who had instantly become new Old Friends – his words – who'd rallied round after Mum had died.

'Hungry?'

'Starving,' he said, bending down to pull a nearby trainer out of Pickle's mouth.

He followed her to the large kitchen table and as she watched the scene unfold, she felt that her heart might burst: *this* is what family was about. Lulu shrieked and stood up and gave him an enormous hug, Simon held out his hand which he shook vigorously, James embraced him warmly – 'Good to see you, Eric' – as Izzy and Jake leapt up, their teenage personas left at the table as they both said 'Grandad!' in unison as he took one under each arm like he used to do when they were five – this was a memory embedded in her mind for life.

They'd been at a park when the twins were toddlers eating ice cream on a bench. Her dad had been picking dandelions, then blowing them, as the twins watched, in rapture, as the seeds floated upwards to heaven. *Where do they go Grandad? They go to the moon and they plant themselves there.* For about a year after that whenever Izzy saw the moon she'd say, 'I wonder how Grandad's dandelions are doing?' He would often sit with them like that, a twin under each arm, tell them stories, or read, or tickle them under their arms.

Her dad eased himself into the seat next to James, as he carefully moved aside and reset his place, squeezed her dad's shoulder affectionately and poured wine into his glass.

'Now, Simon, tell us all about yourself and if you're good enough for our Lulu here?' Eric sat back and folded his arms, never one to worry about social pleasantries. Just then, Pickle leapt up into his lap. 'Easy, Pickle, I don't know if you're allowed at the table.' He shot Victoria a guilty look. How could she say no? She glanced at Simon, who looked a bit seasick. Then Eric suddenly let out a snort.

'Only joking, lad! I think it's a terrific idea. Tell you what, why don't we take a walk with Pickle after lunch,' he said as he rubbed the pup's belly, 'and we can have a good old chat?'

'Mushroom risotto?' Victoria passed the bowl to him.

'Risotto, pet? No thanks,' he said shaking his head. 'None of that muck for me. You can give it to Pickle later when nobody eats it. Where's the roast beef?' He glanced at the dishes on the table.

Jake stifled a smirk as Izzy glanced at Victoria with wide eyes.

'Dad!' Lulu giggled.

'*Dad*, Izzy is part-time vegetarian now,' Victoria explained, frowning at him.

'Bloody ridiculous,' he laughed, but he took the bowl and spooned a little onto his plate. 'Bit like being part-time pregnant, isn't it?'

A wave of emotion suddenly hit Victoria. Part-time pregnant. It unleashed something inside her brain. Images flashed across – a cot, blankets, the baby mobile – tiny blue butterflies suspended on a pink glittery cord; her staring up at it, because she was lying on the floor. Why had she been on the floor? These weren't happy memories from Izzy and Jake, no. Where were they from? Victoria's hands shook as she placed the bowl back on the table. Her memory wasn't helping her now. It wasn't helping her at all.

22 LULU

We're sitting by the fire in the lounge and Dad is in a big armchair with Pickle on his lap. Simon has left to get some work done at home and whispered that my dad was lovely – *protective, but lovely*, he'd joked as he got in the car – after they took Pickle for a walk earlier, he also said he thought it would be good for me and Victoria to spend some time with Dad alone; James is in the study and the kids are watching something on Netflix.

It's five o'clock and Victoria has just placed a tray with a pot of Earl Grey tea and some slightly burnt-looking brownies on it, on the small coffee table in between the sofa and the chairs. She's sitting on the sofa with me, her feet tucked up under her. Pickle is fast asleep; and Dad's stroking the pup's forehead methodically.

'So girls, you bloody gave me a fright,' I can see he is trying to be brave, but his voice breaks a little. 'Lulu here told me not to come down, said everyone needed to get back to normal first?' He's screwing up his eyes, looking at us both.

It's the same look he used to give us when we hid the biscuit tin under our beds.

'How are your ribs, pet?' He looks over at Victoria.

'Much better.'

'I could kill that woman.' He suddenly says.

'Who?'

'The other driver!'

'Wasn't *her* fault, Dad,' Victoria leans across the coffee table and adds milk to her cup.

I drop my teaspoon onto the saucer with a clatter. 'The police told us she swerved to avoid a deer in the road, Dad,' I say.

'Actually, the police were on the phone the other day,' Victoria continues. 'She was from the Isle of Wight, here for the day, I can't remember the details, but she has admitted it was totally her fault; I need to call the insurance company in the morning, it's all a bit foggy, really – James has been dealing with the police. There's paperwork I must sign.' She attempts a weak smile as my heart hurts for her.

'You need to be careful, pet. The doctors told you no more stress, right?'

'Well that's pretty hard when your husband's frosty, your kids have gone from ten to sixteen overnight and you don't recognise your "best friend" – thank God I've got *you* both.' She pulls her dress down over her knee. Is she about to cry? How awful must it be to wake up in a semi nightmare? Yet my inner critic is telling me that some of it is her own making. If James is off with her, then maybe it's up to me to tell her why? That she wasn't being the best wife, that they had grown apart, that she became more interested in kitchen appliances, one-upmanship at the gym, endless 'appointments' and that new friend Zoe.

'Lulu?' My dad's voice is soft. 'Can you remember much of the accident?'

The fire crackles in the grate and a log falls off. 'Not much,' I lie.

'More than me, though, sis. I think if I could understand more about the accident, remember what happened, it might trigger something. Maybe I'd be able to recall more? I don't know.' Victoria sounds exhausted. She shifts on the sofa and pulls a cushion across herself and hugs it. It's as if she's wrung out from her 1950's housewife performance.

I can feel my cheeks flush. 'Hey, Vicky, it was all a bit of a blur – I mean, I remember noise, the screeching, then suddenly a bang. But I didn't take the full impact because I was in the passenger seat.'

'I'm glad I'm here,' Dad says adjusting Pickle in his lap. 'Seeing you both in the flesh has reassured me a bit.' He strokes Pickle's tummy and then looks up at us. 'Girls, you know that you both mean the world to me, especially after your mum died, I've been quite lonely, no, no, don't say anything,' he puts his hand up to stop us interrupting. 'All my neighbours have been great, and especially my walking group, it feels like home now, it's just that you can't replace your *family* – do you know what I mean?'

I open my mouth to say something, but he looks over at me and I let him carry on. 'And I'll tell you what, after I came off the phone to Lulu about the accident I was beside myself.' He takes a deep breath. 'But I want you both to promise me something?'

Victoria puts her cup and saucer down and leans back. She looks pale.

'What?' I ask.

'I did a lot of thinking on the train on the way down – well, when Pickle wasn't eating the seat covers or darting under someone's seat – and I want you both to promise me that you'll live your lives, no regrets? When your mum and I moved to Yorkshire from here ten years ago it was because she had always wanted to live there, to go back home. And although we only had one year together before she died, I am so glad we did. The community there, the Dales, the walks we've had, the weather,' he laughs, 'all of it; we did that together. She got her dream. And now, I have a fantastic circle of friends. I do feel at home there. We'd always have wondered "what if" if we hadn't gone.'

Victoria's voice is croaky: 'My biggest regret is what I've done, you know, between me and James. I don't know what I can do to sort it out.'

'Well, I don't want to pry, love, but if you think it's worth fixing, then you need to do just that. And, just remember Vicky love, it's up to James to fix things too.' He frowns at Victoria, who nods. Just then, Izzy bursts into the room, clutching her phone. She looks startled.

'I didn't think anyone was in here,' she sniffs.

'Iz, what's wrong?' Victoria asks.

She glances at her phone and puts it in her back pocket and shrugs, moving away. '*Iz?*' she says to her mother, with a touch of sarcasm. 'Oh nothing, just some stupid kid at school. It's fine.' She beams at us, but the smile doesn't reach her eyes, then she turns abruptly and walks out of the room.

'I need to go see her,' Victoria sighs deeply and gets up, following Izzy out the room.

Poor Victoria. It's all such a mess. Imagine waking up and losing six years of your life? I want to help her, but they need to fix their marriage. Somehow the gap just widened. One minute they were the perfect couple hosting children's birthday parties and cuddling when nobody was looking, the next thing, life had moved on and her lens changed. Everything wasn't quite right; she seemed bored, frustrated. Then they lost the baby… And then the attention started to be focused on herself. She became *busy, busy, busy*.

And there's that little voice asking me who *I* am anymore. *Don't waste your life.* Is that what I'm doing? My chest feels like there's a band tightening across it. Married. Do I feel like I'd give anything to be with Simon? Do I feel that − maybe in some dark part of my soul − I'm running away *to* Simon, like he's a safe island, rather than facing conflict? But surely that's what a marriage is about, about shared experiences? About being a team? Answering those questions is going to take some time. The only problem is − I glance at Dad to see he's fallen asleep − with a wedding less than two weeks away, I'm not sure I have much time left.

23 VICTORIA

Victoria sighed as she headed up the stairs to see Izzy. She'd heard her bedroom door slam shut. *Don't have any regrets.* The problem was, she couldn't actually remember what she had regrets *about*. Her last memories of her family were smiling faces, toothpaste on a tie, sunshine, ripping Christmas paper off presents, Disneyworld, Paddington movies and finding popcorn in her bra. And now? Nobody was speaking to her. Not properly anyway. Not if you don't count 'I'm going out' or 'The marmalade's finished'. And somehow her kids just didn't speak to her either – not *really*. Was that because of something she'd done – something before the accident – or was it, as she was learning, because it was a Teenager Commandment? One of the many she was slowly getting used to.

Thou shalt be surly to your parents, thou shalt ask for something precisely two seconds before you need it, thou shalt leave about 489 wet towels on the floor at any one time, thou shalt dress like you just woke up in your clothes (Jake) or change outfits at least fifty times a day (Izzy), thou shalt never look away from your phone, lest the dragon of death descend on you and thou shalt certainly not actually talk to your parents – always WhatsApp (she knew what this was now) them instead, especially if they are in the same house.

She knocked on Izzy's door gently.

'Go away.'

'Darling, let me come in.'

'All you'll do is lecture me. Give me some kind of bloody TED talk.'

'Honey, let me in so I can at least sit with you, I know you're upset.'

'No shit, Sherlock,' came the reply.

She's just sad, that's all, Victoria reminded herself. She's a *teenager* now. Victoria stood a little taller and then twisted the door handle. It turned in her hand. It was open after all.

Izzy was sitting cross-legged on her bed on top of her quilt. It was one that they'd created together. It was a patchwork of all of Izzy's old T-shirts. When she'd been about seven – this memory had stuck like glue – Victoria had been doing a clear-out and Izzy had come in the room and found her putting all her T-shirts, glittery tops and tights into a bin bag for charity. Izzy had gone mad. So rather than tell her she'd outgrown them, Victoria had found another way of keeping them. They'd sat and selected all the clothes which really meant something to Izzy and sent them off to a wonderful woman who offered this service on Facebook. Two weeks later, a beautiful quilt, lined with soft velvet, had arrived in the post. Izzy had adored it.

Victoria sat down on the bed next to her and reached out for her hand, the one that didn't have her phone clamped to it.

'Grandad's fallen asleep downstairs, he looks quite peaceful with Pickle on his lap.'

Her daughter pulled her plait. 'He's a cute puppy. It's

been really good to see Grandad.' She leant back on her headboard and looked down at her lap, her long eyelashes fluttering.

'Izzy, what's been upsetting you? You seem a bit more moody lately. And we saw Mrs Brown recently and she's worried about your grades. You have important exams next year.' *Was this the right thing to say?*

She glanced up at Victoria and pulled a face. 'Doh! Yes, they're GCSEs!'

'Yes, yes, I know. And are you moody because you're worried about them?'

'Mum! Really? Haven't you heard of periods? I mean, look!' She pointed to her forehead and Victoria peered at it looking for clues, but all she saw was Izzy's dark fringe. Had she had a tattoo there, perhaps? If she had, she reminded herself to be *very calm* about it, teenagers were experimenting that's all. She had read that on her Get Up To Speed With Teens website recently.

'Darling, what?'

Izzy swept her fringe off her forehead. 'Spots! Zits! Bloody everywhere!'

'Please stop swearing Izzy.'

'Is that all you can say? I am covered in spots and you're worried about a bit of swearing?'

'No, it's just that you don't need to get this upset. I can't see anything.'

'Because I've covered it in concealer, doh!' She shrugged. 'Don't you get it?'

Victoria stared at her daughter, with her long dark plait hanging over her shoulder, her face covered in make-up and wanted to take the anger and hurt away. *Spot-face.* Poor, poor girl. And, of course, she was moody because of PMT! Good God, how could she not remember these things. Because in her mind she was still her little '*itsy-bitsy*' Izzy. There were years missing. Who had gone with her to fit her first bra? She certainly hoped it hadn't been James. *When* would her memory return to normal? And then a thought struck her – *will* it ever be normal? Maybe she'd lost six years of her life, never to get them back?

'Izzy I'm sorry, I do "get it", if you've got your period, you'll get break-outs, be moody – do you want to talk about it?'

'What? Like discuss it again? We've done that, Mum! Remember the books, the lift-the-flap question-and-answer one you got out the library for me when I was twelve? No, thank you, I'm *on it*. Don't worry.' She folded her arms.

'OK, but is there anything else you want to discuss?'

'Like what?'

'Anything, you know, bothering you, things you need to get off your chest? I just want you to be happy, you know?'

'Really? Coz last time I looked, I don't know, it was sort of like you couldn't really be bothered. There was always something else you were in the middle of. You just want me to be happy to make life easier for *you*.'

'Izzy, that's not—'

'Sorry, Mum.' Izzy shifted on the bed and looked at her. 'I mean, you did stuff for us, but you were sort of absent.'

Absent? Now that hurt. 'Look, *I'm* sorry, Izzy. I need to do better. I will do better, I promise. I just, well, you seem a bit withdrawn, not yourself.'

'Yeah, Mu-u-m, coz the "myself" you remember was like ten and a half and used to wear *Frozen* underpants. Well, Mum, newsflash: she grew up.'

Victoria took a deep breath. This was much harder than she'd imagined. Her website *had* warned her, but still. 'And, um, Izzy – I don't want you to have any secrets.'

'Ha! What like *you* don't! Everyone's got secrets Mum, get real.'

'What do you mean?'

'Seriously? You, Aunty Lulu – we all have.' She folded her arms. 'Look, I'm really tired.'

It was Izzy's cue that she'd had enough mum-daughter time. But Victoria was determined. 'Just ask me anything, Izzy, and we can sort it.'

Izzy looked up at her and started to fiddle with the end of her plait. 'Can Pickle sleep in my bed tonight?'

———

As she left Izzy's room with the promise of a puppy to be by her side tonight, Izzy was visibly happier. Jake was just bounding up the stairs two at a time when she passed him.

'Pickle did a poo! Classic. I helped Grandad cover it up with kitchen roll! It's still there in a pile. He was using air freshener to spray all over it! Don't look at me like that, Mum, I found the lavender one, the one you *like*,' he said proudly and then raced up the rest of the stairs.

She *wished* she could remember more about her kids. And as for her marriage – where to start? She glanced at a picture on the wall – it was taken when they were on holiday in Morocco before she got pregnant – they were *trying* to get pregnant, she recalled, smiling to herself. She remembered that holiday, how she'd look over at him across the dimly lit table and think *he's gorgeous*, or at times *we're married*, that sense of belonging. The silly look he'd give her when he tucked a napkin into his shirt, the way he could find his way round all the backstreets whereas she would get lost just turning out of her hotel. Where was that feeling now? It was miles away, buried under years of hurt, it looked like. She gripped the handrail. There was a bark from downstairs. 'Vicky, love?' her dad called out.

She sighed. It was time to deal with lavender-scented dog mess.

———

Victoria was on her hands and knees on the floor in the hall, next to the lounge door, spraying sanitizer on the floor and inwardly rolling her eyes about potty training pups. Pickle was by the door, nudging it open. Victoria put the pup on her lap and he let her tickle his tummy. She kissed the top of his head. Just as she was about to put him down she heard her name. The door to the lounge was ajar and she could hear voices, urgent whispering.

'I don't know what to do Dad, she doesn't remember *anything*!' It was Lulu.

'How bad did it get?'

'There wasn't one kind of "bang", it was more a slow fizzle. I mean, after the miscarriage things got bad. She was on anti-depressants for a while, poor thing. And she and James, I don't know, they just somehow grew apart. She turned her attention on herself, on things she could control; they both just lost sight of what they had, I suppose. They were both hurting. But she can't *remember*. She thinks it's all sweetness and light now. But it's not.'

'I can see that.' Her dad's voice gentle, the sound of a log falling inside the fire.

Miscarriage? The word hit her like a thunderbolt. The pink ribbon, the dull ache. It all started to make sense now. *A family of five.* She used to hold the secret to herself, she remembered now. Another baby after several years of trying. The twins had been so easy then – nothing. She held Pickle close as tears seemed to come from nowhere along with flashes of half-formed memories: the blood one morning on her sheets, the pain in her stomach, the hospital with James, *him* crying? She heard the fire crackle and pop, she stroked Pickle's head.

'When she got pregnant, I think they both thought that would be a fresh start – I mean there was nothing really wrong, just, you know, life. But then when she lost the baby – well.'

There it was again: the miscarriage. How much damage had it done to her, between her and James? How much pain was pent up and had been vented elsewhere? She leant against the wall as Pickle licked her face.

'What have the doctors said?' Her dad's worried whisper.

'That she'll regain some memory but not all of it. It's weird because she can drive, set the alarm but doesn't remember stuff like where the kids went to school, her wedding day, the big stuff. Yet she does remember the twins being born, their seventh birthday party; it's kind of pot luck, her memory, that is.'

'I'm sure most of it will come back, but it's hard for her. James seems very wary. But you know, Lu, she seems, well, I don't know how to say this, but I feel I've got my old Vicky back. My girl.'

There was a silence. Victoria's heart was thudding. 'I know what you mean,' Lulu said, and she heard the clink of a teaspoon on a saucer.

Victoria held her breath.

'I know she was upset about the miscarriage, I know there was pain there, but she sort of "switched off" from the kids for a bit.' She heard Lulu sigh, 'It's like *she's* wound the clock back – but the others haven't. Everybody needs to remember what's gone on. Do you think they'll split up? It would be such a shame.'

She heard her dad cough. 'I hope not. I'll speak to James. But really, Lu, it's up to the two of them to piece these things together and work it out for themselves.'

24 LULU

'Oh, sorry.' James is standing by my chair with a cup of tea. 'I didn't know you were in here.'

I smile. 'I must have nodded off – quite a feat with Dad snoring over there.' We both glance at Eric who is making harrumphing noises every second breath. Pickle is by his feet, next to the fire.

'Mind if I join you?'

'Of course not.'

'I can make you some more tea?' He glances at our pot on the small table, it must be cold now.

'That would be lovely.' I feel drowsy, it's probably all the wine and it's so nice to sit in companionable silence with Dad. When James comes back with a steaming cup of tea, I stare out the window to the pretty borders in the garden, little splodges of vivid pink amid the green bushes.

James clears his throat. 'You must be excited about the wedding?'

A pang of guilt overwhelms me because people keep asking that. 'Yes,' I beam at him, because, really, I don't want

James to feel awkward. My ring glistens in the dim light of the lounge and we both sit in silence for a while, the only noise the soothing crackle of the fire. A log tumbles in the grate, and James reaches over to reposition it and throws another one on.

I decide to dive straight in.

'How are you and Vicky?'

He jerks his head up to me and as he looks at me, there's a softness in his eyes that wasn't there at lunch. 'Well, it's complicated.'

I nod. 'I'm sure it is. Her memory is like playing Russian Roulette. One minute she remembers an event, and then next, when I speak to her, she hasn't a clue what I'm talking about.'

'Exactly.'

'Must make it hard for you two to discuss the future, you know, and what's going to happen?' My voice rises at the end – I'm wondering if he'll talk to me about it.

He sighs. 'Well, nothing's certain, she's – well, she's different.'

'You mean like she was before you two drifted apart? Good different?' I hold my breath.

He stares at me and I'm not sure if he's going to get up and walk away. 'Yes and no. It's like I've got a stranger – well, an old friend – back, actually. It's a bit unnerving.' He leans forward and puts his head in his hands and looks up at me. 'It's so confusing to be honest, Lulu. I, we, well let's just say there's a lot of water under the bridge and I don't know if we can go back to how we were – I know *she* thinks we can.' There's a long pause and Pickle flips on to the other side by Dad's feet. 'But I'm not so sure.'

I take a sip of tea and wait for a moment before I speak. 'You should have seen her at the hospital, James. When I told her you were getting divorced – it was like wounding a baby seal. She just stared at me, like I'd said the most terrible thing.'

James stares out of the window, the only sound between us is Dad's light snoring.

'We just lost our way,' James says eventually.

There's a rustle of paper and the newspaper falls off Dad's lap and he startles, then the snoring resumes.

'But I do feel sorry for her, even if I don't show it.'

I sit up. 'She doesn't want your *pity*, James, she needs – I don't know, her marriage back.'

'Easier said than done, Lulu, after everything that's gone on. I know she needs our support right now, I realise that, but sometimes I just think a clean break would be better. Before the accident, well – I lost the Vicky I married, let's put it that way.'

'And have you not got her back, son?' It's Dad; he's awake. James glances over to him.

'Well, I have in one way, Eric, but—' he rubs his temples. 'I'm just so confused.'

'I can see she's changed, back to my old Vicky.' Dad coughs. 'Listen, I need you to take what I'm about to say in the right spirit, son.' He picks up the paper and folds it in his lap.

'What's that?' James lets out a long breath.

'It takes two to give up on a marriage. Just ask yourself if it's what you really want.'

James doesn't say anything for a while. Instead, he gets up and crosses the room to the fire. There, he kneels on the floor, picks up a nearby poker and starts to prod the glowing logs.

'She'd always wanted a big family, James – she used to say she could tell you'd be a good dad, you know, before you two got married, and she was right.' Dad pauses. 'But not being able to have any more kids, that would have hurt her.'

'I know,' James says quietly, standing up and going back to his seat. 'It hurt me too,' he says sitting down and running a hand through his hair.

Dad sighs and turns to me. 'I'd give anything, anything to have Maggie back, you know.' I can hear my dad's voice catch.

'I know, Dad.'

'Don't make the mistake I made, you two.'

James tilts his head to one side and looks from Dad to the fire, then he looks down at his lap.

'To assume you've got forever. Life's short. If there's one thing that Maggie passing has taught me, it's that. You never really know what's ahead of you. Imagine if Vicky hadn't walked away from that accident?'

'Dad!'

'It's true, Lulu.'

I shiver because I just don't want to think about it. 'I think this calls for more tea,' I say, standing up and stretching, glad to leave the room.

25 VICTORIA

'I think this one is lovely.'

They were back at My Little Wedding Dress shop and Marjory was fussing over Lulu at the back of the shop – handing her a tiara, which Lulu dutifully placed on top of her bouncy curls. 'The final touches,' as Marjory had said. With the wedding only a week away, Marjory was brimming with excitement.

Victoria was sitting on one of the gilt-edged chairs at the side of the room. Miscarriage? Her mind kept flashing back to that word. But she didn't want to spoil Lulu's day. It was her job as big sister to be brave. She took a deep breath, pushed the feelings down and studied Lulu who was beaming at Marjory and the shop assistant. And then, when they weren't looking, she glanced at Victoria and rolled her eyes. She'd always been a great actress, Victoria smiled to herself. She was looking, well, like Lulu, but not quite 'the radiant bride' in her ripped denim jacket over a skater skirt with cowboy boots. Her slim legs were encased in purple fishnet tights. Simon seemed like a really nice bloke. But that was the problem. Victoria stood up and went over to a rail of dresses, felt the soft fabric between her fingers then turned around and looked at the cubicle door. Lulu had *never* gone for nice blokes. She'd gone for the edgier ones. The *bad boys*, Lulu used to say, with a smirk as Mum and Dad would ask where she was off to, and she'd come back, hours later, smelling of cigarette smoke and cheap cider, telling Victoria about the 'gig', who'd signed an autograph for her. Once, Victoria remembered, her and Lulu were in stitches in the family bathroom desperately trying to remove indelible pen from Lulu's cleavage where a band member had signed his name. Lulu kept hiccupping, *Mum will kill me!* Then bursting into laughter. But maybe things had changed, too, with Lulu – the last six years were a mystery to her, after all.

'What do you think?' Lulu was standing just outside the changing room in a beautiful flowing veil with her hands on her hips. She looked demure, she *did* look bridal finally.

'It's very nice.'

'Hmm, that's the problem,' she peered into the mirror. 'I'm not really striving for *nice*.' She cocked her head to one side.

'Well, gorgeous, then,' said Victoria fussing with the veil. 'What will you do with your hair?'

'That wedding hair try-out I had was a disaster!' Lulu sighed, fiddling with her veil, 'Markie could barely talk to me, he was pissing himself so much!'

'Markie? Why does it matter what he thinks?'

Lulu stopped tugging at her veil and looked in the mirror at her. Victoria caught a flicker of something in her face. Then she turned around, and stuck her tongue out at her. 'Nice' she mimicked in the mirror and they both started laughing.

'What's the joke, girls?' Marjory waddled up to them,

175

looking between the two of them as the assistant bustled over and started to fiddle with the hairgrip on the veil. Suddenly Lulu said, 'Hold on, I've got an idea – let's see what it looks like on *you*.' She whipped the veil off and placed it on Victoria's head.

The assistant was pulling the veil this way and that and for a fleeting moment Victoria felt bridal. A flutter of nerves rippled over her. Imagine getting married again? To James? To start all over. It would be enough to just hold James's hand, quite frankly.

Marjory stood back. 'Oh my word, it does look amazing on you, Victoria, with your beautiful mahogany hair. What was your veil like when you got married, sweetie? I bet it was stunning. Right, I'm going to look at the shoes. Join me in a minute, will you, Lulu darling?' And she toddled out of the room with a swish of the curtains.

That was just the problem, thought Victoria, staring in the mirror. When she searched for a wedding memory, it was like hauling out pictures from a water-damaged photo album: they were just there, but fuzzy. She stared at her reflection, the veil, the way it hid her face, and had a flash of memory – a cathedral? She remembered James winking at her, a glimpse of his grin, something about the wind, the sweet smell of honeysuckle. She should look for a video, a DVD. Jog her memory. Try on her veil – see if it unearthed something. She pushed the veil back and rubbed her forehead. Marjory was out of earshot, looking at shoes in a glass case by the window. 'Lulu, what happened? I mean what really happened between me and James?'

Lulu's cheeks flushed. 'We don't actually know, sweetheart.'

'I think I might have been having an affair!' whispered Victoria, glad of the veil to cover her burning cheeks.

'*What?*'

'I found some messages on my phone, Lulu, actual messages.' Victoria spluttered.

'From who?'

'*I don't know*, that's the problem!' Victoria hissed, then glanced at Marjory who turned round. Victoria waved at her, then leant in to Lulu again. 'I think they're from someone called Andy. Do I know any Andys?'

'Ah, here's another one.' The assistant came up behind Lulu and placed another, shorter veil on her head. 'I think *this* is the one.' She held onto Lulu's shoulders and beamed at her, then walked briskly off.

'And Lulu,' Victoria couldn't help it. She had to understand, 'did I have a miscarriage?'

Her sister stared silently at her from behind her veil. She couldn't make out her expression hidden beneath the netting. Then she started to nod slowly as Victoria tried to ignore the nauseous snake winding its way around her stomach.

Lulu reached out and took both her hands in hers. 'Talk to James, Vicky,' she squeezed her hands tight. 'You two need to talk, to talk through the pain.'

26 VICTORIA

So many emotions filtered through Victoria's mind on the way home from the wedding shop; she knew that box under her bed held many memories, good and painful. She pulled on her handbrake and parked the car by the garage. Perhaps another trip down memory lane would jog some memories.

She bolted upstairs and nearly tripped over Pickle at the top of the stairs. He was wagging his tail, barking at her, with one of Izzy's bras in his mouth. She scooped him up and tried to rescue the tangled bit of white lace from his jaw. 'Hello, Mr Fluff!' She cuddled him and tickled him under his chin, then he scampered off.

'Dad!' she called to her father, wondering where he was.

'What is it, love?' His voice came out of the spare room.

'Dad, we can't have him upstairs! He's pulling things out of Izzy's drawers!'

'Sorry, pet,' he said, shuffling out the doorway, his hair standing on end, and glanced at Izzy's room. 'Or from her floor!' He grinned at Victoria. 'I was just lying down for a little nap and he crawled up beside me.' Pickle was now by her feet; she bent down and tickled him under the chin. When she stood up, she followed her dad's eyes.

He was looking over to her bedroom. 'And is that James's bed in there too – or there?' He nodded to the box room, the one with the single bed, the one you slept in only if you really had no other choice, where all the suitcases were kept under the bed, and children's school folders were piled up, destined for sorting out; he'd moved in there when her dad had arrived. Her heart sunk. Her dad wasn't stupid after all.

'You noticed.'

'You need to sort it out, Vicky, love.'

'I know.'

'Why don't you talk to him? There's a lot that went on, some of it you don't remember, I know, but try to talk.'

'I'm trying.' As she said it, her heart sunk. Suddenly Pickle charged down the stairs.

'I'll go after him, Vicky. Why don't you go lie down, pet, you look a bit peaky? I'll get someone to bring you up some tea.'

Peaky. People kept saying that. She remembered what the consultant had said. Tired. Fatigue. But she couldn't give up. She needed to find a way of not just re-energising herself, but connecting with James. To keep loving him until there was enough love around for him to believe her, to fill up his heart and hers too, so that he felt whole and could trust her again. Only, it would help if she knew what she had actually done.

She wished her scan was sooner. Perhaps the consultant would look at the results and announce that all would be well with her memory in a few weeks. A timetable for amnesia. *Now, Mrs Allen, your memory has just been in contact with me and it will be back in a fortnight.*

Victoria closed the bedroom door behind her and sunk to the floor. She sat there for a while feeling the fibres of the carpet under her hand, rough against her fingertips, alone with her thoughts. She needed to remember the car crash. She knew the key was in there, somehow, to her memory. She reached for the box under the bed and hauled it out, opened it slowly and found the tiny ribbon. She felt its soft satin between her two fingers and let the tears fall down her cheek. What had happened? Just then, she noticed another small, old phone nestled under the veil with its charger. She frowned. It looked oddly familiar, yet also strange. She knelt on the floor and plugged it in to a socket on the wall and sat back on her heels.

What if she could nudge her brain into gear with other physical things? If a pink ribbon could help her remember, what else could? She stood up from the bed and opened her wardrobe doors and looked at her clothes. They looked completely unfamiliar. And then, right at the end of her wardrobe was a long dress encased in a silk covering. That must be her wedding dress. Perhaps it would jolt her brain to remember the day. Or just, for heaven's sake, remembering the last few years of her life.

She unzipped the protective cover and felt the material of the dress between her fingers. It was beautiful. Satin silk, spaghetti straps with little daisies sewn in under the bust. She kicked off her shoes and undressed. Then she pulled the dress up over her hips. It skimmed over her like a silk glove, but she couldn't quite reach the fiddly fasteners at the back so she left it undone. She slid her hands across her hips to flatten it and looked at herself in the mirror, hoping for a memory. She saw a slim, busty woman with mahogany hair falling over one shoulder, a fringe swept to the side, pink lipstick and a pale face. The woman in the mirror wasn't smiling. Suddenly the door opened and James walked in holding a cup of tea; her hands flew up to her chest where the dress was loose. He opened his mouth to say something, looked at her, then stopped in his tracks. 'Oh.'

'Hi.' She smiled at him, searched his eyes for clues.

'Your dad said you needed some tea.' He glanced at her, blinked, then edged past her and put the cup down on the dressing table. He turned to her then. 'You're in your wedding dress. You —' he stopped mid-sentence, 'look beautiful.' He tilted his head to one side and spotted the pink ribbon on the bed. He reached over and picked it up, twisting it in his fingers and closed his eyes for a moment. When he opened them he looked straight at her. 'What are you doing?'

'Looking for memories.'

His eyes darted between her and the ribbon. 'Some memories are probably best left hidden, Victoria. The consultant warned against stress.' He handed the ribbon back to her and their fingers touched briefly.

'I don't want them hidden, James.' She sat down with a thump on the bed, with her back to him, but she caught him staring at her in the mirror. And she saw something in his eyes; it was fleeting, as his gaze flicked to her briefly and looked her up and down. But she saw it. And unless she was very much mistaken, there was the tiniest flicker of desire there.

James sat down on the bed beside her and took the ribbon from her hand and put the soft pink satin up to his face.

'James, I—'

'You were eighteen weeks. You woke me up one night telling me you were in agony. Blood all over the sheets.' He looked out the window and then back at her. Sunshine flickered across his hair picking up the blonde. 'We went straight to the hospital. We had a scan – there was no heartbeat.' James moved the ribbon to his other cheek, rubbed it slowly across his face and then handed it back to her. 'Can you remember any of it?'

'It comes and goes. The pink ribbon stirred something in me that I couldn't dislodge. A deep ache inside, but I can't—'

'Remember. I know.' He looked down at the carpet. She was aware how close they were sitting. She could smell soap, shaving foam. She wanted to rest her head on his shoulder and let him take away some of the pain.

'And James, we—' Before she could finish, his phone started to ring. He glanced at her and then fished it out of his back pocket and frowned.

'I need to take this.' He looked at her, then reached out and touched her shoulder. It was the briefest of touches and it was almost formal. She sat on the bed for a while, processing it all, unable to move as he walked out the room.

She must have fallen asleep because when she woke up her tea was cold beside her bed.

She sank back on the pillows and picked up her phone, played back their conversation and then immediately felt furious with herself for playing with fire. *Who* had she been texting before the accident? *Some memories are better left hidden.* James's words echoed in her mind. Enough was enough. She jabbed at the phone and dialled the number as her heart rate gathered speed. But it went straight to an automated voicemail. Just then Izzy walked into the room.

'Hey. What are you doing? Are you OK?'

Victoria quickly put her phone down. She could feel the heat rising up her cheeks.

'Why are you in, like, fancy dress?' Izzy squinted at her.

'Oh, right. The dress. Yes. I was just—' Victoria managed her best Be Nice Smile. 'I'm trying to remember stuff – um, lots of things, like my wedding. Looking for triggers like the doctor said.'

Just then the old phone lying on the floor bleeped. Izzy looked over at it. 'What's, like, *that?*'

Victoria couldn't help a small laugh at Izzy's tone. 'That's my old phone.'

'Like *really* old, Mum!' She went over and picked it up. 'Fully charged. Amazing. It's not even a smartphone.' She handed it to Victoria who stared at the screen, then instinctively went to look at her messages. James's was the first contact in her messages. She pressed the first one. Izzy leant over. 'It looks like something from a museum.'

J: Hey how are you? Cold here.

The next speech bubble was obviously hers.

How so? It's June.

J: Because you're not here to warm me up. And it is blooding freezing too! Hotel room boring on my own.

She snuck a sideways look at her daughter, her face lit up by the screen light.

She smiled and stroked the old Nokia flip-top phone with her thumb. Where had he been? She couldn't remember.

J: How are the donuts?

They're good. Cheeky things! What time will you be back?

J: Friday, after work, four hour drive.

Miss you.

J: Not as much as I miss you. Hotel bed too big. Can't sleep. First presentation at 9am. Nervous as hell.

Good luck.

She had memories sliding in and out of her brain. Where had James been? Newcastle? A Premier Inn? Did they still have them? She looked at the thread again.

J: Don't go!

I'm here.

J: Night, SV. xxx

'Who's SV, Mum?'

She rubbed her shoulders. It was getting cold; she lay back on the pillow. She looked up to the ceiling shade with its red fringes and wondered what had made her buy such an awful lampshade. A tear slid down her cheek, she sniffed. 'Oh, it used to be Dad's nickname for me.'

'Which was?'

'Squishy Vicky, if you must know.' And just as they both started to giggle, Izzy opened her mouth, but before she could reply, the doorbell went.

Izzy stood up and peered out the bedroom window. 'Oh, it's Cupcake Queen. I'll go let her in.'

Had she arranged for Zoe to come round? She really couldn't remember. She hauled herself off the bed and clutched the banister as Zoe breezed in.

27 VICTORIA

'Hey, sexy thing! Look at *you*!' Zoe let out a long wolf-whistle, just as James walked past and glanced at Victoria.

'Nice outfit! What's the occasion?'

Victoria could feel herself get redder. 'Well, nothing really. I thought it might jog my memory, if I'm honest. Come in.' She took Zoe into the kitchen and flicked the kettle on. 'Tea? Listen, let me just pop upstairs and change first.'

When she got back to the kitchen, they settled into the cosy seats by the window. Zoe took a sip of tea. Pickle was now sitting on the floor by her feet, enjoying the April sun filtering in through the window.

'You OK, hun?' Zoe leant in and touched Victoria's knee. 'You look a bit peaky.'

There it was again. *Peaky*. 'Yeah, I'm fine,' Victoria took a sip of tea and felt like she was in a pantomime of her own making.

'That dress looked great. Shows off your figure.' Zoe moved her handbag out of the way and put her cup down on the small coffee table between the two chairs. 'Hey, I've got an idea.' She tilted her head to one side and studied Victoria. 'Why don't you wear something similar to your sis's wedding? You said she wanted you to be maid of honour?'

Victoria wiped some tea from her mug with her thumb and looked out to the garden. 'You know what, I might just do that.' She jutted out her chin and smiled.

'Anyway, I'm not here to talk about your sister's wedding, I thought I'd pop round, sweetie, clear a few things up.' She craned her neck to look at the kitchen door.

'Clear what up?'

Zoe took another furtive look over her shoulder and whispered. 'Thought I'd better explain about the whole texting game. You know. Our little secret?'

Victoria swallowed hard. Too many secrets. She just wanted to press 'Rewind' on her life. *She wanted the Old Victoria back.*

'Zoe. I hate this: my husband treats me like a houseguest, my kids are distant and my dad despairs. My sister thinks I've lost my mind, well, I have, I suppose…' She looked up at Zoe and then they both burst out laughing; Pickle stood up and started to bark at them. But then, the laughter slowly morphed into great big sobs as Victoria took a gulp of air and let the wet tears trickle down her cheek.

'Hey, sweetie, don't cry.' Zoe held out a tissue. 'It's all OK.'

'It's *not* OK! I've got these *messages*. On my phone,' she hissed. 'What a mess,' she wiped her eyes and looked at Zoe.

'I can explain.'

'What?' Victoria tucked the tissue into her jeans' pocket and quickly glanced towards the door to make sure they were alone. She looked back at Zoe.

'Look, it was *my* idea, honey,' Zoe whispered, putting her cup down. 'James and you, well, you two were – how can I put it – a bit "broken" and I thought it might be a good idea to spice things up a bit, see if he got jealous. I used one of my old phones and sent you flirty messages. You were going to leave your phone lying around, hoping that he saw it.'

Victoria's mouth fell open. A *game*? She hadn't had any affairs?

'It was one night when James was away on business and you were pouring your heart out to me, telling me the kids didn't seem to need you anymore… I was talking about my date the next day, and then you grabbed my phone and asked me to show you my dating app – we'd had *far* too much to drink, by the way – after that we came up with the idea of the game. Bit of harmless fun. You were up for it,' Zoe said, her lip-gloss shining in the kitchen lights. 'Victoria?'

Victoria just nodded, relieved that the whole thing was a prank.

'Anyway,' Zoe carried on, 'I just wanted to make sure you knew what we'd done, what with this,' she flapped her hands at Victoria, 'memory thing you've got. And I could see how stressed you were.'

'God, Zoe,' she whispered, 'that's the point. I can't *remember*. Everything's so confusing. My marriage seems to be hanging on by a thread.'

'It *is*. Well, it was—' Zoe shrugged and took a sip of tea. 'Look, you guys were stressed after the miscarriage.' Zoe suddenly made a face. 'You do remember that, don't you?'

'I do now,' she nodded. 'James just explained it all, but I'd had flashbacks.' She took a sip of tea and stared out the window. Little pink buds were forming on the azaleas in the border.

'You two just need to get the spark back.' Zoe touched her knee. 'His work, the kids, the miscarriage, it kind of ate away at you both. Plus, nobody's getting any younger. It changes us, this, this,' she put her hands up in the air and shrugged, 'you know, mid-life. We all need a bit of reassurance, don't we?'

'I suppose.' Victoria sighed.

'I have an idea!' Zoe sat up straight in her chair. 'How about—'

'What?'

'We play the game again? Now that you know it's me? Don't look at me like that! Listen, all you have to do is leave your phone out for him to see? See if the spark's still there? What do you say? Bit of good old-fashioned jealousy? No harm done.'

Victoria wasn't sure at all. There had been the smallest flicker of a connection between them in the bedroom when they were talking. She didn't want things to blow up in her face. 'I don't know Zoe—'

'I do,' she said, leaning forward putting her elbows on her knee. 'Did you see the way James looked at you in the hall? Now there's a man who's not going anywhere, let me tell you. Honey, you're halfway there. I bet you two sort things out. He just needs a nudge.' Zoe wagged a green painted fingernail at her.

'I'm not sure Zoe.' Victoria was shaking her head.

'Look, leave it with me. I'll just send a few. Leave your phone around where he can see – OK? That will get his attention.' She grinned. 'I might even send a fake "selfie".'

'I'm not sure he wants to give me any attention, Zoe. I think he's past that.'

'Trust me, he isn't, babe, if he *really* was past all that, he'd move out.'

Perhaps Zoe had a point.

28 VICTORIA

It was the day before Lulu's wedding. They were having a 'girly afternoon' at a local spa with lunch by the pool. It was *Lulu's* day, Victoria had reminded herself as they'd swum a few laps in the pool, splashing each other, then swanned around in white fluffy robes; she told herself to put her problems aside. They'd posed in their gowns and taken selfies – Victoria rather liked this new invention – and sent them to their dad, and she was just scraping the last of her Eton mess from a pretty crystal glass. It was blissfully quiet as they both wiggled their purple toenails, drying their pedicures.

Lulu picked up a strawberry and popped it in her mouth. 'Who was the worst teenager, do you think?' She looked over at Victoria and raised her eyebrows.

'You!' Victoria laughed, then leant her head to one side and studied Lulu in her soft white robe, silver bangles stacked up at her wrist as she wiped chocolate off her robe. 'Remember when you snuck out the house to that party when you were sixteen, hid some cans of cider under the bushes in the front garden? Mum and Dad were horrified!'

Lulu swept some hair off her face. 'Yeah, but it was fun though. And the next morning Mum knew I'd been up to something coz I had glitter all over my face?'

Victoria's hand flew up to her face. 'God, yes. I'd forgotten about that. I covered for you – told Mum we'd played dress-ups. As if!' They both burst out laughing.

'Remember that time I sneaked out the back door so Mum and Dad didn't hear me, to meet that guy – what was his name, the Goth, the one in Upper Sixth?' Lulu grinned. 'Martin, yes. Mum and Dad went mental when they found out I'd been to the pub – but I only did it coz of peer pressure.'

Victoria *did* remember that. She nodded. Lulu had been covered in make-up that day. Black lipstick, spiky blonde hair, before she grew it long and let the curls take over. It was before the days of producing ID and the local landlord used to turn a blind eye to Lulu. Fourth form? The year Izzy is in now. *Peer pressure?* There was a nagging somewhere in her brain.

'Yeah, I was no angel, I did do a lot of stupid things,' Lulu carried on and rolled her eyes. 'Anyway, now,' she said lifting her leg and twisting her foot to admire her lilac toes, 'we're both grown-ups aren't we?' She shot her a look. 'We know better.'

Victoria nodded. There was a well of emotion she was pushing down. 'Yup. We grew up, got married, had twins, before—' She hesitated, not wanting to finish the sentence.

'Before you lost the baby, you mean? Oh, hun.' Lulu reached over and rubbed her arm.

A bubble of longing surged up inside Victoria, and it came whenever she thought about the miscarriage. What had happened afterwards? She pulled the dressing gown tighter across her bust then shook her head. 'I don't want to talk about it, Lulu, this is your day.' She tried to smile.

'It's fine, Vicky – it's good to have some peace and quiet, we can chat.'

Victoria closed her eyes. 'There are pages and pages missing from my life.'

Lulu sat back in her seat and folded her long legs. 'Well, I'll try and fill some in. I remember you told me once that one of your greatest fears was of the twins leaving, "the sound of silence", you said. No one clattering up the stairs, no one opening the fridge, no one shouting at their sister for leaving a million shampoos in the shower, you said it terrified you – not long after that you got pregnant. I know you'd been trying for a while.'

'We'd been trying for years, I can remember that.'

'It was an awful time. You wouldn't talk to me about going to hospital, when you found out you'd lost it—' She reached out and touched Victoria's hand. 'But I knew you were on anti-depressants after that.' Lulu let out a long breath. 'A lot changed between you and James, just small stuff started to niggle you, he was away, you were blaming yourself – both of you took it quite badly, actually, and somehow rather than bringing you two together, it seemed to put a wedge between you.'

My body doesn't work. She had a vague memory of saying it in a heated argument, a door slamming, and then this sinking feeling in the pit of her stomach, like the times when your parents had left you at school, ruffled your hair, said 'you'll be alright' as you stared – petrified – into the classroom. *That* kind of sinking feeling. James driving away. Again. Why hadn't he reached out for her?

Lulu put her foot back down on the sun lounger. 'Things started to unravel. You changed. You said, "my body didn't work to make a baby, but I can make *this* work". And you pointed to your figure. You told me you were feeling invisible. We all told you not to, me, Dad, Zoe, James, but you said it was your body. The consultant who did it, well—' She lifted her shoulder. 'I mean, let's just say I don't think he had your psychological well-being at heart.'

Lulu looked up at her from heavily made-up gold eyelids from her morning's 'make-up try-out'.

'And what did James do?'

'He was always on another project – sometimes away for days. I think maybe he was just putting some space between you both. And I think you thought having a new you would be the solution.'

Vague memories floated to the surface like water-damaged photographs. Late night phone messages. Of unanswered calls. Of curt texts on both sides. Of hurt. Why hadn't she supported James? But had *he* supported *her*? Was it too late to bind together the different ingredients of family life with love and hold it tight?

As if reading her mind, Lulu added, 'He *was* away a lot. You were here with the kids or the "terrible teens" as you used to call them, "being both a mother and a father" you used to say. It was kind of love-hate. You loved them, but you hated how they'd changed.

'James won the bid for that massive shopping centre in North London – remember? No? Anyway, he'd stay up there during the week and come back at weekends.' Lulu had picked up her champagne glass from earlier when they'd had lunch. Her long fingers were twisting the stem, her ruby engagement ring glistening under the spotlights above the pool. Victoria shook her head. In her mind, he was still a junior executive at the firm. She couldn't get used to the fact that he was now partner – with a *secretary*.

'Lulu, I'm finding this difficult, piecing things together.' She put her head in her hands and looked at her little sister, her words ringing in her ears. *Putting some space between you both.*

'I know, sweetheart, but it will take time, remember what the doctors said: patience.'

'Patience, patience…' she felt impatient just thinking about it.

Lulu suddenly stood up and took off her robe. 'I'm going for a dip. Last one as a single woman.' Victoria noticed a look cross her face, then it was gone again. She draped her robe over the back of the chair and dived in.

Victoria sat staring at the ripples of water from Lulu's dive and decided once and for all that she needed to put the past behind her and move on. In fact, she wasn't exactly thankful she'd had the accident, but – and she was damn sure about this – it was certainly a day that changed everything. Tomorrow was Lulu's wedding: she was going to plaster on a smile, she was going to be charming to everyone, she was going to support her sister and walk her down the aisle but – the most important bit – she was going to win James back.

29 VICTORIA

'Right, I've put you both in the smaller honeymoon suite,' the woman at the front desk beamed at them. She was wearing a grey mohair cardigan, bits of fluff from it were dancing in the sunlight behind her shoulder, a string of pearls looped round her neck and her lips were covered in crimson lipstick. They had just arrived at Treetops Country House Hotel, a boutique hotel nestled in the depths of the Sussex country-side. It had a private chapel attached to it, and twenty guest bedrooms. The wedding was at 3 p.m. Lulu was already there, her dad had hired a car and had made sure they were both there by 11 a.m. on her 'big day' and he'd sent Victoria some selfies of Lulu, him and Pickle in the grounds, Pickle with his new 'wedding' collar. He was allowed in the chapel, but not the hotel, so Victoria had found a local dog-sitter to take Pickle later.

'And the, um, children are booked into an adjoining twin room next door,' she continued checking her computer screen. She seemed very pleased with her room planning. Victoria was almost expecting her to wink at them.

'Do you,' James asked, 'have any twin rooms, by any chance?'

Her face fell. It wasn't her fault that she didn't know Victoria and James hadn't shared a *room*, never mind a bed for the last couple of months. She tapped away at the keyboard regaining her professional air, then looked up at them both: 'I'm terribly sorry, no.'

'Not a problem,' he murmured, taking the keys from her.

Maybe tonight things would be different? Victoria's stomach did a little somersault as James picked up their bags. 'Thank you.'

Lulu was going to get some rest by the sound of her last text, but the signal was bad here, and texts were not always coming through. Victoria wanted to check on the chapel, check where Markie would be standing so Lulu wouldn't see him till she was walking down the aisle as he was singing; she did a little fist pump – her secret arrangement would be brilliant! It was all very well having hymns, but Lulu would want proper music at her wedding, and Markie was the man for that.

She also had to make sure the flowers had arrived and were tied on the end of the pews – Marjory had arranged lilies. She had to hang up her dress (she'd found a beautiful midnight blue silk one on sale online), because Izzy and Jake had sat on it by mistake in the car. She had to sort out her hair, and find out if the in-house catering manager had some soft drinks on hand for the twins. An image of Izzy drinking wine on the skiing holiday flashed up. Well, maybe she could have one. *Relax*, she could hear Lulu tell her. Well, maybe she would, just a little. Her stomach did a little rollercoaster flip at the thought of James's face when he saw her. She knew the dress looked good. No, she wouldn't focus on that right now. James opened the door and they walked in. A memory nudged her brain as she glanced out the window. Then it was gone. She could hear the twins arguing in the next room, shouting about who had the TV remote. She smiled. They might be sixteen, but some things never changed.

James dumped their bags on the double bed and looked around as she fiddled with the kettle flex and plugged it in. 'Tea?' He turned and stared at her, then let out a deep sigh.

'You do remember, don't you?' Her eyes darted to him and studied his frown, the way he was standing by the window with his hands in his pockets. 'We had this room before.'

She stared at him. 'We were *here*? And stayed in this *room*?' He nodded.

'I don't remember.'

'It was a weekend getaway.' He coughed. 'A romantic weekend away. Lulu had the twins.' She wandered over to the window and stood next to him. Maybe the desire for a twin room wasn't what she thought. It was because this was bringing back too many memories, memories of a happy time. But surely they could get that back? She had the killer dress... all they needed was—

'Don't think this is easy for me, Victoria, because it isn't.' He exhaled slowly. 'I just, we just—'

'Need more time?'

'Maybe.' He smiled at her and for the first time in a long time, it reached his eyes. She thought of the divorce papers in the hall desk, she thought of the special make-up she'd brought for today, she glanced at the bed and then up at James.

'Look. I'm going along the corridor,' he eventually said. 'See if I can find Simon, wish him luck. I'll see you later, OK?'

She nodded, then glanced at her watch. It was two

o'clock. She needed to get a move on. The wedding was in an hour. She quickly went downstairs and practically skipped along the corridor towards the chapel. She opened the wooden doors and stepped inside; white lilies were tied at the end of each pew with lilac ribbons twisting prettily from them. The wooden organ at the top of the chapel was magnificent, silver pipes towering heavenwards, ready to accompany her sister down the aisle. It was cool and quiet in there, the pews a silent witness to thousands of weddings and emotions, and they seemed to have seeped into the fabric of the place. She studied the altar at the far end. Lulu would be there soon. She tried to imagine herself standing there, next to James, squeezing his hand. Maybe by tonight she *would* be holding his hand? Weddings had that effect on people, didn't they?

'Oh, darling, there you are, I was just checking on the flowers!' Marjory came bustling up. 'Don't they look magnificent?' She shuffled down the aisle in her hotel slippers, towards Victoria.

'It looks lovely,' Victoria agreed. 'Beautiful flowers.'

'I know. She's going to love them!' Marjory beamed.

Victoria quickly pulled her phone out of her pocket and texted Lulu. *Good luck, sweetie! Do you need any help?* She'd told Victoria she didn't want any fuss, wanted to be on her own. Lulu had insisted that she'd do her make-up herself. Marjory was retying one of the bows on the lilies, then she stood up. 'Everything's going to plan!' she said, as she walked past and gave Victoria's shoulder a little squeeze.

30 LULU

I'm in the honeymoon suite. I lean forward. '*Of course* we've been given the honeymoon suite, silly,' I wave my mascara wand and admonish my reflection in the mirror, 'we're getting *married*,' I giggle. Then I wait. For a feeling to register, for some emotion. I glance in the mirror and notice rose petals on the bed. I take a slug of vodka from my water glass.

There's a knock at the door. Izzy pokes her head round. 'Aunty Lulu?'

'Hi darling, come in!'

'Mum said you wanted to be left alone but I thought I'd show you my outfit. What do you think?' She does a twirl. I swivel round from the dressing table and stare at my niece. She is in a white one-piece jumpsuit with a halter-neck. She looks terrific. The jumpsuit reminds me of David Bowie – not that she *looks* like David Bowie, of course, it's just that she owns that vibe. Young. Sexy. Her whole life ahead of her. I remember when I first listened to David Bowie; I was trans-fixed and from then on was the biggest fan. The organ's just started up downstairs in the small chapel. Hymns. Did I choose actual hymns? I reach for a tissue.

'Oh Aunty, Lu, are you alright? You must feel overwhelmed. Getting married, imagine!' Izzy walks over to me and gives me a hug. Overwhelmed? Yes, I am overwhelmed. And – there's an emotion I can't place. I look at myself in the mirror then I take a sip of my drink. It's such a big day. My mind flashes to another day where I felt a surge of anxiety. No, not today.

'Do you need any help? With your make-up and stuff?' Izzy's hand is on my shoulder and I look at her in the mirror standing behind me, so young and willing.

'Yes please.' My hand's shaking. 'I had a make-up try-out at the Spa, but I just can't do it myself.' I lean in to the mirror and judging by the Alice Cooper look I've got going on with my mascara running, I certainly need Izzy's help. And quick. Vicky's just knocked with a 'I'm not stopping and you have five minutes' from behind the door.

Izzy has her hands on my shoulders. 'A bride should look like herself, Aunty Lulu, only *better*.' She pats my shoulder and opens an eyeshadow palette.

I glance at her young face in the mirror and a thought crosses my mind. I get up and open the minibar. I pour her some of the hotel's free 'celebratory wedding prosecco' into a glass and bring the bottle to the dressing table. 'Cheers!'

Izzy looks at me then takes a sip. 'Right, here we go!' she says draining her glass. Then she refills her glass, picks up one of the brushes and tells me to close my eyes. The room seems to swim, but as I sit with my eyes closed for a while, I enjoy the gentle bristles on my cheek, the soft touch of Izzy's fingers pressing on my temple, the fluttering feeling of a brush on my eyebrows, the smear of blusher on my cheeks.

About ten minutes later, Izzy squeezes my shoulder. 'Open your eyes Aunty Lu.'

I stare at the woman in the mirror. She looks good. She looks young, she looks demure, she looks, well, great. With a veil clasped to her now-straight locks, falling to shoulder length, and tiny pearls in her ears she looks bridal. But she doesn't look like me. Another slug of drink. I want to shove a denim jacket over this whole number and feel normal. My eyes go in and out of focus at the itsy-bitsy satin shoes sitting neatly next to the bed. I stare at the ruby ring on my left hand, whispering to me, reminding me that I am about to walk down the aisle, and I think about that kaleidoscope of emotions, about the dark hungry ones eating away at me, about the crash, about my guilt, about events in the past that terrify me and about how safe I'll feel, about how this will make it all go away, that I will no longer be an in-debt children's entertainer, and I pick up my drink from my dressing table. 'Let's do this,' I say to Izzy as I pour a slug of vodka into both our glasses and we finish off our drinks.

———

I am poised at the top of the stairs, my sexy matron of honour by my side. Well, it's Vicky, but she looks a million dollars in that dress she got online. 'Vicky, darling, you look amashing in that dress! Good choice!' I grab her arm. Her hair is tied up in some bun-y thing – Izzy probably did that – and there are wispy bits framing her face. My big sister is totally *owning* it. God, I *love* my sister! And Izzy! And Jake! And maybe James a bit! And – no.

'Lulu, are you alright? Here, hold your bouquet and give me your other hand, Dad's waiting for you at the entrance to the chapel, OK? Ready, honey? One step at a time.' She passes me a small bouquet of pink roses and gypsophila, it's very pretty – did I choose that? – and guides me down the stairs gently like I am an OAP, and the thought makes me snort out loud. I am shaking with laughter. I brush my veil to one side and it catches in my ring. I yank it and the veil rips. 'Oops!'

'Lulu! Careful, sweetheart.' Vicky is using her passive-aggressive mummy voice. I know this because it's the voice she used when the twins were potty training at the same time and I'd visit her and she'd say everything was *very, very fine* when it was very, very not.

'Oh, nobody will notice!' I let out a hiccup. We are at the bottom of the stairs now. 'They will all be looking at your cleavage.' Peals of laughter. Oh, they're coming from me.

'Lulu, have you been *drinking*?' She squeezes my elbow.

'Nope. Nope. Absolully nope. Yes.' I'm nodding. 'Just a teeny-tiny bit.' I hold up my left hand and squeeze my thumb and forefinger together. 'For the nerves.'

Vic's eyes widen at me. 'Right,' she says. I can tell she's Trying to be Calm. Her eyebrow twitches when she's stressed and concentrating; I want to giggle again, but instead I purse my lips shut and look away. Then I realise that I probably have lipstick on my upper lip. 'Vic, stop power-walking! Too fast! Hang on, have I got lipstick on my upper lip, like a granny?' More peals of laughter.

Victoria stops dead, just by the door to the chapel, and fusses with my lipstick, using a tissue she has had hidden somewhere – it's an art mothers have, having a clean Kleenex to pull out like a magician at a moment's notice. She always has one, *somewhere* about her. Even in a sexy frock. Am-a-z-ing as Revel Horwood would say. Just as I'm thinking this, she dabs it on my upper lip, then produces a lipstick from somewhere. How did she do that? Did she carry that in her bra or something? I peer into her cleavage.

'What are you *doing*, Lulu?' She stands back a bit.

'Nothing, nothing, sorry.'

'Right,' she says in her Mother Voice. 'Ready?' And those huge blue eyes look at me, like they've done a thousand times before, when I started at sixth form college, when Mum died, when I went for my West End audition and she was shoring me up, being brave, being on Team Lulu. I want to cry. But not now, not in front of Vic. She will be *really* mad.

'As ready as I'll ever be,' I say instead as I hear Bach's 'Jesu Joy of Man's Desiring' (I'd have preferred The Killers) start up and Victoria opens the doors of the chapel. Dad is standing there in a navy-blue suit and pale blue silk tie, a carnation in his buttonhole; I don't think I've ever felt more love for him, a rush-y kind of swelling in my heart. Bless him. Pickle is beside him, barking, with a curious flashing bow tie collar – absolute genius – at just about the same time as I feel an awful lurch in my stomach.

31 LULU

'Lulu, pet, you look smashing.' Dad reaches for my hand. I'm shaking. His hand is soft and warm and it reminds me of my first day at school. Mum and Dad on either side of me, but it was Dad's hand I remember, because it was huge, covering my tiny, shaking fingers. Mum's hands were always cold. He presses my fingers and my engagement ring pinches me and I flinch. 'You look, beautiful, my girl. I'm very proud.'

I glance up the aisle and see Simon. He's shifting his weight from one leg to another in a nervous sort of jig. Then he glances towards me and beams as there's a crescendo in 'Jesu Joy of Man's Desiring'. I've never liked this hymn. It's as if I'm in a movie of my own making. It's so familiar, very *Love Actually*, and yet here I am, standing with two feet firmly on the ground and unable to move. I look up at Simon again and will myself to feel a pull. He's in a light grey morning suit with a yellow silk cream bow tie. A vision of my old headmaster flashes before me and I take a deep breath. Looking at the guests in the pews, at Simon waiting at the top of the aisle, my breathing starts to quicken and – especially behind the veil – the whole thing takes on a dream-like quality. Where's the voiceover telling people that the bride has arrived, that this is the moment? I smile to myself, but then, all of a sudden, I feel nauseous.

The organ stops and Pickle starts to bark. My eyes roam the chapel: there's Marjory, standing solidly, hair sprayed into a stiff up-do. She looks like she might burst out of her too-tight turquoise dress with pride; there's Izzy grinning at me, doing a discreet thumbs up, as I sway slightly into Dad, and he squeezes my hand again. Jake's in a tweed jacket and tie – he looks like he's about to be in a school panto; I have the strongest urge to laugh – and there's James, immaculate in a dark lavender suit and white shirt. His head is tilted to one side, looking at me; they all are. Smiling and looking at me. And then he nods, it's a tiny gesture, willing me on, sending positive vibes. My brother-in-law, in fact, looks absolutely drop-dead gorgeous today.

Victoria squeezes my hand on the other side. I'm in a sandwich, between my sister and father. A huge burst of giggles escapes. 'Sorry, sorry,' I mutter, grateful for the veil to hide my smirk. And I *am* sorry, sorry for the confusion, for the mess in my brain, for the kaleidoscope, for the vodka. What have I done? I stare blankly at the congregation through my gauzy protection, glad my veil is covering what must be written all over my face. Everyone is looking expectantly towards me. And I stand there, realising that this is the moment, everyone expects me to follow a code. To know what to do.

And then there's a rushing in my ears, followed by silence. The flowers at the end of each pew are beautiful white lilies, their faces smiling up at me. I notice how they are missing their delicate stamens and this confuses me; but, at the same time, their heady perfume is making me feel sick. I look up. There's the rustling of hymn books, someone coughs and then the quiet seeps into me. Suddenly, out of nowhere, a guitar is being played, the opening riff of Eric Clapton's 'Wonderful Tonight'. I stop breathing. *Not that, not here.* It's one of my favourite songs – it takes me back, but I don't want to go there… that was another time… And then the voice. It's low and it's mellow and it's Bruce Springsteen crossed with Chris Rea, but it's not, and I'd know that voice anywhere because it's—

Markie.

He's standing to one side in an aisle of his own, strumming his guitar and looking right at me as his lilting voice washes over the whole congregation, soothing the air. His Adam's apple bobs up and down as he sings, and he's taken care with his clothes, I can tell. The leather jacket has been replaced by a tuxedo top and open-necked shirt – and jeans. He rests one foot on the pew, to steady his guitar and he flicks the hair off his face with a nod of his head backwards. He's smiling at me. He wants me to enjoy my Special Day, he wants to do this for me. He does not want to break my heart. He has no idea how the image is tearing into my ribcage and clawing at my chest.

Are his eyes misty? I can't tell. And then it's back: the kaleidoscope, twisting the lens, dark emotions, the panic, the fear, security, all mixed together – only it isn't security, is it? Markie's smile, my Dad's hand, the waves of terror. It's another panic attack. The last time I had one of these… No. Everything is fuzzy. I can't see straight. The aisle is going in and out of focus and it's all swirly, bright colours around me. I can't breathe, I feel blood rushing to my face.

'Breathe.' It's Victoria, rubbing my upper arm. I take an enormous breath. Only it makes me feel worse. My chest is tight. It's as if I'm breathing in a vacuum. I look up at the ceiling, then at the stained-glass window casting a curious rainbow of bright orange and sapphire blue beams across the walls as I realise all eyes are still fixed on me. I feel like the whole world has tipped to one side and I'm the only one clinging on. And I can't be in this world anymore, it's not right.

'Lulu, are you OK?' Victoria has taken my hand and is now standing in front of me, frowning. I notice her glittery eye make-up and try to focus on that for a while. It's some-thing solid and real to look at, I tell myself, hoping things will start to feel normal soon, because glittery eyeshadow is normal, my sister is normal, I tell myself, it will be alright. *Will it?* says that voice.

'I feel dizzy, faint, I feel, I don't know, I'm not quite—' I mutter.

'Nerves are normal, Lulu, you're about to get *married*.' She gives my hand a couple of pats.

But then I catch sight of Markie again as the music starts. I just need to walk, to put one foot in front of the other, only I can't. It's like I'm stuck in cement. My legs won't move. All I can see is Markie, his head tilted to one side, mouthing 'Are you OK?' and all I want to do, all I've ever really wanted to do comes tumbling to my brain at once, the hours, the days, start to mix together, to form a cloud in my brain, brimming with fury and I want to run, to run to him. And I can't move. I can't go anywhere, I'm rooted to the spot, staring at the top of the aisle where Simon is standing with his hands deep in his pockets, staring at the floor.

The vicar coughs. 'Everything alright?'

I swallow, then take a tiny breath and step forward toward my new life.

'Well done,' I hear Victoria whisper beside me, 'not far to go.' But it's too much and I look up at Markie again and my gut twists and I know that every step I take towards the top of the aisle is a step towards a new future – to safety, to security – but every inch forward in these bridal shoes that are killing me takes me away from what I really want. I force a smile and wish I hadn't drunk the vodka. Not today. Not on one of the most memorable days of my life. But it's too late now. Swallow. Take a small breath. Bright shiny shards of my life mingle with the sickening feeling. I look at Markie again who is nodding, willing me to go on, my safety net in the sea of staring faces. Go on, Lulu, I tell myself. Go *on*.

And I do. I go on. Running down the aisle until I can't stop, until I reach the door of the chapel, to the roses tied on the doorknob, knocking them off as I rush past. Until I reach the hall outside, to where I can hear the murmur of voices from inside the chapel, and hear Marjory cry out, and I can feel the wet tears streaming down my cheek and the sorrow at how hurt Simon must be, and the startled look on the receptionist's face, and the blurry sight of all the catering staff in black and white poised in the hall with trays of champagne in their hands for my Special Day, and I will go on up the stairs, running now, away from my married life, away from the man strumming the guitar who has stolen my heart, away from the gossip and into the cool of the first room I see at the top of the stairs – and onto the bed, where I can sob loudly and leave my trail of destruction behind.

32 VICTORIA

'How's Lulu?' James rubbed his forehead and looked at Victoria. She was leaning on the solid wooden surface of the hotel bar sipping a large red wine. She couldn't really remember if she liked red wine or not, but it was taking the rawness out of today. How could she have not known how Lulu felt? She supposed there was a *lot* she didn't know – and the accident was just the start of it.

'She's upstairs in our bedroom, on the bed, poor thing, I found her there, collapsed on top, still in her wedding dress. She started to try to explain, all sorts of things she was saying weren't making sense, so I've given her some paracetamol, got her out of her wedding dress, made her a cup of tea and covered her in a blanket. She's tired, emotional—'

'And single.' He shrugged. 'Poor girl.'

'I had no idea she felt this way. Well,' Victoria took a sip, 'I had a *niggle*, but I just thought it was wedding nerves. It all just came out in the room, she wasn't ready, she couldn't cope with commitment, but,' she swept some wisps of hair off her face, 'it's not *just* that, James, she kept muttering about some "dark stuff" from the past or something.'

'Poor Lulu. She just needs some time on her own, to figure things out. She'll be all over the place at the moment, Vicky, don't worry.'

There was a fire crackling in the grate; even though it was April, it was a chilly night with frost forecast for later. She shivered. She was still in her flimsy dress. She took another gulp of wine and looked up at James in the dim lights of the bar. He looked like he did in their wedding photo, handsome in his dark lavender suit which set off his fair hair. She bit her lip, trying to remember if she'd bought it for him, or if he'd chosen it. Then she noticed his left hand, wrapped around his wine glass and gasped.

'You're wearing your wedding ring?'

His eyes skimmed over her, briefly, and she felt a tiny jolt of electricity. 'Thought it might be appropriate, we're at a wedding after all. Or were.' He took a gulp of wine. 'Listen, I'm just going to check on Simon, I don't know if anyone's thought about him, poor bloke, he's upstairs.' He put his glass down on the bar and ducked his head under the arch of the small entrance to the bar. It could have all been so perfect – a second chance for her and James, but little did she know how wretched Lulu must have felt, how terrified she was standing at the aisle. Dear Lulu. She vowed to be a better sister to her.

Her thoughts were interrupted as she heard James swear and then laugh. She looked over. He was grinning and apologising to a woman with long blonde hair in a silver cocktail dress, his hand resting on her elbow. The woman was all giggles as James leant in. Victoria could feel something rising in her stomach, a twisting sensation. Jealousy. James smiled at the woman then strode off. It was harmless enough yet it bothered her. Imagine if things had been different? Suddenly she was forced to imagine what life might be like if he'd met someone. She felt panicky just thinking about it. Just imagine, she thought, taking a sip of wine, what it would be like if he'd brought someone new into the lives of Izzy and Jake? Bringing some new woman to family gatherings, watching the two of them cosy up, sharing little jokes.

How close had they been to ruining their marriage? Their family? *Close*, said that voice. Thinking of her family, she suddenly realised she hadn't seen Jake or Izzy in a while. After Lulu had fled down the aisle, she had told them both to go to the bar and get a soft drink and wait for her there. She cast her eyes around the bar. She could see Jake, playing snooker – but where was Izzy?

Markie was strumming his guitar quietly in a corner, singing an Irish ballad next to the snooker table. His voice was mesmerising, but he stopped when Simon walked in, James by his side. By the looks of it, Simon had been drowning his sorrows. He staggered towards the bar. The room fell silent as Simon stood, swaying slightly on the tartan carpet, and surveyed the room blearily. He pulled up his sleeves. Markie stopped strumming.

'You,' he said, pointing to Markie, 'It's all *your* fault.' He walked over to Markie, raised his fist towards him, just as Markie grabbed his wrist and held it there.

'Steady there, you don't want to do that. You'll regret it in the morning, so you will.'

'No, I won't.' Simon's voice slurred. 'You and your bloody children's parties, spending all that time in your clapped-out van, your guitar, and "sweet voice" she used to go on about, I should have put a stop to it.' Simon's face twisted as he said it. 'You know what, her face used to light up when she thought about going to work, about cavorting around in caterpillar outfits, Bloody Bo Peep. What the fuck sort of career is that?'

Markie let his wrist go. 'It's what she wanted to do.'

'Is it?' Simon sneered.

'I think you need to calm down, mate.'

But Simon wasn't finished. 'Calm down, *mate*? I'm not your *mate*. I've just paid £15,000 for thishh.' He waved his hands around the bar and gestured to the chapel. 'But you know what – you can have her. She's all yours. Frigid cow that she is.'

And then, as if it was a scene from a Western, Markie swiftly lifted back his arm, his hand curled into a fist, and punched Simon square on the jaw. 'Don't you *ever* call her that,' Markie growled as Simon winced and clutched his face, then staggered to a nearby seat and slumped into it. It was then that Victoria noticed Lulu swaying in the doorway. She'd witnessed the whole thing. She had a phone in her hand and was shivering in a thin cotton nightdress. Victoria walked over to her and put her arms around her shoulder. 'Lulu, you shouldn't be here. What's wrong, sweetie?'

'There you are, darling.' Her dad came over to both of them. 'Let me get you a whisky, Lulu.'

'She doesn't need a whisky, Dad,' Victoria said, rubbing Lulu's arms.

'No,' stage-whispered Lulu to Victoria, 'I think *you* will, sis, when you see this!' She held up Victoria's phone and swayed to the left a bit and started to giggle.

'What?' Victoria looked at the phone she was clutching in her hand. 'Why have you got my phone?'

'Because you left it on your bedside table, silly, and these notifications kept coming up!'

Good God. Lulu was still drunk. 'Give me my phone,' Victoria said with forced calmness.

Lulu staggered slightly and then handed over the phone. Victoria looked at the screen. There was a half-naked man with his hands on his hips, winking in a photo sent to her.

Victoria's mouth felt dry. 'Oh, it's nothing.' She had wanted to talk to Zoe about this new game, and it certainly wasn't meant for everyone to look it. In fact, she wasn't sure—

'What's up?' James was standing next to them just as Victoria dropped her phone.

James picked it up and turned it over. 'This yours, Victoria?'

This really wasn't the moment she'd have chosen to play a trick on James – and that's if she was even *sure* she should be playing this kind of prank. She'd started to have doubts and had already deleted the last few texts and pictures Zoe had sent. She could lie. She could somehow wiggle out of it, but it clearly was her phone and it would look worse if she lied.

'Yes.' And then she watched as James's beautiful face twisted into contortions as he frowned at the picture. And all Victoria could do was watch.

'James, it's not what you—'

'What the Jesus fucking Christ are you playing at Victoria? Just when I thought we were—'

She held her breath.

'Moving forward.' He let out a sigh. And with that he pulled off his wedding ring and placed it on a nearby table with the phone. Victoria stared at it, the circle of gold symbolizing no beginning, no end; well it certainly looked like the end of something.

Suddenly, Lulu shook her shoulder. 'Victoria, look! It's Izzy on your phone!' She nodded drunkenly to the phone buzzing on the table, with Izzy's picture flashing up. James snatched up the phone again.

'Why? *What*? Yes, Izzy's father.'

Lulu had fallen quiet and James was listening intently, the phone clamped to his ear.

'No. Yes, officer. No, no, James Allen, her husband. Heath Farm, yes I know. We'll come now.'

'*What?*' Victoria and her dad said in unison.

'It's Izzy, there's been an accident. A car overturned.'

Victoria felt like her world had gone inside out. She held her breath. 'A *car overturned*? Is she *alright*?' Her voice didn't sound normal.

'Yes, yes.' James nodded. 'Shaken, but she's OK. They were only going twenty miles an hour, something about a dare.'

'I didn't even know she'd gone anywhere! It's very unlike her.'

'We better go,' said James sharply. Victoria leant against the solid wood of the bar and stared at all the colourful drinks lined up. What had Izzy done? Victoria started to shake. Images of Izzy lying helpless on the side of the road flashed through her mind. Her mouth was dry. Suddenly she needed her husband, she needed him very much – just as he was walking away from her.

'I know the Heath Farm Estate,' croaked Lulu, 'it's her friend, Bella, it's her parents' farm. I've picked her up from there before, when I was babysitting a while ago.'

'Oh Jesus.' Victoria squeezed her fingers into her eyes. 'Right, think. Think. We need to get to her. But I've been drinking, James's been drinking – oh Christ, what a mess.

What a mess. How far is it, Lulu?' Lulu shrugged then hiccupped. Victoria's heart went out to her; she looked so fragile in her thin cotton nightdress. She mouthed 'sorry' to Victoria who just shook her head, she'd have to deal with James later.

'I'll drive.' It was Markie. 'I haven't touched a drop because I was,' he coughed and glanced at Lulu, 'um, the wedding singer. Let me take you there.'

Victoria waved to Jake to come over. 'Jake, what do you know about Izzy. Where she went?'

Jake stared at both Victoria and James as if summing something up. 'Yeah, she said the whole wedding thing was a mess, and that she'd just got a message about a party,' Jake said.

'Party? What party?' James shook his head. 'How did she get there?' he asked.

'Uber. You let her have the app – remember?'

'What's Uber?' Victoria was lost.

'That was in case she needed to get home, be safe, *not* to sneak out to a party without telling us!' He wrung his hands together. 'Sorry, Jake, it's not your fault.' Then he turned to Victoria. 'It's a taxi service – sort of.' James suddenly sprang into action. 'Right, Jake, you stay here with Grandad and Pickle. We're heading to Heath Farm.' Then looked at all of them. '*Now!*' he bellowed.

'Good God,' said her dad. 'This has been quite an afternoon. First, our Lulu, now Izzy.' Pickle barked up at him. 'Come on, lads,' he said to Jake and Pickle, 'let's get you both to bed.' And he scooped the dog up under his arm. 'To hell with hotel rules.'

Ten minutes later, Victoria, Lulu, and James were all piled into Markie's van, bumping down the country lanes.

What had got into Izzy? But thank God she was alright. Victoria stared out the window at the hedgerows flying past in the dark, and could feel the icy tension from James in the seat next to her, his back to her, staring silently out at the deep indigo sky.

33 LULU

I'm acutely aware of how near Markie is to me at the moment, staring ahead and concentrating; it's a look I know well, even in the dark. We have a name for it. It's his 'satnav' frown. He isn't speaking. He's studying the road ahead, which is full of potholes and extremely uneven. The lane twists all the way up to Heath Farm, as far as I can remember. Everybody knows that some of the old farm outbuildings are used for parties, or 'raves' as they were called in my day, by locals from the village. There have been a few drug raids there in the past, too. But Izzy? Why had she been led astray? Normally Izzy is level-headed. I try to piece together my thoughts. I need to be strong for Victoria, but I'm shivering, I feel dreadful about today – and the reason today happened is sitting in the seat right next to me.

'How you bearing up?' Markie whispers into the silence.

'I've been better.'

I glance at my sister in the rear-view mirror – she's biting her nails, staring out the window. Markie turns onto an even smaller farm track and we bump along a bit further. It's a small private road and the farm is up in the distance, lights on at the window. I came to a party here once, with Rich, my 'first love' – when I was eighteen and on the back of a motorbike. When we got here it was full of drunks, people smoking weed, not my scene at all. We'd split up soon after that.

I look up at the sky. It's like someone has cut out a circle in the navy heavens and let a torch shine through. I can make out the empty fields on either side of us, waiting to be fertilized, before they spring into life with crops. It's peaceful here, not like the turmoil of emotions running through my brain. I can't quite believe what I did. And yet the sense of relief is enormous. It's like I've been wearing a jacket with a thousand weights in it and suddenly I feel lighter. And I know I've hurt Simon, I've really, *really* hurt him, but standing there, looking down the aisle at my future, and then at Markie. My heart skips without warning. *What have I done?*

'It wasn't like I *planned* it,' I lean towards Markie and whisper. 'I just couldn't—' I cough. 'I couldn't go through with it.' I shift in my seat. The cotton nightdress feels flimsy against the vinyl of the seat. I'm grateful for Markie's coat, which he handed me before we got in. I pull it across my lap. We pull up next to some cars. Blue flashing lights are casting an eerie glow over the field and hedgerows, as if we've arrived at a music festival too late. I can see a car on its side by the ditch and my stomach lurches.

'Over there!' gasps Victoria. 'Look at the car! It's in the ditch. Hurry, Markie.' Victoria's voice is urgent from the back.

When we pull up, two figures are huddled in blankets by the side of the road. James slams his door shut and goes over to talk to the police.

'Is Izzy alright?' I can hear Victoria, panicky, her feet on the gravelly road as she walks purposefully towards one of the figures, then sobbing as she takes one of them in her arms: Izzy. There are paramedics next to them and they usher over James. The four of them are huddled together. The other figure stands alone. I peer towards them and can just make out the face: Bella. What was it Victoria told me she'd heard Jake say about Izzy's new friend? 'Bad vibe.'

The air is freezing around my face as my breath billows out. Markie is standing next to me, his hands in his pockets; he turns to me. 'This is going to be hard for your sister, Lulu. I wonder what got into Izzy? I presume you told her? About your accident? About what you told me?'

I whisper it as I am too ashamed to admit it even to myself. 'No.'

Markie shifts from one foot to the other. 'Lulu, for feck's sake,' he hisses, 'she needs to know. Especially after something like this – it will shake her up again,' he whispers now, scraping the toe of his shoe in the gravel.

'I know, I know, Markie, but—'

'You've got to tell her,' his voice is exasperated in the dark. Then he turns to me: 'I don't know what you're hiding from, or what you're running away from, Lulu, but you need to talk to her.'

I nod in the dark. 'I'm just so confused at the moment. There's more to it than— look. I—' But I can't explain this to him. Especially not tonight. There's a silence for a while and I look at his face, lit up by the moon. At his square jaw, and then he touches me briefly on my upper arm.

'Sorry I got angry. It'll be alright.' He says it into the night, almost to himself as well as me.

34 VICTORIA

Victoria sat, clenching the seat with her nails, a silver blanket wrapped around her shoulder, and bumped along the rough track to the main road in the back of the ambulance. James was sitting next to Izzy on the bench, a paramedic holding Izzy's wrist, taking her oxygen levels with a little clip on her finger.

'She's at 97 per cent, mate,' he shouted to the driver.

The first paramedic looked at both Vicky and James. 'She's fine, but we need to take her to A&E to get checked over, few scans, it's a matter of course with an RTA.'

Victoria nodded mutely. Being back in an ambulance was making her shiver. James's face was unreadable as he sat, his tie askew, his arms protectively around Izzy, whose eyes were closed. Victoria took in the lines of her beautiful daughter: the angle of her cheek, the curve of her neck, and wanted to pick her up and carry her away from all this mess. Her hair was in a tangle, and her mascara was running in little black rivers down her cheek; she hoped the paramedic was right. What had she been thinking? To get in the car with Bella who'd been drinking, and for a dare? Was it because Victoria had been so absent? Why did she feel she needed to prove herself? What had happened to her strong, sure-footed Izzy? The one who had told the boys to 'get lost' at nursery school when they tried to pull up her dress. The Izzy who had told Victoria she wanted to be 'the doctor for the animals' when she grew up after they'd had to get their hamster put down, because she was sure she'd have been able to save Nibbles. Who now, as far as Victoria could remember – blast her memory – still wanted to be a vet.

Once they got to the hospital, things happened fast. Izzy was taken away from them for a scan and she and James sat on the cold plastic chairs, waiting for news. Lulu was outside in the car park in Markie's van, waiting to take them home. Tentatively, James put his hand on top of hers for a brief second, then pulled it away. 'She'll be fine.'

'You don't know that.'

'I do. She takes after you.'

Victoria allowed herself a smile in that cold corridor with the linoleum flooring and bright strip lights. She was grateful that James had briefly showed solidarity, because when it came to their children, despite all their differences, despite the chasm that had opened up between them, there is an unwritten rule in parenting: you will be strong for them, you will unite.

After what seemed an eternity, and two dreadful vending machine coffees, a doctor in a white coat walked towards them. He had a pink tie, loosely knotted underneath the white coat, brown hair with white temples. The bags under his eyes suggested that he was on a long shift. Had many more patients to see. 'You're Izzy's parents?' he said softly, and they nodded.

'She's fine. She had quite a lot of alcohol in her bloodstream, but nothing else.' He glanced at his notes. 'No drugs.'

Victoria hadn't even thought of that. She gasped. Poor Izzy.

'We've put her through the MRI, everything is fine. I expect she'll just feel weary. Might be a bit of bruising across her abdomen from the seatbelt, but they weren't going very fast. It was lucky she was wearing her seatbelt. Even at twenty miles per hour you can do damage.'

'Thank you, doctor.' They had wanted to keep her in, but pressure on beds meant there hadn't been space. Victoria and James assured the doctor they would watch her.

'If you have any concerns, call us. Any vomiting, if she passes out, that kind of thing. Headaches.' And then he was gone. Onto the next patient in his twelve-hour shift, requiring Herculean strength and caffeine to get through.

———

Standing in her shiny kitchen at 2 a.m. Victoria stared at her reflection in the kettle. She saw a woman with wild brunette hair escaping a bun and dark circles under her eyes. Izzy, James and Lulu were in the lounge and she was making Earl Grey tea for Lulu, hot chocolate for Izzy and had poured a large gin and tonic for James – who had been stony-faced as he opened the front door to let everyone in. Poor Izzy had been mostly silent on the way back but had mumbled sorry a few times as Victoria shushed her, cradled under her arm in the back seat. Markie had waited patiently in his van at the hospital with Lulu, and had just dropped them all off on the doorstep, and sped away hurriedly, even though James had asked him to come in. Markie had offered to carry on and take Lulu back to the hotel but Lulu said she couldn't face going back there in case she bumped into Simon or Marjory – who could have stolen a butter knife and might stab her. That raised a tiny smile from James, but other than that he'd been silent; Jake would be safe there with their dad overnight, so Victoria had agreed.

'Here you go.' Victoria placed the steaming mug of hot chocolate on the table in front of Izzy and then rested her hand on Izzy's cheek. Izzy looked up at her – her bravado had evaporated like steam from the kettle, and in its place was a glimmer of her little girl again. She and Lulu were snuggled up on the couch under a blanket while James turned on a few lights around the room.

'I don't want to start by sounding like a Victorian dad, Izzy,' he said pacing the room like a Victorian dad, 'but you might have killed yourself, you know.' Victoria glanced at him and he looked away. She knew he was worried about bringing up the car accident in front of her, but she also knew Izzy would listen to him.

Izzy took a sip of hot chocolate. With her make-up-less face, her red eyes peeping out from under a blanket, she looked about ten years old. 'I'm really, really sorry,' she sniffed. Victoria wanted to rush over and hold her and tell her not to worry, but she knew James was right. Izzy had to understand what she'd done was wrong.

'But, but it wasn't my fault.' She was twisting a strand of hair around her finger.

'I think leaving the hotel and going to that party without telling anyone *was* kind of your fault, don't you think?' James said, sitting down on a chair with a thump. He folded his leg over and sat with his legs crossed in the armchair looking at his daughter, as if searching for clues. He'd grabbed one of Jake's hoodies in the kitchen as he was cold, and the sleeves were halfway up his arms. It made him look more adorable than ever.

Izzy started to cry. Lulu put both her arms around her.

'Hey, darling.' It was James. 'You must remember, we still love you, everything is OK,' he said softly, leaning forward and placing his elbows on his thighs.

How was he being so cool? The James-dad she remembered would not have been cool with this at all.

'I'm really, really sorry. But, well, I did WhatsApp you guys, but you were busy in the bar,' Izzy sniffed, 'and you know – with all the confusion—' she looked sideways at Lulu '—I just thought I'd get out of there. Too messy.' She shrugged. 'Plus I'd already had some vodka, so maybe I wasn't making the best decisions.'

'I'll kill that barman!' James whispered.

'It wasn't from the bar, it was my fault.' It was Lulu. 'Izzy helped me with my wedding make-up and, well, we were having some pre-wedding drinks, having a laugh,' she grimaced.

'A laugh, Lulu? Vodka?' James stared at her with his mouth open.

'Sorry, sorry.' Lulu shook her head and slid under the blanket.

'Anyway,' James carried on, 'Izzy, what were you doing in the car with Bella, she can barely drive, she's only just started lessons.'

Izzy shrugged. 'S'pose I just wanted to prove I could.'

'Could what?' James asked.

'Could *do* it!' Izzy raised her voice and then her lip quivered. 'They were all chanting at me, it was doing my head in, I just—'

'It's OK, Izzy,' Victoria said gently.

'They're always teasing me. You haven't *noticed* have you?

223

I don't belong with the cool kids, but Bella sort of took me under her wing and it felt good. Except sometimes,' Izzy screwed up her nose, 'she can make me feel crap, too.' Izzy faltered, as if reflecting on this for the first time. 'I mean, she says things like as if she's my friend, and then somehow I find myself doing things I wish I hadn't. Like just now.'

'Go on.' James's voice was soft.

Victoria's mind flashed to Jake telling her about the WhatsApp group at school where Izzy was called 'Spot-face' – Mrs Jennifer had left her a message a few days ago and said that the admin on that group was Bella. With all the wedding hiatus, Victoria hadn't done anything about it. But now, if she could get her hands on those kids – especially Bella – she'd wring their necks.

'Well tonight, she said, "I bet you won't come with me in my car, will you, you're too chicken scared. Your mum had an accident so you probably won't, you're too much of a baby." And I'm like, no, you're not going to get to me like that. So I went. I said, "Sure, I don't care." But,' Izzy said with a sigh, 'I do care, I mean—' She shrugged. 'I thought she would be OK. She knew the roads, it's, like, her farm. And the others – they were cheering me on. It was sort of good-bad to be in the gang.' She wiped away a tear as Lulu hugged her close.

'What else?' Lulu said.

'Well, I felt this good vibe – for a bit. I felt popular, like I could be one of them. They were looking at me, seeing if I could do it,' she said, then lowered her head, adding, 'I know it's crazy.'

'It *is* crazy, honey,' Victoria ventured, 'but it's understandable. But do you really want to be with people who make you feel rubbish, who get you to do things you don't want?'

Izzy shook her head.

'Sweetheart, you need to realise that Bella is not "cool", she's *cruel*,' James added.

Izzy pressed her lips together and pulled the blanket closer. With her smeared eyeliner, she looked like a baby panda peeping out from behind the blanket as Victoria's heart melted.

'Hey, remember in nursery, when you were little, you told those boys to "get lost"? When they pulled up your dress?' Victoria came and sat on the edge of the sofa next to her and placed a hand gently on top of her head.

A small smile lurked on the edge of Izzy's mouth. 'Yeah, yeah, I do.'

'You have to be that girl. The one who says, "get lost".' She took a deep breath. 'It's not just crazy, it's − well, a bit stupid to get in the car with Bella. I mean, she'd been drinking, hadn't she?' Victoria remembered what the police officer had said. The breathalyser. They'd said there were no charges to be placed on Izzy, but that they were going to have a serious word with Bella's parents about allowing her access to the car when she was not only without a licence to drive it alone, but had been drinking. They were pretty sure it would affect her chances of ever getting a licence.

'Stupid? Yeah, well, we all make mistakes Mum, even *you*.' She shot her a quick look. The fiery teenager was back.

'Of course we do, sweetheart, I know, but to mix drinking and driving − I mean—'

'Why don't you ask *Aunty Lulu*?' Izzy nodded to Lulu next to her, who had been remarkably quiet.

'Ask her about drinking and driving.' Izzy sat up, and moved away from Lulu.

'Izzy,' Lulu said quietly, picking at the edge of the blanket. 'Not now. I will tell your mum, but—'

'Izzy, we've all had a long day,' James's voice of reason started, 'I don't think—'

'*She* pulled the steering wheel in your car when you had your accident, Mum! *Ask* her.' Izzy stared at her then pulled her shoulders back.

'Izzy, don't be silly,' Victoria found herself saying as she looked at her sister for confirmation that it wasn't true. 'How would you know that?'

'Coz I overheard Aunty Lulu confess to Grandad – didn't I? They didn't know I was there. I was in my bedroom and they were standing outside, whispering.' And with that she burst into tears.

'Izzy, darling, why don't you get ready for bed? It's been a very long day. Mum will come up, OK?' James stood in front of her and held out his hand. Izzy nodded mutely, took his hand and quietly left the room with a glance back to Lulu. A silence filled the space as Izzy left.

'It's true,' Lulu whispered quietly, looking back and forth from her to James once he was sitting down again. 'I did. I never for a moment meant to hurt anyone, you have to believe me, but—' She looked at Victoria with red-rimmed eyes. 'I was stupid, really stupid and I haven't had the guts to tell you. I – I don't blame you if you hate me, because you know what? I kind of hate myself at the moment.' Tears were streaming down her cheek.

Victoria studied her younger sister with a blanket pulled tightly around her and her heart went out to her. She moved closer to her on the couch and put her arm around her. She was glad she hadn't married Simon, she was glad she finally knew why the accident had happened the way it did. She realised she didn't *blame* her at all. She was her sister. Careless, drunk maybe, needed help, definitely, but she hadn't done it *on purpose*, had she?

'I'd been drinking,' shrugged Lulu, 'at the Wedding Fayre, and it all got too much, the chat about the dresses, the flowers, the pressure, and Marjory telling me what food I should have and Simon's voice going round and round in my head, that I had to get things right – oh, God, just everything.' Lulu swept some hair off her face. 'And I was so wound up about it all, I wanted to scream, but I didn't. Instead, I just drank – all that free prosecco, I just wanted to blur the lines, remove myself from reality, fudge the edges – you know? And then, in the car, when that car was coming towards us, when those lights were blinding us, I pulled the wheel because I thought you were going the wrong way, I was trying to get you to *avoid* it.' She looked up at Victoria. 'Only, it made it worse.'

'Lulu, I can't remember what happened – that car came into our lane because of the deer, that's what the police said, that there would have been no way of avoiding it. Look, it's OK. I don't hate you, Lulu, I love you,' she said, rubbing her back gently. 'I have and will always love you – you're my *family*, my little sister – I mean, and anyway,' she found herself saying, 'I'm glad we had the accident.'

There was a hush in the room as she said it. Nobody spoke and a lightbulb flickered on and off. After a while James coughed. 'What, on earth, is that supposed to mean?' he said, pacing over to the window. 'Have you *any* idea what the impact of this has been on the family, Victoria?'

Victoria stood up. 'Yes, I do, James. And I think it's been necessary.' She glanced over at Lulu who was screwing her eyes up at her, shaking her head. 'I was careering headlong towards self-destruct wasn't I? Because I was hurting?' she carried on, 'becoming someone nobody liked, my kids, you.' She turned to Lulu. 'Why don't we all admit it? I overheard you and Dad, Lulu – now, that *did* hurt.' She came and sat back down on the sofa's arm. 'But maybe I had to hear it, you know, "the old Vicky is back". So no, I don't hate you, because the old Vicky *is* back. And it's because of you, Lulu, the accident, my memory, well, it's probably saved my family and I hope—' she looked over at James who had his arms folded next to the window and was staring out of it, 'my marriage.'

He swivelled round. 'You think? You think that the accident might have saved your marriage? I don't really think so Victoria,' he sighed. There was such sadness in his eyes. 'I did see those texts before the accident, and I used to wonder what it was all about. But we were getting a divorce anyway. And then, recently, I thought you'd changed, but now – I'm not so sure. I think the damage between us was done a long time ago and some things are too hard to repair.' He looked up to the ceiling, and opened his mouth, then closed it again. He seemed to be considering something. But then he strode out the room.

Victoria slid down from the sofa's arm. Lulu leant her head on Victoria's shoulder and then burst into tears. 'I'm so sorry, Vicky, I really am.' Victoria pulled her close. 'It's all a mess, everything,' Lulu sobbed. 'That day. I was just,' she sniffed, 'overwhelmed, it was a whole bucketful of things. And now your phone, James.' She wiped her cheek with the back of her hand and scrunched up her nose. 'Who was that person, anyway? Oh, look, I'm just so sorry.'

Victoria touched her cheek. She was worried about Lulu, she was worried about Izzy – but knew this wasn't the time to tackle any of it or explain anything. Her heart was hammering after what James had said. Life turns on a sixpence, thought Victoria, as she studied the weave of the sofa's covering. One minute you're hopeful for the future, the next, a split second could change everything. Her problem remained how to convince James that she did love him. But first, she had a daughter to look after.

'It's not all your fault. Look, right now, I think you need sleep.' And, as any good older sister would, she took her by the hand and led her upstairs to bed for the second time that day.

Once Victoria had tucked Lulu up in Jake's room, she popped her head round the door to check on Izzy. She crept into her room and stood by her bed looking at her sleeping daughter. Her breathing was steady and there were smudges of black on her pillowcase. Then she bent down, and stroked her forehead for a while before kissing her on the cheek and whispering, 'Love you.'

Just as she was closing the door she heard Izzy turn over and murmur, 'Love you too, Mum.'

———

When she got back downstairs, she heard a noise in the kitchen. James was standing by the leather chairs with a bag perched on one of them. She stared at the holdall as if it were a bomb.

'James, you're—'

'Leaving,' he said, zipping the bag shut. 'For a bit. I think we need some space.'

'OK.' She was using her Calm Mummy voice, like when Izzy sliced her finger and they had to go to A&E when she was seven, and when Jake told her he'd put the hamster in the microwave. She had to remain calm, but see if she could persuade him otherwise. All she wanted to do was scream, 'No!'

She went to the fridge and opened a bottle of wine, placed two glasses on the kitchen island in front of him and looked at him expectantly. 'Why don't we talk?' she said, sitting down and pouring out two glasses, a tiny life-raft in the choppy waters of acrimony.

'No thanks, Victoria.' He glanced at his watch. 'My Uber's here in ten minutes.'

'What do you want to know?'

'What were you doing?' A look of pain flashed across his face.

This bit she knew. This bit she could explain. 'It was just a game, James. It was Zoe's idea. To make you jealous.'

'A game? You expect me to believe you?'

'But it was!' She took a huge gulp of wine.

'Even if you're telling the truth – did you really think it would be a good idea now?'

She looked down at the red wine in her glass and swilled it around. 'No. I don't really think so, not now. But I just couldn't reach you, I wanted to – I don't know, make you realise what you had, what you could lose.' But as she said it, it sounded hollow, fake to her. 'I just want to go back to the old Vicky, for you and me to go back to how it was.' Victoria took a deep breath and continued. 'I *am* the old Vicky. The one who loves you.'

Victoria studied her husband. Although fragments of her memory were patchy, she could remember how it would often take just one look, one smile and they'd both know what the other was thinking. She used to love that about her relationship. They used to finish each other's sentences, struggle to keep a straight face if someone said something funny. Not now. She had no idea what was going through his head. She waited for her husband to answer, for his voice to soften, for him to come over and wrap his arms around her, tell her that they would talk it through in the morning. But there was a beat until he said anything. 'But it's not as easy as that, *is it?*' he said softly.

And when she looked at him waiting by the window for his taxi out of their home, with his tired eyes and beginning of a five o'clock shadow, she willed him to say something. She would have preferred shouting. Throwing wine. Anything but the silence.

35 VICTORIA

Victoria slumped down on the sofa and pulled a cushion towards her. The sound of the door slamming was still echoing in her mind. She could just imagine James now in the taxi, his mouth set in a firm line, pushing his glasses up the bridge of his nose like he always did when he was stressed. Where would he go? To Simon's, where they would both burn effigies of her and Lulu?

She wanted to take away his quiet anger, she wanted him to understand, but hell, even *she* didn't understand. She felt so messed up. There was so much that had led to this point. All of it twisting and turning into a ball of confusion. She remembered something her mother said to her once, that harrowing events can have a habit of putting more strain on a family, not bringing them together. The demons of blame and hurt would join forces producing a lethal cocktail that would seep into any little fissures already there. Rather like ice forming in the cracks of a pavement and bursting it apart. That's what she felt had happened to her and James. The miscarriage had sent them scurrying back inside themselves, rather than reaching out to each other; it seemed that she had taken solace in the routines of home, the control that that brought her, while he'd hidden at work, surrounded himself with new projects and busy schedules and pushed out any emotion and feeling. Feelings that *hurt*. She wished now that he'd only opened up to her. Imagine if he had, and the two of them could have coaxed each other out of their mutual pain rather than make the suffering worse?

Her face was wet from crying, the cushion was damp as she looked around the room – at the baby photos on the mantelpiece, at the crooked 'sculpture' Izzy had made in primary school of four little pigs in a sty. *See, Mummy, that's you, the mummy pig, there's Daddy the daddy pig, and here are me and Jake the twinny piglets!* She had pointed at each one with her chubby little fingers. It was painted brown and was hideous, yet Victoria had proudly displayed it on her mantelpiece for seven years because Izzy had made it with *love*, had made it for her parents. If the house ever caught fire, she'd challenge any burly fireman and run into the lounge and grab it.

Victoria threw the cushion to the other side of the room. Enough was enough. She needed to sort things out. She stood up, took a look at the woman in the mirror hanging over the fireplace. Her hair was all over the place, her carefully constructed 'wedding face' was now a mess of smudged lipstick and smeared mascara. She stared at her, as if willing her to challenge her. Then she swept her dress up and marched into the kitchen. She found an old cardboard box in the storeroom, hauled it out and then pulled the Italian coffee machine from its home next to the hob, and threw it in the box. Next was the expensive mixer and then she grabbed all the flavoured herbal teas from the cupboard and, packet

233

by packet, threw them into the box, quite satisfied with her aim.

Then she stomped upstairs. When she got into her room, she yanked her wardrobe doors open. Out came dresses, out came cashmere sweaters and out came designer handbags. She looked at the scissors gleaming in her hand. There was no doubt in her mind what she needed to do. Holding up the navy leather bag – the one she'd first seen at the hospital, she snipped off the handle, then she cut off the Godawful metal clasp; next she picked up a cashmere jumper embellished with silver threads running through it. *Snip, snip, snip.* That would do. She carried on, smiling to herself, pulling another outfit from her wardrobe and cutting it into tiny pieces. She carried on like this for about half an hour until there was a little heap of clothing strips at the bottom of her bed, on the floor. *That's the New Victoria, in pieces, right where she should be.*

Next, she stood in front of the mirror and started to chop at her hair. Little tufts fell to the floor. She kept cutting until her tresses had been tamed into a shorter cut. A very *uneven* cut, but it sat at shoulder length now and she felt satisfied. *There*, that would do. She put the scissors down on the dressing table with a thump. *Bollocks to poncy hairdressers*, she said in her head and stifled a smile.

'Vicky?' Lulu was standing in the doorway staring at her.

'What are you doing?'

'Sorting out a few things.'

Lulu let out a whistle. 'But your *hair*?' Lulu wandered over to her and put her hands on her shoulders. 'Vicky?' Lulu was shaking her head. Her blonde curls were tumbling down her shoulders and her make-up had vanished. She looked as if the fight had left her.

'That's right, the old Vicky.' Victoria turned around and looked at Lulu. 'You alright?'

'No. Couldn't sleep,' Lulu shrugged. 'I heard cupboard doors bang and James's voice?' Lulu turned around and sat on the bed. 'What happened?'

'He's left.'

'For how long?'

Victoria lifted her shoulder up. 'I don't know. He's confused, I need to let him go.'

'I didn't help though, did I? Your phone – sorry.'

Victoria looked at her. 'Look, I created the mess. It was a silly prank. It could have happened anywhere. I wanted it to happen but it backfired on me.'

'How do you mean?'

She sat down next to Lulu on the bed and explained.

'Whoa.' Lulu fixed her eyes on her and they widened. 'Does James realise it was fake?' It was the question that Victoria had been turning around in her head all night.

She shrugged, reaching a hand up to pull at her hair, then realising it wasn't there. 'I hope so. But what I do know is that *I* wouldn't threaten my marriage for anything, and that's what James needs to know. I can't talk to him right now, but when he's ready to listen, I will. Far from making him jealous and running into my arms, he's just run the other way.'

Lulu was staring at the floor. She was twisting her night-dress between her fingers. Victoria watched a tear drop onto the fabric and soak in. 'I just want to say sorry again. I just kept remembering me pulling the wheel of the—'

'Hey, Lulu, stop,' she said putting her hand on her knee. 'You were drunk. In fact, you're probably harder on yourself than I could ever be.' Victoria stood up and stepped over the pile of clothes, then turned around. 'I know this isn't the time or the place, but you need to think – you need to ask yourself why you were so drunk on the night of the Wedding Fayre, why you turn to drink when things get tough, why you nearly walked down that aisle to another life with someone you don't love?' Lulu glanced at her sideways. Victoria came back and sat next to her and said softly, 'And I'm not expecting you to say anything, it will take time to figure stuff out. But why don't you go home, I mean *home*-home and spend time with Dad? Take some time out?' She placed a hand on Lulu's knee and gave it a squeeze.

Lulu nodded, and looked down at the floor; mascara was still smudged under her eye. Victoria reached out and gently rubbed some off with her thumb. 'Right, I'm going to bed. And so are you,' she said, pulling her sister up off the bed and leading her to the door. 'Night sweetheart.' She held onto the top of Lulu's shoulders. 'Look at me,' Victoria said gently. Lulu looked straight at her with red-rimmed eyes. 'I love you,' Victoria whispered, touching her cheek, 'and what you've got to do is love yourself. This is your big sister talking.'

Lulu smiled wanly. 'Easier said than done, sis, damaged goods here,' she muttered, turning away from her. Victoria watched her wander back to Jake's room, then close the door. *Damaged goods?* But her brain ached from today. She didn't have any more energy left to solve it tonight. She swept the clothes from one side of the bed to the other – the *empty* side – carefully took off her dress and threw it over a chair, then fell into an exhausted, fitful sleep.

———

She was being smothered, she was in a dress shop, naked, trying on new clothes and the assistant was telling her how marvellous she looked. When she looked in the mirror, she had no hair. The assistant grinned. 'Nice to have the old Vicky back,' she said and then she was crying, being pulled, she was drowning, in the sea, but it was like quicksand; she was so, so heavy, but she *had* to swim. She couldn't breathe. But she had to get to Lulu, to Izzy, there was a light, the light of an ambulance—

'Mummy, Mum! Wake up! What's going on? What's happened to your *hair*?' It was Izzy by the side of the bed, pulling her arm. She had turned on the bedside light.

'I had a nightmare, sweetheart.'

'More than a nightmare. What have you done? Why are there clothes all over the floor, and—' Izzy said, rubbing her eyes. She nudged the pile with her big toe, 'they're in shreds? And there's hair everywhere,' she whispered, blinking at Vicky. 'Have you been, like, drinking, Mum?'

Vicky sat up in her bed and wiped her damp forehead and laughed. Then she glanced at the mound of cut up clothes. 'No, I've been clearing out.'

'Are you sure you're not, you know, a bit, um, because of the accident?' Izzy screwed up her eyes and peered at her.

'No darling, I have never felt more sane in my life. Listen, come here.' And as her daughter leant into her, she realised this was the first proper embrace she'd had from Izzy since she'd been back from hospital. She took in the smell of her hair, the essence of *Izzy*, pulled up the soft duvet and switched off the light.

But despite being exhausted she couldn't sleep. Thoughts tumbled around her brain, from the day's events, to the look in James's eyes as he left, the state Lulu was in earlier, Izzy in a foil blanket by the side of the road. Her husband had just walked out, her sister had partly caused her dreadful accident and was having some sort of crisis, and her daughter got in the car with a drunk driver. She lay awake for what seemed like half the night, worrying how on earth it would all be resolved. And yet, as she listened to Izzy's soft breathing beside her, one thing she was certain of: despite the tangled web of confusion, her family meant more to her than anything in the world.

36 LULU

Pickle scampers ahead of me, his little white tail wagging in the breeze. His paws make a kind of clip-clip noise on the road as he trots ahead, pulling on the lead, then he turns back to look at me as if to say, 'hurry up'. He meanders into the verge of the road sniffing the grass. We're at the back of the village where Dad lives, Nidder Bridge, a small cluster of houses, a pub and small shop to the north of Harrogate, on the edge of the Yorkshire Dales. We're following a dry-stone wall around a bend, then there's a small bridge over a tinkly stream where Pickle usually stands up on his hind legs and barks at the water. Fluttery ferns line the edge of the road and I breathe in the sweet smell of wild honeysuckle as Pickle yanks the lead again. Up ahead the road peters out and becomes a path, taking us up towards the small foothills. As you get nearer, the ground gets boggy, then there's a steep climb towards the viewpoint. I've been walking him here for the last two weeks while I stay with Dad, every morning up at 8 a.m., then out and about with him, even if it's raining, by 9 a.m. I've come to love our little walks. Occasionally I've met another dog walker, but mostly I'm on my own, lost in thought – which is really where I need to be, both physically and mentally.

I've been thinking about my kaleidoscope again, those dark fragments along with the light, and I know that I need to reset myself in many ways. I've come to realise that I'm using drink to stop me *feeling* sometimes, and yet that's exactly what I need to do. Except some of the feelings I have are more than I can bear – they hurt too much. But I can't hide inside a bottle. I need to cut down and face some of the music on my own. Pickle's off the lead now and he barks and I call him. He comes bounding back to me, eager for a treat. I fish one out of my pocket and give it to him. He scampers ahead. His love is so simple, isn't it? And so unconditional. Markie's words weave in and out of my mind. *Love yourself.* Only it's not quite as simple as that, is it?

Pretty stone cottages dot the road on either side, and there's a bright red post box attached to a wooden post. The lambs are all huddled next to their mothers in the field by the fence. Pickle and I carry on, following a dry-stone wall, one that I know leads to the path up the hill. I call him towards me and then crouch down and give him another treat.

He scurries ahead of me, then stops and looks back. The sky is a milky wash of blue and white; it's just nine o'clock and a pocket of darker clouds are smeared across the horizon. There are a few chinks in the sky though, letting through a ray of sun here and there, falling on the lush grass. It's glorious here, and with the vastness of the moors stretching ahead it makes me think things through, and when I do, I feel lighter, as if a burden has been lifted. I take a deep breath, stuff my hands in my pockets because it's pretty chilly, even in late April. Pickle darts towards the fence, sniffs, then scuttles over to the other side. I stand lost in thought, looking at the bubbling stream, the water frothing at the edges, the calming whoosh of the water, wild yellow primroses in clumps by the water's edge. My fingers find my phone inside my pocket and I wish, not for the first time, that it would bleep, that there would be another message. I take it out and look at it anyway. One new message. My heart thuds, but it's a message from Victoria.

All OK? Call us later, will you? Speak to you and Dad then. Hope you're resting! V x

I carry on with Pickle along the path for about another mile. There's a noise above, it could be a plane, and there are some thick clouds gathering. I look up at the sky and can feel a change in the air. It was so beautiful about half an hour ago. I call Pickle who comes up to me and starts to trot next to me as I feel a sprinkle of rain. 'We'd better get back, Pickle.' As we walk together in the drizzly rain, I make a decision. I will call that number Markie texted me, see if the counsellor has any spaces. I know it's the first step on a long road, but it's a start.

When I get back, Dad's laid out the brunch things – it's become a daily treat – and by now it's raining quite hard. I'm due to leave tomorrow, take the train back. This afternoon Dad and I are going into Harrogate to look at a new dishwasher for him. I'm going to miss him and Pickle, and our walks.

Dad's lit the fire in the sunroom and we take our bacon sandwiches, mugs of tea and toast through there. The toast is thickly sliced and covered in homemade apricot jam from one of his neighbours, Liz. She's a widow and they seem to have hit it off. He's started to look after her dog for her when she goes to visit her mum in a care home in Bradford. Pickle curls up beside me on the sofa as I swing my legs round.

'Good walk?'

I nod and take a bite of toast. 'Yep. Going to miss them, actually.'

'And Pickle will miss you, and so will I.' Dad looks at me and I wonder how I didn't notice before how he's aged a little, his hair is just that bit thinner on his head, his skin more papery.

'Me too, but I need to get back.'

'Course you do, pet. And face the music.' Dad takes off his reading glasses and fixes me with his pale blue eyes.

'Well, I need to see Simon,' I say, taking a sip of tea. 'I owe him an explanation.'

Dad nods. 'And then what?'

I shrug. 'I don't know. But I do know that I don't want to marry him, I should never—' I stop because I don't want to burden Dad with too much – there's only so much he could cope with. 'I should never have gone down the aisle.'

'He seemed like a decent bloke, Lulu, but somehow he wasn't really your type, was he? Ah well, you won't make that mistake again.'

No, I won't, I think, stroking Pickle who has curled up by my feet. It was wrong to look for security with Simon. I did it for all the wrong reasons, I realise that now. It was just so easy to get wrapped up in the wedding, in running away, in being safe, *in being someone that wasn't you*, a little voice says.

'Do you remember what I told you and Vicky when I was staying, about your dreams?' I look up at him and nod. 'You need to follow them, Lu,' he carries on. 'I don't think you were ready to get married. There's too much you want to do. Mum only had one year here,' he waved his hand around the lounge and gestured to the view outside. 'But she did it – we followed her dream.'

He stands up and walks towards the mantelpiece. There's a photo of Mum and the two of us, on a swing chair. I'm about six and Vicky is a teenager, maybe seventeen. She's wearing a lemon-yellow dress and beige wedges; I'm sitting in Vicky's lap, looking up adoringly at her. Mum's looking at the camera, her blonde hair cut into a short bob. I take after mum, with her fair hair and blue eyes, Vicky has always been more like Dad, darker hair and skin, but you can see we're sisters, it's in our slightly wonky smile.

Dad picks up the photo and turns it round in his hand. 'This was taken on Vicky's seventeenth birthday, we'd just been to Brighton for the day.' At the mention of Brighton all I can think about is Markie, his broad smile, the smell of fish and chips, the ice skating, his face when I was bearing my soul to him. It's such a fond memory and suddenly I have such an urge to go home.

'I will follow my dream – well, dreams, Dad, believe me, I will.' I tell Dad about one of my dreams, about an agency I've contacted, who put out-of-work actors and singers in touch with productions that need help, understudies, extras, just to get you back on the stage. It's not the West End, but it's the first step. And it's not hiding underneath caterpillar outfits anymore.

'And there's something else, Lulu love. Your mum, she had two life insurance policies. Now, I don't want you to say anything, but I want you to have half of one, for now. I'm putting away Vicky's share, but I want you to have yours now.'

My heart sinks. 'No, Dad, I can't take your money.'

'It's not my money, pet, it's *yours*. Don't argue,' he says standing up and getting his coat from the hall. 'Come on,' he says shaking out his coat, 'we've got a dishwasher to choose. Get your jacket on.'

———

In bed that night after a warm bath, with Pickle curled up beside me, I listen to the rain on the roof and I think about my future. *Drum, drum, drum.* And I let my mind drift to Markie and to our time together. Victoria's told me that she's seen him and Miss Perfect, his new assistant, at the village hall and that he's waved to Victoria once or twice when he's been in his van, and *she*'s been in the passenger seat. I frown and pull out my phone. I quickly find his business Facebook page and I scroll through all the new images of him and her. I feel a stab of envy, even though I know I have to leave that business behind; it's not just that it's—

I decide to text him.

Dear Markie, How are you? I'm fine but I really miss you.

I delete that.

Hi Sexy,

Everything's GREAT. Dad's great, Pickle is a little terror, everything's fine. How is Little Bo Peep without me?

I delete that too.

Hi. It's good being at Dad's, walking on the moors with Pickle has cleared my head a bit. But I'm ready to come home. How are things with you? Be good to catch up.

I press send.

I'm getting the train back tomorrow – another five hours to think about the future and mull over how I get back to being the me I want to be. But I already know what I want. Follow your dreams, said Dad. I frown as I tickle Pickle's tummy. First, I owe Simon an explanation.

37 VICTORIA

'No, fat arse, I said I wanted Hawaiian.'

'Jake! Don't talk to your sister like that!'

'But she's being really annoying and not making up her mind. Last week she was vegetarian, now, not only is she *so* not vegetarian, she wants a Meat Feast. I mean, is she for real? I'm having a Hawaiian,' said Jake mutinously.

Victoria held the phone to her ear to complete the pizza order and practised her deep breathing. 'Anyone for Coke? Sides?' she said brightly. 'Apparently today's a Family Fun Special.'

The twins sat at the kitchen table and glared at each other. She put the phone down and listened to the rain pelting down outside. Perhaps the only thing to look forward to *was* a slab of dough with melted cheese. Did she even *like* pizza? The absence of James was making everything so much harder, but she had to try, try for the kids, to keep things as normal as possible until she could talk to him. It had been a week since Lulu's not-wedding as Jake liked to call it. A week since James had left and all she'd had was a brief text telling her that he was collecting some things; he'd made sure he came over when she was out. He was staying at an Airbnb in the village. A week since Lulu had been wandering around the Yorkshire Dales sorting out her head, or at least Victoria hoped she was. She'd seen Markie a few times, normally driving past in his clapped-out van with some blonde at his side.

'So maybe we could watch a family movie later, what do you think?' Victoria said, getting knives and forks out of the drawer. Izzy looked up from her phone and squinted at her. 'Mum, we don't live in an Enid Blyton novel. We don't want to watch Jurassic Park!' Izzy stood up and wandered over to the fridge and pulled out some orange juice. Victoria closed her eyes momentarily. This was exhausting. A week of silence, sleeping badly, checking her phone, refreshing her emails, double-checking her WhatsApp. Nothing. And why should he contact her? Because she wanted him to?

It wasn't Izzy and Jake's fault that their parents were confused – and it wasn't their fault that it had rained every day of the Easter holidays. Jake had been stuck in his room on his iPad, either watching movies or working on his 'projects'; Izzy has been glued to her phone and was eating so many chocolate biscuits that Victoria worried about a new outbreak of spots to send her into orbit, yet couldn't really say anything as she was so touchy. James was avoiding her and her sister was miles away in Yorkshire. She felt terribly alone.

'How about some David Attenborough? I've recorded some great shows,' Victoria suggested, beaming. But by the glares she got from her children, she could already tell that saving her family was going to be harder than Saving The Planet.

'Right where do you want these?' It was the week after Family Pizza Night and the weather was still foul. She'd got up early, with a new sense of purpose. She was holding up two bin bags full of designer clothes, handbags, shoes and gym gear, dripping wet from the rain outside in front of the nice lady at the charity shop. She'd had another sort-through as there was little else to do in the rain. She'd also visited her hairdresser, to gasps. But they'd fixed her hair. It was shorter, messier. It felt more like the old Vicky. And her cupboards were practically bare when she'd banged them shut. But it suited her. New start, she'd thought, surveying the empty rail. She'd rested her hand on her wedding dress and carefully stroked it, and considered getting rid of it. But she'd shook her head, and hung it up on the back of her bedroom door. *No, you'll stay where you are.*

She glanced out of the shop window; the rain had turned into drizzle, drizzle which would go down the back of your neck and seep into your pores. She'd rather have torrential rain. At least with that you knew where you were. She'd almost suggested pizza again last night, but remembered what a disaster it was last time. They'd all had their pizzas and the twins had gone to their rooms and she'd ended up watching *The Holiday* with a large vodka tonic – it was *so* romantic. She'd tried for a week to jolly them up, take them for a walk, watch a family movie, bake some brownies. She'd tried to stop checking her phone every five minutes for news from James, too.

'Just over there, dear,' the woman from the charity shop motioned, bracelets clanking on her forearm.

'And this?' She gestured to the coffee machine in its box under her arm.

'Ooh, that's super. Just pop it on the counter here.'

Victoria placed it on the top of the glass counter with a thump. 'Good riddance,' she said, and felt the woman's eyes on her back as she strode out of the charity shop. When she got outside she felt a sense of freedom and was more determined than ever to erase the New Victoria from her life. Back in the car, she watched the raindrops chase each other down the windscreen. She switched the engine on and blasted the windscreen with hot air. Just then her phone beeped. She practically emptied her bag onto the seat looking for it in case it was James. But it wasn't. It was a Google Calendar message reminding her that her hospital scan appointment was tomorrow.

'Oh shit,' she said out loud, as she flicked on her windscreen wipers. James had said he'd take her when they first got the email. What now? Lulu was in Yorkshire with Dad, and Zoe was away. Victoria had been told she shouldn't drive back from it, because of the possibility of taking medication at the appointment. How would she manage? She dearly wanted James to be there, even if he wasn't speaking to her, just to be a solid physical presence. She *needed* him.

She held her phone in her hand for a long while, watching the wipers swish this way and that, thinking of various messages to send him.

Need help.

No that sounded too dramatic. She deleted that.

Brain scan tomorrow, please advise.

No, that sounded ridiculous. She deleted that.

Hospital visit tomorrow, at 12, are you able to help?

She pressed send and bit her lip.

She sat in the car holding her phone and looked at the village through the rainy windows. There was the village hall across the road, with the Little Norland Coffee Shop, the park in the far distance with the wooded hillside rising up from it, she looked across the road to the small independent grocer, a fruit and veg shop, a newsagent and the bridal shop. She stared at the little boutique with its flower display neatly adorning the window outside, and wondered how many other brides-to-be would walk in, clutching not only their bags but their hopes and dreams close to their chest, imagining a bright, shiny future. Suddenly her phone pinged to let her know there was a new message.

Of course. Pick you up at 10am at the house. J.

As she released the handbrake, she felt like she'd won the lottery. *He cares.* She drove home with a ridiculous swell in her heart and kept telling herself not to get too excited. She was going for a *brain scan*, after all, she reminded herself, not a date.

38 VICTORIA

It was a quiet journey down to the hospital as she sat lost in thought about what it had taken to get them to this point, to being perfectly polite strangers, and the cold chill that ran through her when James opened the car door for her in silence on their driveway this morning.

'How's your, um, accommodation?' she'd asked, a few minutes into the trip. 'Grim,' was the swift reply. 'And you don't want to come home?' she'd asked, biting her lip. He'd hesitated for a while, as they were at a junction and she tried not to read too much into it, until he said, 'Not at the moment,' navigating his way around a tricky roundabout. Then he'd told her that, when he dropped her back home he would be collecting a few more of his things. Her heart sunk. To take her mind off it, Victoria stared at all the new houses that had been built on the outskirts of Little Norland. 'Look at all these new houses,' she remarked to James, to measure his response.

He simply looked over at her sideways. 'They were here when we bought the house, Vicky.' They fell silent as flashes of countryside whizzed past and privet hedges blurred into a line of fuzzy green and beige beside the road. Spring was truly on its way now, it was early May and the countryside seemed greener and fresher. Tiny lambs dotted the fields and clumps of daffodils broke up the grass as they sped past. They made their way through the small country roads twisting and turning across rural Sussex as James flicked the wipers and screenwash on; they swished intermittently across the smeared windscreen somehow emphasising the quiet in the car.

After a while, James opened his window for some fresh air. A chilly blast went through the car. 'How's Lulu?'

'She's at Dad's sorting her head out. I think it's good for her to be there – away from all this,' she wasn't sure what she meant, she just knew that Lulu hadn't been herself. 'From this place, from memories, I don't know, from who she was trying to be. She needs to figure out what she wants.'

'I guess that makes two of us.'

Victoria glanced at James. His hands were gripping the wheel and he was looking straight ahead. She looked at his temples, greying slightly, and wondered when time had marched on so fast. His jaw was a little slacker, but still strong and determined; it was a profile she'd know anywhere – memory loss or no memory loss. He was wearing a white shirt and his now-familiar reading glasses perched on his head. The rain had finally stopped and the sun had emerged from the mushroom-coloured clouds just as they'd set off from the house earlier. And there was a warmth to the air which had surprised her as they crunched across the gravel driveway to the car. She'd left her coat undone and stood and watched two blackbirds scavenging in the leaves by the holly bush as she'd waited for James to put his coat in the boot. I nearly threw this away, she'd thought, watching her silent husband move things around in the boot. The hum of a leaf-blower in the background had been soothing until James had slammed the boot shut and said they'd better get going because of the traffic.

The road opened up ahead of them into a dual carriageway and the trees became denser on either side as they drove over shiny roads towards the hospital. She was dreading going there, revisiting the terror of that night, but a part of her was grateful, glad that at least there might be some more answers.

They slowed at some traffic lights and James let out a sigh. 'Traffic's always bad here,' he muttered under his breath. Was it?

Do you love him?

She took a deep breath and closed her eyes, weariness overwhelming her.

————

Half an hour later, they were pulling into the car park. She still couldn't believe the hospital had been built. It was going to take *years* they'd said. Years she'd never get back.

'OK?' he said as they passed the hospital entrance sign.

She nodded. 'I'll feel better when someone has given me a few more answers. It's so tricky playing cat and mouse with my memory.'

'One step at a time,' he said, slowing down and easing into a parking space.

She went to touch his sleeve, but then slid both hands under her legs and leant forward instead and looked out onto the striped yellow lines reserved for ambulances.

'I guess so. I know that nobody said it would be easy, but nobody said I'd forget this much. I just feel so hopeless at times.' She shrugged and felt something inside her deflate. In the old days James would have said, *No you're not.* He'd prop her up, hug her maybe, they would have found something funny to laugh about in the car park, he'd have tickled her under her chin and pulled one of their funny faces, made her laugh. He certainly wasn't going to go anywhere near her chin today.

'We'd better go.' James reached for the door handle.

'James?'

He looked over at her and she noticed how wide his pupils were and she wanted to say more, she wanted *them* to be more, but she felt wrung out, unable to make amends from the past. Even a past she couldn't quite remember.

'Nothing. Let's go.'

———

The consultant took off his glasses and pointed at the image on his screen.

'Most of this looks normal, Mrs Allen.'

Most.

'What can you tell us, Mr Anderson?' James crossed his legs and looked over the consultant's desk to the screen.

'As I've told your wife when I first saw her, retrograde amnesia is a funny thing.' He nodded to the screen again. Victoria could hear a voice in her head: *I'm not laughing now, doctor.* 'And in your wife's case, things seem to be following a familiar pattern.'

'Familiar?' James scratched his head.

'As I explained before, she can remember all the things from a while ago – say seven years plus, but even then there will be holes, but recent memories, from just before the accident, they will be gone.'

'Like the actual accident, doctor?'

'Yes, I doubt you'll remember what actually happened.' He smiled. 'But it might be for the best, don't you think? These things are normally pretty traumatic.' He looked over at Victoria.

'I wish I could feel the same, but somehow everything seems to be hinged on that day.'

'It's possible that something just prior to the accident will be at the forefront in your brain, but you are associating it with the accident. And the brain is a mysterious thing. We still only know so little about it. It looks like your working memory is fine – for example, if you played chopsticks on the piano as a child, you'll remember that. Recent memories will be the most affected. But looking at your MRI scan, I'm satisfied that things are progressing as they should.'

Chopsticks? What bloody use was playing some parlour piano song when she couldn't even remember exchanging her marriage vows?

He leant back in his seat. 'It will take patience, Mrs Allen. Some memories will come back, others, I'm afraid will be lost. The damage has occurred to the memory storage areas of your brain. Some people will lose maybe a year or two, others,' he coughed, 'decades.' He adjusted his tie. 'You could try looking through more photos, talking about shared memories with friends and family, find physical things which might trigger a memory, you know, significant things, or a favourite possession, ornament – he looked over and shrugged. It could be anything which sparks things off.'

'Right. I see.' She didn't see at all. It just seemed that because she was living and breathing, the fact that her family were semi-strangers was just an annoying consequence of the accident; it felt as if all the consultant really wanted to know was that she was basically alright.

As if reading her mind, he pulled on his tie and said, 'Have you tried hypnotherapy? Visualisation?'

She shook her head.

'Right. Well, in terms of your scan, everything looks normal. You will, of course, have bouts of tiredness and any stress will make this worse.' He looked at his watch. 'Unless you have any more questions, then I'm afraid I need to see my next patient. I'm running a bit late.'

———

The sun was hidden behind some clouds when they left the hospital and the warmth she felt earlier had disappeared. She pulled her cardigan tight around her and shivered. The sky was slate grey now with pockets of blue remaining. The air was damp. They walked side by side back to the car, their footsteps in time with each other. They seemed to fit together, be two pieces of one puzzle, and she had a memory, a hazy one, of walking somewhere like this with James, the sound of the road beneath her feet, the staccato clip-clip of her shoes, James's arm around her. The hospital, the blood, the ache in her stomach, the awful antiseptic smell. She was walking away from it, he was there, he was – what? He was squeezing her shoulders, they were in this car park, she was sure of it.

She stopped and rubbed her arms, he carried on for a few paces. 'When we were last here, James, I mean before the accident, it was the baby, wasn't it?' He turned around and looked her in the eye. She saw the strain on his face, the way he tilted it to one side. She saw the man she loved weigh up what to say.

'Yes, we were coming for the scan. And yes, it's when we lost her – the baby.' He closed his eyes and took a deep breath. Then he opened them again and walked back to her and touched her arm. 'Let's get you home.'

The doctor said she would find it hard to locate memories, but this wasn't just a memory, it was a wrench in the pit of the stomach, a twisty-turny emotion like seasickness, with no name, flashes of images were popping into her brain unbidden – a glittery mobile, humming as she washed baby blankets, the scent of sweet baby powder. The sun popped out again briefly from behind the grey overhead and she could feel its fleeting rays on her cheek, yet she shivered. The pink ribbon. It all made sense now. James was still standing next to her. His arms were folded. 'Come on, it's cold.' And they both walked back to the car.

James slid the key in the ignition and turned towards her. 'I know this is hard for you, Victoria – and,' he looked up at the car ceiling briefly, 'it's bloody difficult for me. The wife who's been distant, who you feel has given up, she has an accident. Then she's,' he shrugged, 'different. Like time-warped back to another era, when, I don't know, when things *were* different, when she loved you. And then, *then* pictures of half-naked men on her phone… I mean, one minute it's going in one direction, then,' he tapped his thumb on the steering wheel, 'the next,' he let out a sigh, 'well, I really don't know what's going on.'

'James, I do love you. The phone? That was a prank, a joke. Maybe not the best timing, I know. When I think back, losing the baby – I don't know, perhaps I didn't know what to do, perhaps I couldn't *reach* anyone.' Her eyes slid across at him. 'Maybe I just didn't know what to do, so I started to focus on myself which meant I stopped focusing on the pain.' He nodded and stayed silent.

'But James,' she coughed, 'you made decisions too – we both made choices.' She closed her eyes as a wave of exhaustion flooded over her. When she opened them, he was sitting looking out in front of him, his hands in his lap. She studied the familiar shape of his mouth. How powerful his scent was as she sat next to him, inhaling every breath, and she frowned.

'Choices,' he muttered as she stared at the specks of dust dancing in the air around her.

'James, I don't want to go back to how it was before, whatever that was. It sounds awful. *I* seemed awful.'

'You weren't awful, Vicky, you—'

'Were probably a bit lost,' she said.

'Yes. We both were.' He glanced at her then and looked down at his lap.

'James, all I know now is that I want to go back – to how we were. I may have lost some of my memory, but I never forgot you were my husband.' Her stomach was twisting in a little dance, one of nerves, of *reaching* him after all the days of silences.

'Hey, we shouldn't be discussing all this, the doctor said no stress.' He brushed some invisible dust off his trousers and looked over at her.

Victoria let out a long breath. To hell with stress, this was her marriage. 'The one thing I do know, is that right now, the woman sitting in front of you, the old Vicky, she's sorry about what happened, the baby, the pain, the distance between us, and all she wants is her husband back, to pull funny faces with, to laugh with, to have him fold her into his arms,' she sniffed, 'to stop the ache at night in the pit of my stomach when I think I've lost you, to put the missing piece of our family jigsaw back in to make it whole again.' She took a deep breath. 'The old Vicky, the one right here, she really, really wants you back.'

James shifted in his seat and handed her a tissue.

'Can we at least try again?'

'Maybe.'

A feeling blossomed in her heart as he turned the engine on. It was as if she'd seen a pot of gold at the end of a rainbow. It wasn't a definite 'no', it wasn't 'absolutely not', it wasn't 'I don't think so', it was 'maybe' and it gave her hope – a rising feeling of anticipation that her heart clung to all the way home.

39 VICTORIA

It wasn't exactly easy at home, but tensions had lifted a bit and the kids were back at school. James had been away for three weeks now and it was early May. He'd told her that he just wanted some space, that it was probably a good thing for both of them. She hadn't wanted to push it any further and was trying to live in the moment as much as she could. She and the twins had fallen into a routine of domesticity – Izzy and Jake went to school, she had time on her hands to cook or to garden, and to just spend some quiet moments with herself, at home. May had produced some beautiful sunny days. The azaleas were blooming in the garden, the wisteria was fluttering next to the kitchen windows and she was discovering that she actually liked weeding, pruning, digging over the rich soil, she loved the silence, the therapy of tending to a patch of soil and standing back and looking at her work, watching it grow. Perhaps James was right. Time on her own had been healing.

Lulu was due back in two days. She'd been at their Dad's for nearly a month. Last time Victoria had spoken to her on the phone she sounded brighter, she said she was ready to come home and 'face the music' and follow her dream, whatever that meant, but Victoria hadn't pushed her. She was just glad she was in a more positive mindset. She'd also told Victoria that she had really cut down on her drinking. Said she just didn't need it there. That she felt happier and more positive – and that she'd agreed to some kind of counselling, but would tell Victoria more about that later. Oh, and that all her jeans were too tight because she and Dad had been 'treating' themselves to home baking almost every day. Victoria laughed at that bit. She was glad Lulu was looking after herself.

It was Saturday afternoon and Victoria was sitting at the kitchen table in her grey leggings covered in soil, her gardening trousers, a floppy hat and a dirty blue V-neck T-shirt. She was flicking through emails on her laptop, catching up with admin, when an email from Izzy's school caught her eye. She had just spent two hours weeding a small patch under the lilac tree at the front of the house. Jake and Izzy were playing tennis, she could hear the thwack of the ball every now and again. It didn't cease to amaze her that they had a tennis court still, it just seemed so *unlike* her, them. A tennis court built by the New Victoria – someone she very much wanted to distance herself from.

Thinking of distance, her eyes flicked to her phone to see if there were any new messages. She and James were still skating around on polite ice, there had been little more than communication on text about arrangements for the kids. The connection she had felt in the hospital car park had gone for the time being. Some texts were meant for her, where he asked if she was feeling alright. He just wanted facts, not an emotional outpouring, she could tell. There had been no more mention of the divorce. She held her breath every time a message came through in case it was about that. She could hear Jake and Izzy speaking to him almost daily; she heard laughter in the bedroom at night, listened as they joked with him as she went past the corridor, and she tried not to mind. They'd emerge later and say things like 'Dad says hi and you need to make sure you double-lock the French doors' or 'Dad says don't forget the car needs its MOT tomorrow'. Domesticity without the intimacy. But she'd take that for now.

He was due any minute to pick up some things and take the kids out. They were being very *civil*. But despite the civility, there *had* been a few tiny step-changes. She replayed them in her mind: hovering on the doorstep just a fraction longer than he normally would when he dropped off the kids, noticing that she'd had her hair cut – *'looks great'* – her handing him homemade chutney when he last dropped the kids off from school. She felt that a piece of the twining in their relationship that had been pulled taut was being teased out a little. She jumped up, dashed upstairs to change her T-shirt, wash her hands and put on a smear of lip-gloss.

As she was coming down the stairs she could hear the car on the gravel. Registering a small flutter in her belly, she walked back into the kitchen and moved the rack of newly baked brownies to one side of the kitchen table. She heard keys in the lock – he usually knocked and waited by the door. Then suddenly he was in front of her, standing in the kitchen. 'Hey.'

'Hi, James.' She forced herself not to fling her arms around him and instead clutched the edges of the kitchen counter.

'You look different,' he said. She tilted her head to one side and looked at him. 'Messy,' he lifted an eyebrow. 'Suits you.'

She walked past him towards the kettle. He smelt slightly different – of shower gel, like limes. 'Want coffee?'

He glanced at her and at the cafetière and nodded; his eyes scanned the kitchen. 'Where's the machine?'

'Gone. To a charity shop. I expect some uptight bitch with nothing better to do than whine about coffee will have snapped it up.'

He held her eye for a split second; there was the beginnings of a smile around his lips, then he carried on rummaging through a pile of post. She came over with the coffee and two mugs. She moved the rack of warm brownies between them. He picked one up and bit into it at the same time as she did. It was gooey and warm and her best yet. She stole a look at James in his crumpled polo shirt as he wiped his mouth.

'These are good,' he said brushing icing sugar off his jeans.

She moved her laptop to one side. 'Well, they're not fat-free anyway. Can you imagine? Tell me, did you used to compliment my cooking?'

His lips twitched. 'I did, as a matter of fact.' He nodded to her laptop. 'What have you been looking at?' They had forged a small step forward, surely? He was *in the house*. She wanted to celebrate. In fact, what she really wanted to do was to grab his reading glasses from the top of his head, put them on upside down, make a funny face, the way she used to do, and say, 'And now for the ten o'clock news!' in a mock-serious voice to make him smile. Instead, she kept her hands clasped together and looked back down at the screen, then up at him.

'A fun mini-duathlon, for the anti-bullying campaign at Izzy's school.'

He moved the screen to read it. 'Really?'

'Yes. Perhaps – I was, er, maybe…' Where was she going

with this? She wasn't really sure, but he seemed interested. 'It might be a nice gesture for Izzy, to um, to, you know, do it,' she blurted out before she had time to think. 'What do you think?'

'What, together? I think that's the sort of thing the old Vicky would do,' he met her gaze and bit into another brownie.

The gauntlet had been thrown down. Not only would this be good for Izzy to see, it would mean she could spend some time alone with James. Do something on his terms, duathlons were certainly not something she'd normally do, for lots of reasons. 'The old Vicky?' she said calmly. 'She's right here. Let's do it.'

He stopped chewing mid-bite. 'You want us to do it? Seriously?' he said.

She nodded.

'Wouldn't you, you know, chip a nail or something?' He stared at her, deadpan.

'I'm willing to risk it.'

His eyes darted to her quickly, then back to the brownie between his fingers. 'OK then. What are the distances?' he said, licking his fingers.

She pulled her laptop towards her. *What had she said?* Blood rushed to her ears as she started to scroll. She hated swimming, ever since the – well, it was a bit hazy. Anyway, she would worry about that later. Her stomach was flipping around as if a million butterflies were trying to escape. She put down her brownie, she suddenly wasn't hungry. She peered at the screen. 'It's a 3k run in the woods round the school, followed by a two-hundred-metre swim.' She gulped. Last time she looked, she could barely run for three minutes when she'd been chasing after Pickle. Even though the New Victoria seemed to be toned, it was more down to bendy-type

Pilates classes and very upholstered gym wear. And what about her new 'enhancements' – how could she run with those? James would be fine – he'd won third place in the Sussex Sevens, after all, and although that was years ago, he still went to the gym, often boasting about how far he'd run on the treadmill, competing with colleagues.

Just then Izzy and Jake flew in the back door, Izzy trying to whack Jake with her tennis racket. 'Stop it, you loser! You're just pissed off coz I won! Hey, Dad!' and with that she flew at James, who got up and held his arms out for her as she tumbled into an embrace with him. Vicky chewed her lip; witnessing such a tender moment, she nearly started to cry.

'Whoa! Steady, Venus! How are you?' he said, kissing the top of her head, then gently put some hair behind her ears. For once it hadn't been locked into a plait and was falling about her shoulders.

'I just won at tennis!'

'You so *cheated*!' Jake stood with his hands on his hips.

'Sore loser.'

'Hey, Dad.' Jake stood awkwardly in the doorway.

'Jake! Come here and give me a hug!'

He was over in a shot, and then, somehow as Victoria cleared away the coffee cups and stood with her back to the sink watching them, Jake and James were play-wrestling on the floor. *This is what I want.* She wandered over to them. 'Careful, he's only sixteen!'

'Yeah, with muscles,' mumbled James from under Jake's arm.

Izzy was sitting at the table. She'd poured out two orange juices and pushed a glass over to Jake. 'Hey, loser brother, here's some juice.' She grinned. 'C'mon. Truce?' Picking up her glass, she nodded at Victoria's laptop. 'Mum, what's this?

You doing this anti-bullying thing? Melanie was talking about it at school.'

Melanie was one of Izzy's new friends. She was a sweet girl, Victoria had met her on a few occasions, and they had had her round for a sleepover. That was exhausting. The girls had stayed up till 4 a.m. chatting, even when Victoria banged on the wall. But she was happy to encourage the friendship. Melanie's skills were being able to find Domino's pizza offers where others failed, and she was not into competitive one-upmanship the way Bella had been.

'Maybe. Possibly with your dad.' She held her breath.

James and Jake stopped wrestling on the floor.

'What about the swimming?' Izzy said, screwing her eyes up at Victoria. 'You sure, Mum? What about—'

Victoria nodded vigorously. 'I'll be fine.' There was a memory lodged somewhere that was niggling her.

James sat down and drained his coffee cup, then placed it back on the table. 'I could ask work if they'll sponsor us – they should donate a reasonable amount.'

Us.

Victoria stared at James's mug. It lived at the back of the cupboard and was slightly chipped but she couldn't bear to throw it out. Here was a memory she *did* remember. Jake had decorated it at one of those Pottery Café's when he'd been about four. It was for Father's Day and Jake had decreed that 'Daddy likes dinosaurs'. The mug had been plastered in sponge imprints of various dinosaurs with 'Happy Father's Day' written in very wobbly letters across the base. He took a deep breath. 'I'm in,' announced James. 'If we both get some sponsorship then we could raise some decent money for the school's anti-bullying campaign. I think that's important. What do you think Izzy?'

'Cool,' she said, smiling. 'Me and Jake will watch, won't we?'

Jake stuffed two brownies into his mouth at the same time and nodded vigorously, then wiped his mouth with the back of his hand.

'Right,' said James, scraping his chair back, then he turned to Victoria. 'Tomorrow at 7 a.m.? At the school running track?' he said breezily, heading for the kitchen door. 'I'd warm up a bit first.' She nodded, too overwhelmed to say anything. Was this a *date*?

'Let's go, you two,' James shouted to the twins, holding onto the kitchen door handle. And then it was a flurry of phone-grabbing and hoodie-finding as they headed off with James to find yet more pizza. After the din of banging doors, shouts of 'where are my other trainers?' and the crunch of tyres on gravel, the kitchen fell silent, leaving Victoria alone with her thoughts.

40 LULU

'How could you, Louise, Lulu – whatever bloody name you want to be called?' Simon's running his hands through his hair and scowling at me. We're in his kitchen. He's leaning against the sink. He looks pasty and his eyes are red. He is scratching his hands intermittently, probably the eczema has flared up. I feel a stab of guilt. He told me once, it does that when he's stressed. I'm sitting at the stainless-steel table. There's a wooden planter on the table housing a raspberry-pink hyacinth with fluffy green moss spread out over the base. The perfume is pungent and heady and it's making me feel queasy. Sun streams in from the enormous Victorian sash windows, across the table, and the ruby in my engagement ring sparkles.

The ring is sitting next to the hyacinth.

I feel exasperated. But it's not his fault. How can he know what's going on in my mind if I haven't even told him? If I haven't even admitted it to myself yet?

I didn't want to face Simon but knew I had to. I spent a lot of time on the train journey back here chewing it all over and knew he needed a decent explanation. We'd been corresponding by short messages. He asked about Izzy. Then he sent me a curt message when I was at Dad's saying that he'd packed up my few things that I had at his place – my toothbrush, a few dressing gowns and my favourite mug ('the lumpy one'; it's one which Izzy made me at nursery, which he's always hated) – and put everything in a box and said he'd appreciate it if I could collect them. As I stood on the porch a moment ago, I studied the box lying out in the cold. Our relationship, reduced to a cardboard box.

'Look, Simon, it's all my fault.'

'You're damn right it's all your fault.'

I pick up the ring and then put it back down again. 'Sorry.'

He spins round, walks toward the kettle and flicks it on angrily. Now he's slamming two cups down on the kitchen surface. 'My mother is beside herself.'

I grimace. 'I'm really, really sorry.' And I am, I am sorry for the hurt I've caused. 'I'll pay for my half of the wedding, I swear.'

Simon turns to face me; his cheeks are pink and the redness has reached the tip of his ears. He pulls his shoulders back. 'It's not about the money, Lulu. I mean, I thought we were going to spend our lives together, I had it all planned out.'

'But that's just the problem, Simon.'

He glares at me, lips pursed.

'The planning, *your* planning—' I continue.

'But I thought you liked that, you told me you didn't know who you were anymore and that you liked the security I brought. Those were your words.'

I bite my lip. Had I said all that? Maybe I'd said it when I was drunk, hiding from the truth. I don't know. I suppose some of it is true. 'I did want security, I *do* want a plan, Simon. But maybe not always *your* plan.' I don't expand. How can I tell him it's just that I don't want that plan to be with *him*? 'I had lost my way, that's true. But I don't feel so lost anymore. I've done a lot of thinking up at my dad's, it's cleared my head a bit. I've spent hours on the Dales with Pickle on long walks just chewing things over. How much I was drinking, my future, I want to sort it all out.'

He puts his arms out and leans backwards on the kitchen counter, and tilts his head back, as if he's summing me up. 'Well, good for you. I wish you'd done your thinking *before* you agreed to marry me.'

It's a fair point.

'Do you know how mortified I was, standing there in the chapel?'

I meet his eye. 'Listen, could you sit down? There's something I need to explain, something that should hopefully make you understand – well, everything,' I say softly. He brings the coffee over and sits down opposite me, arms folded. I need to tell him about *it*. About how I want to get over it and get back on stage and prove to everyone that I can do it, and about how I've come to be so messed up and why the safety net of marriage made sense – but my rehearsed explanation is cut short.

'It's all *me, me, me*, isn't it, with you?' he says pulling back his chair. He folds his legs over each other and sighs. 'Do you ever think about anyone else? Good God. Anyone would think that you'd had the memory issues, that *you'd* lost your mind, not your sister.'

I'm speechless. I'd planned to tell him everything, to make him understand, but I just can't. I look out the window and can just make out a foal in the fields in the distance, huddled close to its mum. My throat catches.

'And what about Markie?' He says his name as if it's poison.

I shrug. 'He's with someone else, so Victoria tells me.'

'Lost your chance there, didn't you?'

In all the months I've known Simon, and despite the fact that I truly deserve the blame for what's happened, I have never put him down as spiteful. My mouth falls open. I look at him sitting across from me in an ironed shirt, gold cufflinks shining and I look at his mouth twisting and turning with words of hate for me, and I notice how beady his eyes are and that they're staring right at me. A tiny bit of spit escapes from his mouth as he's talking. 'Are you listening?'

'My mother warned me, you know,' he says flicking some imaginary dust off the table with his hand and his cufflinks clink on the surface. 'Said I could do better than you. What did she say? Oh yes, said you were the flighty type. "Cheap", I think she said when she first met you.' He pauses. 'And I defended you. Shouldn't have bothered.'

I wipe my cheeks with the back of my hand. I know he's hurt, but I can't explain anything to him now. It's not worth it. How can I empty out my soul into this sea of hatred? 'I needed some space,' I say instead. 'Need to figure things out.' That much, at least, is true.

'You can have all the space you want, Lulu. Now get out.' He pushes his chair back as if he's about to get up, ready for battle. But he doesn't deserve to know the truth. And with that last comment, I slide the ring across the table towards him, stand up and leave.

41 VICTORIA

God, it was *freezing*. It might have been May, but at seven in the morning Victoria pulled her fleece down over her bum and stamped her feet to keep warm. She was standing on the edge of the school's running track. How she had managed to drag herself away from under her warm duvet on a Sunday morning was anybody's guess. She rubbed her hands together and waited as James fiddled with his GoFit watch. Didn't the God of Sunday say it belonged to either lazy sex – no hope there – lounging around in PJs, or reading the papers in bed with a croissant and decent coffee?

'Right. We'll calculate how long it takes you to run a lap, then we can see how much progress you need to make so you can keep up with me on the actual run.'

'I'll be fine,' she said indignantly.

'Let's start slowly – OK? You don't want to do too much too soon. Especially in your condition.'

My condition? A little voice told her that James was just being practical in light of her ribs, but another, more competitive one, the one that wanted to get back to normal, was saying: *you can do this*. James took off round the track. She started to shuffle slowly. She was halfway round the first half lap and she was taking deep lungfuls of air. Good God, this was hard. Her breath clouded around her face in the freezing air and when she breathed in, the cold air was sharp in her throat making her cough. She kept putting one foot in front of the other, even though her legs were beginning to hurt, and her tits were killing her – despite the two sports bras she'd worn. Just a few more paces to go. There! She'd done it. James was waiting for her with his hands on his hips. He glanced at his watch.

'Well done. Ready for the next lap?' *Next* lap?

She nodded because she couldn't actually speak. Then she gulped some air. 'OK! How many laps are we doing today?'

'Just five – so one kilometre. It's a third of what we have to do on the day.'

A third? Vicky didn't think she could do one more lap, never mind five. What on earth had she been thinking? But she *had* to do it, to prove to Izzy – to James, but, especially, to herself that she could. And she was with him. They were *together*.

James had already started off, jogging at quite a pace. There was no way she was going to catch up with him, at one point he seemed to be racing round a corner. For goodness' sake! Then he slowed down, sped up again. When he got to the finish line he looked back at her and grinned. He *was* watching her suffer, but it was a grin nonetheless.

'Alright?' He bent over with one leg stretched out in front of him, stretching his hamstrings, as she panted towards the white line.

She rested her hands on her kneecaps and inhaled the cold air. In and out. Steady. Finally, she raised her head up, sweat building on her forehead despite the chilly morning. 'Yup. I'm alright,' she managed, standing straighter now. 'Again?' Where had those words come from? She must be insane.

'Fine. I think you should just do a fast walk this time – OK?'

She glared at him, then gave a brief nod. He was off, jogging in front of her. She glanced at his broad back, at him effortlessly pounding along the rusty-coloured running track and swore under her breath. It was easy for him. Do this for Izzy, she reminded herself. She kept going, striding this time, reminding herself to breathe. Keep going. All that mattered was that she finished this lap, she'd suggested it after all. Her lower back was aching, her chest tight, but she took a long inhale in, then out, kept on walking briskly to the finish line.

'Not bad.' James stood, not a drop of sweat on him. 'Why don't you sit down,' he carried on gently. He nodded to a bench by the pavilion. 'Looks like you could do with a break.' She screwed up her eyes. The sun was glinting across the dewy grass and she could just make out a wooden bench in the distance. 'I'll keep going; I won't be long,' he said, holding his hand up to shield his eyes from the sun. Then, he crossed over his arms and yanked off his outer running top. She caught a glimpse of his firm torso, it was so normal, yet so intimate. She looked away.

'Vicky?' He was staring straight at her. She caught his eye and smiled at him, but he just nodded and set off. He was running faster now, without her, following the white lines, his tall, athletic body making it look easy, striding purposefully along the track. It took her back to that video, watching him with the twins when they were tiny. *Her James.* She sat down on the grass and hugged her knees to her chest, listening to the sound of birdsong and took in the sweet smell of newly cut grass.

———

'I think we did OK out there.' Victoria was sitting next to James in his car, in the queue for the carwash. James had handed her a coffee. 'That's a proper one,' he'd said. 'No soy muck.' And grinned. It had been his idea to head here after the run. She had other ideas about how to spend the rest of Sunday morning, and it hadn't involved mechanical car cleaning, but she didn't protest. She stole a glance at him. His muscular legs were encased in running shorts, the smell of sweat mixed with his aftershave mingling in the air. *His* smell. She imagined reaching out squeezing his thigh. *No, Vicky, that won't do*, a voice said.

James was humming as they inched forward towards the mouth of the carwash, keeping the car within the metal parallel lines. She always found it so hard to do that; once, she'd actually got out of the car to check that she was within the lines and the machine had actually *started*. She'd been soaked. Now, the fluffy black brushes whooshed towards them, swallowing them up like the mouth of a hungry hairy caterpillar. She laughed out loud.

'What?'

'Oh, nothing. I'm just imagining that we're being swallowed by a huge prehistoric caterpillar.'

James looked across at her, his eyebrows knitted together. 'Been watching Jurassic Park again? I think that you need to go back for another MRI scan!' Then he glanced at her. 'Sorry, God sorry, Vicky, it was a joke, I didn't mean—'

'It's alright, it's alright. This keeps happening, one minute

I'm fine, next I can't remember things and next, I'm gabbling about caterpillars.'

'Patience, remember, that's what the consultant said.' He took a sip of his coffee, then placed it on the dashboard; steam rose from it and spread across the windscreen.

'I know, but—' she faltered. 'I can't help thinking about how things were, six years ago, I mean, when I woke up in hospital, from the crash, it *felt* like it was six years ago, to me, anyway – and yet so much has changed.'

'We've been through this, Vicky.'

'I know, but I was so hopeful in hospital. I was so perplexed why you didn't come running to my side.' She glanced over at him but he was looking the other way. 'Why did we let it change, James? What went wrong?' She stared at the soap bubbles on the windscreen, the mist on the inside and listened to the clatter of the brushes beating at the car.

'Life just got in the way. We let things slip.' He let out a long breath. 'We lost sight of each other, I think. You put the twins first,' he carried on, 'over our marriage sometimes. I put my work first and I was away a lot. When I got back home, though, I felt like I was just another place setting at the table, Vicky. You never really asked how I *was*. I know it was hard, but you forgot I was a person, a man, your husband. The one you used to write notes to in his lunchbox – remember?'

Of *course* she remembered that memory, and she was so glad he did too. 'I do remember that, but maybe, well, maybe I forgot some things James.'

'Like me,' he whispered.

'And *I* felt the same, James. Forgotten.'

They fell silent.

'And then of course – you know,' he picked up his cup

and took a sip as the foam from the brushes obliterated the view from the side windows.

'The baby.'

'Yes.'

'Do you blame me?'

'Victoria. How can I *blame* you?' He moved his arm, and for a split second Victoria thought he was going to hold her hand.

'I mean for even trying to have another baby. For, I don't know, what it did to us. I can remember bits, some bits before and then the tears, the—' She had wanted to say 'your coldness' but she didn't want to spoil this cocoon. It wasn't exactly romantic, sitting in the car with a coffee – but at least they were alone. Because even if he'd taken her home, there would have been a work call interrupting them, or Izzy breezing in wondering where she'd left her make-up or Jake barging in to ask if he could order pizza, like *now*. She absent-mindedly drew a heart shape on the mist on the inside of her window with her finger.

'I remember feeling guilty that I wanted another one, we already had two, but that longing was there.'

James looked over at her but said nothing for a while.

'Me too – I mean about the longing,' he finally said. He took a gulp of coffee, placed the lid back on it and clamped it firmly in the cup holder. 'We both wanted another one, Vicky. It was when the twins were about nine, Lulu had them for the weekend so we could get away – remember? Anyway, we went to the Lake District – we walked, went to some cosy pubs, we talked, we stayed in that dreadful hotel with the creaky floorboards,' he laughed, '—remember, the Windermere Inn? That's when we decided to try for another baby, over dinner that night – in fact, you said she was conceived that evening.' He looked at her from under his eyelashes.

She did have a bit of a memory of that night, creaky floorboards, creaky bed; it was only a tiny double bed she remembered. Far too small for James's long legs. 'Didn't your feet stick out the end of the bed?'

He nodded. 'Yup.'

'And the duvet cover – revolting yellow – right?'

'You said it reminded you of snot.'

'But afterwards,' she carried on, 'I mean, after we lost the baby, I have flashes of memory, it wasn't a good time, was it?'

He let out a breath. 'No. We both withdrew into ourselves, really and that's exactly when my job became more demanding, several bids were accepted at once, I was away, it was the perfect storm, really. You and the kids seemed to cope without me, it was, I don't know, as if you didn't need me. You became unreachable.' He shrugged. Bubbles of soap were smeared across the windscreen. It felt oddly intimate, enclosed in the warm air of the car. 'But maybe I should have tried harder. I didn't appreciate how much you were hurting. I mean, if I was feeling wretched, God alone knows what you would have felt, after what you went through in hospital.' She peeked over at him, but he was looking out of his window the other way. Then he turned to her. 'When the twins were young and needy, it all seemed fine,' he looked up to the roof of the car, as if for inspiration, 'I mean we had a purpose, both of us, you had your role as a mother, I was working, then we were trying for another baby – that was a purpose too – but after the miscarriage, we let weeks slip into months, we didn't talk – I mean properly talk – and I'd come home at the weekend and feel like a stranger in my own home.'

'I was on anti-depressants, James.'

He nodded silently. 'I didn't realise the impact on you. I suppose we both needed each other but just didn't say.'

The noise of the brushes buffeting the back of the car filled the space between them. James said nothing, but sat staring out the window.

'I didn't help by distracting myself with my appearance, did I?' she offered. 'But, you know, I can only imagine I was doing it for you – to make you appreciate me.'

'And games on your phone?' He turned to look at her and was smiling. 'Look, I did appreciate you, Vicky, but you changed. You were—'

'Grieving.'

'Do you think about her?'

'Of course I do. Some parts are so clear now. Bits and pieces have come back since I found that pink ribbon, like how we decorated the nursery, the butterfly mobile, how excited we were that we'd be a family of five. Choosing names… you liked, was it Amelia? I was stuck on Ashley.' She glanced at him. 'Did we never get beyond A in the baby books?'

James smiled briefly then scratched his cheek. 'We spent ages looking at those books in bed at night. We felt like it was a gift. You were sure you wouldn't get pregnant again. But then after, I don't know. I lost you.'

'We both lost each other.'

A thousand thoughts flitted across her brain, half-formed memories and flashes of images from the past. The nursery, the tiny pink blankets with white embroidery she'd allowed herself to buy. The aching feeling after the hospital. She couldn't remember the hospital, somehow that was still blank, but she remembered the grief, the loneliness. Looking after the twins when they still needed her. Pushing it all from her brain. Telling everyone she was fine; always a smile and a cheery 'OK' when in fact she was crying inside; those fragments were coming back.

She was feeling light-headed. She gripped her seat and dug her nails into the soft leather. The rollers were coming back down over the windscreen, whirring and beating on the glass, *thwack, thwack, thwack,* and it was then that Vicky's heart started to race. A scene flashed across her frontal lobe, the headlights, the scraping metal noise and suddenly she was back there with the thundering sound, the brushes blurring the windscreen, the drumming in her head, her breathing sharp, her chest constricted, moisture on her upper lip. It was like being sucked into a vortex of panic, things were blurring and she kept seeing the pink ribbon flash through her mind, then the bright lights of the accident, the smoke on the bonnet. She looked at the brushes rolling up towards her, faster, louder – gaining speed, coming right at her. She started to shiver uncontrollably.

His hand was on her cheek, pulling her face towards him. 'Vicky, Victoria, are you alright? You're burning up.'

'No.' She shook her head. 'No, the noise, the accident. I—'

'Let's get out of here.' Just then, James started the engine, pressed his foot on the accelerator, even though the brushes were still on the roof, and sped out of the carwash. Vicky glanced to the left to see one of the attendants on the forecourt waving his fist at them. If she didn't know better, she'd think James actually *cared*.

___

He was crouched on the floor when she came in.

'James?'

He looked up at her, and wiped his eyes. His hair was dishevelled, like he'd been tugging at it; it was sticking up on one side.

'Alright?' She smiled at him and then knelt on the floor and sat next to him as if he were an animal she didn't want to frighten. He uncurled his legs and stretched them out and leant on the wall. He smelt of sandalwood and pencil shavings as she sat next to him, their legs side by side.

'How are you feeling?' he said gently.

'Better.'

'You've been asleep for ages. I asked Izzy to check on you.'

She nodded and touched his knee lightly. 'What are you doing?'

'Oh, I thought I'd wait to see how you were. I, well, I was just looking for some of my stuff to take away with me from under the desk and I came across this.' He smiled thinly. He was holding onto a small DVD case with a silver DVD in it. He handed it to her.

'What is it?'

He opened up the box and took out the DVD to show her and turned it around in his hand, holding it between his thumb and index finger; it glistened in the sun's rays. He handed it to her. There was purple swirly writing on the disc.

❤ James & Vicky. September 2001. ❤

Tiny purple hearts were next to their names.

'Our wedding DVD?' she whispered.

He nodded.

'Have you watched it?'

'Not yet.' His voice was hoarse.

'Shall we have a look? It might – you know— It might help.' She eyed him sideways to see how he'd take it. She could see the beginnings of a five o'clock shadow across his jaw and she longed to stretch out her hand and touch his skin, feel the roughness of his cheek against the back of her hand. In fact, what she really wanted to do was to curl up and lay her head on his lap and let him tell her a story, transport her out of this pain, be the couple they used to be again.

He took the DVD from her. His hands were trembling. 'OK,' he said softly. Then he knelt up and grabbed his laptop and put it on his knee. As he opened the little drawer for the DVD, Victoria felt slightly short of breath. She put her hand to her forehead and tucked some hair behind her ear. The air in the room had turned heavy. It was about six o'clock, a beautiful sunset was spreading its golden fingers across the treetops; birds were chirruping their evening song outside. A thin ray of light was reflected on the screen and then – suddenly – there they were. She was laughing and throwing her hands in the air – a moment, no – a lifetime ago – captured on a silver disc. They looked joyous. She was throwing her bouquet in the air; a cheer as someone caught it – Lulu! She looked radiant in a lilac dress with a halo of daisies resting on her long blonde curls like a Glastonbury babe. More laughter, the video showed the guests following James and Vicky, like the pied piper, and a sea of well-wishers were gathered behind them, the cathedral providing a stunning backdrop.

'Where's that?'

He cocked his head to one side and seemed to be summing her up. 'Winchester Cathedral.'

'We were married *there*?'

James's eyes widened at her as he smiled and nodded. 'We were. It was a magical day.'

She took in the majestic buttresses of the stone cathedral behind them, the guests milling around, a swarm of pastel-coloured dots as the camera angle had now switched to a higher vantage point. Silk shining in the sun, confetti nestled in up-dos and on men's shoulders as if the heavens had opened and showered multi-coloured rain on everyone.

'You looked—' James nodded at the screen. 'Stunning.'

He was blinking rapidly. She desperately wanted to reach out and touch his hand but she daren't break the flimsy connection in the oddly intimate moment, sitting side by side on the floor.

Memories faded and then returned as she studied the two of them holding hands. It was like watching a movie, and yet – it was real, too. James spinning her round, then standing under a stone arch, the perfect backdrop – that's where the picture in the lounge had been taken, she realised now – and he pulled her tight towards him, hands on her waist, and kissed her fully on the lips.

'We were happy,' he murmured, pressing 'Pause' on the screen.

She pulled the fabric of her top down and smoothed it over her legs. The hum of a distant lawnmower was the only sound for a while. They sat surrounded by their thoughts and breathing as the sun slid further behind the trees, its rays flickering over the oak tree, casting shadows through the window. She pulled her mohair cardigan tight around her. James closed the lid of the laptop, lifted it onto the chair and knelt on one knee to stand. Stretching his arms above his head, he looked down at her. Then, slowly, he extended his hand to her, offering his help for her to get up. She took it. It was the first time they had properly touched since she came back from hospital. His grip was warm and he wrapped his fingers around hers as he pulled her up to standing, then suddenly they were face to face. The urge to touch him was overwhelming *and* his hair was still sticking out.

'I'd better go,' he said, smiling as he squeezed past her towards the door.

42 VICTORIA

'You had a panic attack in a carwash?'

'Well, yes. No. I mean yes, Lulu, it was awful. But then, actually, James was so sweet.' Victoria switched the phone to her other ear and told Lulu what happened. But not the bit about after he left. That that one sound of the door clicking shut had elicited a thousand emotions in her.

'Vicky, you OK?'

'Yes, I'm fine now.' And she was. She had slept so much better the past two nights. It was as if she and James had crossed some invisible bridge.

'Well, actually my legs are *killing* me, I could hardly sit down earlier, but it was worth it.'

'I can't believe you two went *running*. By the way are you sure you should have been running? Did you check with the doctor?'

'Yes. No. I lied, I told him it was a charity *walk*.'

'*Vicky!*'

'Oh, don't worry, I probably *will* walk some of it anyway. Look, I need to do this for James, for us, for *Izzy*. Listen, I wanted to ask if you'd be up for running with me? Just a bit – today, to get some fresh air, and – well, I've got to get all the practice I can get.' She cleared her throat. 'Please?'

She heard Lulu let out a long whistle. 'Good work, sis.'

'He hasn't even moved *back* yet, Lulu but—'

'Progress, right?'

'Yeah, I think so. Anyway you've been cooped up at home since you spoke to Simon. If I didn't know better I'd say you were hiding from something – or some*one*,' she said pointedly. 'See you at the rec. Twenty minutes.'

'What like twenty minutes, *twenty minutes*?'

'Don't be late,' chirped Vicky and then she hung up.

———

'You're, running, again, Mum? As in jogging? But you can't even walk properly after the last time.'

Victoria was crouching down in the hall, adjusting her shoelaces. She stood up and put a hand on her lower back. 'Ow. Well, no, you're right, but I need to keep practising.' She pulled her ponytail tight then winced as a pain shot through her backside.

'Didn't think you were serious. I thought it would be one run and it'd be all over.' Izzy did her 'fish-eyes' as Jake called them, where they bulged out as she opened her eyes wide. For such a pretty girl, it made her look like a fly.

Victoria stared at her daughter. Those teenage hormones must be pretty potent. She really, *really* wanted to support Izzy through all this anti-bullying, but, at this very moment, she could hit her. 'Yes, Izzy. I am. Three kilometres, in fact, and then swim. To raise money for *your* school, to help *you*. With your dad, OK?'

Izzy jutted her chin out and shifted her weight to her

other hip, her crop top revealing a slice of brown midriff. 'Yeah, well, I didn't ask you to.'

'I know you didn't. We want to do it. And I'm meeting Aunty Lu today, it's a park run.'

'Whatever.' Izzy rolled her eyes. 'Just make sure you wear a decent bra,' she said, glancing at Victoria's bust.

Victoria's mouth fell open as a hundred retorts zoomed across her brain. She was amazed all these sarcastic slogans were still lying dormant in her consciousness, waiting to be used. Where had they come from? But no, she wouldn't say anything. Izzy was just finding it tough, she reminded herself. Since the Heath Farm incident they had discussed moving schools, but Izzy was insistent on staying. 'I don't want Bella to think she's won,' she'd said. 'And anyway, she doesn't talk to me now.' And, of course, she had a new circle of friends, including Melanie. The feisty girl who was on her guard the whole time was slowly being replaced by a newer, softer Izzy. Her grades were improving and she was no longer wearing quite so much make-up. 'It's her mask,' she'd told James. 'She can't face the world without it, or so she thinks.' There had been less make-up, more Izzy.

Victoria suddenly had an idea. She marched towards the hall table where the little basket of keys lived and grabbed the car keys. 'You know what, why don't you come with me, too? It would be good for Aunty Lu to see you,' she said, dangling the keys on her finger.

'What, like, and run?'

'Yes. Come on. You haven't seen Aunty Lu for weeks. She could do with some cheering up. Look, it's just a park run, like I said, three kilometres, nothing too strenuous. We can walk a lot of it. Be good for you,' she said, then quickly added: 'For us. To have some time together.' She smiled at her daughter. She badly wanted to do this, to prove that she could do this for Izzy, for James, and well, for herself. It was important for her to show Izzy that she was taking it seriously, that she wanted to support her not just with seeing the teachers at school, not just with talking her through and actually implementing the online bullying guide, and not just with getting her to go to the school counsellor, but to run, to raise money, to show her that *Mum was present*. She wasn't on her phone, distracted. Even if Izzy couldn't see it at the moment.

Izzy hesitated at first and put her hand on the banisters as if to go upstairs, not looking at her mother. Victoria was sure she would shrug and walk up the stairs, but instead she turned round. 'OK then. I'll come. Give me a minute to get my stuff on.' And with that, she bounded up the stairs.

Half an hour later they were pulling into the small car park next to the field that had become the starting point for Little Norland's Park Run. The weather was warm, with a cool breeze blowing. The sky was a milky blue and she could see a kite soaring above in the sky, gliding on the thermals. She looked at all the other runners lining up, chatting and joking, and searched for Lulu. It was the first time she'd seen her since she'd been home to Dad's in Yorkshire. They'd texted and had a FaceTime call – especially after the Simon incident, but Victoria knew she'd wanted to chill on her own in her flat. Time to get her head straight. She spotted her standing by the fence in stretchy purple leggings and an orange running top. She had to hand it to Lulu, she certainly got into the role when she'd made up her mind. She waved at her and went jogging over.

'Hi!' She gave her a big hug and then stood back. 'You look great!' And she did. She'd put on a little weight, her cheeks had filled out and her complexion was glowing. The fresh air of the Dales seemed to have done her a world of good.

The officials in high-vis jackets were dotted about the field, directing people about where to stand. There was a carnival sort of atmosphere about. They were due to start at 10 a.m. Victoria really needed to get this distance under her belt to know she could do it. Last week she had managed to do two kilometres running and walking. She was building up to three. As for the swimming – well, she'd be fine, surely? Breathe in slowly… then out. She knew she was a strong swimmer. But since the car accident, she'd been having these terrible nightmares about being underwater, looking for things in underwater caves and not being able to speak, she'd open her mouth and no sound would come out. She'd usually wake up and reach over for James, forgetting he wasn't there. And she'd tremble, alone, reliving the nightmare without anyone there to put their arm around her. She picked up the pace because that was easier than letting her mind dwell on anything else.

'Hey, slow down!' Izzy was panting by her side.

Victoria laughed. 'C'mon slowcoach!' She nudged her in the ribs and saw Izzy shake her head and roll her eyes at Lulu. 'Mum's now, like some personal trainer.' And the three of them laughed as they set off up quite a steep hill. It felt good to laugh together, to be outside enjoying the fresh air and smile at the other runners, feeling a sense of achievement with Lulu and Izzy.

After a while, Izzy broke into a fast walk. 'You two go on, see you at the bottom,' she puffed, then picked her way through the runners as she walked back down the hill. Victoria and Lulu carried on. Lulu had always been super-fit. It came with the territory of being twelve years younger – and she'd been pounding the Dales at Dad's as well. Sweat built up on Victoria's forehead, but she kept up with Lulu and ran the last loop steadily to the top of the hill. They were close to the finish line and she could see Izzy standing by an official, waving at them.

———

Half an hour later, the three of them were sitting on the grass on a picnic rug Victoria had found in her boot. Astonishing, she'd thought, hauling it out and shaking it, how New Victoria got so organized. They were sitting in the sun enjoying iced coffee from the pop-up coffee shack in the field. Children were running around with ice creams, dogs were barking, the noise of a lawnmower in the distance – the atmosphere was relaxed. Victoria wondered why on earth she hadn't done this with Izzy or Lulu before. It was right on her doorstep.

'Look!' shouted Izzy, and they all turned to stare as Markie's brightly coloured van pulled up in the car park and Markie swung open his door. He started to walk then hung back a bit. 'Hey! It's Markie, maybe he can sit with us? I wonder what—'

'Shh, Izzy. I don't want to see him.' Lulu pulled up her hoodie top and yanked it over her face.

'Don't you? Why not?'

'Not really. I'm embarrassed. I got hammered at my own wedding, ran down the aisle. I mean, he's messaged me, a bit,' and her face lit up suddenly, 'he's sent me a couple of emails, work stuff, but – never mind.' She glanced over at where Markie was walking side by side with a woman with long blonde hair and shifted her position. Then she sat with her legs underneath her, frowning.

'Oh look! He's with someone! God, she's fit!' Izzy peered over at Markie and his companion.

Lulu slid down and was nearly lying on the rug. 'Hmm,' came the mumbled response from Lulu.

'Hey Aunty Lu,' said Izzy taking a huge slurp of her coffee through a straw. 'What happened, anyway? That day. I mean, I never really asked you properly? You nearly got married, I mean… *Really*?' Izzy jiggled her straw in and out of her cup, waiting for a response. When you are sixteen you can shoot from the hip like that.

'She saw Markie, Izzy, that's what happened.'

Lulu frowned at Victoria and shook her head. But then she let out a long breath. 'Well, I guess I realised in time that getting married wasn't really my dream.'

'Or getting married to *Simon*,' said Victoria pointedly. Lulu shot her another look.

'What *is* your dream, Aunty Lu?' Izzy said, lying down on the rug and stretching her arms above her.

Lulu shrugged. 'Acting, singing, if I'm honest. Simon never really "got it". He thought it was just something I did to fill in time. He forgot I'd spent four years at drama college. I just couldn't see myself married, kids – not the way Marjory was imagining, not just right now anyway.' She shook her head and some of her blonde curls escaped from her hoodie top.

'Then why didn't you go for it when you had the chance? That *Mamma Mia* audition, Mum told me about it, but you never talk about it, Aunty Lu.'

'I wasn't good enough,' came Lulu's curt reply. Victoria knew when not to push things with her sister. Seeing Markie had obviously unnerved her and brought wedding day memories back. She tried to catch Izzy's eye, doing a 'bug-eye' at her, but Izzy wasn't looking and she sat up again. 'But, Mum, you always tell me and Jake not to take no for an answer,' Izzy carried on, picking at her purple nail polish.

'You know, you *should* follow your dream, Aunty Lu. It's what you always wanted, right? Remember when you took me to see *The Commitments* at the West End – and then later, *Cats*? You said you'd be on stage one day.' Izzy shifted her leg. 'I remember it so clearly. Your eyes were, like, really bright – and you were wearing this cool green glittery eyeliner, but anyway – you loved it, Aunty Lu. It was, like, your *world*.'

'You're right, it's just—' Lulu looked into the distance.

'What?' Victoria touched her sister's knee, but Lulu remained silent.

Victoria decided to change tack. 'Hey, I'm about to run three kilometres with a new bust,' she grinned at them both, 'then swim two hundred metres, cheered on by all the parents at Izzy's school – so if I can do *that*, then I think you need to be brave too.' Victoria picked at some nearby daisies and started to thread them into a daisy chain.

'How do you mean?' Lulu tugged at her hem of her running top.

'That's up to you to decide. But follow your dream, whether it's getting back to the West End, or telling Markie how you feel.' Lulu glanced at her from under her hood then. 'Be yourself,' added Victoria.

'And just what is *that*, Mum?' Izzy said, staring straight at her. 'It's been bloody Jekyll and Hyde with you! One minute you're some uptight super-mum before the accident, and now, you're like, well,' Izzy lifted a shoulder to her ear, 'you're, well, nicer.' It was the biggest compliment Victoria could hope for at the moment. She fought back tears.

'Izzy, shh.' Lulu poked Izzy in the ribs and smiled at her.

'No, it's true,' Victoria held up the daisy chain and placed it round Izzy's neck, then bent in for a quick kiss.

'Eurgh, that's *way* too much, Mum!'

'Remember when we used to make loads of these in the

garden,' said Lulu, piercing a daisy stem and looking at Victoria, 'then bring them in and put them on Mum and Dad?'

Victoria nodded and cast her eyes over to Markie who was striding back to the van holding a cup of coffee with his companion. He hadn't seen them – or if he had, he wasn't about to come over. 'Lulu, why don't you go on, go over there and speak to him?'

Lulu glanced at the couple in the distance and shrugged. She shook her head and yanked her hood over her head a bit more. A cloud suddenly blotted out the sun, casting a long shadow over them.

'No. I don't want to speak to him, to *them*,' Lulu mumbled.

But from what Victoria could sense, she had never seen her sister want something so much in her life.

43 VICTORIA

'Go, Jake!' James was red-faced, yelling at his son as he sprinted in the relay. She stole a glance at him. A week had slipped by and it was now June. It was the last week of term with all the craziness that brought, from art exhibitions, to fayres, to camp-outs, sleepovers and cricket matches. Today was Sports Day. Victoria was standing next to James at the side of the track, next to the ticker tape. The atmosphere was relaxed: there was music in the background, sweaty kids darted between parents clutching melting ice cream, the muffled announcement on the Tannoy about which event was next, the earthy smell of newly cut grass. Victoria pulled the brim of her sunhat down further to shade her shoulders. It was the dads' race next. She squinted in the sun at James. She was just contemplating a playful nudge in the ribs when a booming voice interrupted them.

'James!' It was Mike, one of the dads from the school, standing next to them. 'Hi Victoria. All better?' He leant over and gave her a quick peck on the cheek.

It was easier to lie. 'Yes, fine.'

He turned to James: 'Racing?'

James hesitated.

'Maybe you shouldn't bother. Because I'll probably beat you though.' Mike kept a straight face.

Victoria's memory might be shaky, but she knew her husband's reaction to being baited like this. He'd be up for any kind of race – it was one of the things she loved about him. 'You're on.' James punched Mike in the arm and sprinted off ahead of him as Victoria focused on the motley crew of dads lining up at the start line. Some were stretching out quads, some tying shoelaces, others were just chatting as if they were at a drinks party.

Jake ambled over to her. 'Hey – good race,' she said and stopped herself just in time from swooping in and giving him a hug. 'You run like your dad.'

'Now that's a compliment,' he said, smiling and held his hand over his forehead, squinting into the sun. 'Dad racing?'

Just then, Mrs Jennifer appeared on the side-lines next to Victoria. 'Hello Mrs Allen, can I have a word?' She gestured to a shady spot and they walked side by side as Mrs Jennifer told Victoria that Bella was leaving the school. 'She's moving on. Her choice. I had a long chat with her parents and they feel that a new start is a good thing.'

Victoria nodded. They hadn't asked for Bella to move, and Izzy was coping alright, but there was always the spectre of her, the memories Izzy had to face on a daily basis. And she knew Bella was repentant, they'd had a letter from her. But would that be enough? It would be much easier on Izzy if Bella wasn't around the whole time, reminding her of her past.

'Well,' Victoria replied, 'I wish her luck in the new school. Thanks for telling me.'

'That's alright,' Mrs Jennifer said putting her hand up to

shield her eyes from the sun, then added: 'Izzy's grades are improving. She says she's interested in becoming a vet? That's a tough course. But her grades are on track.' She started to move off, then turned back. 'Oh, and thank you for participating in the duathlon, raising money for the anti-bullying project. I saw your name on the list.'

Victoria nodded as her stomach did a little squeeze. *She would be alright.* Suddenly, the whistle sounded and the dads were off. She dashed back to where Jake was standing to watch. They were all in the same position for a while, then a rangy-looking man with baggy red shorts started to fall back, he turned to the crowd on the side-line and shrugged his shoulders, to laughter. Another, with cropped blonde hair, was running in his socks – he began to skip, to cheers from the onlookers and he saluted them; suddenly it became clear this was a race between James and Mike as the two of them took the lead. She looked up – they were head to head with fifty-or-so metres to go. James was fast – but Mike was just that bit speedier and the space between them was opening up as everyone cheered them on, especially Mike as he was nearly at the finish line. James's face was a fusion of red cheeks and clenched jaw as he flew past them. Victoria clutched Jake's arm. 'Go James!' she shouted. He was making up some of the ground, from where she was standing he had a chance, she put her hand up to shield her eyes from the glare and peered again. Just as she did, James took a huge spurt – and then, somehow, lost his footing and tumbled to the ground, clutching his knee.

'Dad's gone down, Mum! Look!' Jake sped off but a first-aid woman was already there applying an ice pack to James's knee. Jake crouched down beside him, and after a while James started to laugh. Mike had jogged over to them by then and pulled James up by the hand. James limped slowly, taking Mike's arm as Jake jogged back over to her. 'Dad's got a small graze, the big noodle,' Jake said smiling. 'The first-aid woman says just clean it properly when you get home and has Dad had a tetanus?' Only James wasn't meant to be coming home today, was he?

———

Back at the house Victoria added ice to a jug, cut up some lemons, and poured in some cloudy lemonade as the others sat outside. She had insisted James come home with them to clean up the cut, and he hadn't resisted. Especially when she'd had a brainwave and told him they were having Moroccan chicken later.

James, Jake and Izzy were all sitting in the sunshine at the small table on the patio looking over the garden when Victoria came out with a tray of lemonade – and a first-aid kit. She stopped abruptly, the tray in her hands and took in the scene. *Her family.* They were sitting there in the June sunshine, laughing together, Izzy in a pair of shorts, poking Jake in the ribs for some reason, James's head thrown back, shoulders shaking – one leg up on the nearby chair.

She carried on towards them and glanced at the garden. The grass was growing over the edges, but the small planters she had made up earlier in the month were glorious. Bright pink splashes of geranium poked through the magenta lobelia, and tiny white carnations bobbed in the breeze. The shrubs she'd planted in the borders were flowering, blousy peonies, upright lupins and red-hot pokers were all vying for attention in the summer sun. She placed the tray on the table and glanced at her handiwork. Jake filled up everyone's glass, while she reached inside the first-aid kit for an antiseptic wipe. She bent down next to James and started to dab his knee.

'Ooo!' James grabbed hold of her shoulder and gave it a squeeze. She almost forgot what she was doing as little sparks flew inside her chest and she had to concentrate on getting all the grit out.

'Sore?' She made a face at him.

'I'll live.' He smiled at her as she swiftly placed a plaster over the graze, then stood up and refilled everyone's glasses as Jake and Izzy stifled a giggle.

'What's the joke?'

'I just said to Izzy that maybe Dad's not as young as he used to be!' Jake raised his eyebrows at his father. 'You know, getting beaten by Mike.'

'I'm not over the hill yet, you know. I would have definitely beaten Mike if I hadn't fallen over.' He chucked the ice cubes from his glass on the grass and grinned at Jake. 'Hey, the grass is a bit long isn't it?'

She sat back on her seat and took a long drink of lemonade. The grass *was* pretty long. She'd been meaning to cut it last week, but life had taken over. And it badly needed doing.

'Jake, can you cut the lawn today – maybe with Dad's help?'

A bit of lemon flew out of Jake's mouth. 'Dad? Cut grass? You must be joking! Dad and lawnmowers don't mix!' Didn't they? She couldn't remember.

James narrowed his eyes at Jake. 'I'm perfectly fine with a lawnmower, thank you very much.'

'Yeah, right Dad. The last time you got the mower out, we had to call Grandad to ask about the parts, and send him pictures on your phone, you didn't know how to start it!'

'That's enough Jake,' he was slightly red in the face. Was he trying to defend himself in front of her? She felt oddly touched. James scraped his chair back. 'No time like the present.'

'What about your knee?' Victoria placed her glass on the table and frowned. James stopped and turned to look at her.

'It's fine.' Then he strode towards the shed. 'Jake, come and give me a hand, son!' he shouted.

'Sure.' Jake winked at Victoria. 'See? Can't do it himself.' She swirled the ice round in her glass and smiled. They were nudging each other as they walked to the shed at the back of the garden, then they disappeared inside.

She refilled her glass and closed her eyes, enjoying the sun on her face.

'Bella's leaving,' Izzy said quietly to her. Victoria opened her eyes and looked over at her daughter. She'd been so much more relaxed at home, the snarky comments had lessened, she even gave Victoria the briefest of hugs the other day.

'I know, Mrs Brown told me today. Relieved?'

Izzy shrugged. 'Yeah. I mean I've got new friends now, but I think it's better for both of us that we wipe the slate clean.' Izzy went back to looking at her phone just as there was a noise and swearing from further down the garden. She could see James pulling the starter cord but the machine was silent. After a few more goes, James kicked it and Jake started to laugh. He shoved James out the way and grabbed the cord, gave it a mighty pull but nothing. Then James took over again. He pulled it so hard he almost fell backward. Then he steadied himself and kicked the lawnmower and swore. For someone who designed vast shopping complexes and understood the exact proportions in a technical drawing of a fifteen-storey building, he was hopeless with a piece of garden machinery, it seemed. She fought the urge to giggle, then felt a rush of sadness. It was such a perfect, domestic scene, yet things were far from normal. She closed her eyes, feeling a breeze on her cheeks, and willing herself to find some more memories of the last six years she could hold close to her heart.

———

Much later, she was sitting with James on a blanket at the bottom of the garden. It was the best spot to catch the evening sun before it disappeared. His knee was still painful and he had his leg stretched in front of him. They'd had a late lunch – the Moroccan chicken had fallen off the bone, the French bread had been warm and crunchy and James had made a salad of nectarines and goat's cheese. At one point, she'd felt the wine going to her head and she'd closed her eyes briefly as Izzy went back to the kitchen to get salad servers; she'd listened to the sounds of summer, to Jake and James laughing, to the clank of cutlery and the birdsong, and imagined it was always like this, the four of them around the small garden table, the sun shining and the smell of freshly cut grass around them. Then she'd been flustered, as she'd opened her eyes and caught James staring at her.

Once lunch had finished, Jake and Izzy had cleared up, to lots of coughing and nudging and 'We'll leave you two to catch up' then, one by one, they'd wandered off – Jake to go skateboarding with a friend, and Izzy disappeared into her room. She'd been sure James would bolt off then, saying he had things to do, but he'd stayed for a cup of tea, and now, she'd just poured them two glasses of wine.

'Garden looks good.'

'Thank you. It's given me time to think.'

'That's good.' He took a sip of wine. 'You never used to have time for it.'

Didn't she?

They were silent for a while as they both enjoyed the last of the day's sun dancing over their bodies, dappled from the nearby silver birch. She lay down on the blanket and twisted the fringed edges between her fingertips. The sky was a tapestry of colours now: hazy burnt tangerine, with crimson and ochre streaks painted across it, and smears of white, as if someone had spread meringue mixture across the heavens.

'And what have you been thinking about?' James took a sip of wine.

'Meringues. What? Oh, everything.' She sat up on her elbows and laughed, but then felt a pang of regret. 'I'm sorry, James.'

'You've already said that – quite a few times. And I am too.'

She looked over at him. He looked vulnerable, sitting with his legs crossed at the ankles, sipping his wine. One thought kept looping round her head and now felt like the right time to bring it up. She knew she'd made mistakes, but it took two to break a marriage down, surely?

'Well, I am. But I also mean I'm sorry things went wrong between *us*,' she said quietly.

James shifted his position and glanced at her. 'I can't help feeling,' she continued, 'that I was testing myself, testing our marriage.' She took a sip of wine and stroked the blanket. James sat silently watching her, his long fingers wrapped around the wine glass. She could feel his gaze and she looked to the left, studied the sun disappearing behind the trees, fearful of what his eyes held. But then she sat up and looked right at him. 'What I mean is,' she cleared her throat, seizing the moment of calm between them, 'it takes two to mess up a marriage, doesn't it?' He jerked his head towards her. 'What happened to us, James, to *you*?'

He let out a long breath and she watched his shoulders rise and fall. 'We both changed,' he shrugged. 'After the miscarriage,' he stopped. 'Things were never the same. You used to cry. I felt wretched that I didn't know how to reach you.' He spread his left hand out on the rug and then clenched it into a fist. 'I'm sorry, Vicky, if I wasn't there enough for you. We'd had months of trying, and I didn't know what to say or do anymore.' He rubbed his temple. 'I blamed myself, I blamed the science and then, eventually, I kind of switched off, retreated into work, left you to deal with the day-to-day because the bigger stuff was too hard and I guess you put your energy elsewhere – into other things. I understand that now.'

'It sounds to me like maybe I couldn't reach *you*.'

He shrugged. 'I suppose so. I was thinking about it the other day, it was kind of like we were both walking along in the same life, the same *house*, and yet there was an invisible Perspex screen between us. Two people who loved each other, but neither of us reaching through the screen.' His eyes were glistening when she looked round and she touched his forearm.

Loved each other. 'I remember bits, James, snatches, more the feeling than a proper memory. Like the emotion of it all, but not the facts. I remember a feeling of failing somehow.'

'You hadn't failed, Vicky.'

'But I *had* failed, hadn't I? At least that's what I felt, I think. Failed to produce another child.' That now-familiar grieving feeling that would grip her, she knew what it was now. But she'd been allowing herself to feel these things again, and had spent so much time in the garden where she was lost in these thoughts; perhaps she was healing, perhaps she was letting the pain run its course, run out through her fingertips and into the soil.

'How can having a miscarriage be a failure? It's just your body and it—'

'Didn't really work, did it?'

'No, it did work, it gave us two beautiful twins.' His mouth turned up slightly at one side and then he was smiling, properly grinning. 'Donuts – remember?'

How could she forget? The 'mini jam donuts', she and James used to call them. After that first scan, when they were so shocked it was twins, they'd gone to a nearby coffee shop and bought something sweet to celebrate. Mini jam donuts. Raspberry. Too cloying. But they didn't care.

She nodded. 'Raspberry, right? And you hate jam.'

'I do.'

'And the next day you said we should order everything we already had – the cot, the blankets, the car seat – all over again. "We need to go big, Vicky", you said. Remember?' She touched his foot with hers and he smiled. She poured them both another glass of wine and stared out at the garden in the disappearing light. Hazy memories were surfacing. And then she found she could remember one time very clearly, and she recalled it for him, when she was in the bath once, and was sure the lump was a baby's heel, pressing on her insides. James had said, 'Definitely the boy—' they'd known by then they were having a boy and a girl, '—looks like a left-footed striker.' And he'd laughed as he'd soaped her back and knelt down and chatted to her bump, whispered to her tummy that the only team to support was Arsenal, wasn't it little bump? And he'd told the bump where his favourite team were in the Premiership as she'd laid back and put a hand through his sandy hair and sighed. She remembered that so clearly.

'James?' She took a sip of wine as he looked over at her.

'Can you tell me more – about what happened at the hospital? When we lost—'

'Her,' he said quietly.

She nodded.

'Do you really want to know?'

'I do. I feel like it's a piece of a jigsaw that I'm trying to put back together and I need to know how it fits with everything else, it's just a hole at the moment, a dark hole.'

He reached over and squeezed her fingers briefly. James took a long breath. 'When they couldn't find a heartbeat, they got several consultants to have a look, to check. You weren't talking. I couldn't reach you. They said—' James's voice was thick and he coughed. 'They said you'd have to deliver the baby. Which you did. The nurses, they wrapped her in blankets and showed you, and she was wearing a tiny hat with a pink ribbon on it. That's the ribbon that's in your box.'

Victoria let the tears fall. Although she couldn't actually remember it, she could *feel* it and the ache in her heart now was from something she was beginning to remember. When she looked up she could see James's cheeks glisten in the dusky sunlight. Silence surrounded them, interspersed with the odd chirrup from the blackbirds, as they sat, both lost in their own memories.

After a while, James rested his glass on the blanket and leant back on his elbows. 'I didn't know how to reach you after we lost the baby, Vicky. My way of coping was to throw myself into work, I admit it, and well – I'm sorry. And I'm sorry you felt lost. You used to say that to me. I know now that I let you down. You used to say to me you felt lost because the twins were growing up, and lost because we never had the baby.' He stretched out his legs. 'I'm beginning to see it much more from your side, but you know what: the twins still need you, Vicky, you must know that, they always will. You're a great mother.'

She pulled herself up to sitting cross-legged and leant forward towards him and took a deep breath, inhaling the sandalwood smell of him. 'And you?'

It was a beat before he answered. 'So much has gone on, Vicky, I just don't know.'

———

Victoria shivered in the breeze and glanced at the empty wine bottle. They'd carried on talking for a while more and covered some inconsequential things, then talked about Izzy, and about Lulu. 'I think we better go in.' James hauled the blanket up from the grass and shook it vigorously, then swayed slightly to the left and almost lost his footing. 'I,' he hesitated, 'I'd better not drive.' He tucked the blanket under his arm. 'Can I stay here? Or, or,' he hesitated. 'Would the Victoria I'm looking at not agree to that?' He bit his lip. She had the two glasses in one hand and the bottle in the other. She stepped towards him. 'The Victoria right here would like that very much.' She started to walk back to the house, but stopped and faced him. 'After all, this is your home,' she said to her husband, silhouetted in the fading light.

44 VICTORIA

James had stayed the night after the sports day, and the night after that. He went back to the Airbnb on the third day to gather up his things. Victoria had watched, twisting her wedding ring round her finger, as he'd pulled his duffel bag from the boot of the car and marched into the house, swinging it over his shoulder and then dumping it in his room upstairs. They were still very much in separate bedrooms, but there had been a tiny gear-shift. He had started to come in to use the en-suite bathroom in the mornings, muttering about the kids' bathroom being 'in a state' and 'Izzy's make-up all over the place'. This morning he'd brought her a cup of coffee. Usually he swept in and out, but today when he'd handed her the coffee he seemed to want to say something. He'd hesitated by her bed, a towel tied around his waist, as her eyes flitted across his chest, then she'd looked away as he'd placed the coffee on the bedside table. Finally, he'd glanced at his watch and hurried off.

It was the middle of June, one week till the event. Victoria had been walking and running, using an app on her phone, gradually increasing the distance until she was comfortable going at a steady pace for three kilometres. She was never going to win any races, but that wasn't the point. She could regulate her breathing now, keep going and, most importantly, even though her legs ached by the end of it, she knew she had the – what did Jake call it, 'headspace' to do it.

Zoe was in the park with her today for some 'moral support'. *Can't run to bloody save myself, sweetie, but I'll tag along and cheer you on.* She had turned up in glittery leggings and a pink headband. Victoria burst out laughing.

'What are they?' she said pointing to her leggings.

Zoe frowned. 'They're the latest Lululemon, darling. *You* used to get the new leggings every season.'

Had she? She supposed on another planet far away she would have cared, but right now she didn't care if she ended up running in her pyjamas. She smiled at Zoe and started to jog to warm up. 'They're great. Come on!' She laughed. 'I've got to do the full distance today, just to prove I can.'

'Right-oh! Course you can!' Zoe was panting next to her. 'Jesus, sweetheart, this is serious!'

They jogged a bit further, then Zoe stopped. 'And the swimming, are you training?'

'Yes, soon,' she said as she jogged ahead, blocking out the little voice reminding her of the nightmares – were they real memories or not? The water, the fear. She couldn't tell. She would think about it all later.

Victoria completed the three kilometres, the app on her phone motivating her all the way. She didn't walk once, she ran the whole course – three circuits including the hill. Zoe had bailed out at about one kilometre and Victoria could see her perched on a bench, scrolling through her phone.

When she got home, James's car was reassuringly in the driveway. He'd been away the night before, in Newcastle visiting a client, and had got back late last night. The house had felt bigger, more lonely, without him – even with Jake and Izzy's banter. She'd missed him and a small part of her brain was worrying that he wouldn't come home. When she'd heard the key turning in the lock at midnight, she'd relaxed then, turned off her light and fallen into a deep sleep. He was home.

————

She was just picking up the last raisin from the floor as James walked in. 'Is the coast clear now?' She nodded.

'No more low-flying flour?'

'Nope.' She wiped her hands on her leggings and straightened up.

Half an hour ago it had been a different story. Somehow, her, Izzy and Jake had ended up having a food fight when she got back from the rec. They'd tried to bake some chocolate chip biscuits together, Victoria had come in and found Jake and Izzy locked in debate about the temperature of the oven and, to diffuse the situation, she'd lobbed a handful of flour at each of them. Izzy had squealed, 'Mum!' and it had resulted in open warfare as they'd retaliated with handfuls of raisins, pelted chocolate chips at her and she'd thrown more flour across the table at them. She hadn't laughed so much in ages. Despite the mess of the kitchen, despite the food all over the floor, it had been the look on James's face when he'd come in the kitchen to find her, Jake and Izzy covered in flour, wrestling on the floor that had set them all off giggling again.

'Where are the food-fighters now?'

'They're playing tennis – letting off steam.'

'Good idea.' James put the kettle on. 'Tea?'

'Please.'

'How was your run this morning? Time?'

'Twenty-five minutes.'

'Not bad. Maybe you'll be able to catch me up at some point.'

She flicked a tea towel at him, grinning. 'Maybe I will!'

'One week to go,' he said glancing at his watch. 'Are you ready?'

'Course,' she said, and he gave her a high-five as she passed. She felt better than she had in a long time. The running was invigorating her. Was it making her memory come back? She didn't know, but it seemed to be doing her good, the fresh air, the exercise, something for *her*. She eased herself into one of the comfy brown leather seats at the end of the kitchen, and winced as she slid her trainers off. Her muscles had taken a beating. The doors were ajar letting a cool breeze in, as the tiled floor lit up with shafts of sunlight.

'And you're sure you'll be OK? You know, about the whole event?' He seemed to be studying her closely.

'Yes. The consultant has said as long as I go at my own pace.' She omitted to say that he thought she was *walking*, but she felt fit. It would be fine, she reassured herself.

'Right.' James placed the two mugs of chamomile tea down on the glass-topped coffee table between the chairs. 'Anyway, it was nice to see you three having fun just now.' It *had* been fun. She couldn't remember when she'd last let go like that with her kids. A voice was telling her: *a long time*. Perhaps she'd lost sight of that over the years. And she reminded herself that despite the fact that her children were growing up, they still needed her. Yes, they didn't need their shoelaces tied or toothpaste wiped off their face, but she was still their mother. Look at what Izzy had just been through.

She glanced at the framed photograph on the dresser.

Izzy and Jake in fancy dress, both with their black antennae bobbling on their heads, their little cheeks painted yellow. The bees. They had been the most adorable bees. James followed her eyes.

He nodded to the photo and let out a small laugh. 'Remember Vomit Boy. What was his name?'

She opened her mouth to reply but then shut it again. It was gone. 'Can't remember, but I do know that we said after that, that bouncy castles and cake don't mix.'

'They don't.'

'Was I a good mother, James?'

He picked up his mug and looked at her. 'Yes. *Are*.'

'Because I don't remember, well, a lot of things.' She shook her head. 'I mean, a lot of people would have thought that I was unambitious, that looking after the twins – being a *wife* – was a second choice. That I gave up my career.'

'Well, you did, but that was admirable. Anyone can be a marketing assistant for a charity, Vicky, but not everyone can be a good mother.'

'But I don't *remember* James, I know I was *there* for lots of firsts – first steps, first words. They were important. I do sort of know that. Some things are very clear. But so many of my memories,' she searched for the word, 'they've evaporated. They don't feel solid.'

James leant back and took a sip of tea. 'Well here's one: you called me in the middle of a meeting years ago – do you remember? – it was the one I had with the boss from New York, I'd been waiting to speak to him for two weeks. He was signing off the project and was extremely difficult to get hold of. He was flying out later that day. The twins must have been about eighteen months – and he was sat right *there*,' James nodded to an imaginary person opposite him '——you'd texted before to say it was urgent, so I took the call – it was on FaceTime.' There was a flicker of a smile on his face.

Victoria was getting a fuzzy memory, but it wasn't clear. 'Go on.'

'I told my boss it wouldn't take long and you only called in emergencies, so he said go ahead. Then there you were, on my screen grinning at me that they had both done a poo. They'd been constipated for several days and it was a break-through. You shouted, "they just poo'd their pants!" just as Izzy and Jake said, "Dada" at me on the screen, then you were laughing. I turned bright red, coughed and then pressed end call and had to try to finish the meeting. Luckily, my boss laughed, he had older kids.'

'Did I really do that?'

James nodded and leant forward, then turned to look at her. 'You were—' he cleared his throat, 'you *are* a great mother, Victoria. Sometimes maybe too good.' He looked straight at her and smiled. She noticed how white his teeth were when he spoke.

'You've never said.'

'Vic, you've lost your memory, so let *me* be the judge of that.'

Good mother, but not such a good wife, a voice was whispering to her. She desperately wanted to reach out and touch his hand. Instead, she enjoyed the moment of peace. 'I'm sorry,' she whispered. And in her mind's eye she could see wet cheeks, foggy memories of the twins, blurring in and out of focus, she could see their faces, feel the touch of warm fingers on her cheek. And when she opened her eyes, her vision blurred by tears caught in her eyelashes, it was James's hand brushing away the wet, his thumb tracing a semi-circle under her eye just as the sun flickered across her face.

45 VICTORIA

There were about 200 people lined up along the start line with huge numbers pinned to their chests. It all felt very real. Victoria pulled her T-shirt down over her stomach. This was the day. The duathlon. She was nervous, but she was determined to do the event for Izzy. And, if she was honest, for herself.

It was a humid, cloudy day in June. The air was thick. The heat had been building all week and it was due to break today. James had checked the weather the night before and frowned in front of his laptop. 'Thunder – heavy rain. Not ideal. You need to watch your footing. The part in the woods will be hard with all the tree roots.'

'I've been round that route a thousand times,' she'd said confidently.

Victoria zipped up her light waterproof and looked heavenward. She didn't feel that confidence now. The sky was painted aubergine with black clouds building on the horizon. Izzy, Jake and Zoe were milling around next to the start line. Izzy beamed at her and waved crazily, her arms in the air;

Jake had his hood up, arms folded. Where was Lulu? Izzy spotted her again and started to wave. 'Go, Mum!' Victoria felt like she'd won the lottery. She was going to *do this* for her daughter. They'd raised over a thousand pounds on JustGiving, she couldn't back out now.

'Alright?' James was towering over her. He was in a bright orange weatherproof top and black tri suit underneath. She looked up at him and nodded. She couldn't actually speak, her throat was so dry. She hopped from one leg to another to distract herself, looking down at the electronic tag on her shoelaces.

'I'll wait for you at the pool, OK? Don't worry about your time, just finish the race.'

That would be the *last* thing on her mind. Merely completing it was the major hurdle. She just wanted to get the run over, then she'd see James at the indoor pool and the rest would be fine.

Just fine, she reminded herself. They were just silly nightmares. Fragments of dreams. Nothing solid.

'And try not to worry about—'

'Yes, yes,' she said impatiently. She knew what he was about to say. She jigged up and down, hoping that the start whistle would go off soon.

'Remember we're doing this for Izzy, alright?'

She nodded. *Izzy*. Focus on Izzy. A man with a loud hailer was telling everyone a few health and safety issues, about the water stations, that there would be officials along the way. The crowd was getting restless now, some people shouting and laughing. Some of the runners were wearing fancy dress; there was a man in red stripy tights and red stripy top, with black-rimmed glasses and a sign that read 'Where's the Bullying?', a take on 'Where's Wally?' A group of women were huddled together; one of them had a short veil on her head, the others in tiaras. They were wearing T-shirts pronouncing 'Tanya's Hen Do'.

James stood next to her, stretching out his hamstrings. They'd agreed that they would start off together but that as he was clearly faster than her, he'd go ahead. Three kilometres, she could do this, she knew she could do this.

Once the whistle went off, there was a loud cheer and then a thunderous noise of feet and the crowd clapping. At the start, everyone was shuffling away from the finish line with lots of arm jostling, cheering, the smell of sweat and deodorant mingling among the runners. A few of the contestants at the front sprinted ahead, but most people were slowly jogging along, waiting to get more distance between them and the person in front. James nudged her arm. 'OK?'

She nodded. Blood rushed to her ears as a sea of people surrounded her.

'Good luck,' he said, striding ahead. The problem was, one of James's strides was about five of her running steps. She increased her pace, pumped her arms and tried to keep up.

Despite the weather, the mood was jubilant, people were chatting, Tanya's Hen Night girls were ahead of Victoria, giggling, one was applying lipstick with a compact mirror, another girl was pulling up her socks; they were adjusting tiaras and screeching to each other. She pulled back her shoulders and picked up her pace.

She'd lost James by this point and it had started to drizzle. She carried on, up past the edge of the woods feeling the dampness on her face and back of her legs. She was in a 'tri suit' – an all-in-one suit designed for going straight into the water. The ribbon of path running around the woods was covered in wood chip and easy to run on, but as the path continued deeper into the woods it narrowed and was inter-laced with slippery tree roots.

Victoria rounded the bend at the end of the woods and took the path deeper inside. There was a yellow arrow directing her, although she knew the way. She carried on up a steep hill, a marshal on her left, waving her on and holding up a '1 km' card. Thank God, a third was over. She continued up the hill, the rain was getting heavier and she knew the steepest part was yet to come. The air was thick with rain and humidity, and the smell of the damp soil filled her nostrils. She shivered as rain seeped down the back of her waterproof. Her feet were aching and she tried to ignore the sensation; she knew that she had nearly completed the steepest part. Just then a runner barged past her and knocked her off the path. 'Oi,' she cried out, as a woman in a tiara pounded ahead. It was one of the Hens.

Taking a huge lungful of air, Victoria could see the top of the hill. Just keep one foot in front of the other, she reminded herself. Out of breath, she reached the top of the hill, but she didn't want to stop. She glanced at her watch and was thrilled to see it was the fastest time she'd ever made it up the hill. Galvanised by her time, she sped down the other side, knowing that when she came out the woods, it was an easy lap round the edge, then towards the finish line. She carried on, the path was thick with mud now and she could feel it splattering all over the back of her legs.

Her arms were pumping by her sides, she tried not to slow down, but it was incredibly slippery. Loose stones had made her slide a few times over the mud but she had steadied herself. Now, she could just see the edge of the wood meaning that the finish line would be in sight when she emerged from the trees. She sped up, increasing her stride, glanced at her watch, and, just as she did, she miscalculated jumping over a tree root and felt her foot jar against it – suddenly she was up in the air, the soil beneath her coming closer and closer until – wham! – she was face down on the path, her right knee felt jolted into the soil and her right hand took the full impact. All the air had been pumped from her lungs and she took heaving breaths, lying on the path, her ribs still slightly tender. Rain carried on beating down on her and she sat, feeling the dampness soak through her jacket. She studied her right hand, it was covered in blood and ached. Her right knee was throbbing and a trickle of red liquid made its way down her leg, seeping into her socks. She sat for a moment, in the pouring rain on the muddy path, knowing she had two choices. She could either burst into tears, or get up and carry on. She thought of the accident, of Izzy's face the night at Heath Farm, and she hauled herself up onto her knees, onto all fours, winced, and then gradually stood up. There was nothing for it but to start to run again, slowly, putting one foot in front of the other.

By the time she emerged from the woods her hand and knee were throbbing in time to her footsteps. She could see the finish line. Izzy and Jake were huddled under a green golf umbrella. Now, she just had to get to the swimming pool and finish off the last part. She ran towards the finish line to cheers, let the official take the tag off her foot, waved to Izzy.

'Go Mum!' she heard Izzy call, and that cheer carried her forward as she sprinted towards the pool – just as a new kind of pain shot through her chest. A tightness. No, she would not allow herself to panic. A nauseous sensation wound its way around her stomach as she entered the hot fug of the pool – her body seemed to be taking over. There was the tightness again. She looked up and could see James lining up for his heat of the swim. She could do this.

46 LULU

I creep around the back of the village hall. There are flowerbeds beneath the windowsill and it's hard to see in, but I find a spot in between two planters of pansies and geraniums. I edge my way through them, and rip my tights just as I approach the window. *Damn.* The windows are dusty and there are cobwebs on the outside, I brush them away and peer in.

I clench my hands on the window ledge and take a deep breath. My knuckles go white. I lean closer. Markie is there with Katia. She's in *my* dress, she's singing songs *I* wrote the lyrics for. Children are milling around her like she's bloody Santa Claus. Swish, swish goes her long blonde hair that doesn't seem to have fuzzy bits that stick out. I'm reminded of a time when I was about five, I was in Reception at school. This little girl Nula wore my dress. Every day, just before our Rich Tea biscuit, we were allowed to play dress-ups. And every day there was an unwritten rule that we all wore the same clothes and played the same parts. I was the Princess. There was Baba – a big felt elephant's head – but nobody

315

wanted that, because Denise used to hide in it and pee; there was also a pirate outfit, and a knight made of stretchy silver elastic and bits of tinfoil – and the Princess dress. But one day, I went to the toilet and when I got back Nula was wearing the Princess dress. 'I'm the Fairy Princess today,' she'd said, waving a sparkly wand at me. When I looked at the others they were all dressed up too. I was bereft. The teacher came over and chided with me, told me that everyone had to have a turn in different outfits. I looked in the dressing-up chest and there was only Baba left. I burst into tears.

That's how I feel today.

Markie is sitting on the upturned box, strumming his guitar and grinning at the enthralled kids. I can just make out his voice. But then my heart stops. Because it's his eyes, he's looking at her and it's the admiration, it's unbearable as she twirls around. It shouldn't matter but it does.

A spider scuttles along the window ledge and I gently move it out the way. I flick some hair off my face. *What am I doing here?* When I look up, Markie and Katia are packing away their things, and the children are collecting their party bags. Mums and dads are appearing and collecting their offspring. After a while, the hall clears out and Markie and Katia are chatting by the piano. He's gesturing with his hands and she's throwing her head back laughing. Then their faces look serious – *oh God, is he going to kiss her?* I feel ashamed that I'm peeking in on such an intimate moment and yet I can't pull myself away. Another few quiet words and then he leans in and he hugs her, puts both his strong arms around her shoulders and pulls her tight and kisses her on the cheek. I close my eyes. I'm too late.

Suddenly there's something fluffy by my feet coupled with loud barking.

'Shush, Mustard! No! Sorry, *sorry*!' A woman in a light blue tracksuit is tugging at the lead of this furry friend who is yapping at me and jumping up on my legs, snaring my tights.

'Oh, gosh, sorry!' Her voice is high pitched.

'Don't worry!' I say, reaching down to pat him. He reminds me of Pickle, but he's determined to be the centre of attention, and leaps around me, twisting the lead and I'm caught up so much that – no! I trip over and fall into the flowerpot as the dog's owner lets out a shriek.

She yanks the dog away apologising and then fusses around the dog trying to make him sit. I'm covered in soil now and the pansies are squashed, the ladder in my tights is running right up my thigh. I am trying to haul myself out of the wooden planter just as I hear a voice I recognise above me. *No, no, no.*

'*Lulu*? Is that *you*?'

I'm stuck in the flowerpot, my skirt up to my waist with ripped tights. I look up at Markie and make a face.

'What, exactly, are you doing in the flowerpot, you eejit?' He grins at me. And I can't help it but we both burst out laughing. It's the first time I've seen him since he dropped us back at Victoria's on my 'wedding' day and he's leaning out the window, his hair flopping over his forehead, shaking his head at me. It's a bittersweet moment: I'm overwhelmed with the joy of hearing his laugh and sorrow about what I've just seen.

———

I shrug. 'I was just passing.'

We're sitting in The Little Norland Coffee Shop, next to the village hall. I love this place. It's a family-run business and all the food is made onsite. The chairs and tables don't match, there are comfy leather sofas dotted around and fresh flowers on every table. Newspapers are stuffed into a stand next to the cash register and the place is warm and cosy, the smell of freshly ground coffee in the air.

'Passing the back of the village hall, and you got stuck in a flowerpot?' His face is deadpan.

'I told you, it was the dog.' I bite the inside of my cheek to stop myself saying any more as I look at his cheeky grin. 'Oh, alright. I was spying on you.' It just comes out. It's too hard not to be honest with him.

'Your voice's snippy again, so it is.'

'I'm not snippy.'

His eyebrows rise and I feel I owe him an explanation. 'Because, well, I just wanted to see, you know, what you were up to and how you were coping – without me.'

'Coping?' His mouth twitches. I could hit him. 'Well, Katia is doing brilliantly, so she is. She's deadly.' I've got used to Markie's quirky Irish expressions now. 'She's got a great voice, a knack with the kids.' He looks at me and opens his mouth as if he's about to say something. Then his expression changes. 'And how're *you* going, Lulu, how's your old man? How's Pickle? Did you think about what I said?'

I'm glad we've moved on from Miss Amazing. Seeing her was enough. And I have thought about what he said; he messaged me when I was on the train, to let me know that Katia was permanent. It was a blow, even though I know I've got to move on, move away from kids' parties. He told me get a 'proper job' as an actress or singer, with a smiley face. Sent me the link to that agency I told my dad about. I know he meant well, but it still hurts. I fold my arms across my chest and nod.

'I did – and I spoke to Victoria, that night, I told her. Actually Izzy blurted it out,' I confess, pushing my sleeves up and looking at him. 'But I was going to tell her, and then I told her everything, absolutely everything, I swear, about being drunk, about pulling the wheel, the way I felt, the pressure, everything I told you.' I shrug. 'All of it.' There's this odd need to be totally honest with him, as if he pulls it out of me.

'Good. And how was she?'

'She didn't blame me at all. In fact, you know what she said? She said,' I feel my throat catch. 'She said she loved me, that she knows I didn't do it on purpose.'

'Go on.' Markie touches my knee and my heart does a little flip.

'In fact, she said she's glad we had the accident.'

Markie leans back on the sofa and moves a cushion. 'She said that?'

I nod.

'How so?' He tilts his head to one side.

'Because she's glad that she's time-travelled back six years, I suppose. She said she prefers the old Vicky, the one from six years ago.'

Markie puts both hands above his head and stretches. I can't help but glance at his shirt as it opens up at the collar and notice how smooth the skin is there. 'I see. And what did James say?'

'Don't know. I went to bed, but there was something else going on between the two of them and, well, he left for a bit. But I think they're patching things up now.'

'Relationships, eh? Messy.' He stares at me and pulls at his earlobe where the guitar earring sits. 'How did, er, Simon take it?'

I roll my eyes. 'God, I can't believe I was about to—' I shake my head, 'to share my life with him, I mean, he was horrible to me. I was going to tell him about— Anyway.' I shift in my seat and pick at my laddered tights. Something stops me going any further. 'I know he lost his first wife, but he was cruel, told me I was "cheap". Those were his words.' I lower my eyes and stare at my boots. I still feel ashamed.

Markie lets out a long low whistle. 'Never can tell.' He finally says.

'What?'

'People aren't always what they seem, and we don't know what they're hiding, what they're running from.' He stares straight at me, and it's as if he knows.

A young girl with blonde hair in a high ponytail comes up to us wearing an apron. She's the owner's daughter, and asks if we want anything else, but I shake my head. She puts a bottle of water on the table and smiles at us.

'I did some serious thinking at Dad's,' I say, 'and I know I've been a bit messed up, I've been running away—'

'I know you have, Lulu. It's obvious. When you first started working for me you told me you'd auditioned for the West End, but then next thing, you're happy to be stuck with me.' He shrugs. 'I mean, I know I'm a great guy and all that —' He stops and looks at me; it's as if he can see right through me, then playfully punches my arm. 'I'm kidding, but what I mean is, I'm ten years older than you Lulu, I made my choices, it's my business. But you? You're wasted here.' He waves his hand around, I assume he means Little Norland.

I open my mouth to speak. There's so much more I want to tell him. More than anything, I want to let these demons go. But just then my phone pings. A text from Izzy.

Where are you?? Mum's done the run and now it's the swim.

'Oh shit, shit, shit! I was meant to be there!'

'What's up?' Markie is staring at me. 'You're doing that sucking-a-lemon face.'

'It's Victoria, I can't believe I missed her run!' I glance at my phone for the time. 'But there's still the swim to do.'

'Her duathlon, you mean?' I'd texted him and told him all about it on the train on the way down. 'I saw all those signs at the car park on the way here. You need to be there.' He jumps up. 'I'll drop you off on the way.'

I grin at him, thankful that he can always see what needs to be done.

He looks at his watch. 'We're doing Caterpillar at five o'clock.' He rolls his eyes. 'So there's time.'

A little splinter lodges in my heart. *We.* I attempt a shaky smile. Then my eyes follow him as he walks out the café, one hand yanking up his jeans, the other slinging his guitar over his shoulder and I'm rooted to the spot. I want to run after him, but I stop myself. I slowly pick up my handbag, take a deep breath and head to the door.

She sat on the raised edge next to the pool, shivering in her tri suit, and tried to stem the blood from her hand. She'd managed to nip to the Ladies' quickly and wipe down her leg and wash her hand, but they still stung. An official was standing next to the swimmers with a clipboard, talking. She was in white shorts and T-shirt with a lanyard round her neck, laughing and joking. In her hand were coloured wristbands she was giving to each swimmer. Victoria watched her mouth move, saw her check her watch, issue some more instructions, and then nod at them. But Victoria couldn't hear. Instead, she was staring at the choppy water, the noise of the pool and the crowds thrumming in her ears. Swimmers were gliding up and down, like underwater missiles, chasing their own personal-best time, slicing through the water. Suddenly, the whistle blew to signify someone finishing, then an electronic bleep as the next wave of swimmers entered the water.

They were next.

'Alright?' The official was bending over. She leant in

closer. Victoria could see tiny hairs on her face. 'I said, are you alright?' A wave of bile rose in Victoria's throat and she swallowed it down. She stared at her toes, crunched them up to focus her mind on the present, as the din of the water, whistles and booming announcer smothered her like a claustrophobic blanket. It was for Izzy. She had to be brave. Just like Izzy had been when she'd gone back to school with her head held high in front of Bella.

Victoria nodded mutely. She kept her eyes on her pink neon wristband. She twisted it round and round, no beginning and no end. *No beginning, no end.* She gulped. James was about to enter the water in his wave of swimmers. He was mouthing to her, 'You OK?'

Her hands were shaking as she gave a thumbs up, took a deep breath of the fuggy air. And then her row was up, ready for the water. They were all walking to the start line. She stood next to the diving boards as an official checked their names. She forced herself to look at the surface of the water. *This is real*, she told herself. She shuffled towards the edge of the pool, the smell of chlorine stinging her nostrils, beads of sweat forming along the tight line of her swimming cap. The noise in her head was like a swarm of bees.

'Are you OK, dear?' The timekeeper had his hand on her elbow. She nodded. 'Only, you need to start or you will be disqualified.'

Victoria stared at him. He had kind blue eyes with little flecks of black in the irises and short grey hair. 'It's fine, I'm fine,' she muttered, then edged forward, pulled her goggles down over her eyes and did a pencil dive straight into the deep end. It was ice cold, the liquid surrounding her and the tang of chlorine filled her nostrils, water filled her ears as she emerged from her dive to slowly start to swim. One arm over the other, kick your legs. Keep going. She looked up towards the end. Tiny water droplets on her goggles obscured her vision; the end seemed miles away. She gulped and took in some water, started coughing. She hadn't swum anywhere since, well. Just *since*. It was all a muddle.

She put her head back in the water and carried on, trying to get going. She took huge lungfuls of air, left, right, kick. *Breathe, breathe.* Her knee was aching badly and her hand was throbbing. She knew she wasn't breathing properly, she felt suffocated. She told herself to stay calm as the water slapped her cheek. She froze, took in a mouthful of water, coughed and inhaled more water; her goggles were steaming up, she was swallowing chlorine. There was no air. *Keep going* she told herself, but then, from out of nowhere, she was back to the nightmare: water in her ears, screaming, the acid tang in her mouth, her limbs felt like lead, as if she was swimming through cement; she stopped, looked wildly around, she knew she was thrashing, gasping for air, one minute above, the next submerged, muffled noises, a siren, the water deafening in her ear, her hand stinging. Then suddenly pressure under her arms, a strong grip. She was being hauled up, the muffled noises turned to carnival noise above the water, a hand on her head.

It was James, dragging her to the edge of the pool, hauling her along the water, then an official was kneeling on the side, his mouth opening and closing, eyes wide, reaching for her. And she was staring at the ceiling, bright neon strip lights hurt her eyes, her head on the hard surface, grit under her legs, a hand on her shoulder. Shivering uncontrollably. And then it went black.

48 LULU

James has just texted. Victoria is fast asleep – thank goodness she is OK. I'm back at my flat, letting them have time alone. I can't shake that image of seeing her submerged in the water, I just lost it, I jumped up and started to scream. It was like nobody could see her. Then James was suddenly next to her, thank God it was the shallow end; that image of him hauling her up under her arms is awful. I shake my head. The whole event had to be stopped. I can't get Vicky's pale face out of my mind. The senior lifeguard said she was alright. Her colour had come back to her cheeks and she'd had a cup of tea before James got her in the car. Izzy had been awesome; holding her hand on the side of the pool, telling her it would be alright, the mum-daughter role reversed.

There's a knock on my door. I glance in the mirror and it's a sight to behold. Wet T-shirt from helping Victoria and James, bird's nest hair. I glance at my watch: seven o'clock. When I open the door, I inhale sharply. It's Markie.

'Hello.' I can't help a grin spreading across my face.

'I was, um, just passing,' he says and gives me a wink. 'But there were no flowerpots to fall into.'

'Very funny.' I stand back to let him in, my heart thudding.

'Cute flat.'

'Thanks.'

'I got your message about Victoria, I came to see how you were,' he says taking off his leather jacket and placing it on the arm of the sofa.

'*I'm* fine,' I say, quickly smoothing down my hair, 'it's more Victoria I'm worried about.'

'And how is she?'

'The family are all with her, at home. The first aider at the pool said she'd be OK. That it looked like a panic attack. She was a bit shaken.'

'I'm sure you are, too.' He stares at me as I nod and somehow, I feel tears threaten. I'd been holding it all together and it's as if Markie can touch the soft centre of me that nobody else sees and I just seem to crumble. But I can't be like this.

'Do you want some tea?' I say, to take my mind off things.

'Ach, OK. But no poncy nonsense, OK? Just builder's.' He smiles at me and takes a seat on the sofa.

When I come back with two mugs of tea, I put them on the small table in front of him and sit next to him on the green faded sofa. I pull my knees up and hug them.

'What are you thinking?' he says after a moment's silence as we sip our tea.

'I was so worried when I saw her. Because Victoria's always been the capable one, the bigger sister, the one who'd take over, who'd read to me at night when Mum was tired.'

'That's a nice memory.' Markie crosses his long legs at the ankle.

I look out of my window, at the fields stretching into the horizon. The rain has stopped and a few chinks of light are appearing in the sky through the blue-grey clouds. I think about Victoria's life, about how she put on a brave face, kept going and it makes me think of my own demons.

'Penny for them?'

I look at him, with his crumpled white T-shirt, at the guitar earring in his left ear, shining in the sun's weak rays and his open, smiling face and I think about the last time I tried to tell this story. Not only had Simon not wanted to hear it, he hadn't even given me a chance. I take a long breath in. 'It's a lo-o-ng story,' I say pulling a cushion over my knee.

'The ones that matter normally are.' He leans back on the sofa and folds his arms. My heart misses a beat as I start, but then I open my mouth, see Markie smiling, and ready to listen to me and I begin.

'You've always asked me why I didn't carry on with my West End dream. Izzy asked me, too. Victoria can't remember how I changed. And I, well – everything changed that day. My dream was put out.' I pause and look down at the tea in my cup.

'What day?'

'It was the day of the *Mamma Mia* audition, I remember it well. I'd been anticipating it for a month, practising my lines in the shower, in the kitchen. I was seeing the producer at 2.30 that day. I'd bought a new £35 wrap-over dress, worn my denim jacket, cowboy boots and spent ages on my make-up. I also went into a department store on the way and covered myself in expensive perfume because I couldn't afford to buy any.' I shrug. 'I can't stand that perfume now.'

Markie nods at me.

'And I took the train to London, then the tube to Piccadilly Circus. I found the hotel where the audition was taking part, and I went to the front desk. They said he was already in the room, waiting for me. I didn't think it was odd; I had never been to an audition before. He'd emailed me and told me that it was too noisy at the theatre, that we'd be able to speak better at a hotel. I was beyond excited. I would have travelled to the bottom of the sea, you know?' I shrug at Markie as I feel my throat catch.

I cough. 'Anyway, I go up in the lift and then knock on the door. This guy opens it, he's about maybe sixty, I don't know, and he shakes my hand, asks me to come in. Neatly dressed, suit. I look around expecting there to be an assistant, a team of people interviewing me, a camera, something, anything. He tells me to sit on the chair and then he starts asking questions. Asks if I want a coffee, but I'm too nervous to drink anything. It starts off fine, he asks about my previous experience, about my college degree, he asks questions about my ambition, what I want for my career. He tells me that it's a small role in the show, but it's a prominent one; he says I will be alone on the stage for some time, that I need to make an impact. Then,' I take a breath, 'I notice how much he's looking at my legs, he seems distracted, and he moves his chair closer and I smell garlic, I smell cheap aftershave. He tells me he needs to see how *much* I want it.' My stomach curdles at the memory. 'He tells me how pretty I look, and I'm flattered.'

'Go on.' Markie sits up and makes a fist with his hand.

'Then he tells me that he's interviewed a lot of girls for this show and that the person he chooses has to be someone really special. When he said "special" he looked me up and down. That's when I started to have misgivings, but I still wasn't sure. I'd never done this before. I was naïve. But I was, by then, way, way out of my depth, I can see that now.

'And then,' I can feel tears. 'Sorry Markie, this is,' I swallow and carry on, 'hard for me.'

'You don't have to say any more, really Lulu.' He's leaning towards me now, deep frown marks on his forehead, studying me.

'No, I do. I have to deal with it. So,' I sniff, 'he tells me that having good legs is critical for the role, that I'll have to wear heels and he says he has to check how I walk. He produces a pair of high heels and tells me to put them on, and walk towards the bed. And I do, I put them on.' I shake my head at the memory. 'I stand up and walk to the bed. And before I know it he's behind me, he's pushed me onto the bed, has my hair in his grip and he's hurting me, really hurting me. He tells me to sit up, that he wants me to "do something for him, to see how good an actress I am". He yanks me up by my hair and tells me he likes me, that I might get the job, but first I have to act out a role, do something.' I shudder. 'Then he unzips his trousers and he looks at me, says "is there a problem?" I felt sick, I didn't know what to do, I remember feeling trapped. Then he sat next to me on the bed, pushed his mouth on mine, it was disgusting, but I really wanted that part. I didn't know if I should be acting or —' I shiver as my voice starts to break. 'Running away.' Markie pulls a blanket from the arm of the sofa across me. 'I remember shouting "Don't" as he pulled the sleeve down on my dress, ripping it. I sat there humiliated. He stared at me then, then ordered me to take my bra off.' My cheeks are wet now as I hang my head and I feel this stabbing pain in my gut, as I recall the events of that awful afternoon.

'Lulu, it's OK, you can stop.' Markie touches me briefly

on the knee and I look down at his hand with the silver ring on the thumb and take a deep breath.

'He tried to kiss me again. I froze. I felt like I was watching myself. He told me I was a "good girl" and part of me felt it was my fault. I guess I know that's wrong now, and yet—' I stop. Tears trickle down my face and I am back in that small hotel room with its revolting geometric wallpaper, cheap carpets and the smell of garlic. 'He pushed me down on the bed. I remember the feel of his hands, they were rough, he was wearing a wedding ring. He said if I did what I was told and acted well I would get the part. And,' I pull the blanket over my knee and look at Markie, 'I wanted that part, I *really* did.' Suddenly I am that girl lying on the bed, staring at the ceiling, her heart hammering in her chest and I feel disgusted with everything.

'I tried to get up. He slapped my face, he told me I shouldn't dare. That it would ruin my career. But from some-where, I just felt this fury, you know?' I look at Markie and our eyes meet. 'I slid off the bed and I bolted, I reached the front door and I ran down the corridor, my dress ripped. I pushed through a Fire Exit door, ran down to the next level and then sat there, on the cold concrete steps, trying to get my breathing back. Once I had calmed down, I went down another set of stairs and found the Ladies'. I stayed there for ages, crying. Then I washed my face, pulled my dress up and went home on the tube.

'I never told a soul.' I blink away some tears and look into Markie's green eyes. 'Until now.' He fixes me with a stare, his eyes, the colour of emeralds, with tiny amber flecks in them in the dim light, they're dewy.

'Jesus feckin' Christ, Lulu. I don't know what to say. What a complete bastard. And you've never told anyone?'

I shake my head. 'A year later, that's when I applied for

the job with you. I was "better", I told myself.' I shrug, then carry on. 'I mean, the nightmares had lessened, but I don't think I'm over it.'

'Will you see someone, talk about it, get some help?'

I nod slowly. 'I did some research, sent some emails, when I was at Dad's.' I fiddle with the edge of the blanket.

'You can't deal with something like that on your own.'

'I know, I suppose I went into myself for a bit, looking back, that's when the drinking got worse. I could still be "fun Lulu" because it took the edge off, be someone who I used to be, only I needed the drink to forget the pain.' I straighten out a leg and circle my ankle round, thinking about it. 'Drink sort of melted real life away. I get these flashbacks; the drink, it makes me take a "holiday" from myself – know what I mean?' I lift a shoulder to my ear.

He nods.

After a while he speaks. 'I'm glad you've told me.' He reaches over and places a hand on my knee briefly. 'But, you know, someone once said to me, "you can't expect anyone to love you if you don't love yourself".'

'I think I know what you mean,' I sigh and hug my knees up to my chest.

'I know you, Lulu. Every time you drink, you change. Whether it's pulling a steering wheel—' he stops to look at me, 'or being a bit crazy at a Bubble Disco,' he smiles. 'If you loved yourself more, you wouldn't be like this.'

I nod. I can feel the tears threaten. And it's not because I'm sad, it's because I know he's right – but more than that, it's because, I realise, he *cares*. 'At my dad's up in the moors, it was wonderful. I took a long walk every day, cleared my head, cleared my thinking. Decided what I wanted.'

'And what's that?'

'Well, obviously I need to talk to someone, I know that,

but there are two things I've been dreaming about.' I feel the colour rise in my cheeks. I get up and walk to the window and move the curtains to one side and stare at the damp fields outside. One of them is obviously out of my reach now, judging by what I saw at the village hall, so I concentrate on telling him about the other. 'Well,' I say, walking back to the sofa and sitting down, 'I'd like to get back to the West End, to try my luck again, or maybe sing professionally, I've contacted that agency, thanks for sending that to me. They're pretty cool, like a middleman between booking you a gig and finding places to perform.'

'Good stuff.'

'I have an interview in two weeks. It's a start. You know, following my dream. Dad reminded me about Mum,' my eyes well up when I think about it. 'Reminded me that she only had one year of her dream.' My eyes find a spot in the middle distance. My fur rug is covering an old wicker chair; when Simon was last round he picked it up with two fingers as if it was contaminated. I sigh thinking about it. 'So, yeah, West End here I come – second time round. And anyway,' I venture, 'looks like you don't need me anymore.'

Markie gives me the briefest of playful punches on the shoulder and it's all I can do not to reach out and clasp his hand. 'Hey, you're fabulous, you know that, but it's not what you want to do is it? Katia's grand, she's really good.'

A little spear jabs at my heart, but I nod enthusiastically. 'Great that's just – yeah, great.'

His tone is soft: 'I went off the rails a bit, you know, after Esme died. That's why I could see it in you. Looking back, I was just trying to blot out the pain. Threw myself into my music, out every night, gigs, didn't let myself really feel anything. But eventually it catches up with you – you need to confront it.'

I smile, feeling this sensation wash over me. Grateful for his guidance, pleased that he wants to share his experiences with me. It's relief and exhaustion rolled into one. We're silent for a while, both lost in our thoughts. The sun is streaming through the window now and my purple voile curtains diffuse the sunlight as it makes a pattern on the floor.

'Shouldn't you, you know, tell Simon all this, tell him everything you told me? Explain?'

'I tried. He didn't want to know. I wanted him to under-stand – well, some – of what happened, of who I'd become. I know it was wrong, but, you know, we make mistakes.'

Markie purses his lips and doesn't say anything but he's looking straight at me. After a while he leans back and clasps his hands behind his head. My eyes flick to the soft skin next to the sleeve of his T-shirt on the underside of his arm. 'Everyone makes mistakes, Lulu.' He stretches his arms in the air then sits forward. 'Anyway, I think we could both use a decent hot chocolate, what do you say? As much as I like tea, I think this calls for sugar. I'll make it.'

I nod as Markie wanders into my kitchen and starts to rummage around. Imagine if this was what it was like all the time? I allow myself a brief fantasy where Markie is in my kitchen, where we are a *couple*. But I force myself to stop. It won't happen now.

'Here you go.' He places a perfect hot chocolate in front of me. There's even some cream on the top, with chocolate powder sprinkled on top and a teaspoon in the mug.

'Thanks,' I say, picking up the mug from the table.

'Here's to new starts.' We chink mugs. I stare at his funny dimple in his chin and nod and I realise I desperately want to tell him what the other thing was I'd been dreaming about. The problem is, it's just too late.

49 VICTORIA

'Vicky?'

Someone was squeezing her shoulder. 'Wake up. I've brought you tea.'

'OK,' she whispered. Her throat hurt. Lulu was standing by the side of the bed wearing a purple fringed leather jacket and a frown.

Lulu waited till she'd sat up properly then handed her the tea. 'There.'

'You sound like Mum.'

'You sound crap.'

They both smiled at each other. It was the day after the event and Victoria had spent most of it in bed, but she'd woken up that morning feeling much better and had been dozing since. It was now about midday.

A head poked round the door. 'Are you OK, Mum?' Izzy came in and sat on the edge of the bed, her fingers fiddling with the bedsheet. 'You've been asleep, like hours, Dad told us to leave you alone, and I—'

'I'm sorry, Izzy.'

'You gave me a fright.' Izzy folded her arms across her chest. And suddenly Victoria watched her sixteen-year-old morph into the ten-year-old she *did* remember. She sniffed. Her cheeks were red. She reached up and pulled Izzy close. 'I'm fine, I feel much better today.' She breathed into Izzy's hair, kissing the top of her head. 'I'm sorry. I didn't mean to give you a fright, I was just trying to finish the race – you know, Dad's such a good swimmer and I suppose I—'

'Did too much.' Lulu cut in.

Izzy looked up at her and rubbed her eyes. 'Next time, Mum, *no* swimming, OK. It just reminded me of—'

'I know, sweetheart, I know. My memory was playing tricks. One minute I thought it was just a nightmare, the next I worried it was a memory. Turns out it *was* a memory.' And as Victoria lay in her dimly lit bedroom with her daughter held to her chest, and her sister by her side, she was engulfed in a feeling of gratitude that she was here, that nothing had happened and that she *was* able to hold her like she'd never let her go. Because no matter if Izzy was sixteen or six, Izzy needed reassurance, she needed *her*.

'Izzy, I'm fine, really. I had a good sleep and I feel good. I really do.' She gave Izzy her best Coping Mum Smile.

Lulu was looking out of the window, her arms wrapped around herself. She suddenly turned to face Victoria. 'I said I'd take them out, to give you some peace. We'll get the bus into town.' She walked towards the bed and stroked Izzy's hair.

'Yeah, don't forget you promised ice creams from that new place,' beamed Izzy and suddenly the sixteen-year-old was back in the room. Lulu nodded. 'Of course, your majesty – and will you have sprinkles with that?' Lulu nudged her in the ribs.

'Hey, don't let your tea get cold Mum,' Izzy scolded, sitting up.

'I won't, promise.'

'I'm meeting Lara – remember, Melanie's friend? I told you about her, she's cool.' She raised her eyebrows at Victoria. 'Then maybe some window shopping. Aunty Lu can decide,' she smiled, yanking down her top.

Just then Jake put his head round the door. 'Hey, Mum. You OK?'

'Yeah, I'm good, I'm great. Don't worry.'

'I'm not worried,' he stage whispered, looking over his shoulder, 'but Dad *definitely* freaked out last night, and he's been pacing the kitchen floor all morning.' Jake's eyes widened. 'Oh, and his cooking is a bit crap; last night he made us burnt sausages, raw pasta and some weirdo potato salad from the fridge, dated, like 1988 or something. So, if you've nothing better to do than recover from like, drowning, could you make our dinner tonight?' He grinned at her and leant on the door. 'And maybe don't do that semi-drowning thing again.'

'I'm sorry. Hey maybe we could bake some cookies?' She winked at him.

'No way.' He came over and gave her the briefest of hugs. Then he looked at Lulu. 'We off?' She nodded.

'Take it easy, Mum.' And as they all left the room, she collapsed back on her pillows and wished more than anything that they could all be a family again.

When she woke up, little ribbons of sunlight were creeping around the curtain and lighting up the wall. Tiny specks of dust danced before her as she groggily realized where she was. Looking at the clock, two more hours had passed. It was two in the afternoon. She could smell something cooking in the kitchen, it smelt like bacon or onions, or both. She was ravenous, but she sank back into her pillows to the sound of cupboard doors banging and the occasional clip-clip of men's shoes in the hallway. Then silence.

She must have slipped back to sleep because a while later there was a tiny knock on the door. 'Vicky?'

She opened her eyes and James was peering round the door clutching a tray. 'Are you OK? Only you've been asleep for a long time. I popped my head round every twenty minutes but you were always asleep.' He leant on the door frame. 'I was,' he shifted his weight from one foot to the other, 'um, a bit worried.'

'I'm fine. Thank you.'

'Well, I'm just keeping an eye on you, like I've been told. And I think you need to eat.' He started to walk towards her.

She flopped back onto the pillows. 'That smells good.'

He came over to her bed and placed the tray on the side table and helped her organise her pillows to sit up in bed. 'You did too much, took on too much, especially after what you've been through. I spoke to the consultant.' He narrowed his eyes at her and she looked down at the fibres of the sheet. 'Anyway,' he carried on, 'I brought you a pot of tea and some bacon and cheese scones drowning in butter—' He stopped mid-sentence. 'Sorry.' He shook his head. 'That was insensitive.'

'Hey,' she placed a hand on his arm, feeling the soft wool of his jumper under her fingers. 'It's OK.'

He looked down at her hand on his arm. 'It's just that it's not OK, is it?' His voice was strained.

'I thought I could do it, I—'

'But you couldn't, not really, *could you*?' he took a deep breath. 'Sorry,' he rubbed his forehead with the back of his hand. 'It's probably my fault. I shouldn't have pushed you in the running, and I should have warned you about the swimming, about the— But I didn't want to stop you being brave. It seemed so important to you. I thought you'd remembered, but – anyway, and when I thought I'd lost you, like *really* lost you…' he looked out through the window and then back at her, his forehead crinkled in worry. 'First the car accident, now this, and it just brought it all home, speaking to your Dad, how he lost Maggie—' She stared at his strong jaw and the way he was wringing his hands together. 'And it terrified me,' he whispered.

She took a sip of tea and didn't want to disturb the fragile silence between them. After a while she spoke. 'James, what was it that I couldn't remember? I was having these nightmares, drowning, what actually happened? It seems they were memories, not dreams.'

'We were on a canoeing holiday years ago, the kids were little. We'd been off the coast of Dorset, hired canoes. You were with Izzy and I was with Jake. It was choppy, it had been raining heavily, we probably shouldn't have gone out. But,' he half-smiled, 'the kids had draped themselves over the sofa, crying, and so we'd decided to go for it.' He stopped and looked out the window. 'But the coastal swell had been huge that day and you and Izzy went out too far. You capsized, the lifeguards had to get you.'

'I don't remember,' she said quietly as he lifted her hand into his and started to stroke her knuckles with his thumb. They both sat like that for a while, lost in their own thoughts. The air was stuffy. She didn't want the moment to end. He held her gaze and he was back, *her* James. And after all the turmoil, here he was, laying bare his soul. She loved him more than ever.

'But you didn't lose me then, or now. I'm still here, I'm still your wife.' She squeezed his hand. There was a beat until he glanced at her and smiled.

'I'll leave you to rest.' And he got up and wandered out the room. She ate the two cheese toasted scones then sank back into the pillows. She lay there for a long time, sipping her tea, trying to make sense of what had happened the last time she'd been in the water. She picked up her phone and scrolled through it, images flashing in and out of her consciousness, but she couldn't concentrate on any one thing. She put it down and fell into a light sleep, with the sunlight playing on her face.

After a while, she woke up, her head groggy with memories and dreams. She slid out of bed and hauled her treasure box out from underneath the bed. She opened the cardboard flaps and started to rummage through her keepsakes until she found it. She pulled it out with a flourish and gave it a shake. The tiny daisies sewn around the edge of it, their yolk-yellow centres and delicate petals still in perfect condition. Victoria sat on her dressing table stool and slid the veil's clasp through her hair, then pulled the veil up and over her face. She smiled at her reflection in the mirror and turned from side to side. My wedding, she sighed to herself. Would she *ever* remember?

Sitting back down on the edge of her bed she flicked the veil back over her shoulders and scanned the tray. Her stomach rumbled. She fancied something sweet. *Ice cream.* Yes. She tiptoed downstairs over the soft carpet and wandered into the kitchen. She could hear the low rumble of the radio in the lounge. The fridge was humming quietly and the afternoon sunlight was flooding in across the tiled floor. She crept over to the freezer and opened it up. There were two tubs of chocolate ice cream and one rum and raisin. She lifted out a tub, and closed the freezer door with her foot, humming to herself. Then, she stood at the kitchen counter and peeled back the plastic seal and dug a spoon deep into its velvety centre. She leant back against the counter, closed her eyes and was just savouring another spoonful when she heard a noise. Her eyes flew open and James was standing in the doorway staring at her, with his head cocked to one side. His expression was unreadable. Was he angry?

'What are you doing out of bed?'

She shrugged. 'Sorry, doctor, but I'm hungry.'

He grinned. 'But you don't like chocolate ice cream,' he said, his eyes darting to the spoon.

'Oh, don't I?' she stopped mid-lick.

'Nope,' he said folding his arms across his chest. 'Never have.'

'Right.' She caught his eye. 'Maybe *you* should have it, then?' She took a big lick then held it out to him. His eyes flicked over her, and he looked up at her face. He approached her slowly, as a predator might stalk a deer. The floor felt solid beneath her and yet everything else in the room seemed to tilt on its axis. She held out the spoon to him, biting her cheek, as he stood next to her and gradually opened his mouth. She looked at his shiny white teeth as she slid the spoon in.

'Delicious,' he murmured, holding her gaze. She studied his face, his tired, kind eyes searching hers.

'Isn't it? So – why don't I like chocolate ice cream?'

He tilted his head to one side and licked his lips. 'Beats me. It's rich, chocolatey, more-ish, gives you tingles down your spine; can't think why not.'

'Then what *do* I like – or love? Because I've sort of lost my memory, you see. And perhaps I need some help remembering. In fact, maybe if you tell me what *you* like, I'll remember.'

'Alright then,' he said, leaning in towards her, and lifting up the veil on her shoulder with a finger. 'But first, this way.' And he held his hand out to her. She placed hers inside it, as he wrapped his warm fingers gently around hers as her stomach plummeted towards her feet, and then seemed to lift up again. It was the same sensation as being on a roller-coaster. Only she wasn't in a rollercoaster, she was in the kitchen with her husband and the noise of blood rushing to her ears was almost deafening. He tugged at her hand, leading her back up the stairs, her bare feet treading slowly on the soft carpet. He looked back at her every now and then, pulling at her hand gently as tiny sparks lit up in her belly.

'You asked what I love?' he said, nudging the bedroom door behind him closed and stood in front of her. 'Well,' he said, pushing the veil over her shoulder softly, as her heart raced, 'winning races, chocolate ice cream, skiing, beautiful buildings, and my two glorious, grumpy teenagers.' He touched her chin. They were by the edge of their bed and she stood there in her veil and pyjamas, her heart strumming as he placed his hands on her shoulders and pushed her softly down onto the bed, where she sat in front of him.

She looked up at her husband and fiddled with the netting of her veil, rubbing it between two fingers.

'Is that all?'

'No. Another thing I love…' He knelt down and held her face in his hands, his thumb tracing tiny circles over her cheek, 'is being at home, with you – *this* you.'

And then he kissed her, taking his time and she melted into the moment, everything was about his touch, his breath on her lips. He stood back and carefully peeled off her pyjama top and let it fall onto the bed, then slowly traced a line from her chin to her breasts, where he circled his thumbs around each nipple. She could feel the desire welling up in her, she could hear her heart hammering in her chest as he slowly lowered her to the bed, where he whispered in her ear all the other things that he loved.

———

She was still out of breath when James threw off the bedclothes, grabbed her by the hand and yanked her out of bed. 'Come with me!' He leapt out of bed and threw on his jeans.

'What are we doing?' Victoria wrapped her silk dressing gown around her and flew out the door after him.

'You'll see.' He grinned at her then raced down the stairs, two at a time. He went to the hall table and opened the drawer. Pulling out some papers he said: 'This is what deserves to happen to these.' Victoria stood beside him with her head tilted to one side as her husband, the one she so nearly lost, neatly ripped one, then two, then three of their divorce papers into shreds; then he got the shredded pieces from the floor and started to tear them apart again. After that he placed the whole lot in the palm of his hand and threw them up in the air, letting them shower over them. He folded his arms and turned to look at her. 'That should do it,' he said, grinning.

They wandered back up the stairs, tiny flecks of paper in his hair and flopped on the bed laughing. After a while, they were silent, lying side by side in the tangled sheets, legs inter-twined. The sun was just visible behind the trees outside, and the open window let the sound of blackbirds chirping their evening song flood in. Her veil was thrown over a nearby chair and her pyjamas lay crumpled on the floor. She looked up to the ceiling and then her eyes settled on James. He was lying with his eyes shut, his long lashes grazing his cheek. It just felt right having him next to her. It was solid and real and *normal*. Whoever she'd become, *this* was what she wanted. This kind of normal. And it felt more real than anything had in the last five months, that much she did know.

'What made you change your mind?' She nudged his leg with her big toe.

His eyes opened and then he sat up on his elbows and leant towards her. He stroked her cheek with his hand and she pulled the sheet up around her and snuggled under his arm.

'Well?' And she could feel tears threaten, because she was so happy, yet so sad they'd had to travel down such a long hard road to get to this place. She knew life was complex, she knew it was made up of light and shade, but she was, well – emotional.

'I didn't *change* my mind, Vicky. It was never one thing—' he looked out the window and then back at her. 'It was countless things: watching you with Izzy, seeing you puzzle over the coffee machine, it was difficult not to laugh; how you put your family first, wanting desperately to hold you at the hospital when you had your scan but I was confused then,' he sighed. 'And then how sorry you were, for well – everything. Being in that dreadful Airbnb and missing you all – and it gave me time to think, to realise that what your dad said was right: it takes two to give up on a marriage, and I lost sight of that, I lost sight of *my* part in it – and I'm sorry.'

He altered his position. 'And, if you must know,' he said, pushing some hair off her forehead, 'seeing you standing there in the kitchen in your pyjamas and veil, with chocolate ice cream on your chin, you looked simply adorable. And vulnerable – and as far as tipping points go, that sent me over the edge. I stood there and I just wanted to hold you.'

She leant over and laid her cheek on his bare chest.

'There's been a bit more than holding going on here…' She slid her hand around his waist and held him tight.

He kissed the top of her head and pulled her close. 'And I also realised, when you were in the water, when I looked over and saw what had happened, I just froze. Then I couldn't act fast enough, I was desperate, I wanted you out, I wanted us to go back to how we were, I knew it was our second chance and—' but he didn't finish his sentence because the door was flung open wide and Jake screeched in.

'Mum! Tell Izzy – whoa! Is that, like *you*, Dad?' He squinted in the dim evening light.

'Yes, Jake, it is.' James sat up in bed just as Victoria lowered herself down a little under the covers. She started to giggle.

'What's going on?' Izzy was standing behind Jake, her hands on her hips.

'Enough! Enough! Reverse! I'm heading downstairs. Netflix calls!' And with a bit of shuffling, her children backed out of the room. Jake tried to close the door behind him, only it wouldn't shut properly as there was something in the way and it clicked when he tried to shut it.

Her wedding dress.

James sat up and reached for her hand. 'It's obvious you don't remember our wedding, do you? I was watching you when we looked at that DVD together.'

'No,' she said quietly, enjoying the feeling of his finger tracing a line over her wedding ring. They both stared at the dress, dangling from the hanger, the satin shimmering in the dusky rays, the sequins in the diamante daisies casting tiny shards of light across the carpet.

'Then let's do it again.' His eyes darted around the room. 'We'll have a party, I don't know, call it what you want, an anniversary party – a mid-summer party, and you can wear your dress, we can renew our vows. Or is that too cheesy?'

'Too cheesy.'

'Right.' He sank back down on his pillow.

'But I like the party idea,' she added hastily, planting a kiss on his chest, not wanting to deflate his enthusiasm.

He squeezed her hand as she grinned to herself. It was the second-best feeling she'd had all day – especially as an idea suddenly popped into her head which made it all the more exciting.

50 VICTORIA

Victoria looked out of the bedroom window. It was a beautiful day in late July. They'd been lucky with the weather. It had drizzled earlier and she'd been worried about the flimsy pop-up covering the guests and the dancefloor. But James had said he'd checked the forecast and it would be fine by about six o'clock, when all the guests were arriving. She'd hired a small acapella band to sing – and she'd asked Lulu if she'd mind doing a song – it was a duet, but she'd said their dad would do it with her, just for fun. Nothing too tricky, let's mark the occasion, she'd grinned, hugging her secret to herself. Lulu had been delighted. 'It's been a while since I sang with Dad – Christmas karaoke ten years ago!' she'd said at the time. Victoria had just smiled.

She spotted Izzy stringing lights up around the cherry tree, her hair loose and not confined to a plait for once. She was reaching up and carefully looping the lights across the branches, the sun catching the top of her tanned arms. Victoria felt fiercely protective and it made her think of Lulu, about the dreadful assault. Victoria had been speechless, had listened to her recount it with tears streaming down her face. But it all made sense now: that man had taken away her innocence and replaced it with fear; her sister had turned into a shadow of her former self – for a while. Victoria had seen such a change in her over the last few weeks. Nothing would happen overnight, yet she'd had her first counselling session and her eyes had been shining when she'd told Victoria about her meeting with the talent agency – there was nothing concrete yet, but she knew these things took time. At least she was on the road to being who she wanted to be. Her 'old' Lulu was back, the feisty sister who grabbed life by the shoulders and shook it up – not the sister who was about to throw away all her dreams and hide behind a shoddy marriage for security.

She looked up at the sky. It was a brilliant sapphire blue, with a few white clouds stretched above her like candy floss. Below, the garden was doing a great job of showing off. The wisteria was fluttering, pockets of perky lupins swayed proudly in the border and the red-hot pokers stood majestically above all the other shrubs, their fiery orange petals looking magnificent in the sun. The lawn had been cut – by Jake – and even though it wasn't dark yet, the fairy lights across the cherry and apple trees at the bottom of the garden were twinkling in the sunlight.

Her dad and Pickle were both having a nap; they'd arrived on the train yesterday. But that wasn't all. Standing shyly on the doorstep after the taxi had dropped them off was Liz, Dad's neighbour and her little dog, standing obediently by her side. Her dad had been like a teenager around Liz all morning. It made her heart swell. Jake was just helping James put cutlery and glasses on the table outside, and Izzy had added some finishing touches here and there: small jam pots of marguerite daisies around the garden on tables and sprinkled silver horseshoes across them too. '*It's for good luck, Mum!*' She'd bought an extortionate amount of ready-made party food – who could be bothered cooking? Zoe was bringing dessert – no fat-free brownies, Victoria had insisted – and Jake and Izzy were going to help with the drinks.

She stared at herself in the mirror in the bedroom. She'd tied her hair up in a messy bun and put her two new clips on either side – daisy clips – Izzy had given them to her as a present; they were made from tiny mother of pearl petals. And Izzy had also bought her and Lulu both a necklace – it was a silver necklace with a sweet daisy pendant. She said that it reminded her of being in the park that day and making daisy chains and it was the day she'd begun to feel 'well, connected to you' again, she'd mumbled as she'd handed Victoria the little charm. Victoria twisted the solid daisy around between her fingers. Her darling daughter. Her make-up was a bit of blusher and mascara followed by a slick of lipstick. She'd meant to paint her nails, but in the end, didn't have time. Her wedding dress still fitted her – just – and she slipped on a beaded bolero jacket over her shoulders as she knew it would be chilly later – and it just made it look less formal.

'Hey, look at you.' James came over and kissed the back of her neck. Since the ice cream evening, they'd been inseparable. It was like he couldn't get enough of her. He was in his dark lavender suit, with a white shirt, open at the neck. She spun round and put her arms around him and he drew her in for a kiss. She opened her eyes for a peek at them in the mirror. They looked like a couple on their wedding day. It was perfect – perfect for today, and perfect for forming new memories.

'Are we ready?' She smoothed down the back of her bun.

He glanced at his watch. 'I think so. By the last count there are about 500 sausage rolls in the oven, and from what I can see, Jake is in charge of cocktails, which are a lurid orange. Pickle is wearing a flashing collar and Liz's terrier has a bow. I'd say we're ready.'

The acapella group were milling about singing various covers; there was a female lead vocalist and she had a beautiful, lilting country vibe. She reminded Victoria of Miley Cyrus. Guests gathered next to them in the late afternoon sun and sipped their drinks, some clapped, listening to the music. Victoria spotted Zoe talking to one of the school mums and went over to her.

'Hey, sexy mama, check you out!' Zoe gushed and gave her a peck on the cheek. 'I *knew* that you'd wear that dress again! It looks dynamite.'

'Thank you.' It had been a great idea to wear her dress. She would probably never get the chance again. Just then, Lulu appeared – in a stunning white halter-neck jump suit as Izzy let out a squeal.

'Aunty Lulu! Nice! That's just like—'

'Yours, yes, it is. I remembered where you said you bought it and ordered it specially.' She did a twirl – she looked fabulous. Her cheeks were rosy and her shoulders and arms were a golden colour from her new hobby – running a couple of times a week in the woods. She'd told Victoria that she'd enjoyed walking in the Dales so much, she didn't want to stop exercising just because she didn't have a dog to walk, so had started running instead. Her tanned skin glowed beneath the white suit; and the white halter-neck accentuated her long, slim neck. Her blonde curls were untamed and were bouncing around her shoulders as she did a mini curtsey. She looked the happiest Victoria had seen her, well, for months. Lulu clasped the daisy necklace between her fingers. 'It looks great on you,' Izzy said, giving her a hug.

'Thanks, sweetheart, I love it.'

Eric appeared in smart trousers and jacket with a blue shirt, grinning from ear to ear. 'Oh pet,' he said, giving Lulu a hug and then standing back. 'Nobody told me it was Abba fancy dress.' His face was mock-serious.

Lulu leant in and gave him a kiss on the cheek. 'Thanks, Dad! I can always rely on you to make me feel good!'

'Only kidding, poppet. You look radiant.' And she did. That was the perfect word for her. Just then, Jake appeared holding a large silver platter in front of him with a mountain of sausage rolls. 'I reckon if you eat twenty each, we might get through these sausage rolls.' And with that he quickly lobbed one towards Pickle who was sitting patiently by his feet. Victoria pinched his cheek then put her arm around him.

'Oi, Mum, I'll get ketchup all over you!'

'I don't care,' she laughed, popping a sausage roll in her mouth.

James came over and started to fill up everyone's glasses, then slid his arm around Victoria with his free hand. She leant against him, feeling his solid warmth next to her and it was the best feeling. Her fingers found his hand at her waist and she squeezed it, tracing her thumb over his wedding ring, in its rightful place. 'Good party,' he said to everyone, then turned to Victoria, 'Sure you don't want to renew our wedding vows, wife?' *Was he serious? That was far too cheesy!* 'Have you lost your mind?' she joked.

'No,' he said, as he headed over to a table and popped the bottle down, then sped back to the group. '*You* have!'

There was a hushed silence from everyone as his words sunk in. James bit his lip. Izzy was doing her 'bug eyes', looking from her to James, Victoria took a sip of wine and started to cough, but then she burst out laughing. Lulu spat out a bit of sausage roll as she was giggling so much. Jake mouthed '*phew*' at his grandad and wiped his brow with his free hand. Then James lifted up Victoria's arm and twirled her round in her satin wedding dress and pulled her close. As she glanced over his shoulder to see if her plan would come together, he whispered in her ear: 'But I'm incredibly glad you did. Welcome back, Vicky,' to the sound of cheers from everyone standing around them as he then kissed her fully on the lips.

51 LULU

It just goes to show, joking about your wife's amnesia is a good party trick. I'm thrilled for them, they deserve this – and to make some new memories. The band have finished their sets; now the DJ is setting up his decks, encouraging everyone to hit the dancefloor later. Victoria's asked me to sing a song with Dad while they're doing that – she says she's sure I'll know the words. Whatever it takes, I don't mind. I'll sing 'Wheels on the Bus' if she wants; this is *her* day and I'm so happy for her.

Suddenly, a song strikes up that I recognise. Victoria's waving frantically at me, motioning for me to go and get the microphone. I haven't performed for adults for a long time, and all I've had to drink was a peculiar orange-coloured 'mocktail' made by Jake. It tasted of toothpaste. Here goes. It's a melody I'm familiar with – oh, God, it's the opening guitar riff from *A Star is Born* – 'In the Shallow' – surely that can't be right? Where's Dad? Victoria's nodding at me to start – maybe she doesn't know it's a duet and I open my mouth to start to sing the male part when, from behind me,

Markie appears – and starts to sing. There's a hush. He's standing tall, on the edge of the dancefloor, staring at me, singing *to* me, his beautiful voice, his eyes searching mine and shining. My legs turn to jelly and I feel like there are a million emotions flitting across my brain. Why's *he* here? Then suddenly it's my turn to sing, and I know all the words, it's one of my favourite songs and I open my mouth. I take a huge lungful of air and I'm singing, looking at a sea of eager faces, willing me on, then Markie is right beside me, holding his microphone, his green eyes smiling. The tempo changes and we're both singing the finale and it's raw and it's powerful and tears are streaming down my cheeks. This song has always moved me to tears, and now, today, standing next to him, it's almost unbearable.

When we take our last breath and finish the duet, I can see Markie's eyes are leaking a few tears. He wipes them away hurriedly. I scan the room, looking for Katia.

'That, Lulu, was awesome.' He holds my hand as we both take a bow, to huge applause. When the noise dies down, he turns to me and whispers in my ear. 'Hold on, there's someone I want you to meet.' He squeezes my hand, then lets go as he dashes off the dancefloor. The moment's gone and my heart sinks, because as much as I wish him well, I don't want the moment to end, I don't want to see him and Katia together, to tersely wish them well. I'd rather ram fifteen sausage rolls into my mouth in the kitchen to muffle my crying.

I step off the dancefloor to various people saying well done. I nod and smile, but it's as if I'm underwater. I can't hear the noise, the crowds. My eyes are fixed on Markie. He wanders into the crowd and I follow him with my eyes. My heart tells me to run away, into the house, into the quiet and yet I'm rooted to the spot. I can't face this. Then suddenly I see him snaking through the crowds. He's holding someone's hand. But it's not Katia. A woman in a gold sparkly top with bows on the shoulder and black trousers with huge heels totters towards me and holds out her hand. Her lips are painted deep red; they match her fingernails. Oh, *God*. He has another girlfriend.

'Lulu, this is Gina.'

My stomach clenches. Why is he doing this? Why would he look at me that way when he was singing and then introduce me to his girlfriend? I want to hide in the loo, anything but go through with this.

I blink and look over the sea of people. The DJ is playing popular hits now and the makeshift dancefloor is crammed. It's dark, but I can make out Dad and Liz shimmying in the distance; Izzy and Jake are doing some weird dance with their hands in the air, taking selfies, and Victoria and James seem to be waltzing to Pharrell Williams's 'Happy'. I smile despite this awkwardness. I turn to Gina, determined to get through this. 'Nice to meet you. How did, er, you two meet?' It's excruciating doing party small talk. I'd rather eat Pickle's dog food.

'Lulu, I asked Gina to come along tonight. To hear you sing.'

'You knew I was singing?' I look at Markie and I see a twitch of a smile.

'Yes, Vicky set this up. The duet,' he says.

I'm confused.

'You've got a great voice, Lulu.' Gina nods at me and takes a sip of her cocktail.

As I open my mouth to say thank you, Markie butts in: 'Gina heads up an indie record label, and she's looking for—'

'You're not his *girlfriend*?' I blurt out. I just can't help myself.

'No, sweetie, my girlfriend is over there.' I follow her gaze to a woman in a peacock blue dress, who's sitting in one of the chairs with Pickle on her lap, stroking his fur.

'Oh,' I manage as the realisation sinks in. I look between her and Markie. 'You like my voice?'

'I do. I've seen some of your work on YouTube.'

'That seems a lifetime ago,' I say, fiddling with my necklace. 'But I did upload some stuff recently.'

'I know. It's good.' She opens up her handbag and rummages around. She hands me a business card. 'I'm on all the socials, look me up. But why don't you give me a call, then we'll take it from there.' She winks at Markie and then disappears off. I hold the card in my hand, too stunned to talk.

'Shall we get some air?' Markie nods and we both wander out of the pop-up tent, across the lawn. There's a question I'm dying to ask and my eyes flit across the garden and back to the pop-up looking for the answer, before I take the plunge.

'What about Katia?'

'What *about* her?' Markie's lilt travels through the air between us. I study his face for clues and his eyes are dancing. He's standing inches away. I can see tiny bits of stubble appearing, and smell fresh soap on his skin.

'Well, aren't you two, you know, together?' I say, my breath catching in the cold night air.

'What makes you ask that?'

'Because I saw you hug and kiss! At the village hall.' It's out before I can help it.

'Oh, for the love of Jaysus! Yes, but that was a friendly peck on the cheek, so it was. I won't deny it. Want to know why?'

I take a step back and stand with my hand on my hip, my heart thudding. 'Yes.'

He starts to walk towards the cherry tree. I follow behind him. We are slowly making our way down to the bottom of the garden. The fairy lights are glittering like stars that have fallen from the sky. It's much darker now and I feel a cool breeze across my shoulders.

'I told her about you,' he begins, 'about what had happened – an edited version.' He stops and turns to me. 'She was at college with Gina – and well, she offered to get in touch, when I'd explained everything and, y'know, I kinda got over-excited and kissed her on the cheek.' He shrugs. 'Satisfied?'

Most of me wants to believe it, but my faith in myself has taken such a battering, I almost don't trust myself to hope for this.

'You don't believe me, do you?'

I look up at him, his earring glinting in the fairy lights.

'I *want* to believe you but—' Just then Pickle comes bounding up with a pink strappy sandal in his mouth. Markie manages to scoop him up, retrieve the sandal and pops it in his pocket, then gently lets Pickle down and ruffles his head. He stands in front of me, puts both hands on my shoulders and I am aware of the warmth in his fingers pressing down on my skin.

'Well, perhaps this will change your mind.' He takes his hand and strokes my cheek with the back of it as little electric shocks dart across my skin. Then he places it back on my shoulder. 'I have always loved you, Lulu, from the moment you stumbled into that marquee on the very first day when your heel broke, from when you opened your mouth and sang, when you do your crazy, stupid, brilliant Macarena dance, I love that you care about the kids as if they're your own, I love you on stage – and,' he pauses, 'I even love you in the Caterpillar outfit,' his eyebrows jiggle a little '—but the problem—' he rubs my shoulders as a thousand fireflies are released in my stomach, my tongue is stuck to the roof of my mouth and all I can feel are his hands on my bare skin as I look into his shiny eyes – 'the problem,' he says again, and takes a breath, 'was that you didn't love yourself. I could never understand why – until you explained it all to me.'

I'm nodding slowly. 'And do you believe that I love myself now?' I tilt my head and look up at him.

He walks his fingers down from both my shoulders slowly, then grips my hands tight in his and pulls me in towards him. 'Yes,' he whispers in my ear, as I feel his breath and his rough skin next to my cheek, 'I do.' Then he stands back and grins, cocks his head to one side as if he's heard something. 'Will you dance? Because I think you'll like this.' And he squeezes my hand, and pulls me towards the dancefloor as I hear The Killers starting up – and I simply laugh, running alongside him. It's all I can do. I can't speak, because I'm just too happy.

————

If you enjoyed EVERYTHING HAS CHANGED then you will love A YEAR OF SECOND CHANCES, one of Kendra Smith's fantastic and heartwarming novels!

ACKNOWLEDGMENTS

Writing this novel has allowed me to provide an overarching tip for any writer: do not agree to write a book over three lockdowns with four males in the house and a new puppy. With a 90,000-word novel deadline looming I would turn a blind eye as the teens 'trained' the puppy to 'high five' – as well as other questionable canine party tricks.

And now for the serious bit. I had a head-on car crash a couple of years ago and it changed me. My psych review said that was normal. That people who have a 'life altering' event – especially at a younger age (I'll take that, doc, thanks) feel different afterwards, after say a stroke, a heart attack or car crash; they feel more vulnerable. Hell, yes. And sometimes I feel stronger. And sometimes not.

In writing this book I wanted to explore how much of an impact these things can have – the ripple effect. You witness the stone fall into the water, burst the surface tension of those molecules. What's less obvious are the concentric rings spinning out from that one single event. How much do people change? What kind of trigger could it be? I played with that idea, as authors do. Could it change your personality? Yes. Your memory might go. That too. Long-buried frailties from the past might surface. Absolutely.

For Victoria and Lulu, the car crash triggered different things – an avalanche of consequences for our two heroines which they had to deal with. And I hope you've enjoyed reading their journey.

On a more practical note, I've put some distance between the accident and this book in order to write it. I have applied some fictional leeway with my heroine who had a brain injury and amnesia. I feel qualified to poke fun (only in the pages of my novels) as I have had first-hand experience of a trauma, of MRI scans, and of the scary world of PTSD. My heroine pulls through and she questions who she really was, so for her it's a positive experience. You don't really want to know about the nitty gritty of real-life, the actual legalities, and so on. That's why you're reading fiction, and that's because I'm trying to do my job. So apologies if there are any factual inaccuracies, because they are all mine, for the purpose of the story. However, I am grateful to Jenny O'Brien for reading through the trauma and amnesia sections and pointing me in the right direction.

Thanks too to Aidan and Karen Murray (again!) for checking over Markie's Irish sayings to make sure they were 'on point'.

Thanks also to my lovely goddaughter Maddie Turner for checking over Izzy's teen dialogue in parts of the book.

A big thank you to my gorgeous family – warts, puppy-training techniques and all. It's through the pages of these books that my gratitude shows, in rejoicing the meaning of family. I hope you can see that.

Thanks too to the DWLC – to Adrienne Dines, Claire Dyer, Kerry Fisher and Alison Sherlock for moral, email and emotional support and encouragement for all things writerly and beyond.

The first chapter of this book was also shortlisted for the Elizabeth Goudge award by the RNA. That was a real boost! Thanks to Alison May, chair of the RNA at the time for all her input; and to the whole RNA 'family' out there.

And a huge thanks to my editor, Hannah Todd, for enjoying my novel and making superb suggestions which have (I hope) only made it better. Thanks to the whole team at Aria for producing this book – and to the cover designer Leah Jacobs Gordon, I love it!

And lastly, thanks to the bloggers, reviewers and of course to you, the readers.

ABOUT THE AUTHOR

KENDRA SMITH was born in Singapore but educated at boarding school in Scotland and then at university in Aberdeen. Her list of achievements range from being an aerobics teacher in the Nineties, climbing the highest mountain in South-East Asia, working in women's magazines (including *OK!* in London, at the BBC, and *Cosmopolitan* in Sydney). She currently lives in Surrey and spends her time looking for odd socks or chewed tennis balls – and other random duties associated with being the mother of three boys and a Springerdoodle.

With dual British-Australian nationality, she has lived and worked in both Sydney and London. She has been a writer and journalist for over twenty years. She now writes contemporary women's fiction and this is her fourth novel. Kendra can move from keyboard to cooker with ease. She can rustle up a 100,000-word novel, but finds it hard not to burn boiled eggs. Find her on Twitter @KendraAuthor or on Facebook @kendrasmithauthor.